DANCE

A Paranormal Murder Mystery

by

Cara J. Swanson

Published by Nighthawk/Raven Publishing
Denver, CO

Printed in the U.S.A.

Nighthawk/Raven Publishing
Printed in the U.S.A.
www.TheWritingRaven.com
www.carajswanson.com

When Demons Dance

ISBN-13: 978-1508530084

ISBN-10: 1508530084

LLCN: 2015905800

Immensely gripping....a story that couples dark spirituality with self-awareness....5 out of 5 stars!

- *San Francisco Book Review*

Dedication

In memory of the strong, amazing women who were taken from us far too soon; Tamara, Theresa, and Robbie. You are still missed.

And for Jill and Eric; without your friendship and amazing support, this book would never have happened.

And always, for Shawn.

A huge Thank-You to Lt. Brett Johnson, CIB Commander of the [real] Grand Forks Police Department. Without his patience and willingness across the span of four years this book as you hold it would not exist. Rest assured that any errors found within are mine, and mine alone.

Also by
Cara J. Swanson

Fiction

Blood Cult: Book I of the Elvestran Chronicles
Daigu: Book II of the Elvestran Chronicles

The Long Journey: tales of a world yet to come

Nonfiction

Hey, I Wrote a Book! What do I do now? A Writer's Guide to Self-Publishing

WHEN DEMONS DANCE

A Paranormal Murder Mystery

by

Cara J. Swanson

PROLOGUE
UNFORTUNATE SOLUTIONS

The great mystery is not that we should have been thrown down here at random between the profusion of matter and that of the stars; it is that from our very prison we should draw, from our own selves, images powerful enough to deny our nothingness.

- André Malraux, *Man's Fate*

I'm on the dark side of the dawn
Just waiting for the end of black December.
- Hellyeah, *Black December*

The past gives way to a cold winter field
The ground below, hard as steel.
- Clutch, *Gone Cold*

PROLOGUE

Discovery minus 78 hours

Eyes closed, her lips moved silently as she prayed, teeth gritted against the shivers that threatened to rattle them loose from her skull. The gold necklace around her neck began to burn against her skin as the frozen air did its work. She could feel the tiny cross in the hollow of her throat, and she imagined the inscription on the back being written into her very body. It seemed a fitting vision, considering the words that *were* written – albeit in ink – not so far from the cross.

She heard the heavy steel door scrape against the concrete floor. Footsteps tried to echo and fell short, defeated by the minus temperatures.

"Please," she whimpered, her voice catching on the acrid smoke of the burning talisman being waved around her head. "Please, I changed my mind."

"I'm sorry," came the response. But the voice didn't sound sorry; it sounded happy; excited, even. "You know this is the only way."

"It hurts," she groaned, trying to curl up around herself, to warm her core, but the restraints wouldn't let her.

"It won't take long," she was assured. "I promise."

And the voice was right. Even the pain from her face, the long jagged mark of a burning iron that had been bright-hot with agony a few minutes ago, was beginning to fade.

The last thing she felt was a tug as the necklace was jerked from around her neck. The force made her head flop forward, and she knew herself to be falling, at long last, into the deepest of sleep.

BOOK ONE
DISCOVERY

incubus

[**in**-ky*uh*-b*uh* s, **ing**-] /ˈɪn kyə bəs, ˈɪŋ-/

noun, plural **incubi**

1. an imaginary demon or evil spirit supposed to descend upon sleeping persons, especially one fabled to have sexual intercourse with women during their sleep.

2. a nightmare.

3. something that weighs upon or oppresses one like a nightmare.

I will walk, with my hands bound
I will walk, with my face bloodied
I will walk, with my shadow flag
Into your garden
Garden of stone
After all is done
We're still alone
I won't be taken
Yet I'll go.

- Pearl Jam, *Garden*

CHAPTER 1

Discovery

I hate early mornings. Detective Olivia St. George of the Grand Forks Police Department, Criminal Investigation Bureau, sighed heavily as she looked down at the very dead, very frozen, corpse. It was early January in North Dakota, the wind was gusting at a brisk ten miles per hour, and at only fifteen below the temperature was almost mild for the season. A native Dakotan – a native Native, as she would put it - her long black hair was tucked up under a fleece cap and her feet wore heavy boots lined with thick sheepskin. Her sturdy five-foot-two frame was surrounded by a double-quilted fleece-lined winter coat. Still, she shivered, her olive complexion pale and waxy from the frozen air as her body ached for the warm bed left behind only minutes before.

The corpse was at the bottom of a ditch, mostly covered by a drift of wind-blown snow and broken brush debris. Only the head and one naked foot, sticking out from the end of dark-colored pants, were visible. Red hair, matted with frozen mud, was tangled with twigs and decaying leaves. Half of the corpse's face was gone; from chin to occipital, the musculature on the entire left of the face had been nibbled away, leaving the cheekbone and sinus cavity as stark features in a deserted landscape. Where both eyes had once been, only emptiness remained, mutely staring out at the night.

The elegant span of neck and the femininity of the foot were the only hint to the corpse's gender. With the red hair and white skin surrounding the dark emptiness of her face, she was a pale dead flower against the frozen dirty snow.

The crime scene, by comparison, was a bright spot in an otherwise pitch-black night. Three portable spotlights powered by a too-loud gas generator had turned the victim's last resting spot into a circus side show. A small crowd of uniformed officers, two Detectives, and the farmer who had found the body completed the transformation.

"Why do these things always happen in the middle of the night?" Olivia grumbled, glancing at her watch and blinking as the glare from the lights reflected off the watch-face and into her eyes. At three-thirteen a.m., it could be considered either very late at night or very early in the morning, depending on one's temperament. No matter what, it was a sucky time to be standing in the freezing cold, looking down at a dead body.

The corpse was stretched out in a ditch along a rural farm road several miles off Highway 2. If it hadn't been for a nearby farmer's dog coming home with a scrap of fabric in its mouth, she probably would have laid in the ditch, unnoticed and unfound, until spring. The farmer, thankfully suspicious, had followed his black mutt back to its prize and then called 911. He was seated now on the snowmobile he'd used to follow the dog, his proud mutt on his lap and wrapped in the farmer's warm embrace.

"So what do we know about her?" Olivia asked louder, stepping out of the way as the two Medical Examiner technicians walked up with cameras and lights in hand.

The other Detective, Matthew Gossett, flipped open his leather-bound notebook and cleared his throat, pushing golden locks away from his eyes with one gloved hand. He was fashionably dressed, as always, and somehow seemed impervious to the cold despite wearing street shoes and only a camel-brown double-breasted overcoat. His gloves were thin calfskin and even his cap was more fashionable than serviceable.

"White female, red hair, maybe mid-twenties. Hard to tell. No identification that anyone's found yet. She's been out here awhile – coyotes have obviously gotten to her pretty bad."

"I'm done with the long shots," one of the technicians said, lowering his camera. "I can do the close-ups now if you're ready."

"Maybe her car broke down," Olivia mused, not really listening to either man as she kneeled to take a closer look at the victim. She began brushing off the snow, slowly revealing the rest of the dead woman as the camera flashed. The nearest house was still nearly a mile away; if her car had indeed broken down on the highway, she would have had to have walked for miles in the cold before finally collapsing here.

The dead woman's only clothes seemed to be a pair of large woolen pants, a nondescript linen shirt and an oversized man's tweed coat. Besides being strikingly unfeminine, her attire was also starkly inappropriate to the season.

"What do you think?" Olivia asked, leaning back on her heels.

"From her clothes, I'm guessing a vagrant."

Olivia was startled into a laugh. She looked around the harsh landscape, shading her eyes against the wind. "Vagrant? How many vagrants do you know go walking across North Dakota in the middle of January?"

Matt shrugged. "It's just a guess."

Olivia donned a pair of plastic gloves and went through the woman's pockets.

"No ID," she said finally, "but there is this." She raised a blue-clad hand and opened her fingers to reveal a small golden cross dangling from a delicate, broken gold chain.

"There's an inscription on the back," she realized, squinting. The spotlights drowned the miniscule letters out entirely. She stood, *urf*ing painfully as her hip popped loudly, and moved into the shadows.

"Matthew, bring your flashlight over here."

He sighed dramatically, leaning over her and shining his light at an angle across the tiny cross.

"Can you make that out?" she asked, looking closer. "Damn but I must be getting old. I can barely see those letters."

"I think it's a Bible reference," Matt squinted. "But it's hard to tell."

Olivia slipped the necklace into a plastic evidence bag, labeling it before stowing it in her coat pocket for safekeeping. She fumbled off the plastic gloves, flexing her fingers to bring blood back into her already-numb hands as she pulled her winter gloves back on.

"Did anyone find her shoes?"

"Uh, she wasn't wearing any," Matt responded.

"There's no way she walked all the way from the highway, in this weather, with no shoes on," Olivia grumbled. She hated half-assed police work. "Either she got dumped or they're around here somewhere."

"Coyotes," Matt said again, trying to be helpful. "They could be anywhere by now."

"Look again," Olivia said harshly, then winced at her tone. "I mean, I'll help you look again." She resented being paired with Detective Gossett. In her opinion he was sloppy and lazy, cruising by on the good looks gifted by his Scandinavian forefathers and his version of 'charm,' which Olivia found grating and inane. At six-foot-six he towered above everyone and, she thought, liked to use his height to make others uncomfortable. Even though they were technically peers she couldn't help treating him the way she saw him – as an inept, overgrown child. She hated working with Matt but she hated even more that he brought out the worst in her.

Matt sighed loudly to convey that he was just placating her. "Alright, let's scour this whole road!" he yelled to the uniforms securing the scene, as if he'd just thought of it.

Olivia shook her head and pushed Matt Gossett to the back of her mind. She couldn't believe she'd once slept with him. What a horrible morning-after that had been. At least it had been the final push she'd needed to get back to AA – a silver lining on an otherwise dark, dark, *oh* so dark cloud.

After another thirty minutes it was obvious that neither the dead woman's shoes, nor her identification, were anywhere close by. The cops and both Detectives had looked under every scrubby bush and the entire length of the ditch, on both sides of the road, for at least a hundred yards in both directions. Everyone was completely frozen when they finally called it quits. They'd spent so long searching that the ME's van had already left with the corpse, leaving only a tangle of yellow police tape to show where the dead woman had lain. The techs, with the assistance of the uniformed officers, had filled a plastic garbage can with the snow and debris immediately above and below the victim, leaving the site cleaner than it had been before.

"Coyotes," Matt said again smugly when they finally regrouped. Olivia ignored him. She had a gut feeling that wherever the dead woman's shoes were, they weren't being gnawed on by a skinny North Dakotan coyote.

Finally Olivia limped back to her car, her hip a red-hot mass of angry nerves. Being on her feet for over an hour out in the cold had awoken every old injury she had.

She sat back in the driver's seat, closing her eyes for a moment and resting her mind as the engine warmed. It was at moments like this – half-frozen, stiff with cold and pain, frustrated about her life and career – that the drink called to her worse than ever. But she knew if she just rested a moment, centered herself, it would pass, as it always did.

A noise startled her out of her reverie. It was Matt, honking as he passed by on his way back to the office.

"Great," she grumbled under her breath. Just what she needed – a reminder that they'd be working together on this case. It was definitely the icing on what had already been *such* a delightful morning.

She went straight to the Medical Examiner's office, knowing the corpse would beat her there. Hopefully the doc would already have begun an initial examination and she could put a better label on the victim than 'faceless dead woman.' The ME's office was in the basement of the Grand Forks Police Department, and on a cold winter's day the chill of stainless steel was indistinguishable from the chill of the frozen air.

Olivia was pleased to see that Detective Gossett was nowhere to be seen. She figured he was probably shuffling papers around on his desk, trying to look busy while avoiding doing any actual real work.

"Ah, my favorite Detective," Doctor Whitney Johansson said cheerfully as Olivia walked through the door. The ME was examining a string of x-rays clipped into the lightbox, her bright-red hair a hot flame in an otherwise cold and colorless room. "How they hanging?"

"Lower every year," Olivia joked back, giving her two 'girls' a pat. It was a standing joke between them, a private female ending to a common and very *male* greeting, and it earned her a funny look from the young technician across the room. "So, anything on my victim?"

"Well, we haven't gotten too far yet, so hard to say," Whitney answered. "It's way too soon to say for sure, of course, but at the moment it's looking like death by exposure. Accidental, or even possibly suicide, although that's rare and hard to prove."

"Suicide by exposure? Surely there are easier ways," Olivia mused, watching as the doc peered at the backlit x-rays hanging on the wall.

"How do her feet look?" Olivia asked, picking up the thread of the conversation after a long silence.

Whitney glanced over at her. "Not too bad, considering. I'd say she was only barefoot for a few minutes before dying, or her shoes and socks were removed shortly before death. Taking clothes off is a common reaction to hypothermia. No signs of frostbite – just postmortem freezing. And she definitely wasn't walking around barefoot. Her feet are clean."

"Were they chewed on, or anything like that?"

"Like by animals? No. Wholly intact, ten toes and all. She even has manicured toenails. Come take a look."

That got Olivia's attention. "Really?"

She followed the doc down to the end of the room where a steel table held a still-thawing young woman. Her red hair had been combed free of debris – not to improve her looks, but to check for evidence – and she now resembled a sleeping and extremely pale Snow White, instead of a frozen homeless woman. Her clothes had been removed and neatly folded into plastic evidence bags that were still sitting on a side table, along with several other smaller evidence bags, all sealed with red tape.

"Come on over," Whitney gestured her down to the feet-end of the victim. Olivia leaned over, trying to see past the thawing, porcine skin to the humanness that had once been. The toenails had been polished and painted with a clear glossy coat, trimmed just far enough from the toe to give a hint of femininity without attempting a French manicure. These were toes meant for sandals, Olivia mused, but for walking in, not lounging on sandy beaches – utilitarian with just a nod towards fashion.

"Hmm." She stood back up. "We didn't find shoes or socks at the scene. Matt thinks she was a vagrant, walking her way across the

Dakotas and into oblivion."

Whitney had the same reaction as Olivia, her braying laugh bouncing off the tiled walls. "Matt wouldn't know his gluteus from his anconeus."

"His whooza whuzza?"

"His ass from his elbow."

Olivia chuckled. "Very nice." Whitney's ear had been twisted more than Olivia would have liked when she was trying to climb out of the hole she'd dug of her life. She had a sharp wit and fierce sense of right and wrong, matched by a stubborn streak that had kept her at Olivia's side when most people would have gotten sick of her and kicked her to the curb. Olivia knew how lucky she was to have Whitney as a friend; and for a long time the feisty redhead had been her only friend.

Actually, she was still her only friend, Olivia reminded herself.

"It's very unlikely she was a vagrant," Whitney said, returning to where she'd left off. "She was well-fed and healthy, with no external signs of malnourishment, abuse, or disease. In fact, the damage to her face is the only actual injury we've found so far, except this odd inflammation on the inside of her thighs. Some kind of a rash or something. We'll know a lot more once we can open her up."

"How long will that take?"

"Well, unfortunately we'll have to wait until she defrosts before we can do much more. We'll speed up the process as much as we can, but we can't exactly just stick her in the microwave. Angela over there –" she nodded towards the other technician, "is about to get some dental impressions. We've already done fingerprinting."

"Got it," Olivia nodded. "And thanks. Any way to tell how old she was?"

"I'd say she was a healthy Caucasian woman in her early thirties who had regular access to dental and medical care. Oh, and she has a tattoo."

Olivia perked up. "Is that so? That might help identify her, as long as it's not the ubiquitous lower-back 'tribal' tat or band of roses around the ankle."

Whitney chuckled. "Yes, those do get old, don't they? Lucky for you this girl was actually pretty creative. Look here." She turned and pointed towards a computer monitor that still displayed a string of digital photos. "She has something written across her upper back."

"Right on," Olivia said cheerfully, looking over at the screen. "*Vocatus o non vocatus, deus aderit,*" she read slowly. "What the hell does that mean?"

"Something about God, that's all I know," Whitney said apologetically. "I only took medical Latin, I'm afraid."

Olivia shrugged. "It's a start."

They were interrupted by Angela, the student technician, walking over. "Detective, can I help you with anything?" she asked cordially, if somewhat stiffly.

"No, I'm good," Olivia shook her head. "Just make sure I get a copy of those, okay?" She nodded towards the digital photos displayed on the monitor.

"Of course," the girl nodded. "Also, while you're here, I just noticed something on the x-rays."

Olivia followed her back to the light wall where the girl pointed towards a black-and white shot of the victim's pelvis, an inch-long "T" showing in bright white. "She has an IUD," the tech said proudly, as if she herself had put it there. "We should be able to get a serial number off that."

"Fantastic," Olivia nodded, the girl's enthusiasm spilling over. "Great work."

"Hey, before I forget, her personal belongings are over here,"

Whitney called across the room, nodding at the pile of evidence bags. “You can take them to the lab if you want – it’ll be faster. Just sign the clipboard.”

“Will do,” Olivia said, giving Angela the tech a last nod of appreciation. “Was there anything besides the pants, shirt, and coat?”

“Nope, just those three items,” both Angela and Whitney answered simultaneously. “No bra, panties, or anything else.”

“Hmm. Strange. Maybe it is a homicide after all.”

The winter sun had yet to struggle its way over the frozen horizon when Olivia stepped back into the cold, arms full of evidence bags, taking a breath of frozen air and shaking off the smell of antiseptic death. She was faced with a decision; turn right around and go back to the office and risk seeing Matt, or try to get a start on this case without returning to her desk. What she really wanted was coffee, but at this time of what most people would still consider night, the only options were bad police station coffee, bad gas station coffee, or bad homemade coffee.

She opted for the gas station. Few places were open in Grand Forks at five in the morning and the warm, well-lit Chevron down the road was inviting. The night clerk glanced up at her briefly then went back to his graphic novel as she wandered down the aisle. She filled up a 20-ounce Styrofoam cup with fake cappuccino from the dispenser, then sipped on it as she looked over the snack choices.

When she’d first quit drinking, candy bars had been her best friend. The sugar rush and subsequent crash was familiar and comforting, similar to the rise and fall created by alcohol. After gaining fifteen pounds she’d moved on to granola bars, then gum, the pretzels. Anything to keep her hands and mouth occupied, to distract her from the ever-present urge to drink.

Now, sipping on syrupy fake coffee, she tried to decide between a strawberry-flavored Nutra Grain bar coated in 'vanilla' or her absolute favorite, a Reese's Fast Break.

I've been good, she told herself, reaching for the Fast Break and ignoring that she was holding about three hundred calories in her other hand. *Besides, peanut butter is good for you.*

As she picked up the Reese's the clerk coughed, loudly. Olivia shook herself out of her reverie and went up to the front to pay.

"Sorry, I was lost in thought," she said cheerfully. "Just these two things."

"How about that one in your pocket?" he said coldly, staring her down.

"Pardon?" Olivia said, confused. "I don't-"

"I saw you put something in your pocket," the clerk said, rising to his feet. He was tall and wide, at least three hundred pounds, his flabby white face turning red with anger as he loomed over her.

Olivia patted her pockets and looked at him strangely, struggling to keep her temper down. "Look, I don't know what you *think* you saw, but I'm not a thief," she said, her voice dripping ice cycles, staring up at him from her scant five-foot two.

He slammed his graphic novel down on the counter. *Black Dog,* she saw, her eyes automatically reading and storing the title. "Goddamn prairie niggers, comin' in here and stealing all my shit," he snarled, his face now a ripe apple. "Empty your pockets!"

Olivia stared, eyes narrowed, her temper a growing storm. Keeping her eyes locked on his, she emptied her pockets, slamming her wallet down on the counter followed by a stick of lip balm, a half-empty pack of chewing gum, a wadded-up gas receipt, forty-two cents in change, and finally pulled back her coat to reveal her holstered 9-mm duty weapon and the badge clipped to her belt. She stood there, pockets turned out, shaking with furious anger as she kept one hand protectively over her gun.

"Is that good enough for you?" she snarled back.

The clerk looked down at the small pile of belongings, his eyes lingering on the badge and the gun. The red was draining from his face, quickly replaced by the purple of embarrassment.

"Look, I'm sorry, I thought I saw you take something," he said sincerely. "There's no need for all that." He reached over to scan the Reese's and stopped when he saw the look on her face.

"You're a fucking racist piece of shit," Olivia said through her teeth as she returned her belongings to her pockets. "I wouldn't buy from you if this was the last store on Earth." She stalked away, shaking with anger and adrenaline, wishing the door wasn't automatic so she could slam it behind her.

She took her anger out on her car door, hoping the asshole inside would hear it slam shut. The Mudvayne album in her CD player started up automatically when she turned the key, and she turned the volume up to drown out the pounding in her temples. Chad Gray's angry, yet mournful pleas to *scream with me* were a perfect match for the furious beating of her heart.

Of all the gas station clerks in all of Grand Forks, I had to get the one guy who still thinks it's 1954.

As she wiped angry tears from her cheeks, she suddenly realized that since she had drank coffee while in the store and then left without paying, technically she *was* a thief.

"Oh, God," she sighed, laying her forehead on the cold steering wheel, hysterical laughter threatening to bubble out of her. "If that was meant to be a lesson in humility, you've got piss-poor timing."

CHAPTER 2

Discovery + 3 hours

[Man] is quite capable of responding prehistorically to present-day situations…living upon occasion in a world that ceased to exist a long, long time ago. He may at times revert to a dream-time of a sort, responding to contemporary events as if he were still a wild species at large in a wilderness.

- *The Emergence of Man* (John E. Pfeiffer)

Olivia spent the remainder of the morning at the crime lab. It was a ten-minute drive to the lab and she found it soothing, letting the music from her CD player take her mind to better places. Once there, she went ahead and did what tasks she could to make it easier and faster for the lab techs; cataloguing each item, doing initial light and chemical tests for blood stains, rolling for hair, and filling out the top of the checklist. The lab tech on duty, Melinda, signed off on the results before storing everything away in a locker for safekeeping. It was unusual for Detectives to be so proactive, but Olivia was very hands-on and most of the lab techs knew her by first name. She had done a one-year internship in this very crime lab – albeit as a mere lab *assistant* – during college, back when she was trying to decide what path she wanted to take after graduation, so they were more lenient with her than with strangers. The nearness of the lab was one of the attractants that had drawn her to join the force in Grand Forks after graduation; she could have gone anywhere, but the town had begun to feel like as much of a home as she'd ever had.

More importantly, at least on this particular day, working at the lab gave her something to do while keeping her away from the office as well as giving her justification to go home afterwards and catch a few hours of zz's.

Finally arriving back at work, she walked in with coffee in hand (bad homemade version, this time), deep in thought, trying to keep from yawning and rubbing her eyes. Her quick nap had been filled with vaguely remembered, frightening dreams that had left her feeling ill-rested and troubled.

A quick glance around proved Matt was nowhere to be found. *Thank goodness*, she said silently. She just didn't have the energy to deal with him right then.

She was surprised to see a manila envelope with the ME's logo in the corner already waiting on her desk. They were certainly a hard-working crew, tucked away down in the basement as they were.

Olivia, on the other hand, felt herself to be more and more of an automaton as time went by. Whatever reasons she'd had for joining the force had long since been buried in the sludge of day-to-day living.

Olivia opened the envelope and pulled out a sheaf of papers and photos. They had included copies of the tattoo photos, with a ruler included in the shot for size reference, along with printouts of the digital fingerprints, data about the dental impressions and x-rays, and a note that they hoped to have the body warmed enough for an examination by late afternoon. Olivia set those aside for the moment. Later, she'd run all of that information through the system to see if she could find an identity for the dead woman; for now, she was anxious to see what else they might have found. Her eyes scanned down the paper, taking in each new bit of information with an uncharacteristic lack of detachment.

Adhesive residue on chin, wrists, and ankles, consistent in width and viscosity with the use of electrical tape or mid-sized duct tape. Subdermal cellular damage from ice crystals in all digits and bottoms of feet. Blood pooling in lower extremities suggests victim died while *standing upright. Evidence of pre-death 3rd degree burn wound on left cheek, roughly 4 inches by 1 inch. Evidence of post-death removal of damaged tissue from left cheek with serrated blade. Inflamed tissues inside both thighs and vagina, likely due to overuse of detergent or another nontoxic irritant. X-rays show multiple postmortem bone fractures in both legs and torso. Multiple contusions in various stages of healing along both arms; size and shape of contusions match with human bite marks and fingernails (possibly self-inflicted).*

Preliminary cause of death (barring tox screen results): heart failure resulting from severe hypothermia. Preliminary ruling: Homicide.

There was more, but she had to stop there. For the first time in a long time, Olivia was actually shocked. She thought she'd developed a thick skin over time, impervious to surprise at what humans could do to each other; but this had caught her unawares.

She was so lost in thought that she didn't realize Matt Gossett had come in until he sat on the edge of her desk. She jumped when he touched her shoulder, the papers in her hand scattering across her desk.

"Oh, you scared me," she breathed, putting her hand over her heart. "Way to give me a coronary, Gossett."

"Well, geez, it's not like I snuck up on you," he said, offended. "What are you reading?"

Olivia sighed, remembering that since the case was now officially (at least preliminarily) a homicide, that meant she was stuck with Matt for the foreseeable future. Wordlessly she gathered up the report and handed it to him.

She sat silent as he scanned down the page. Finally he looked up at her, eyebrows wrinkled. "Okay."

She stared. "What do you mean, okay? Do you not see the portent of this?"

"The what?"

Olivia sighed, resting her face in her hands. "For once, Matt, just pretend that you aren't an idiot, okay?"

He stood up, finally offended, and tossed the report back on her desk. "Whatever you say, *Detective* St. George." Huffing, he stalked across the room to his own desk and sat down hard, turning his chair so his back was to her. Olivia rolled his eyes at his childishness, ignoring the stares from around the room as she went back to the report.

She had just regained her concentration when her phone rang.

"CIB, St. George," she answered it absently.

"I just want to help," the puerile voice said.

"Oh, for God's sake," Olivia said loudly, slamming the phone down and spinning in her chair. "Matthew, are you *seven*? Don't call me from twelve feet away."

"Fine," he said imperiously, lifting his chair and carrying it over to her desk. He settled in next to her, grinning. "Now we can work together."

"Great," she muttered, turning back to the report and ignoring him.

After a few minutes he cleared his throat. "I really do want to help," he said.

Olivia hung her head, saying a silent prayer for patience. "I just don't want to have to explain every single thing to you," she said stiffly. "You're a Detective, for God's sake." She could feel all eyes on them and she knew what people were thinking. She had previously had a reputation as an ice queen, and when Matt had finally 'scored' with her, it was immediately obvious that everyone knew. Now their public interactions had been reduced to a lover's quarrel without the love, the endless spats that married couples have when their thirty-year marriages are stuck in a permanent loveless rut. But she didn't even have a once-happy relationship – or *any* relationship, for that matter - to look back on.

The worst part was, she couldn't even remember their night together. She had been so far gone on vodka shooters that even the next morning was a blur. All she remembered was waking up next to him, her clothes in a heap on the floor, her body aching as a result of too much alcohol, staying up far too late, and who knew what else. She had shakily slid out of his bed, getting into her clothes and leaving as fast and as silently as she could. They'd never spoken of it – but she knew she wasn't imagining the smug look on his face or the way she was treated subtly different by all the men at work after that. It was as if she'd been moved into a different category in all of their minds; from the 'untouchable' column of an ice queen, to the 'likes it drunk and rough' column. It was unbearable.

Now, seeing the pout on his face, she sighed and tried to regain the mantle of professionalism she had once worn so easily.

"Look," she said with forced calmness. "Just read this page. You see here and here? She didn't die accidentally, Matt. She was bound and frozen, and then dumped. And look at this part – her face was burned before she died, and then the killer removed the burned area, probably because they thought the burn would look more suspicious than if she appeared to have been chewed on."

He read it over again. "Okay, I get it. It's a murder. Didn't we already think that?"

She squeezed her eyes shut for a moment. "No, you thought she was a vagrant, wandering across never-neverland in the middle of winter."

"Well, geez, it was just a guess," he said, offended all over again.

"Don't guess, Matt. This is Crime 101, for God's sake. Deduce."

"Well, I deduce that she's not a local girl."

"Oh?" Olivia raised an eyebrow. "How do you figure?"

“The tattoo.” He slid the 8 by 10 photo in front of her. “How many local girls have Latin tattooed across their back?”

Olivia shrugged. “She could be University. Not local doesn’t mean she didn’t live here. Did you ever find a car?” It had been Matt’s job to research any reports of abandoned vehicles within a ten-mile radius. Not that anyone could have conceivably walked ten miles in that weather, but Olivia liked a big buffer zone.

“Well, no,” he admitted. “But the University thing is a place to start, right?”

“Yeah,” she agreed grudgingly. “But she’s not a kid. She’s early thirties, Doc said.”

He shrugged, leaning back in a way that looked both posed and casual. “She could still be University. A Grad student, maybe, or just someone going back to school a little later in life.”

“True,” she admitted again. “So let’s go check it out.”

“What? Where?” he looked confused all over again, having apparently used up his available brain space on that burst of cogitation.

“It’s only three o’clock. The admin offices at UND will still be open.”

“But we don’t know her name,” Matt said, still confused.

“Nope,” Olivia huffed, hauling herself out of her chair. “But if she’s a Grad student, she might also be an Aide, and if she didn’t show up for class or work for the last few days, someone might actually have noticed. Like you said, it’s a start.”

Matt heaved a mighty sigh before standing up and retrieving his coat. “Fine. But I’m driving.”

Olivia rolled her eyes. “Whatever.”

The University’s business offices were not a far drive for the two Detectives. Olivia spent the time sipping reheated coffee, choking down the urge to comment on his driving and staring out the window in silence. The winter sun was already setting and it cast pink and red glows across the brick buildings, turning windows into stained glass and giving the old buildings a brief respite from the degradations of age.

Apparently her cold demeanor did not go unnoticed. "Let me ask you something," Matt finally said as they walked from the parking lot. "Why didn't you just come by yourself?"

"Because I figured you wouldn't stop bugging me until we did some work on this case together," Olivia said bitterly, the harsh words slipping out before she could stop them.

"Whoa!" Matt stepped back and held up his hands. "What's the problem here, St. George?"

Olivia swiveled on her heel, almost relieved to finally hear him ask that question. "The problem is you, *Gossett*," she spit. "I don't like you and I'm not embarrassed to make that obvious."

"What did I ever do to you?" he asked, his blue eyes going as wide as those of an innocent puppy dog.

"You-" Olivia choked. Even now she couldn't bring herself to discuss what had happened between them, what must have happened between them even if she didn't remember it. Bile rising in her throat, she gritted her teeth and put her hands on her hips. "Do you want to do this or not?" she charged furiously. "Because I am perfectly happy working this case without you."

"I see that," Matt said coldly. "Why don't I just wait in the car while you do this. Alone."

"Fine," she spit and swiveled on her heel, stalking through the double doors before he could change his mind.

Twenty minutes later, she stalked back out of the building, wishing for the second time that day that she could slam the door behind her. Happily she was able to slam the car door, folding her arms and sitting with heavy brow.

Matt ignored her, starting up the engine without a word.

Olivia sat at her desk, looking over the initial autopsy report for the twentieth time. The woman at the Business Office desk had been spectacularly unhelpful, and had basically sent Olivia away in a furious huff. Olivia supposed it hadn't helped that she'd already been in such a foul mood when arriving at the woman's desk. She'd charged in and demanded information, immediately putting the woman on the defensive and giving her no reason to want to help.

Since then, she'd checked in with the two Detectives who were working on getting a fingerprint match (nothing in IAFIS), ran the woman's information through NCIC and checked the Missing Persons pages of every Law Enforcement organization she could think of (nothing, and nothing) and called about the status of the autopsy (in progress). She'd done an internet search on Latin forums and tattoos, hoping to find a picture in some online posting that would pop out as her victim. So far, no luck or hits on anything.

At this point and this time of night, there wasn't much else she could do. Nothing was open, so she couldn't make phone calls or visits; and without even having a crime scene as a basis for beginning it was a needle in a haystack situation. Worse; the dead woman could be from anywhere. She could even be Canadian; Grand Forks was only a matter of a few highway hours from the border, and there was no reason to assume it was the body of an American. It wouldn't be the first time someone had snuck across an international border to dump a body.

Alright, alright, she said to herself, trying to collect her thoughts. Doc said the woman was frozen and then dumped. But she hadn't thawed noticeably between the two events; so either she had been initially frozen close by or had been in a refrigerated truck….

Wait. It was January in North Dakota. The body would have stayed frozen solid in any unheated trunk or vehicle. They hadn't had a day above zero in months; she could have died in October, for all Olivia knew.

Damn. First possible lead down the toilet.

"Uuuuugh," she sighed, rubbing her face. *To hell with this*. She shoved pictures and X-rays and fingerprint cards and report documents back in the envelope from whence they were delivered. She put it in her top drawer and decided to see if Whitney was still in her office. At least it was something to do.

Doctor Johansson was, for once, not elbow-deep in someone else's vital organs. She was at her desk, listening to a technician's digital audio taping from a previous autopsy. She required that everyone make audio recordings during autopsies and liked to spot-check the newer tech's work.

Olivia stopped in the doorway, realizing the recording was about to end and waiting so as to not interrupt. After only a moment, the audio clip ended and Whitney looked up, surprised.

"Hey!" She said, concerned. "What's up? Are you okay?"

"Oh, I'm okay," Olivia sighed. "Sorry to interrupt. I was going stir-crazy at my desk."

Whitney chortled. "I know how that goes. You feel like getting out of here?"

Olivia grinned. "Sounds great."

Twenty minutes later they were parked on bar stools at the Blue Moose, Olivia with a cold glass in hand. Whitney had declined; she hated cold drinks in the winter, but said it was too early in the day for anything else. Strangely enough, she had shown up still wearing her lab coat and the green sweater she seemed to favor these days; Olivia could hardly remember seeing her wear anything else for quite some time.

"Ah," Olivia took a long swallow of her frozen red slush. "Strawberry Margarita mix without the tequila. My favorite."

Whitney chucked. "I've never liked tequila. Wine has always been my thing."

"Ugh," Olivia wrinkled up her nose. "I never did care for wine. Beer, though…" she heaved a great sigh. "Yeah, I definitely miss beer."

They sat in companionable silence for a long moment, lost in their own thoughts as the bar began to fill up around them with the bustle of early diners and drinkers. Jim, the bartender, refilled Olivia's glass, casting eyes towards Whitney the non-drinker. Several new arrivals aimed towards Whitney, veering off at the last moment as she gave them the fuck-off look.

"This case…." Olivia said finally. "It's bothering me somehow."

Whitney didn't respond for a moment. "More than usual?" she asked quietly, her green eyes steady on her friend's face.

Olivia rubbed her forehead. "Yeah. But I don't know why."

"Is it because it's a woman, or the way that she was murdered?"

Olivia thought, then shook her head slowly. "I don't think it's either. I can't put my finger on it. I just keep thinking about her, laying there in the cold and the dark. A woman with no name and half a face."

"Maybe that's what's bothering you," Whitney said shrewdly. "That she's faceless, nameless. Lost and alone."

"Yeah," Olivia sighed. "Maybe so."

"You know, not to pry," Whitney said carefully. "But you don't talk much about your family, your childhood."

Olivia shrugged, raising an eyebrow. "So?"

"Well, I just thought maybe there was something about this case, something about her being abandoned this way, that was maybe, uh, pushing some buttons for you."

Olivia narrowed her eyes. "Uh-oh, are you going shrink on me?"

Whitney laughed, throwing her head back. "Okay, you caught me. No more head shrinking. I'm much better with dead people, anyway."

"So I've noticed," Olivia grinned. "Tell you what. When you start dating again, I'll tell you about my childhood." Whitney's family had been killed in a head-on collision a year before that had put the doc herself in intensive care for weeks. Gossip said that Whitney, the driver, had been drinking; but Olivia knew she would never have risked her own family. She hadn't touched a drop since, though, but had never looked at another man either.

"That's a deal," Whitney raised her imaginary glass again, and they gave a toast to life of both past and present.

CHAPTER 3

Discovery +18 hours

"It must be a dream, it must, it must," said Jill to herself. "I'll wake up in a moment." But it wasn't, and she didn't.
- *The Silver Chair* (C.S. Lewis)

Much later that night, Olivia walked in her front door more than ready to curl up in front of a roaring fire with a blanket and a hot toddy. Unfortunately, she had no fireplace and she no longer drank; so, as usual, she made do by leaning up against the radiator with a steaming cup of chamomile. Her stomach roiled with margarita mix, acid, and untold secrets. She had gone back to the office for several hours after leaving Whitney at the Blue Moose, hoping to catch up on emails and sketch out some notes for the case. In reality, she just hadn't felt like going back to her cold, empty, lonely apartment.

"Isn't this romantic," she sighed, looking around her drab apartment. It was small, just one bedroom off a combined living/dining space and a tiny kitchen. But she kept it clean, if entirely unornamented, and it was in a part of town that didn't yet suffer from frequent explosions of meth labs; always something to consider in a rural agricultural area like Grand Forks.

She did not bring visitors to her apartment. Even Whitney had never been here. Olivia didn't want people to see that she slept on the floor in front of the radiator, or the lack of pictures on the walls. The lack of anything personal, for that matter.

The sleeping on the floor habit had begun as a way to save money. She'd already been sleeping on a single mattress on the bedroom floor; and it occurred to her one day that it was silly to heat a whole separate room just for sleeping in. So she'd drug the mattress and her single dresser out to the living room and closed off the bedroom, which was now as functionally useless as it was empty. Her other furniture consisted of a drabby recliner next to the small table she used as a combined kitchen table and desk. Currently it was covered with old newspapers and a stack of library books that she had yet to open. The top of the dresser served to hold her sole memento from childhood; a graduation photo from her Catholic elementary school. Fifty twelve-year-olds stood awkwardly in plaid skirts, black slacks, and matching white shirts, clutching the paper rolls that declared each of them ready to join the world of teenagers upon start of the next school year. Hers was one of only three brown faces peering out uncertainly from amidst row after row of white.

She closed her eyes, feeling the heat from the radiator beginning to loosen the ever-present knot in her back, and wished for the thousandth time that she had a cat, or dog, or anything living that would express excitement at the fact that she was finally home. And then she reminded herself for the thousandth time that it would be cruel to leave a pet home by itself for fourteen to sixteen hours a day, and she sighed, and she cradled her head in her arms and fell asleep to the rhythm of the radiator knocking and humming.

At first she didn't realize it was a dream. She walked through a thick forest, the trees surrounding her taller and wider than she ever imagined trees could be. The undergrowth burgeoned with bright green ferns, tangled vines, and unfamiliar flowers. The cool air was redolent with scents of decomposing leaves, tangy berries, and moist, damp, earth. The trail beneath her feet was gravel-covered earth, heavy with spongy moss. Her lungs felt suddenly heavy, but it was a pleasant feeling – a sense of much-needed moisture flowing back into her cells.

Olivia looked around in wonderment. She had never seen such an abundance of green life. It was like remembering the paradise from a book she'd once read; a story so satisfying and delicious that it had stuck with her for life, even after the title and author were long forgotten.

She smiled in amazed pleasure, clasping her hands together and looking up to thank God for such an amazing place existing. As she did so, the sky that she belatedly realized was dark and gray opened up and she was drenched in a cold rain. Squeaking with dismay, she took off running down the trail. She had no idea where she was going or how far she'd have to run, but anything seemed preferable to the soaking she was receiving.

As so often happens in dreams, it seemed perfectly normal that the forest around her suddenly morphed into a bathroom. She was standing in front of a dirty mirror, hands clasped on the sides of a chipped porcelain sink. The face gazing at her was one she'd never seen before, and that was when Olivia realized she was dreaming.

The woman who looked back at her had long, curly red hair and startling green eyes. The cheekbones were high, the nose small and elegant. It was as foreign of a face to her as any stranger in an airport.

Olivia screamed and the stranger's mouth opened, letting out a horrific cry of pain. The hands raised, fingers crooked and stiff, and they raked down cheeks and forehead until blood pattered across the chipped porcelain.

Olivia stepped back, holding her bloody hands before her, crying with fear and dismay.

"Please," the woman in the mirror implored her. "Please." As Olivia watched, the woman in the mirror lowered one bloody hand to grasp the small golden cross she wore around her neck.

"Please help me," she pleaded one last time, and Olivia woke, breathless, unconsciously rubbing her hands across her face, leaving her cheeks red and rosy. She almost expected to feel the raised ridges of fingernail scratches running down her cheeks.

It as only when her heart finally slowed and her breath returned to normal that she remembered the small golden cross hanging around the neck of the woman in the mirror. It looked just like the cross that Olivia had last seen in her own possession, at the bottom of a small evidence bag.

It was not like her to forget things, especially something as important as evidence. She rushed to her coat, her heart pounding, relief flowing like cold creek water when her hand felt the plastic bag still in the side pocket. She remembered then how she had put that one bag in her coat pocket so as to not lose it in her car; ironic in retrospect, since she had completely forgotten about it after arriving at the lab.

Cold creek water. Hmm. *That was an odd choice of allegories*. She shook it off, pulling out the plastic bag and taking it into the bathroom where the light was better.

She switched on the overhead fluorescent and held up the bag to the light. The cross was so tiny that even in the smallest evidence bag, it took up barely one scant corner. She could see that there was an engraved inscription on the back, but it was so small and of such delicate script that her eyes couldn't even focus on it. Cursing the vagaries of getting older (although truthfully her eyes had never been 20/20), she set down the bag to pull out the beauty mirror she never used. She'd never given in to wearing reading glasses, and the beauty mirror was the best option she had. It was a large circular mirror, with a small oval in the bottom. The oval held an extra-magnification mirror for examining those *really* small skin defects.

She held the cross up to the oval, peering close at the tiny engraving. The mirror reversed the symbols, but it wasn't difficult to right them in her mind. Across the bar – the 'arms' of the cross - was inscribed *S.L 7:21*; clearly a reference to a passage in the Bible.

The inscription down the back was not so obvious. "*...URSNSMUSMQLLUB*," she read each letter slowly, squinting as she scribbled the letters down in her notebook. "Riiiiight," she groaned out loud. Even as a former Catholic schoolgirl, that one was just beyond her reach.

Bad dream forgotten, Olivia rushed in to work that morning, excited to have another clue – no matter how small – to go on. She didn't even have time to sit down before the Lieutenant's door opened.

"St. George! Gossett! Get in here," Lieutenant Martin growled. He was a tall, grizzled man in his late forties. Where most cops would have either retired or continued to move up the ranks, Martin was happy to stay right where he was. As Lieutenant, he was able to keep a thumb in the ongoing cases while avoiding most of the never-ending politics that imbued the higher positions. Olivia had good reason to believe that his gruff exterior was just camouflage for the big softy he really was.

Olivia, knowing exactly what the impromptu meeting was for, gathered up everything the ME's office had sent over the day prior, as well as her own notes and scene sketches.

"Good morning, L.T.," she said cheerfully.

"Hmph," Martin said as usual. "Sit."

Olivia sat. A minute later, Matt finally wandered in, looking very discombobulated and not his usual smooth self. The Lieutenant raised an eyebrow.

"Everything all right, Gossett?" he asked.

"Fine," Matt said, running a hand through his hair. "Didn't sleep too good."

"Alright, fill me in."

Olivia handed L.T. the manila envelope. "ME's office sent over an initial report," she began. "Preliminary ruling is homicide. It looks like the vic died standing up, and was bound to something to keep her that way. There's still adhesive residue on her chin, ankles, and wrists. The doc sent a sample of the adhesive over to the State Lab."

"So she was taped to something," Martin said, listening while reading.

Olivia nodded. "Most likely to a pole or fence. It kept her upright after death, or so we believe."

Lt. Martin peered at the report. "This says she has an IUD? What's that?"

"An intra-uterine device," Olivia translated. Both men still looked blank, and she had to keep from rolling her eyes. "Birth control?" she offered. "A little plastic tube with copper coating inside the, uh – inside the woman. Lasts for years."

"Ah," he said, finally understanding. "And do these things have serial numbers?"

"Yes," she nodded. "They are getting that for us this morning, along with the rest of the autopsy results. Tox screen should be back by tonight."

"Good. Let's get an ID on the vic *today*," the Lieutenant emphasized. "And what about this necklace? You've got a note about it here but no picture, no details."

"Oh – uh, I haven't processed it through Evidence yet," Olivia hedged, trying not to squirm in her seat.

"What are you waiting for?" L.T. said, clearly not expecting an answer. "Keep me updated." He handed back the envelope and report, waving them away.

"Good save," Matt winked once the Lieutenant's door was shut.

She sighed. "Was it that obvious?"

"Nah. Don't sweat it. We all forget stuff sometimes."

"Yeah, well, I've been forgetting a lot lately," Olivia admitted in a sudden burst of intimacy. She pulled the bag with the cross out of her coat pocket. "I've been carrying this around since yesterday. I completely forgot about it when I went to the lab."

Matt chuckled. "Did you at least figure out the inscription?"

She shook her head. "It is a Bible reference, like you guessed, but I haven't looked it up yet. Do you mind?"

"Sure, I'll take care of it." He took the bag from her hand. "You gonna handle the IED thing?"

Olivia smothered a laugh. "Eye-*you*-dee. Yeah, I'll head downstairs."

"Thank goodness for x-rays," Whitney confided in a low voice, leaning against a wall as the newest student tech clumsily weighed someone else's brain. "We might never have found it in a manual exam. We couldn't even reach it when we did the base internal scan for sexual trauma yesterday. This girl has a *really* long canal and it was way up there." She paused. "Is it weird that I just said that?"

"Well, you are a doctor," Olivia pointed out. "But it's still kinda gross."

"Sorry," Whitney said sheepishly. "Sometimes I forget my audience."

Olivia laughed, then lowered her voice. "That's okay. Matt called it an IED."

"Hah! That sounds like him. Did you tell him that very few of us carry bombs around in our women parts?"

Olivia chuckled. "No, I was nice about it. He was looking pretty rough this morning."

"Late night, no doubt. Anyway, the serial number is in with the autopsy results." She nodded towards the folder in Olivia's hand. "The company is called Praxis. You should be able to find them online, I'd think."

"Thanks," Olivia said gratefully. "What would we ever do without you?"

"You'd have to examine your own dead bodies," Whitney joked. "Good luck."

She had expected to be on the phone all morning, being routed from one unhelpful Public Relations secretary to another. To her surprise, the Praxis switchboard operator sent her directly to the Operations Manager.

"We're always glad to be of assistance to the law enforcement community," the Praxis rep told her. A pretty standard canned response, in Olivia's experience, but nice to hear nonetheless. "But I can only tell you when and where that particular unit was shipped. You'll have to contact the receiving medical facility for anything beyond that."

"It's a start, and I appreciate it," she told him sincerely.

"Let me see." She heard the clicking of fingers typing on a keyboard. "That unit was sent to the student clinic at the University of Washington. The one in Seattle. Is there one in D.C.? I don't know. Anyway, they received it on May 20, 2011."

"How long are those IUD's good for?" Olivia asked.

"Ten years," he said cheerfully. "So your girl still has over six years to go."

"Actually, she's dead, so I don't think she'll be needing it anymore,"

Olivia said bluntly.

Silence. "Aah…yes, I'd forgotten the nature of your call. I do apologize, Detective."

"No worries. Thanks for your help."

When the Praxis rep had said "University," her heart had quickened, hoping he was about to follow it with "of North Dakota." But no such luck. However, it had confirmed an initial hunch; it *was* still possible that the vic had been either working at, or was a student at, one of the Universities in the surrounding area.

Her next task was to look up the phone number for the student clinic at the University of Washington. Olivia knew very well that this might fall under patient confidentiality. She'd probably be able to get a court order requiring the clinic to give up the information, but that would take time and resources, and would be an especially sticky matter considering that the clinic was in another state.

At least it wasn't a medical facility in Canada. That could have brought the investigation to a screeching halt.

The switchboard at UW told her in a friendly yet robotic-sounding recorded message that she could enter the last name of the party she was looking for, or she could wait until business hours to be connected. Swearing, Olivia glanced at her watch before realizing that Washington was two hours behind. It was only six in the morning in Seattle.

Sighing, she hung up the phone and swung her chair around.

"Any luck on that?" she called to Matt. His back was hunched over his desk as he flipped through the thin pages of a tiny pocket-sized Bible.

"How the hell do you find anything in here?" he groused.

Olivia *tsk*ed as she walked over. "Now, now, swearing at a Bible is bad for your health," she admonished. "Where did you get this, anyway?"

His face reddened. "It's mine."

"Nothing to be embarrassed about," she said, surprised. "I just hadn't figured you for one to keep a Bible in your desk."

"Hey, I like to cover my bases," he said defensively.

"I don't think it works that way," Olivia chuckled. "Here, look. This part here was Luke, right?"

"I dunno, I was looking through the S's," he sighed.

"It's not a dictionary in alphabetical order," she smiled. "*S.L 7:21* has to mean Saint Luke, chapter 7, verse 21."

"Okay, hold on. Ah, here we go. *'And in that same hour, he cured many of their diseases, and hurts, and evil spirits.'* Hmm. That's a weird thing to put on the back of a cross, don't you think?"

"Yeah, that is pretty weird, but so's the rest of the inscription," Olivia pointed out.

"Ye-eah, about that…" Matt squinted. "What the hell is that supposed to mean?"

"Beats me," she shrugged. "It's way beyond me, that's for sure."

"Aren't you the one who went to Catholic School?" he quizzed.

Olivia narrowed her eyes. "How'd you know that?"

His eyes skittered around the room. "Just heard it somewhere."

She frowned. "Yes, I did, but it wasn't like that. I'm not Catholic."

"Well, I'm guessing *she* is. Was. Any luck on the IED thing?"

"Matthew, it's not a bomb. I-*youuuu*-D. And no, the clinic it got sent to isn't open yet. I'll call again soon."

He shrugged. "Okay. You'd know about that stuff better than I would."

Choking back a retort, Olivia walked back to her desk. How did he always manage to piss her off so badly in such a short time?

While she waited for the clinic at UW to open, she decided to try again to follow up on the tattoo angle. It had occurred to her that a tattoo of a Latin phrase, talking about God, was not just creative; it was specific. A person who had such a tattoo would have either had to research the correct way to write and spell the phrase, or would already know Latin. As a person who had a fair amount of tattoos herself, Olivia knew that "*vocatus o non vocatus, deus aderit*" was not the kind of phrase found in most portfolios or binders of examples in your standard tattoo parlor. Combined with the engraved cross, it was likely that the vic had more than a passing relationship with the Church.

She also knew that the placing of the dead woman's tattoo was important. Most women who get tattoos on their upper back aren't planning on the tattoo being seen very often, unless they live in a very warm climate or have a job where they normally wear very little clothing. So far, Olivia had no reason to think that the dead woman fit either of those categories. Seattle wasn't particularly warm and sunny, and although Grand Forks got *very* hot in the summer, it was short-lived and full of clouds of blood-sucking mosquitoes. Neither climate was great for going about scantily clad.

That meant that the phrase, and tattooing of, was important enough to the victim that she had done it more for the personal meaning, rather than the showing off of said tattoo.

Olivia knew that generally speaking, people with tattoos could be grouped into two categories. There were those who specifically planned to show off their tats, and that was part of the reason for getting them in the first place, if not the major motivation. Then there were the people who had personal reasons for choosing to permanently inscribe their bodies, and those people weren't usually too worried about whether or not they showed off their ink. Olivia was in the second category – very few people even knew she had tattoos - and she had a gut feeling that the dead woman was as well.

A boyfriend (or so she had called him, briefly) had once asked her why she had so much ink. It was a hard thing to verbalize, especially to someone who, like him, had none at all. Olivia had thought hard and had finally said, "Because I want my outside to match my inside." How could she possibly explain that every new piece of ink, each extended piece of dermal real estate taken up by an image she had purposefully put there, made her feel slightly more *her?* More at the helm of her own body, rather than just a passenger inside a ship that she'd landed in purely by luck of the draw?

He hadn't gotten it, of course, and the relationship had ended soon after.

But it would more than likely have ended soon, regardless; Olivia was not one to let anyone get close to her, not for a very long time.

She decided the vic might even be a theology student. It was probably a long shot. Were women even allowed to be theology students? As a functioning agnostic, Olivia had no idea. But while she waited for something else to fall in her lap, it was the best idea she'd had so far. And, at least, it was something to work on while she waited.

First she went to the University of North Dakota's website to see if they offered a theology program. She didn't expect that they would, and she was right. Next she did a general search for theology programs in North Dakota and Washington. She came up with a number of universities in both states that offered degrees in theology. She bookmarked the search page, knowing that if the IUD angle came to a roadblock, she'd be contacting *all* the schools to ask if they'd had any redheaded women go missing recently.

Finally, it was late enough that she could call back to the clinic in Seattle. She finally got through to Patient Records. The weary voice on the other end told her she'd need to fax an official request for information, along with a letter from the Coroner's Office stating that the IUD was taken from a deceased person. Then after three to five business days –

"Whoa, whoa," Olivia interrupted. "Three to five *days*? You've got to be kidding me. What part of 'murder investigation' do you not understand?"

"I'm very sorry, Detective, but there's only me here," the tired-sounding woman responded. "It's not just a matter of plugging the serial number in the computer. I have to pull a list of all the students who've received IUD's and do a functional search-"

"But it was shipped to the clinic on a specific date," Olivia interrupted again. "Doesn't that narrow it down?"

Silence, then the voice heaving a sigh. "We get thousands of them, Detective. There's no telling how long we had it in stock before a patient received it."

"What if I describe the patient to you? Won't that make it easier?"

"Well, yes, I suppose so. I could narrow the search parameters-"

"Good. I'll include a full physical description in the official letter. You should receive the fax within the next hour." She hung up, feeling as exhausted as the clinic admin had sounded. She leaned back in her chair, resting her eyes for a moment, then groaning when her phone rang. She snatched it before the clamoring could make her headache any worse.

"CIB," she answered automatically.

"Is this Detective St. Cloud?" the voice said hesitantly.

"Detective St. George, yes," she corrected mildly. "How can I help you?"

"Um, this is, I mean, my name is Melissa. I work at St. Agnes' University. I'm calling about the dead girl you guys found?"

Olivia scanned her mental files for a St. Agnes', but came up blank. "Yes, Melissa, thank you for calling." She leaned over and grabbed her ever-present notebook and pen, flipping it open to a blank page. "Can I get your last name?"

"Uh, it's Thompson. Melissa Thompson."

"You have information about the victim?"

Olivia could feel the girl hesitating. "Even if you think it's nothing, every little bit helps," she pushed gently.

"It's not that it's nothing," the girl said all in a rush. "I just don't understand how she ended up in North Dakota."

"You said you work at St. Agnes' University?" Olivia said, puzzled. "Where are you located?"

"We're in Graham's Ford," Melissa Thompson said. "Washington."

Olivia paused, taken aback. "Washington State?"

"Yes."

Olivia wrinkled her eyebrows. "How did you hear about the victim?"

"Um, I saw it on TV, I think."

"Uh-huh," Olivia said, not believing it for a minute. The news about the dead woman hadn't even been broadcast in Grand Forks yet, much less across the country.

"Um, yeah, so anyway, there's this girl…." Melissa faded off.

"Yes?" Olivia pushed.

Her voice twittered with nervous laughter. "I don't know why I keep calling her a *girl*, she's older than me."

"What's her name?" Olivia pressed.

"Anna Taylor. She works part-time in the library with me. That's where I work? The library? So anyway, um, she stopped showing up for work last week and no one's been able to get a hold of her."

"Can you describe her?"

"Uh, she's about my height so about five foot two, I guess. Red hair, green eyes."

"Did anyone call the local police when she disappeared?"

"Oh, I don't know," Melissa said, sounding surprised that anyone would do such a thing. "I'd have to ask my boss, I guess."

"Has anyone gone to Anna's house, or called her family?" Olivia pressed harder.

"I don't know," Melissa was apologetic. "I'd have to ask my boss."

"And what's your bosses' name and phone number?"

"Oh.....um, her name is Mrs. Pace. Uh, Lauren Pace, I think, except I'd never dare call her that," nervous laughter again. "But she doesn't get in until eleven."

Olivia glanced at her watch. It was just after eight on the coast. "Do you always get to work this early?" she said inquisitively.

"I unlock the study rooms for the graduate students," Melissa explained. "They get priority for the rooms between eight and ten in the morning. Mrs. Pace is really strict about having the doors open *right at eight.* She's kind of a har- harda-"

"Harridan?"

"Yeah, that."

Olivia sighed. "What else can you tell me about Anna?"

"Just that she'd gotten kind of flaky the last few months. When she stopped coming in I thought she'd gotten fired, you know? But then Mrs. Pace finally asked me where Anna was."

"Flaky how?" Olivia pressed. "What was her behavior like?"

"She just got so weird," Melissa said, and Olivia knew she was shrugging on the other end of the phone line. "It was like she got afraid of everything. She wouldn't look you in the eyes, she always kept her head down. She stopped putting her hair up and it just hung down around her face all of the time. And it seemed like she stopped bathing."

"She smelled?"

"Yeah, kind of. I mean, she didn't smell like butt, or anything," her voice twittered again. "Just this weird smell, like burnt herbs or something. I don't know."

"Did she start dressing different?"

"Yeah," Melissa said, her voice lilting with surprise. "I forgot about that. She used to dress so nice – skirts all the time, pretty blouses. She was so pretty." Mournful, the past tense finally hitting home.

"And how did she dress, more recently?"

"Baggy. Grungy. But not *fashionably* grungy, if you know what I mean. Nothing fit anymore. It was like she started dressing out of an old man's closet."

"Men's clothes?"

"Yeah, they sure seemed that way. Nothing fit right and it was all so ugly."

Olivia blew out her breath. So far the description fit perfectly, which just made the conversation that much more suspect.

"Do you have any idea what precipitated the change?"

"Huh?"

"Do you know what happened," Olivia rephrased.

"Oh. Well, she was having some problems with her boyfriend, that's all I know."

"Does he have a name?"

"I don't know. We really didn't talk all that much."

After a few more questions, it was obvious that 'Melissa Thompson' had reached the limit of her information, whether real or imaginary.

Hopefully Mrs. Lauren Pace, if she was real, would have a little more information. In the meantime, Olivia could follow up on the name and see if there was an 'Anna Taylor' that had recently gone missing. She could also see what the computer might tell her about Melissa Thompson in Graham's Ford, Washington, as well as doing a back-search on the phone number the girl had called from.

She quickly put together the official letter for the Lieutenant to sign, as well as a letter for the ME to sign, to be faxed to the student clinic. Twenty minutes of running around and she'd accomplished that task. She settled back at her computer with a new cup of coffee and her notebook.

She first called the number for the mysterious Lauren Pace and as she expected, it went straight to voicemail. After leaving a cursory message, she opened up the portal to the NCIC database, which of course caused her phone to immediately ring. Cursing under her breath, she narrowly avoided knocking over her coffee as she reached for it.

"It's me," said Matt cheerfully from the other end, and she looked over her shoulder and saw his desk was empty. "I made progress."

"Where are you?" She asked belatedly.

"I'm over at that church on State Street, you know, Cathedral of the Holy Cross? They translated the rest of the inscription for me."

"That's great," she said, feeling oddly left out. "And….?"

"Oh, yeah. So, URS and all of that, is a reference to a long passage which translates as, 'Begone, Satan, suggest not to me thy vain things, what thou offerest is evil, drink thou thyself thy poison.' Apparently it's not from the Bible, exactly, but some other text? Anyway, I don't pretend to understand it but I think that's why it's written as a bunch of letters instead of shorthand, like the other one."

"The Medal of St. Benedict," Olivia realized out loud, talking mostly to herself. "I should have recognized it."

"Oh?" Matt said, and she remembered he was still on the line and was instantly embarrassed.

"Yes, the Jubilee Medal, it's called," she continued more or less smoothly. "It's considered to be like wearing a continual silent prayer. St. Benedict is said to have exercised great powers over the spirits of darkness."

"Is it typical to have it on the back of a cross like this?" He asked curiously.

"No, normally it would be on the back of the medal itself. But if the cross was very important to her, she might have felt that inscribing it on the cross was more venerable than just going out and buying a medal. I'm surprised they didn't tell you any of this," she finished in a rush, still feeling a little left out.

"Me too," he said simply, and left it at that.

CHAPTER 4

Discovery + 32 hours

After scribbling their new-found knowledge into her notes, Olivia promptly forgot about it due to several important things happening.

The first was a message delivered by the Desk Sergeant that Lauren Pace had returned her call while she was on the line with Matt. Considering that the number Olivia'd been given had gone straight to voicemail – and not the kind with a recorded name, either, but just a number – and that she hadn't even been sure Mrs. Pace existed, Olivia was ecstatic to have gotten a call back. Of course, it could still be a dud lead, or a hoax, or any number of other things, but it was surely better than *no* call back.

The second occurrence was the second message, delivered by the same irritable Desk Sergeant, that she'd gotten a call from the State Crime Lab regarding a possible match to her unidentified vic's dental x-rays. Reading that nearly sent Olivia into paroxysms of joy – suddenly her day had gone from a minus five to a plus ten on the St. George Scale of Awesomeness.

The third event that sealed her short-term memory loss was her phone ringing yet again. This time it was the Lieutenant on the other end, forgoing even the appearance of small talk.

"I need to see you," he said simply, and hung up.

Tucking the two phone messages into her desk drawer, she walked over and knocked on the Lieutenant's door.

"In," he barked, which translated meant "Come in, please, and shut the door behind you."

Olivia felt as if she was reporting to the Principal's office. The air was unusually tense and the L.T. had a strange look on his face.

"Sit down," he said with only half his normal curtness. "St. George, I have some news, and I'm not sure if it's good or bad so I'll just lay it on you."

She waited expectantly, her palms sweating. Was this it? Was she finally being fired? Or maybe transferred – that would explain the "good or bad" possibility.

He cleared his throat, seeming to be unsure of himself, which in itself was very disconcerting.

"Your, uh – your husband was killed last night," he said, watching her face.

Olivia frowned. "My…huh? Oh….Darren. My ex. What happened?"

He nodded. "Uh, yes, Darren Bernard. They seemed to think y'all are still married. He, uh, he was killed in a prison riot."

Stranger and stranger. "Darren was in prison?"

"You didn't know?" The Lieutenant was looking at her oddly.

"Sir, I haven't talked to or even thought about him in almost a decade and a half," Olivia said, which was almost completely true. "We've been apart longer than we were ever together." She avoided saying *divorced*, since technically they were not. She'd been far too afraid to stick around to serve him the papers and then, eventually, her concern at not being found had ensured that she surrender that time of her life to the dustbin of half-remembered nightmares.

And they'd been legally separated all this time, anyway. States had common-law marriages, so surely there was such thing as a common-law divorce?

"Well, I wasn't sure," Lieutenant said, seeming relieved that she hadn't burst into tears or raked her fingernails down her face or any other dramatic reaction.

"So....he was in prison?" she prompted. As much as she hated to be, she *was* curious.

"Yes, he'd been in for several years," L.T. continued. "Manslaughter, I think, maybe a few other charges thrown in. I can find out the particulars for you-"

"No, that's okay," she said hurriedly, holding up a hand. "It won't change anything." The last thing she wanted was her boss digging into her ex's past, which would eventually and certainly lead him to *her* past.

"You're still listed as his next of kin," he said kindly. "There are some folks in the department that can help you make arrangements." He held out a slip of paper.

"Um....sure, thanks," she said, dazed, taking the paper automatically.

"Listen, St. George," he continued. "I know you hadn't really been married to this guy for years, but I still want you to make an appointment to see Dr. Kennedy."

Dr. Kennedy was the Department psychiatrist.

"Whoa!" Olivia held up a hand. "L.T., I'm fine, trust me."

"Uh-huh," he said, "I'm not buying that one again. Either you make at appointment, or I'll make one for you. Understood?"

"Yes Sir," she frowned. "Not to change the subject or anything, but I might have an ID on our Jane Doe."

"Oh? Oh! Good, good." He waved her away. "Keep me updated."

"Will do," she agreed, pushing the chair to the side as she stepped out.

"And make that appointment!" He yelled at her back as she closed his office door behind her.

After Detective St. George left his office, Lieutenant Martin looked down at the file in front of him. He hadn't been exactly truthful with Olivia; he knew exactly why her husband had been in prison, as well as the man's life history, that part of Olivia's life that had coincided with the dead husband's, and the nitty-gritty details of the man's death. The Lieutenant had done his research, as thorough as he always was, before calling Olivia in to his office. He had debated whether to even tell her about the man's death, but after reading everything in the file in front of him, he'd decided it might be good for her. Closure, of a sorts, if there was such a thing. He just hoped it wouldn't push her into another incident – he'd barely been able to swing keeping her in the Department last time. It would have been a damn shame to lose her. She was everything a Lieutenant could ask for in a good cop; smart as hell, observant, reliable. She'd aced the Detective's exam her first time, despite her protestations that she hadn't had time to study. She lacked the social skills of the more popular crew, but he couldn't care less about that crap. Besides, she was able to keep Gossett in line, and that wasn't easy to do, especially for a female; that damn Swede thought his ass was gold and his charm was unstoppable.

Her last episode had been understandable, in his opinion; her best friend in a brutal car accident that had left Dr. Johansson in intensive care for weeks, hovering on the thin line between life and death. And then when Olivia had finally resurfaced from that pain, she had been slapped in the face with the gossip that Whitney had caused the accident by drinking and driving. Lieutenant Martin had done his best to squash the rumors – they did no one any good, after the fact – but Olivia had descended into a black depression for months, barely speaking to anyone when not engaged in direct conversation about a case. Coupled with what she'd already been through earlier in her life, what happened to Dr. Johansson had just been too much to bear.

Hopefully Dr. Kennedy would send her back with a clean bill of mental health, as he finally had last time, after extensive work on both his and Olivia's part.

Sighing, he opened the folder and gazed at the 8x10 photos that lay on top. The photos showed, in full color, the scars of four bullet wounds – two entry , two exit – that Olivia St. George carried on her body to this day. The old wounds had been thoroughly documented at her initial medical exam upon entering the force, as were every tattoo, mole, and scar that had existed at the time.

Olivia thought no one, other than the grizzled old doctor who had performed her exam, would ever see these pictures. But Lieutenant Martin knew everything about his people; every strength, every weakness, and every old hurt that might wreak havoc on a detective during a homicide investigation. So he knew that Darren Bernard, in a drunken fit of rage, had shot two 9mm bullets through his young wife the night of her twenty-second birthday. The first bullet had passed through the meat of her upper right shoulder and passed cleanly out the back. The second bullet had shattered the ball of her right hip, leading to several reconstructive surgeries and what L.T. guessed was a lifetime of pain, especially in cold weather.

She had refused to press charges or testify against him. Darren, of course, upon sobering up had cited "accidental discharge of a firearm." He had done a whopping eight months in prison. To Olivia's credit, she had used those eight months to change her name, file for legal separation, and leave the state.

Lieutenant Martin knew that she had never dared return home to follow up with divorce proceedings. He also knew that Olivia had not just gone back to her maiden name; she had changed it entirely, last *and* first. Lock, stock and barrel. He figured the primary reason she'd given up on the divorce was so that Darren Bernard would never find out her new name or where she'd fled to.

He also knew she'd continued to go to great lengths to hide her secret, as the years went by. He doubted she had shared details, or even the fact of, her marriage to anyone in the Department. She had never been one to get close to her coworkers; in fact, Dr. Johansson was the only friend Lieutenant Martin knew of. But she was a great Detective, and in the end that was all that really mattered around here.

Sighing, Lt. Martin reached for his phone and dialed Dr. Kennedy's number. The shrink would need to know that his "favorite" patient would be coming in for a tune-up.

Olivia sat down heavily, the paper in her hand fluttering to land on the floor next to her chair. She didn't notice she'd dropped it; her mind was elsewhere. She felt like she'd just been handed an unexpected, monstrously wonderful gift – and at the same time, she felt guilty for thinking of anyone's death as a gift.

But it was the truth. Darren Bernard had done terrible things to her that, please Lord, *no* one would ever know about. Things that had taken her years to stop thinking about. She suddenly felt a wave of anger rise up within her – wasn't it just like Darren, right when she'd finally stopped thinking about him at *all*, he had to go and do something that brought him right back to the forefront of her mind!

As preposterous as it was, Olivia felt that he had somehow planned this. He was that manipulative; to make sure that even after his death, she was being tormented.

That thought brought another, more frightening one; what if he wasn't dead? What if he had somehow faked his death solely to draw her out of hiding?

After all, she hadn't run that far; only one state away. And obviously there were still records in existence that connected her to Darren, since the Lieutenant had known about her marriage, and even the prison had tracked her down despite her name change.

Unaware that she was whimpering under her breath, Olivia's fingers flew across her keyboard, searching for further information about the supposed death of Darren Bernard. She found an old blurb about his incarceration, and once she had the location it was easy to find a phone number for the administrative office at the prison.

She dialed the number, her chest tight with anxiety. *Pick up, pick up*, she prayed silently. *Yes!*

"Hello, this is Detective St. George, Grand Forks Police Department," she said, trying to reign in her breathing. "I'm just following up on a cold case. Do you have a prisoner named Darren Bernard?" The lie came out easily.

"We did," the administrative officer said, "but I hope you didn't need him as a witness, Detective, because he was killed during a prison riot last night."

"Oh, dear, a riot?" she said, trying to sound interested and sympathetic.

"Well, more of a skirmish, really. Only a few prisoners involved. He was the only one hurt."

"Would it be possible to get a copy of the death certificate?" she asked.

"Uh – sure, I don't see why not. What's your fax number?"

She read it off. "Please make it to my attention," she stressed. "St. George."

"Will do. Anything else?"

"May I ask how he died?"

"Shanked right in the neck. Messy as hell, I don't mind telling you. Guy who did it was a lifer anyway – probably a paid job. Bernard wasn't too popular around here."

"Really?" *Imagine that, Darren not popular.*

"Yeah, sexual offenders usually aren't anyway, but he was especially good at pissing everybody off."

"I'm sorry – sexual offenders? I was under the impression that he was in on a manslaughter charge."

Pause. "Well, yes, but that wasn't the only one. He was shacking up with some seventeen year old girl, and one night he got drunk and decided to use her for a punching bag. Not the first time, I might add, but this time she died from internal injuries. So they got him for assault and battery, rape because she was underage, and manslaughter."

Good Lord. "Wow."

"Yeah. I get the impression the local cops had just been waiting for a reason to take him in. It's a shame it had to come to that."

"Well, thanks for your help."

"No problem. I'll get that fax off to you."

She hung up, her mind spinning. He obviously hadn't changed his ways since she'd lived with him. And a seventeen year old girl? *God, Darren, didn't you learn* any *self control?* she thought angrily.

At least it had put her mind at ease. Maybe she'd frame the death certificate and hang it in her bathroom. It would give her something to look at when she was taking a shit.

That's so gross, she berated herself. *Instead, make a hundred copies and use it for toilet paper.*

Chortling in her mind, she opened her desk drawer and took out the two phone messages, eager to get back to work. The message from the Crime Lab included the name and phone number for the dentist who had reported a possible match. Olivia dialed the ten digits, noting that it was an out-of-state area code.

"Tumwater Dental."

"Is this Dr. Basilla's office?"

"Yes it is, how may I help you?"

"This is Detective St. George, Grand Forks Police Department."

"Oh, yes, Detective, I was told you might call. I have that information for you right here. We had a patient named Anna Taylor whose x-rays might match those of your deceased."

"I'm sorry – *might* match?"

"Yes, well, there is some degree of probable error. Teeth are just teeth, after all, not DNA, no matter what you see in the movies."

"I'll remember that," Olivia said wryly. "In other words, Dr. Basilla is covering his rear end by saying only 'possibly.'"

"Exactly." Her wry tone was matched by that of the receptionist. "Although with x-rays being digitized now, it's a lot easier to promise a perfect match than in the old days. What else do you need from us?"

"Do you have an address? Phone number? Parent's names, anything like that?"

"She hadn't been in for some years, but I can tell you the last known address and phone. She wasn't a minor so there's no parent information."

"When was her last visit?"

"Hmm….looks like….June of 2011."

"I'll take everything you can give me."

That task accomplished, Olivia relogged into her computer. This was turning into a bully of a day, and she wanted to see what else she might be able to find on Anna Taylor before calling Mrs. Pace.

Most people – especially the younger generations who had practically been teethed on iPhones and iPads – didn't know, or care, to be wary about how much of their personal information ended up on the internet. Anything they had ever typed or uploaded to a website would exist in cyberspace almost forever. People cried indignantly about corporations and governments accessing their personal statistics, and then they tweeted and Facebooked every moment of every day of their lives to a cyberworld of what amounted to random strangers. It was funny, really.

Like most cops, Olivia didn't have a Facebook page, much less a Twitter or Tumblr account. She knew the value of cyber anonymity.

According to Dr. Basilla's receptionist, Anna Taylor's birthday was August 14, 1980. That would make her just over thirty-four, a prime age for underestimating the power of a search engine when digging for dirt. Oddly, after thirty minutes all Olivia had come up with was a single forum entry by Anna80 in Tumwater, Washington, which might or might not actually be Ms. Taylor. The forum was a familiar one to Olivia; called *Broken Wings*, it was a virtual group therapy room for victims of sexual abuse and sexual assault. Anna80 had tentatively asked,

How can u know 4 sure ur being hurt if it leaves no marks?

Other forum members had left a flurry of responses – 58 in total - many of which spurred further discussions and led to multiple threads. But Anna80 replied to none of them, nor did she respond to pleas to elaborate on her situation.

Olivia did a screen capture and printed it for her file. It was a very thin lead to go on, but did add a checkmark to the "killed by abusive boyfriend" section on the list of possible scenarios.

Finally, she picked up the phone to dial Lauren Pace, who would hopefully still be in her office. Olivia glanced at her watch; it was four her time, which made it only two in the afternoon in Pacific time.

Where had the day gone? She had had no idea it was so late already. Her stomach rumbled as she realized lunch had long since come and gone.

Mrs. Pace's office phone rang and rang, and just as Olivia had begun to lose hope, a chipper, surprisingly young-sounding voice answered. After the description given by Melissa Thompson, Olivia had expected an angry old curmudgeon; the stereotypical wrinkled old librarian brandishing a ruler and a sheath of Overdue slips. The voice on the other end sounded nothing like that.

"Yes, this is Lauren Pace," it chirped. "Thank you *so so* much for returning my call, Detective!"

"Uh, my pleasure," Olivia said, taken aback. "Do you-"

"You see, I have *so much* to tell you," Mrs. Pace interrupted. "I'm just *sure* I can be of great help to your investigation!"

"Wonderful," Olivia said, still dazed. "I-"

That was the last word she managed to get in for quite awhile, and after a few minutes she gave up and just listened. Mrs. Pace was a font of information, and she was *extremely excited* to impart everything she knew to Olivia's willing ear.

"You see, we've all been very worried about Anna," Mrs. Pace said breathlessly. "So *very* worried, you see. That boyfriend of hers – oh my! What a doozer that one is." *Doozer?* "I thought she'd finally gotten rid of him for good, but here he comes yesterday, acting all broken up about her. What a terrible thing! Can you believe that boy even had the *gall* to ask me – me! how he could get in touch with her? Imagine! Well, he might as well be wearing a sign that says 'Guilty,' if you ask me! Had a hangdog look on his face like I've never seen."

Boyfriend already knew about Anna's death. Olivia put another checkmark in the *boyfriend* column in her mental notebook, and reminded herself again to do a background check on Melissa Thompson. Love triangle, perhaps?

"...and that poor girl. Such a *pretty* girl. Wanted to be a nun, you know, before that *thing* with her uncle. Oh! What a horrible man. Who would take advantage of a child like that? And him a *minister*, of all things! Turned her right off the Church for good, it did. Just terrible. Terrible." Mrs. Pace *tsk*ed again.

"Mrs. Pa-" Olivia tried and failed again to break in. The woman's voice flowed like Niagara Falls; overwhelming and utterly unstoppable, yet heartening to behold.

"...and then she finds this boyfriend. *Seamus*. Ugh, such a character. And it was straight downhill for our Anna! Her studies gone to pot, her self-esteem right down the toilet. She went completely to seed. Her looks, hair, clothes, everything. I think she actually started wearing *his* clothes. It was horrible, horrible!" At that she broke down and cried, and Olivia gave her a moment before jumping in.

"Mrs. Pace," she said firmly, determined to get her own boat afloat before the river started back up. "Please allow me to ask you a few questions."

"Oh, I'm so sorry," Mrs. Pace sniffled. "I do go on, don't I? Please, dear, go ahead."

"Thank you," Olivia said, mollified. "How long did Anna work for you?"

"She started here in January of 2012," the librarian sighed. "It was work-study, you see. Part-time work for full-time students. I was so pleased with her that I went to the Dean, and he helped us get a grant for a full-time position so I could keep her on. That was – oh, must have been about a year and a half ago, now."

"And does Seamus have a last name? How long had they been seeing each other?"

"Seamus Kiely, I think it is. Must be about six months now he's been coming around here. I'm not sure how long before that they started going together."

"And how did you hear about Anna's death, Mrs. Pace?"

"In my heart, I already knew," she said flatly. "But Melissa told me this morning when I came in. She said it was all over the television. I don't have one, myself, so I would never have seen it."

"How long was Anna missing?" Olivia asked gently.

"She – she never came back after the Christmas break," Mrs. Pace sighed, and Olivia winced to hear the heartbreak in her voice. "I thought maybe she'd been stuck somewhere – you know, snowed in with relatives or something – but she didn't answer her cell, and I called and called, and she just never showed up."

"Did you contact the police?"

"Yes, I did. They went to her apartment and didn't find anything wrong, or so I was told – I wasn't there – and they said she'd probably just gone off with friends or something."

"But she wasn't one to just 'go off' somewhere, was she," Olivia guessed shrewdly.

"No! Certainly not. Detective, Anna was like a daughter to me, and truthfully she was more responsible than at least two of my own children," Mrs. Pace gave a sad little laugh. "I just knew something *terrible* had happened to her during the holiday break, but I didn't know what else to do."

"I understand," Olivia said kindly. "Do you remember who you spoke with when you talked to the police?"

"Yes – um..." she snuffled for a moment. "They sent me to Missing Persons, to a Detective Carmichael."

“Thank you.” Olivia jotted that down. “What can you tell me about her family?”

“She didn’t have much,” Mrs. Pace said wistfully, perhaps thinking about her own children. “Just that uncle – the bad one – and she mentioned a sister once or twice, but they weren’t close. Some sort of falling-out, I guess.”

They talked for another twenty minutes, by the end of which Olivia had formed a mental picture of all the players thus far in this tragic play. Seamus, the dark-garbed, brooding, perhaps violent boyfriend; Anna, the beautiful, shy late bloomer with low self-esteem who may have been sexually abused as a child by her minister uncle; and Melissa, the flighty, part-time library aide who often showed up smelling like pot and liked to flirt with all the boys.

The only part that didn’t click for Olivia was the massive age difference between Anna and the other two. Mrs. Pace had been surprised herself when Olivia pointed it out – being so much older than all of them, the librarian had never really noticed – but most 34-year-old graduate students don’t make boyfriends out of 19-year-old college sophomores, which is what Seamus apparently was. Anna was practically old enough to be his mother. And Melissa? She was barely eighteen, Mrs. Pace said. The girl had done some sort of alternative study program that allowed her to graduate high school early.

It did add more credibility to a possible love triangle, however. Melissa would have been jealous and perhaps bitter about a woman so much older than the man – boy, really – she was dating, a boy Melissa may very well want for her own.

Olivia could see where the attraction between Anna and Seamus might have come from, although she felt it was stretching logic a bit. A late bloomer, unaware of her own beauty, shy and inexperienced, still emotionally scarred from childhood abuse – as young as Seamus was she might have seen him as safe, closer to her own level of experience and emotional maturity than men her own age.

And Olivia also knew all too well how flattering it was simply to be *liked*, especially for a woman who believed herself unattractive and unlovable.

By time she got off the phone it was going on quitting time. She glanced at her watch, bounding out of her chair and catching Lieutenant Martin just as he was about to lock up his office.

"St. George? Where's the fire?" he cocked an eye at her.

"Sir, I just need a few minutes of your time," she pleaded.

"My wife is waiting, and she *hates* when I'm late for date night," he grumbled. "You've got five minutes."

"Great!" she rushed. "I need to go to Washington."

Pause. "What? Why?"

"That's where our Jane Doe is from!" Olivia was unaware of how chipper she sounded. Lauren Pace's chirpiness was seriously infectious.

"Whoa, back up," he held up a hand. "You got an ID?"

"Well, it's still a *possible* ID, but everything fits," Olivia amended. "Dentals, description, timeframe, even a possible motive – it's all there." She quickly sketched in the framework of what she'd learned in the past few hours.

"What about the IUD?"

"It was shipped to the Student Clinic at the University of Washington in Seattle. I talked to the clerk there. She has to go through the patient records by hand to find a match to the serial number – it'll take her a couple of days."

He frowned. "Have you contacted this Carmichael over there in Missing Persons?"

"Not yet," she acknowledged.

"Call the local P.D. in the girl's hometown and ask them if they dusted her apartment for prints," he directed. "If they did, and you get a match to our Jane Doe, I'll send a bucket down the dry well that is our budget and scrape up enough to fly you two out there."

"Great!" she said. "Thank you *so so* much, Lieutenant. Have fun on your date night!"

He gazed at her morosely. "And do us all a favor, St. George. Cut down on the caffeine, okay?"

As she was looking up the number to call Detective Carmichael, it flashed on her what L.T. had said; *you two*. As in, she'd have to take Matt Gossett with her. *Shit!*

In the excitement of the day she'd forgotten all about him. She turned to look at his desk, but his chair was empty and his jacket was gone. He'd already left for the day, apparently.

Olivia sighed, suddenly exhausted. She hadn't eaten anything all day, running on pure adrenaline to get from one discovery to the next. She decided that after one last phone call, she'd call it quits for the day.

Thankfully, the sergeant she spoke with at Graham's Ford P.D. was helpful and promised to send a team to get prints, if they didn't already have any on file. She explained that it should be an active Missing Persons case, although she had yet to speak with Detective Carmichael, and the sergeant grunted knowingly.

"Wish we could send *him* out there," he grumbled. "Do him good to get off his fat ass. It'll prob be someone from Crimes Against Persons, though."

"Shouldn't it be someone in Homicide or Violent Crimes?" she inquired. "Not to step on your toes or anything…"

"Not a homicide yet, at least for us," the sergeant pointed out. "Now, if you get a *match*, on the other hand….but we'll cross that road when it comes."

"Agreed," she sighed, eager to get off the phone and get home. "Do you mind having them call my cell as soon as it's done? I'll let the crime lab know to expect the prints." She read off her cell number.

"No prob. Should be done by day's end."

Leaving the building, the frigid wind greeted her with a slap in the face. The mercury had held steady all day at minus three but with nightfall was dropping fast. Olivia was reminded of the Lakota name for the month of January; *ċaŋ napopa wi*, "the month when the trees break." Frequent heavy snowfall, occasional ice storms, and harsh winds led to many a tree losing limbs as the weight of thick layers of ice built up on the branches.

She hurried to her car, glad as always that the parking lot was equipped with plug-ins for block heaters. It meant the difference between her car warming up for five minutes or twenty minutes – or not starting at all. She had never sprung for a remote car-starter, because she only thought about it in the exact moment that she opened a door to walk outside. As soon as the block heater was unplugged, cord safely stowed behind the license plate, and she was snug inside the car, thoughts of a remote starter were again forgotten.

Pearl Jam's classic *Black* started up when she turned the key. Eddie Vedder wailed about his lost love and Olivia shook her head, thinking of love triangles and unrequited love gone wrong. It wasn't a coincidence that *that* song came on; it had been just beginning when she'd turned off the car, but it did seem oddly appropriate given what she'd learned that afternoon.

The title *Black* flashed across her mind, and she had a sudden vision of the graphic novel that the asshole gas-station clerk had been reading; *Black Dog*. The cover had truly been an artistic masterpiece, consisting of a half-naked, grossly over-endowed platinum-blond female being attacked by a growling, shaggy, half-man half-beast. The monster clearly had something on his mind besides making her his dinner, as evidenced by the leering expression on his part-human face. The woman had been shrinking back, both hands held up to fend off the beast, but the look on her face was one of weary resignation as if this was something that happened to her all the time.

Olivia shook herself out of the reverie, growling under her breath at the memory. Fuck that clerk and his stupid "graphic novel." She cursed her brain, that it could remember such details about something she'd only glanced at and yet forget important things like leaving evidence in coat pockets and eating lunch.

She'd suddenly had enough *Black* and hit the button to eject the CD and go to radio. The speakers were silent for a moment before delivering the dulcet tones of Soundgarden's *Fell on Black Days*. Swearing under her breath, she grabbed the first CD that was next in her book and shoved it into the player. Her jaw dropped when the first song it launched into was *Black Sunday*, on Black Label Society's album *Order of the Black.*

"Fuck!" she said angrily, stabbing the button and turning it off entirely. "Just too fucking ridiculous."

Happily, home was a short ten-minute drive away. By time she walked in the door, all thoughts of the clerk, man-beast creature, and violent love triangles had been washed away by dreams of a hot shower. She felt cold from the inside out; the short drive, not even long enough for her car heater to really warm up, *had* been long enough for her to get a chill that went straight to her bones. Sometimes she had trouble believing that she was actually native to this climate, as miserable as she was every winter. Some of it was due to old injuries, sure; no matter what the doctors claimed was *supposed* to happen after a wound healed, cold inevitably made things hurt. Some things just couldn't be put back the way they were.

The hot shower was everything she'd dreamed it would be. She settled into her recliner with a microwave dinner of turkey enchilada, limp green beans, and something that the box claimed was "cherry cobbler." It didn't resemble any cherries Olivia had ever seen, but it was hot and sweet and she ate every crumb.

Warm and full for the first time all day, snuggly in the cozy chair with a quilt pulled up to her chest, her eyes suddenly felt very heavy. She had just started on her new copy of the *Wicazō Ṡa Review* but didn't make it three pages before her eyelids closed and her head made a slow-motion descent onto the back of the recliner.

CHAPTER 5

Discovery + 40 hours

On the right they will devour, but still be hungry; on the left they will eat, but not be satisfied. Each will feed on the flesh of their own offspring.

- Isaiah 7:9:20

It was the voice that got her attention. Olivia opened her eyes to see who was there. Sometimes the other tenants got loud, but this voice wasn't muffled by walls or doors. It was a familiar voice, and even as she struggled to place it, the hair on the back of her neck was already standing up at whatever hint of memory had flashed through her mind.

She raised her head to look around for the speaker and found her face to be only inches from a smudged bathroom mirror. She was standing, wearing only her bathrobe, her hands tightly clasped to the sides of a chipped, white porcelain sink. It was the kind meant for smaller spaces; not wide but with a deeper bowl, and without surrounding countertop or cabinetry, leaving the plumbing exposed underneath.

"This is a dream," she stated, and the face in the mirror nodded.

"Yes, it is," the other woman agreed. Olivia recognized her from the dream of the previous night, the details suddenly flooding back.

"Are you Anna?" Olivia asked, already knowing the answer.

"Yes," the other said. She was wearing the same clothes she'd had on when her body had been found in the ditch, and her hair was messy and streaked with mud. But her face was clean and clear, without a hint of decay or injury.

"Are you haunting me?" Even Olivia's dream-self felt awkward asking that question. It seemed such a terribly personal thing to ask someone.

"You're dreaming, Olivia," Anna reminded her from the other side of the mirror.

"So this isn't real?"

"I didn't say that. You must figure out what's real and what isn't." Anna leaned in, an urgent look on her face, staring into Olivia's eyes. "And it's very important you understand that just because something occurs inside your head *doesn't mean it isn't real.*"

As the last word dropped from her lips, a claw-like hand snaked around the side of Anna's head, clamping over her mouth. The redheaded woman's eyes went wide, her shriek of surprise and dismay muffled by the grip of the mostly-unseen attacker. Anna's hands flew up, reaching for Olivia, who could only watch in horror as the woman on the other side of the mirror was yanked backwards with such force that her body folded in the middle like a rag doll. She disappeared into the darkness that had consumed the mirror.

Olivia shrank away, knowing that something bad was coming, Anna's last words ringing in her ears. She tried to will herself to turn away, to run, to go *somewhere* but her body was frozen in place.

"*Oliviaaaa,*" a voice whispered from the darkness. It was the voice that she had heard upon arriving in this nightmare, the man's voice. Only now she recognized it as Darren, and even as her stomach fell his voice changed into something much less than human. It was *deep*, like the growl of a big, angry dog, yet somehow sibilant and whispery at the same time.

"*Oliviaaaa,*" it called again, and laughed a horrid, slimy laugh that made her ears hurt. "*Did you like my gift for you, Oliviaaaa?*"

"What gift," she whispered, tears leaking uncontrolled from her staring eyes. The blackness in the mirror was swirling, smoky, and all-consuming.

"*Your loving husband,*" it answered mockingly, and she felt a hand running up her back. She tried to jerk away but it came to rest on her right shoulder and *pressed*, exerting such force that she could feel her knees threatening to buckle. "*His death was my gift for you, Oliviaaaa.*"

She grimaced with pain, leaning as her right leg began to give way. The old injuries to her hip and shoulder flared into hot knives stabbing into her and twisting inside the joints and muscle tissue.

The voice laughed as she cried out, her hip and knee buckling under the pressure.

"*Or should I say...*Kaya," it whispered cruelly, and then was gone.

She blinked, raising her head and seeing her comforting living room, the quilt that still lay across her lap, and the book she'd dropped. The carcass of her microwave dinner still balanced precariously on the stack of books.

Her relief was palpable. Just a bad, bad, *bad* dream. You'd think that knowing you were dreaming would make it less frightening, but for a lucid dream that was a doozy.

Doozer, her mind amended, remembering Mrs. Pace's unique turn of phrase. She glanced at her watch and saw it was barely seven. She'd only been asleep for a few minutes.

Needing to hear a friendly voice, she got up and grabbed her cell phone from her purse, hitting speedial-2 for Whitney's cell. She knew the doc would answer unless she was deep in someone's body parts.

It rang and rang, and just as she was about to give up it clicked. Olivia waited for Whitney to answer, perplexed, hearing only light static.

"Whitney?" she asked, checking her phone to make sure she'd dialed the right number.

"Whit-" she tried again before being interrupted.

"*Oliviaaa,*" the serpentlike voice slithered from the cellphone, chuckling with malice. "*You're too late she's already* dead!"

"No," she gasped, closing the phone with a hard slap and throwing it down on the floor. "I'm dreaming I'm dreaming I'm-"

The phone rang. She watched the face light up, Whitney's name scrolling across the top as the theme to *Bones* rattled Olivia's nerves. She'd chosen that ring tone for Whitney as a joke but had come to like it, until now.

She eyed the phone like it was a swaying cobra. Finally, cursing herself for what was surely massive stupidity, she gingerly reached down, picking it off the floor and flipping it open.

"Hello," she whispered after a long moment, closing her eyes tight.

"Olivia?" Whitney's concerned voice was almost drowned by the rush of relief as Olivia let out the breath she'd been holding. She opened her eyes and saw she was once again sitting in her chair, quilt still up, book still dropped, everything as it should be.

"Wh – Whitney? Is that you?" she stammered. "I'm sorry, I just had the worst dream. I'm so out of it."

"Are you okay?"

"Yeah. What's up?"

"I had a bad feeling. Can I come over? We can order pizza."

"Um..." Olivia's head was so fuzzy but her stomach growled, reminding her that pizza would be a great supplement to the one tiny meal she'd eaten. "Sure, that sounds good."

"Great!" Whitney sounded so chipper. "I'll be right there."

Even as Olivia folded her phone closed, the doorbell rang.

"How did you do that?" she asked, more than a little freaked out as she let Whitney in.

"I was already here," Whitney quipped. "The beauty of cell phones."

She stepped in, casting a curious eye around the apartment.

"Love the décor," she teased. "I see you've chosen 'early austerity' as your theme. You didn't tell me you were a nun in your off-time."

"Nice of you to notice," Olivia raised an eyebrow. "And why are you only wearing your labcoat? Where's your winter coat? Aren't you freezing?"

Whitney looked down at herself, seemingly puzzled. "No, I'm fine."

"Well, you've got to be cold. Do you want some tea or something?"

"Sure, thanks."

Olivia opened a cupboard, removing two mugs and a plastic bin filled with boxes of tea. She filled both mugs with cold water and put them in the microwave. "What kind of pizza do you want?"

"Anything's great."

They stood for a moment, Olivia watching the timer on the microwave, Whitney watching her. Finally the timer dinged, Olivia plunked in two bags of chamomile, and carried both mugs over to the living room. A few moments later, pizza ordered, they both settled on to the mattress that served as both bed and couch.

As they waited for the pizza to arrive, Olivia's mind drifted back in time. Hearing Darren's voice, even in a dream, had been disconcerting to say the least. As her mind wandered, she gradually became aware that Whitney was speaking to her.

"Earth to Olivia!" The doctor said for what was probably the fourth time. "Geez, where you at, woman?"

An uncharacteristic desire to unburden rose in Olivia's chest.

"My husband was killed in prison last night," she said all in a rush, her eyes wide and intent. "The husband that I have not seen since the night of my twenty-second birthday, when he beat the crap out of me before shooting me twice and dragging me out to die in the ditch behind our trailer." She stared at Whitney, heart hammering in her chest, waiting for her friend to look shocked or horrified or both.

Instead, it was as if nothing Olivia had just said registered. "Ooh, pizza's here," Whitney said, rising from the mattress at the knock on the door. "Can you get it? I need to use the restroom."

Appalled, shaking in embarrassment and confusion, Olivia did as requested. Waiting for Whitney to come out of the bathroom, she ate a slice of pizza silently, her mind once again drifting back in time.

South Dakota, a hot summer's evening. The air is stifling, filled with the buzz of mosquitoes rising over the sodden grass. The girl still known as Kaya – it will be a year before she is Olivia – is hurriedly packing a dingy suitcase, throwing clothes in with no regard for what her hands are grabbing from the dresser. She knows she has to be gone before he gets home; if he catches her packing, his temper – already brimming over earlier that day – will be more than she can handle.

He'd been drinking since breakfast, as he did most Saturdays. His anger these days was ever-present; whatever bit of love he'd had for her, way back, was gone entirely, lost in his need to control and manipulate. His little Indian doll, *he called her, saying it like a sweet nickname, but he meant it sincerely; she was his plaything, to make do whatever he desired. Any refusal or even hesitation was met with the coldest of cold anger; there was to be no denying of his will.*

Ironically, what he wanted was never for her to be with him. In the beginning, all he asked for was an audience for his perverted fantasies; stories that stretched through half a ream of paper, filled with pictures scavenged from porno magazines and twisted plot lines that he himself thought up. If she didn't immediately comply or didn't act excited enough for his liking, he would turn cold and angry. His affection for her was entirely dependent on her doing exactly as he wanted with no hesitation.

Eventually, the stories weren't enough; she had to act out the fantasies, first by herself, then with 'friends' he brought home from the bar or from town, while he watched. The things she had to do for him became increasingly sadistic and strange as time went by, and now his newest plot twist was a mixed-race baby; he had long since been fascinated with anything and everything interracial and already guilted her into being with several black men he'd met in town. Now he wanted her to let one of them get her pregnant. Not that Darren was even capable of loving a child – any baby was just another life-form for him to control, manipulate, and break to his will.

This new requirement to earn his love was the final straw for Kaya/Olivia. Everything she'd already done was horrible enough that she suffered from ongoing nightmares, but the thought of bringing a child into this house made her vomit. She had stalled him for as long as she could, but finally she could stall no longer; he had set up a "date" for her for that very night, and when he came home and discovered she had not gone, his fury would be unstoppable. His will was entire, and there could be no arguing; she might as well argue with the wind.

The air in their small trailer reeked of his heavy cologne and the cheap whiskey he favored. He liked to "pre-game" before going to the bar, and she knew very well the cologne was meant to attract other women. He wanted nothing to do with her *body, but still he got delight from his conquests outside of their marriage bed.*

She thought briefly of his gun, wondering if she should grab it and take it with her, but she didn't know where he kept it and the thought was quickly washed away by the glare of headlights shining into the living room. It could have been anyone driving by – their trailer was at the front of the complex – but she knew instinctively it was him, thrown out of the bar early for acting the drunken fool and pissing off the other patrons.

Gasping for breath as her heart surged, adrenalin pumping into her veins, she abandoned the suitcase where it lay and raced for the back of the trailer. The bathroom window was tiny but it did open, and with the door closed to fool him, might just give her enough of a head-start to actually make her escape.

She was still wrestling with the window when she felt his heavy footsteps on the cheap plywood deck outside their front door. Hot tears began to fall as she tried to angle her shoulder; as small as she was, she couldn't quite fit both shoulders out the tiny window at the same time. Her right arm nearly popped out of its socket as she wrenched it back in, her head and left arm hanging outside, mosquitoes already biting her as she struggled.

The front door slammed, heavy boots striding across the living room and headed her way. He was already grumbling aloud, no doubt in a foul mood from whatever had occurred at the bar, heading for the bathroom to relieve himself.

She wriggled desperately as she heard him arrive at the closed bathroom door, and pause.

"Babe?" His deep voice, thick with alcohol. "What're you doin home?"

She tried to make her voice light, the windowsill pressing against her chest. Her shirt was caught on the latch, she realized in an abstract way, as she turned her head and called to him through the window.

"Done already, baby," she chirped, hoping to sound cheerful. "Just cleanin' up."

Her shoulder popped painfully as she gained another few inches, and the floor creaked as he turned away from the door. She could feel *the moment he laid eyes on the open half-full suitcase, and the whimpering under her breath was second only to her painful gasping.*

"Kaya?" he growled, and there was a thud as he swept the suitcase to the floor. "What the fuck is this?"

"Baby, I'm just putting some stuff away," she called, her voice catching in her throat as she shoved herself through yet a little further, sweat dripping from her efforts. "That dresser is so full, y'know, and-"

"You lying piece of shit whore!" he hollered, and in her hysteria she tittered at his ironic choice of epithets. The bathroom door splintered in its cheap frame as he kicked it open, charging through like a huge white bull.

A heavy hand came down, grabbing the waistband of her pants and wrenching her backwards into the tiny bathroom. The windowsill dug red lines across her stomach, her shirt shredded by the latch that still held it tight, as she was pulled from her escape and thrown against the wall. His fist was the first to make contact, breaking her cheekbone with a red burst of hot pain across her vision, but the boot quickly followed suit, thudding into the side of her thigh over and over again as she screamed.

"Leave me, will ya?" he was breathing heavily, waves of whiskey breath wafting across her bleeding face as she moaned. She reached out for the door frame, trying to pull herself into the other room, and a jagged piece of broken wood stabbed into her palm.

"Don't worry, baby," he grunted, taking something from the back of his pants. "If you want to go, I won't stop you." She looked up through a red haze to see a small black eye looking straight at her; she didn't even have time to realize it was the barrel of his gun before the eye flashed once, twice, and she was washed overboard into a sea of endless pain.

Olivia was jarred awake by her last memory of that night, gasping for breath and staring around her small apartment wildly. She was in her chair, mug of untouched tea on the table next to her stack of books. She stood, her legs shaky, and walked forward four steps to see an empty bathroom. Turning in confusion, she saw the pizza box on the kitchen counter; only her single slice was gone. Whitney was nowhere to be seen; except for the other mug of tea, sitting cold and untouched on the floor, it was as if she had never even been there at all.

CHAPTER 6

Day Three

The Chief and his Tribe went to the American Indian Center at Mission and 16th. They were looking for an Indian. They had walked all the way from the Haight. A lock hung on the door of the Center. They stood by the door, wondering whether they should go back to Haight, wait around, or call somebody. "I wonder where all the Indians are?" one of the Tribe said. "Maybe it's a day off or something," the other Tribe member said.
- *The San Francisco Indians* (Simon Ortiz)

The next morning, Olivia blearily opened her eyes at the sound of the alarm. Out of habit, she glanced at her cell phone and was surprised to see that she'd missed a call in the wee hours of the morn. It was an unfamiliar number from an out of state area code; probably some drunk, she figured, misdialing their cell phone in an attempt to get a cab.

She had to call it back, just to be sure. There was the slim possibility that it was someone calling about another case. And if it *was* some drunk, it would serve them right if she woke them up at six in the morning.

She hit Send and waited as it rang, and rang, and rang. Finally someone picked up.

"Hello," the voice said very quietly.

"Hello, I'm sorry if I woke you, someone at this number called my phone a few hours ago," Olivia said. "This is Detective St. George at the Grand Forks Police Department."

Long pause. "I'm sorry, I think you have the wrong number," the soft voice said, sounding *very* sleepy.

"Who am I speaking with?" Olivia said, putting on her Police Officer voice.

“Laura.” Yawn. “I didn’t call you, I’ve been asleep all night.”

“Laura, does anyone else have access to your phone?”

Long sigh. “No, I live alone. But I only got this number a few days ago, are you sure you mean *last* night?”

“Yes Ma’am I do,” Olivia said firmly, glancing again at her missed calls list. “Someone at this number called my cell phone at three-thirteen a.m. – less than three hours ago.”

“Oh my God, Lady,” the sleepy Laura groaned. “I don’t know what the hell planet you’re on but it’s barely four o’clock now. I have a test in the morning, I’m going back to sleep.”

Click.

Olivia stared at her phone for a moment before flipping it closed. Sleepy Laura must be on the Pacific coast, but who would be calling Olivia in the middle of the night from over there?

It was too early for this. She heaved a sigh and hauled herself off the bed and into the kitchen. She would love to take another hot shower – more for the “hot” part than for the “shower” part – but both her green streak and wallet said No. Water was expensive here, and hard to come by except in the form of snow. No sense in wasting.

She got the coffeemaker brewing and nuked a bowl of instant oatmeal. On mornings like this she missed the days of wearing a cop uniform, when she didn’t have to figure out what to wear.

Lethargically spooning lumpy oatmeal into her mouth, staring at the rising level of caffeinated goodness in the coffeepot, Olivia ran down her mental To-Do List:

- Check on fingerprints from Anna Taylor’s apartment – why the hell hadn’t those guys called her yesterday evening? – and get said fingerprints to Crime Lab

- Call UW Student Clinic, check on progress of IUD identification

Technically the two cancelled each other out, but when it came to identifying a body, a Detective could never be too careful. She'd rather get confirmation on both before trying to contact Miss Jane Doe's family.

- Research Melissa Thompson and Seamus Kiely
- Call Anna Taylor's landlord, find out when she was last seen, and get names & numbers for neighbors in building who might have known her
- Call the University, get names & numbers for Anna's professors and classmates

After the last one her brain stalled out. The thought of all those phone calls made her even more tired; she hated interviewing over the phone. But until she confirmed that Anna Taylor was their Jane Doe, there was no way the L.T. could swing a plane ticket for her to go clear across the country to interview people in person.

Time for coffee. Just smelling it made her feel better.

When she walked in the building, she decided to swing by the ME's office before going to her desk. She felt a little awkward about the night before; the good Doctor had acted so oddly, not at all her normal kind self, and the situation had left Olivia doubting her own sanity, which was a familiar and thoroughly unwelcome feeling. It was a state she had experienced in great depth in years long past.

She was shocked to see the lights off and the door to the lab locked. Whitney was practically always at work, especially since returning from her long stint in intensive care and losing her family. Work was her life, quite literally.

Well, it wasn't the end of the world. Whitney deserved to sleep in. Olivia went back to the elevator and up to her own desk, ready to dig in to another long day at work.

She was, for once, pleased to see a stack of phone messages waiting on her desk. She flipped through pink papers, looking over each one, then walked straight to the Lieutenant's office.

She knocked on the doorframe and stuck her head in, pausing when she saw he already had his nose in paperwork. He held up one finger, finished reading whatever he was looking at, then looked up.

"Yeah," he said, obviously distracted.

Olivia held up the handful of pink slips. "Guys in Washington dusted for prints and sent 'em electronically right to our lab," she said. "God bless technology because the tech guys already got a match. Also, the clinic called back about the IUD. We've got double confirmation that Jane Doe is Anna Taylor. Can I go to Seattle now?"

His eyes widened, then he grinned. "Hallelujah. At this rate you'll have the whole thing wrapped up by dinnertime tomorrow. Go up to Admin, get the billing code for us 'cause I can never remember what the hell it is, then book two plane tickets to Seattle. *Cheap* ones, mind you, department ain't made of gold."

She grinned back and gave a little salute before turning to go. "Aye aye, Chief!" she said happily.

"And don't forget to tell Gossett!" L.T. yelled at her departing back. "You can't just *pretend* you forgot to take him with, like last time!"

She chuckled as she walked away. 'Last time' referred to a departmental picnic. She had been strong-armed into carpooling with Matt, then conveniently forgot all about it and showed up by herself. He'd played it off well, but everyone knew she'd done it on purpose and she still caught ribbing about it from time to time.

The Detective in question had yet to appear for the morning, so she took the liberty of leaving a tantalizingly vague yet direct note on his computer monitor.

M – ID'd vic, we fly out 2day. – O St.G

She was tempted to book the first available flight, but besides being even more ridiculously expensive than the later ones, she had to be fair and give Matt enough time to actually *get* to work before making him turn around to go home and pack. Although, she thought as she glanced at her watch, if he didn't hurry up she'd be well within her rights to just leave him behind.

Sigh. Pipe dreams, and all that.

She finally booked them both on the noon flight out of Grand Forks. It would have been slightly cheaper to fly out of Fargo, being that they had all of four gates versus Grand Forks' two, but it also would have meant a 2-hour drive across the frozen wonderland of flatness that is eastern North Dakota in January. Not that the thought wasn't tremendously exciting, but it was going to be bad enough having to travel with Matt at all without the extra car ride thrown in.

At least she didn't *have* to put them in adjoining seats. Happily, both the commuter flight out of GF as well as the commercial flight they had to catch in Chicago had enough seats available that she was able to pick two widely-spaced seats. *Very* widely-spaced.

At five till eight she glanced at her watch again, sighing in frustration. Still no Matt. Although their work hours were technically eight to five, like most of the other Detectives Olivia normally got in at least thirty minutes early to catch up on email.

At exactly eight he waltzed in, Starbucks in one hand and a donut in the other.

“Morning Ted, morning Jean,” he said casually to those he passed.

“Matt!” she barked, then winced at the sound of her voice. *God, I sound like Roseanne yelling at Dan*, she thought morosely.

“Aaand a good morning to you *too*, Detective St. George,” he said cheerfully yet sarcastically. “What can I do for you today?”

“I got an ID on our Jane Doe,” she said just as cheerfully, slapping a printout of his e-Confirmation against his chest. He juggled for it, almost dropping his coffee, finally balancing the donut on top of the Starbucks lid so he could take the paper before it fell to the floor.

“What’s this?”

“We’re flying to Seattle. The plane leaves in four hours and I’m *not* driving you to the airport, so you better get packed and get yourself to Gate 2 by eleven thirty.”

He looked more confused than usual. “Why are we going to Seattle?”

“Well, I *could* brief you on everything you’ve missed over the past two days, or you could just read this,” she said merrily, handing him a manila envelope. “It’s the report I gave the L.T., along with copies of the medical exam, photographs, and everything the Crime Lab’s gotten so far.” She slapped him on the meat of his upper arm. “Happy reading!”

Olivia got to their departure gate with plenty of time to spare, considering that it only took four minutes to get through Security. One of the nice things about such a tiny airport, she thought to herself as she slipped out of her shoes and put everything on the scanner belt. She’d had to check her gun, of course; even as a cop she couldn’t carry on the plane. It had to be taken apart and stored in a locked container with the ammunition separate.

She wondered if Matt would think of that, or if he’d even think to bring his weapon. Technically they didn’t have any jurisdiction where they were going; but she didn't plan to take her gun *out* of its lockbox. She just liked having it available, just in case.

When she got to the waiting area at the gate she made herself comfortable. She went to the ladies' room and refilled her water bottle, since water couldn't be carried through security (she still hadn't figured out the point of *that* restriction). The vending machines were well-stocked so she emptied her bag of change, then refilled it with plenty of snacks for the trip. They'd be landing in Seattle at four-thirty, but because of the time difference it was actually a six and a half hour trip.

When it came time to board the plane, she still hadn't seen Matt. She fought down the impulse to call his cell phone; she wasn't going to babysit him. If he couldn't even get himself on the plane on time, that was his problem; *he'd* have to explain to the L.T. why he wasn't in Seattle.

She slept most of the way to Chicago and woke up with a crick in her neck. She was still rubbing it and grimacing when she found her connecting gate. She had almost an hour to spare before the next flight, so she found an open seat by the windows and took a book from her bag. It was already overdue from the library, and she was determined to read it and finally get it turned in.

She'd just opened it when a man sat in the seat next to her. The waiting area was just full enough that there was no point in finding a new seat; she'd end up sandwiched between two other strangers. So she ignored him, trying to concentrate on the words on the page.

After a few minutes she felt him looking at her. She pretended not to notice, determined not to give him an opening.

"Is that any good?" he asked finally.

She shrugged, glancing up just long enough to be polite but not meeting his eyes. "It's okay," she said dismissively before going back to the page.

"I've tried to read that author, I just couldn't ever seem to get into his stuff," the guy said.

"Yeah, he's pretty hard to read," she admitted reluctantly. "I keep trying to like it because I feel like I should. It's even on the Recommended Reading list at our library."

He chuckled, turning towards her just a little more. "I know what you mean. I always wonder how many books are on the best-seller list just because we all think we *should* like that author, even though nobody actually does."

She laughed, finally looking up for real. He was mid-thirties, fair, with sandy blond hair and startlingly blue eyes. He wore an expensive-looking dark blue suit and shiny black wingtip loafers. Her cop's eye saw a well-off businessman, probably on his way to an important meeting with a client.

"I'm William Gustafson," he held out a hand. "Bill."

She hesitated, finally taking it and giving it one quick shake. "Olivia St. George," she said.

"Very nice to meet you. What do you do, Olivia?"

She held back a wolfish grin. "I'm a cop," she said bluntly. "And you?"

He smiled. "Good thing I'm not a criminal. I'm a mechanic."

She blinked. "Pardon?"

"Oh…the suit." He looked down at his clothes. "I'm on my way to a funeral. It's a really quick trip so I didn't bring a change of clothes. It's not even my suit."

"I'm sorry to hear that. Someone close to you?" Olivia mentally drew a line through *businessman* and wrote in *mechanic – maybe*. That explained the calluses on his palm.

"Not really. I'm mostly just going to be there for my sister. A good friend of hers passed away."

"That's very...brotherly of you," she said, immediately kicking herself. "Very sweet, I mean."

"Well, she's my baby sis," he sighed. "So what about you?"

"I'm on a case," she said.

He paused. "You mean you really are a cop?"

Olivia almost laughed. "You didn't believe me?"

"No, I...it just seemed like something you'd say as a woman traveling alone when a strange guy tries to talk to you," he admitted. "But that's awesome. I think you're the loveliest police officer I've ever met."

She batted her eyelids. *Oh my God I'm actually flirting with this guy.* "I bet you say that to all the girl cops," she teased.

"Well, I've tried it on the guys too but they just don't respond to it," he said, deadpan. "How long will you be in Seattle?"

"I don't know. Why?"

He flushed just slightly. "I leave on the red-eye tonight. I thought maybe....we could meet for a late dinner or something?"

He's shy! she realized, delighted. "Hmm...well, I hate to make a promise when I really don't know what's going to happen with this case. Can I call you?"

A beautiful smile spread across his entire face. "I would love for you to call me. Here's my cell number and the number at my sister's house. And my name's Bill."

She laughed. "Yeah, I got that. Thanks, Bill. I'll give you a call later today then." She tucked the piece of paper into her wallet.

"That'd be great." He was still smiling. "Um...do you want me to let you get back to your book?"

"Nah, this thing sucks," she admitted, closing it up. "Would you like to get some coffee with me before the flight?"

His smile got bigger, if that was possible. "Yes I would."

Boarding the plane, Olivia felt happier than she had in a very long time. She and Bill had enjoyed a nice, relaxed conversation at Starbucks, and she actually felt good, like someone who was capable of having a normal, *un*dysfunctional life. Whether they had dinner together or not didn't matter, although it would be nice; just the fact that they hadn't met in a bar was exhilarating enough.

She was settling into her seat when she saw Matt coming down the aisle. He looked flustered.

"Hey, you made it!" she called out cheerfully.

"Just barely," he muttered as he walked by. She laughed to herself, shaking her head. *I bet he missed the flight out of GF*, she thought, *and had to jump on the next commuter flight, which would have given him exactly* – she glanced at her watch – *eleven minutes to get to this gate.* No wonder he looked disheveled.

Bill's seat was on the other end of the plane from hers, for which she was glad; they'd left it on a very nice note and it would have been awkward if they'd ended up being seated right next to each other. Only in movies are coincidences like that amusing, she thought; in real life, people don't want to have some stranger continuously shoved in their face, no matter how much 'chemistry' there is between them.

Of course, she added in her mind, *in movies people always fall into bed together right after they meet and I've learned the hard way how much* that *doesn't work out in real life.*

Their flight landed in Seattle on time. She collared Matt on the way off the plane, juggling her carry-on in one hand and their rental car reservation in the other.

"Hey, I have to go to Baggage Claim," she told him. "Then we're going down to the Graham's Ford cop shop."

He frowned. "Won't it be kinda late by time we get there?"

"Unlike you, other cops work *past* five p.m.," she jabbed. "Besides, they know we're coming. Our L.T. promised their L.T. that we'd brief him before we did anything on this case."

"Alright," he grumbled, rubbing his face. "I'll get the rental car while you get the bags."

She cocked her head. "Are you okay?" she asked kindly.

He sighed. "Just tired. Haven't been sleeping good. And I can't sleep on a plane – I'm too cramped in those tiny seats."

"Well, I'll drive and you can rest." She patted his shoulder, putting on a horribly fake Italian accent. "Don't-a you worry, Mama Livia take-a good care-a you."

It worked – she was rewarded with a tiny smile.

Matt *was* tired; by time they hit I-5 his head was tipped back against the head rest, loud snores reverberating from his open mouth. Olivia played with the radio, delighted to find a great rock station almost immediately. She kept the volume moderate in deference to her snoring partner – which was a crime, really, as some music is meant to be really, really loud – but still enjoyed it. She rocked her head along with the music, oohing and aahing under her breath at how lovely the landscape really was. All she had known about Washington and Seattle was that it rained all the time. Granted, a fine mist was forcing her to use the wipers even now, but if that was the reason for how amazingly green everything was in the middle of winter? She'd put up with the rain, too.

The drive passed quickly and before she knew it, they were exiting the freeway. She pulled into a gas station, figuring that Matt would appreciate a chance to wash his face and wake up before they briefed the L.T.

Matt didn't budge, even after the car was parked and the ignition turned off, so she gave him a friendly poke in the side.

"Hey, slugger. Wake up."

He didn't seem to notice so she poked him a little harder. "Matthew, wake up."

He groaned, stretching and yawning widely. She waved her hand in front of her face, grimacing.

"Wow, dude. Here, have a breath mint. I'm going in to use the restroom. You coming?"

He yawned again, following it with a sleepy yet lascivious grin. "Only if we can use the same one."

"Yeah, yeah," she said dismissively. "Here's a comb. Go in and wash your face and put yourself back together."

"Yes, Mother." He gave her a little salute. "Thanks for not drawing on my face while I was asleep."

She winked. "Who says I didn't?"

The Graham's Ford PD was right down the street from the gas station. They introduced themselves at the front desk, showing their badges, and the desk sergeant lifted a phone to his ear.

"Ma'am? They're here," he said and replaced the receiver. "Alright folks, go straight through the door. Lieutenant Alvarado's office is the last door on the right."

The Lieutenant was waiting for them. She was quite tall, towering over Olivia by nearly a foot, with short brown hair and piercing green eyes. She wore a sensible, dark-blue linen suit and black flats. Olivia, sensing a kindred spirit, was immediately delighted, and she didn't fail to notice that Matt seemed somewhat deflated by being almost eye-to-eye with their host.

"Sarah Alvarado," the Lieutenant said, giving each of them a firm handshake. "Please, have a seat. We appreciate you coming all the way to Washington. Very few people would have put out such effort for a Jane Doe."

"Well, we have so little excitement," Olivia joked. "Really, though, thank you for seeing us."

Lt. Alvarado folded her hands on her desk and leaned forward, looking very serious. "Lieutenant Martin gave me the gist of it, but pretend that I don't know anything about this case. Tell me everything."

Matt handed her the manila envelope. "Copies of everything we have so far, for your records," he said. "Uh, I'll let Detective St. George fill you in." He looked very uncomfortable.

Olivia cleared her throat. "Yes, Ma'am, thank you. Vic was found approximately sixty-five hours ago in a ditch off Highway 2, about five miles from town limits. Evidence indicates the woman had been bound with duct tape and left outside to freeze before being dumped. She died while standing upright. The facial muscles and derma from the left side of her face had been removed after death with a serrated blade, but the M.E. found indications of a 3rd degree burn in that same area. No indications of sexual assault or internal trauma, except a strange rash inside her thighs and inflamed tissues in her vagina, caused by some kind of irritant. M.E. ruled death by freezing. No defensive wounds and nothing under her fingernails. The only personal possession on the body was a small gold cross with an engraved inscription. We used her fingerprints and the serial number from her IUD to ID the body as that of Anna Taylor, thirty-four, previously of 1621 Horseshadow Lane, apartment twelve. She had previously attended UW and was currently a grad student at St. Agnes', where she also worked as a Library Aid. Supervisor said she never came back after Christmas Break. Conversation with a co-worker indicates possibility of a violent boyfriend." Olivia paused and took a sheet of paper from her bag. "Here's the list of people we need to interview, their relationship with the vic, and last known addresses." She handed it over to Lieutenant Alvarado, who glanced at it before placing it with the envelope.

"Okay," the L.T. said. "So what do you need from us?"

Olivia and Matt glanced at each other. They hadn't expected this; the briefing was just a formality, they thought, something to ease the awkwardness of stepping into someone else's jurisdiction.

"Ma'am, all we need at the moment are background checks from your local database on those three individuals," Olivia said.

"Easy enough. What else? Manpower? Directions? Hotel recommendations?" L.T. prompted.

"Uh, I think we're good for now, but thank you," Olivia said, raising an eyebrow at Matt. He nodded in agreement.

"Yes Ma'am, we'll let you know if we need anything else."

"Good. I've assigned a Detective to accompany you when necessary, since you don't have jurisdiction here. You'll meet her in the morning."

"Thank you," Olivia and Matt said in unison.

"Good!" She rose to her feet and held out her hand again. "Good to meet you. Keep me updated."

"Will do." They all shook hands again and the visiting Detectives made their way back to their rental car.

"That was interesting," Olivia observed as she slid into the driver's seat. "Are you okay?"

Matt frowned. "Fine, why?"

"Oh, you just seemed a little…uncomfortable."

His eyes narrowed. "What do you mean?"

"Female Lieutenant and all that."

He turned to face her, his face hard. "You think I have a problem with women, don't you."

Olivia turned to face him as well. "Don't you?" she said directly.

He frowned. "You're being antagonistic," he said flatly. "Let's just go."

Olivia rolled her eyes and turned the key. "Yes, dear," she muttered under her breath.

She'd made reservations for two rooms at a nearby hotel. They checked in and dropped off their bags, Olivia securing her weapon – still in its lockbox – in the room safe. She'd been right when she guessed that Matt wouldn't think to bring his.

They had managed to agree on a plan of action. Being that it was already evening, their first stop would be Anna Taylor's apartment building. They'd split up and interview as many of her neighbors as they could before calling it a night.

Anna Taylor's apartment complex was two rows of three story, double-sided tan buildings. Each building had twelve apartments. The grounds were well-kept and even in January, rows of bright flowers lined the sidewalk.

"Pretty nice digs for a grad student," Matt commented. "How much you think her rent was?"

"Let's find out," Olivia said. She'd called ahead to make sure someone from the main office would be available to meet with them. She parked the rental car in a Visitor's spot. A red Prius was in the Staff parking space.

"Have you noticed how everyone here drives a Prius?" Olivia mused.

Matt shrugged. "It's easy to drive an electric or hybrid when it never gets below zero."

"I suppose." Olivia raised a hand and knocked on the front door of the main office. She heard heels clacking and then the knob turned.

They were greeted by an older woman with a helmet of gray-blond hair that had been moussed and sprayed into submission. Her face was heavily made up, with thumbnail-sized gold balls hanging from her ears.

"Hello, hello, come in," she gushed, her voice lilting with a touch of Irish. "I'm Maggie Hofstedt, the owner. You must be the Detectives."

"Yes Ma'am." Matt ducked under the doorway, Olivia following suit. "I'm Detective Gossett, this is Detective St. George. We'd like to ask you some questions about one of your tenants."

"Yes, yes, of course, Anna Taylor. Please, have a seat. Can I get you anything? Water, juice, coffee?"

Olivia perked up. "Coffee would be great." Three chairs had been arranged around a small coffee table in the middle of the room, which looked like it would normally be used as a waiting area. She saw a door on the other side of the room that stood halfway open, revealing a tiny cluttered office almost entirely taken up by an overflowing desk.

"Ma'am, we were expecting a landlord or superintendent to meet with us. I hate to put you to all this trouble," Matt said smoothly. Olivia had to give him credit; he might be intimidated by women authority figures, but he was great at questioning female witnesses. All that masculine charm oozing from his pores, she supposed.

"Actually, my husband and I *are* the landlords, supers, and almost everything else," Mrs. Hofstedt said, setting two mugs in front of them. "We used to own quite a few complexes, but it was getting to be a bit much for us. We sold the others a few years ago, and now we just manage this one. We're semi-retired, you might say."

"And you run the front office?" Olivia guessed, taking a sip from her coffee. "Wow, this is wonderful. Hazelnut?"

"Hazelnut crème, actually," Mrs. Hofstedt smiled, "not that I've ever been able to tell the difference. Yes, I do all the paperwork – leasing, billing, and so forth. My husband takes care of the maintenance aspect."

"He maintains all these apartments by himself?" Matt raised an eyebrow.

"Oh, no. He has one full-time employee and several on-call specialists for electric and plumbing. I also have a girl that helps me part-time here in the office."

"What can you tell us about Anna Taylor?" Olivia asked, opening her notebook.

"She was a good tenant. Very quiet, always paid on time or in advance."

"How long had she lived here?"

"Oh….almost three years now."

"How much was her rent?" Matt interjected.

"She paid six-fifty a month." Mrs. Hofstedt leaned forward. "I gave her a student discount when she moved in," she said in a conspiratorial whisper. "She was such a nice girl and I hated to think of her having to live in a bad neighborhood like so many of the kids from the college."

"Did she have a roommate?"

"No, just her."

"Boyfriend? Anyone that came around regularly?"

"Not that I saw. But that doesn't mean much. I try to give my tenants their privacy, being that we live on site and all."

"Where is your husband? We'd like to talk to him as well."

Mrs. Hofstedt smoothed a wrinkle in her silk pantsuit. "He's actually working in Anna's apartment."

Olivia's heart dropped. "He's not *cleaning* it, is he?"

"Oh, no, dear. He's just installing a new range. We're converting all the apartments to flat-top ranges; they're so much easier for the tenants to keep clean."

"That's very nice of you. Why don't we go visit your husband and Detective Gossett and I can see her apartment at the same time?"

"Of course." Mrs. Hofstedt disappeared into her office, coming back out with a key in hand. "It's in the last building on the left."

The three of them trouped down the sidewalk, Matt towering over both of them like a giraffe with two gazelles.

"The air smells so good here," Olivia commented, inhaling deeply. "Is it always like this?"

"Oh, no dear," Mrs. Hofstedt assured her. "This is such a dreary time of year. I do get so tired of the rain and gray skies."

Olivia kept her comments to herself, considering 'eye of the beholder' and all that. The air was damp and fragrant and at least fifty degrees warmer than back home, and despite the gray sky seemed to her to be anything but dreary.

Mr. Hofstedt was a well-muscled older man with a full head of white hair and two arms covered with ancient tattoos. They seemed to have held up well, though; Olivia could still make out the basic form and function of each picture. He seemed an odd choice for his Mrs.; a clashing of social levels, blue-collar boy sweeps rich girl off her feet.

"Hello, dear," Mrs. Hofstedt said fondly, giving her Mr. a little smooch. "These are the two Detectives I was telling you about."

"How-do," he greeted them, holding out a hefty paw. Olivia gingerly shook it, watching as her hand was enveloped by his callused mitt.

"Uh, Detective Gossett, why don't you speak with Mr. Hofstedt while I take a look around," Olivia suggested, turning to Matt.

"Sure," he agreed. "Mr. Hofstedt, I'd just like to ask you a few questions…"

Olivia walked around the apartment, trying to get a feel for the woman who had lived there. Thank goodness Anna had been in the habit of paying her rent in advance; the Hofstedts said they hadn't even known she was gone until Graham's Ford PD came by, so all of Anna's things had remained undisturbed – at least by them. It remained to be seen if anyone else had a key to the place.

Anna had lived sparsely, like the student she was, but had leaned towards flowered fabrics and wooden furniture. Many of her possessions looked to be second-hand, or she'd had them long enough to take the 'new' off. Her sofa was worn, the armrests a little battered, and the coffee table had overlapping rings stained into the cheap wood. A windbreaker still lay across one arm of the sofa. Several theology textbooks sat on an ottoman next to the coffee table.

Olivia paused at the bookcase. The shelves alternated books and knick-knacks; Anna'd had a penchant for ceramic animals, battered science fiction novels, and quasi-Irish-religious plaques. Many of the little animals had shamrocks on them, despite being stamped "Made in China" on their undersides.

She knelt down, tipping her head to see the books on the lower shelves. The spines were darker, dingier, and much more faded than the novels on the upper shelves. Anna had been quite interested in the darker aspects of religion; she had copies of *Compenium Malificarum, Malleus Malificarum,* and *Grimorium Verum*, not to mention *The Rite, A Guidebook to Demons,* and *A History of Demonology and Witchcraft*. She also had a copy of the Bible, Torah, and the Quran.

"Quite the religious buff," Olivia muttered. She pulled out *The Rite* and opened the front cover. A discolored bookstore stamp marred the first page; Haven Books on Winchester Avenue had been proud to sell this used book.

She slid the frightening-looking tome back in its place and took out her phone, clicking through the menus until she brought up the video function. She scanned the camera eye slowly across the titles, making sure each one was readable.

As long as the video was going, she might as well get the rest of the apartment. She walked carefully through each room, making her own little documentary; "The Furnishings of Anna Taylor."

Anna's bedroom was neat and clean; suspiciously clean, in fact. The bed was even made. Her closet was half-full of skirts, slacks, and blouses. No men's clothes in sight. The bathroom was equally clean; no rings in the tub, no grime in the toilet. Even the mirror was sparkling.

Olivia had wondered if the bathroom would be the one from her dream, but no such luck. The sink was blue, surrounded by a blue countertop, and the mirror was also the door to the medicine cabinet rather than being a free-hanging mirror like in her dream.

Oh well. Maybe it was just a dream; Olivia had certainly had stranger things going on in her head than a simple lucid dream, in years past.

As she was standing there, staring at the clean bathroom, she suddenly realized something looked out of place.

"Hey, Matt?" she called. "Can you come in here a minute?"

"Hang on," he called back. She heard him talking as he finished up with Mr. Hofstedt, then he came around the corner.

"What's up?"

"Do you see anything strange here?" she asked, wondering if it was a figment of her imagination.

He looked for a long minute, pursing his lips in concentration.

"Yeah," he said finally. "There's a pattern in the floor that doesn't quite make sense."

"Right! Like the outline of something, don't you think?"

Matt crouched down, running his finger over the linoleum. "It's....melted," he said slowly. "Just enough to leave a slight discoloration." He put his hand down, following the marks by feel. "Do you have a pen?" he asked Olivia.

"Um...here," she said, handing him the one from her notebook.

"Thanks." He traced the edge of the melted area, using his finger every few inches to make sure he was still on track. Olivia watched as a familiar shape appeared behind him as he crawled across the bathroom floor. He reached the end nearest the tub, and following the melted line, began to come back towards Olivia with the pen.

"It's a body," she said, amazed as she saw it take shape. "The outline of a body."

Matt finished and stood up next to her. He gazed down at his handiwork.

"A woman, you think?" he asked.

She nodded. "The wider hips and narrow shoulders would suggest a female. What could have caused this, do you suppose?"

He shook his head. "I can't begin to imagine. Some sort of....pretend sacrifice, or something."

"Well, let's call it in and have the lab guys tear all this up and take it in. They should also test the walls here for any bio residue or smoke."

"Smoke?" Matt asked.

"Yeah, like from candles and such."

"Oh. Good thinking. They must have been trying to hide whatever went on here – that would certainly explain why the bathroom and bedroom are so much cleaner than the rest of the apartment."

Matt escorted the Hofstedts outside and waited with them as Olivia made the call.

"You good?" Matt asked her. Olivia nodded, tucking her phone into a pocket.

"Yeah, I'm ready," she agreed. "Folks, thank you so much for your time. We'll let you know if we have any further questions. In the meantime, we'll need you to stay out of Anna's apartment."

They all shook hands again. "I'll walk you back to your car," Mrs. Hofstedt said.

Matt and Olivia shook their heads simultaneously. "No need," Olivia said firmly. "We've got some other folks to talk to as well."

"Oh!" Mrs. Hofstedt looked surprised. "Oh….okay then." She watched them leave as they walked away, a funny look on her face. Olivia saw the Mrs. lean forward and say something to the Mr., who frowned and shook his head before they turned and headed towards the office.

"What do you think?" Matt asked her quietly.

"Definitely not telling us something," Olivia said.

"Do you think she was killed here?"

She frowned. "Probably not, considering how far her body would had to have been transported. But it's possible – a freezer truck would have kept her cold."

"Well, let's see what we can get from the neighbors, and hopefully the lab guys will find something. Which side do you want?"

"I'll take this side," Olivia lifted her chin to indicate Anna's side of the complex.

After two hours, she took a break to make a phone call. She walked out into the parking lot, in between a GMC Jimmy and an oversized Escalade. She took the scrap of paper from her wallet and dialed the number to Bill's cell phone.

Her stomach tingled nervously as it rang. She was almost relieved when the voicemail finally picked up.

"Hi, Bill, it's Olivia St. George," she said, trying to sound casual. "I think I can make dinner tonight, if the offer's still on and you don't mind eating late. Here's my cell number…thanks." Click. She hated making phone calls of a personal nature – they were so awkward and uncomfortable.

She sighed, looking down the row of cars and thinking about the neighbors she'd interviewed already. So far, no one seemed to have known Anna at all. She was the perfect tenant; quiet, industrious, with a regular schedule that didn't disrupt anyone else. Only a few people could recall ever seeing her come and go from her apartment, and only the woman directly across from Anna knew her by name.

"She was very sweet," the lady had sniffled after Olivia explained why she was asking questions about Anna. "She always smiled at my little girl and asked her about school. Once she helped me carry laundry up the stairs. I didn't even realize how long it had been since I'd seen her."

Looking at the cars, something occurred to Olivia. She stepped out until she could see underneath the Escalade; a number was painted in white on the asphalt parking space. Most likely, it corresponded to that person's apartment number.

She walked back down the parking lot until she found the space for Anna's apartment – number twelve – situated roughly near the front of her building. A gold Mini Cooper was in the space, parked slightly crookedly. Olivia walked back to the office, hoping the Hofstedts were still there. She tried the door and it opened, so she stuck her head in; both Hofstedts were standing inside, looking at a document.

"Sorry to bother you," Olivia called and stepped inside. "What kind of car did Anna have?"

Mrs. Hofstedt looked up. "Oh…hello dear. I'm not sure, actually, I'd have to look at her lease."

"Was it a gold Mini Cooper?"

Mrs. Hofstedt frowned. "No, I'm sure it wasn't anything that flashy. It was something sensible; a Toyota or Honda, maybe. Something older and kind of beat-up."

"She drove a 1994 brown Toyota Corolla," Mr. Hofstedt said matter-of-factly. "Her tires were always low and I told her they were probably dry-rotted. She said she couldn't afford new tires. The fan belt squealed when it ran."

Mrs. Hofstedt tittered. "He's so good with cars," she said proudly. "Not me, I don't know a hatchback from a sedan."

"Do you know who the gold Mini Cooper might belong to?" Olivia hinted.

"Oh…is someone in her spot? They know they aren't supposed to do that. I'm not sure whose car that might be," Mrs. Hofstedt frowned again. She seemed overly agitated, considering.

Mr. Hofstedt sighed. "It's somebody visiting a tenant," he said. "I don't know which apartment, but that car is here a couple of times a week. Maggie, I've told you that twice now."

"Oh…that's right, you did." Mrs. Hofstedt looked flustered. "I keep forgetting to leave a note on the windshield."

"Alright…thanks, folks." Olivia waited until she was outside to scribble down a note about the gold car. She wished she'd noticed it sooner; she could have been asking each neighbor about it. Well, Graham's Ford PD could run the plates for them tomorrow and clear up that mystery, anyway.

She saw Matt coming down the sidewalk. "Hey," he called. "How many more you got?"

She checked her notes. "Uh…five more. You?"

"Three – the back side of the last building. It's going faster than I thought."

"Yeah, it doesn't take long when nobody knows anything," Olivia said ironically. "I don't know why I thought these people would be any different than *my* apartment building – I wouldn't recognize my neighbors if they fell on me."

"Me either," he sighed. "Hazards of modern living, I suppose. I'm gonna go finish up."

As Olivia was standing at the second-to-last door, waiting for an answer to her knock, a rotund little tabby appeared and wove itself between and around her feet.

"Hey, little guy," she cooed, stooping to give it a scratch between the ears. It leaned into her hand, purring loudly, then rubbed against her leg while she fished a business card from her pocket. She circled her name and cell number, then wrote *Please Call ASAP* in the middle and stuck it in the frame of the door. The tabby followed her to the last door, nearly tripping her as she tried to walk. It wandered away while she spoke to the last person, but when she went back down the stairs it found her again, pushing against her leg insistently.

"Geez, alright," she said with good humor and giving it another scratch. It wore a dilapidated black collar with a faded plastic tag. She rubbed dirt from the tag with her thumb, peering at the faint letters.

Andrew Kiely

555-605-7278

Kiely, huh? She knew *that* last name. Seamus must have a relative in this apartment complex. *Maybe that's how he met Anna,* she surmised. *Coming around to visit someone else.* But she hadn't interviewed any Kiely; maybe Matt had.

Speaking of the devil, she saw him coming towards her.

"I'm all done." He waved his notebook in the air. "Nothing."

"Me either," she said. "Did you interview anyone named Andrew Kiely?"

Matt frowned. "No, no Andrew, no Kiely."

She gestured at the tabby that was lying across her right foot. "Someone's lying, then, because the Pillsbury Dough-Kitty here has Andrew Kiely right on his tag."

"Hmm." Matt bent, scratching the cat underneath its chin. "Maybe someone's cat-sitting for him."

"Possible," she amended. "Or…I did have one door with no one home. What about you?"

He shook his head. "No, amazingly, I got someone at every apartment. It's probably a record."

"Let's go talk to the Hofstedts again, then." Olivia retrieved her foot from underneath the tabby, which promptly jumped to its feet and trotted after them.

"Looks like you made a friend," Matt teased.

"That's me," Olivia nodded seriously. "Making friends wherever I go."

The Hofstedts must have finished up because the office was locked up tight.

"Hmph," Olivia said. "To their apartment, I guess."

Matt glanced at his watch. "Maybe they're eating dinner."

"Could be." The Hofstedt apartment was an attached unit on the back of the main office, accessible by a separate sidewalk that ran behind the building.

Mrs. Hofstedt looked disgruntled to see them again.

"Was there something else you needed?" she said politely. She had changed into more comfortable clothes but her hair and face were still made up.

Maybe she sleeps like that, Olivia thought uncharitably.

"We were wondering who lives in apartment 47," she said.

Mrs. Hofstedt pursed her lips. "Oh dear, I always have such a time remembering that boy's name. Something with an S….Sean, Shane, um…."

"Seamus?" Olivia suggested.

She brightened. "Yes, that's it! Seamus Kiely."

"Does he live alone?" Olivia asked. "I saw the name Andrew Kiely on this little guy's tag."

Mrs. Hofstedt burst into laughter. "My dear, Andrew *is* the cat. Seamus is very serious about it but Anna always called it Andy when she took care of…." Her voice faded off, her face tightening as she realized she'd said too much.

Olivia and Matt looked at each other. "Ma'am, I think you'd better let us in," Olivia said in her Scary Policewoman Voice. "It appears there are some things you forgot to tell us."

The older woman sighed, her face suddenly sagging. "I suppose so," she said, opening the door wider.

Mr. Hofstedt was parked in front of the television, watching a sitcom. He switched it off when he saw them coming, straightening his shirt and looking uncomfortable.

"Won't you sit?" Mrs. Hofstedt gestured at the remaining two seats on the couch.

"No thank you, Ma'am," Matt said formally. "Why did you lie to us about Seamus and Anna?"

"Oh, I didn't *lie*," Mrs. Hofstedt put a hand to her throat. "You didn't ask me if he knew her."

"We asked you about boyfriends," Olivia pointed out.

Her eyes widened. "I really don't think it was like that," she said. "They were just friends. I didn't want to involve him unnecessarily."

"He's already involved," Matt pointed out.

"I'm sorry," she said mournfully. "I couldn't bear to think of that nice boy having anything to do with Anna's disappearance."

Mr. Hofstedt suddenly spoke up. "That kid's a weirdo," he said. "Always dressing in black, always having strange people over. Wouldn't surprise me if he killed her."

Mrs. Hofstedt gasped. "George! Don't you dare say that! He's a very nice boy. Lots of children now are into that 'gothic' look. It doesn't mean anything."

"Have either of you done any cleaning in Anna's apartment since she disappeared?" Olivia asked pointedly.

Mrs. Hofstedt's eyes suddenly darted away. "N-no…not that I recall."

"He did," Mr. Hofstedt volunteered. "That Seamus kid."

"George!" His wife put her hands over her face, collapsing onto the sofa.

"You have to tell them the truth, Maggie," George said firmly, putting an arm around his sobbing wife. "What if he did kill her? You can't let him get away with it."

Mrs. Hofstedt nodded from behind her hands. "He – he came in the office one morning and asked to borrow the carpet steamer," she admitted. "He said…he said he was going to surprise Anna by cleaning her apartment for her while she was on vacation. I thought it was a strange thing to do, but thoughtful, you know?"

Olivia and Matt nodded silently, Olivia thinking to herself that she'd strangle anyone who had the nerve to clean *her* living space without her say-so.

"He had Anna's keys. I knew it was her set because of the little leather fob shaped like a cross. And then…" she stopped, struggling with the words. "The next day I saw him throwing something away, acting kind of sneaky about it. I looked in the dumpster after he was gone and there was a clear plastic bag with a woman's shirt in it."

"What kind of shirt?" Olivia prompted gently.

Mrs. Hofstedt burst into fresh tears. "A bloody shirt!" she wailed. "A flowered blouse just like Anna used to we-we-wear." She sobbed into her hands.

"Did you keep the shirt?"

She shook her head. "No…I put it back in the dumpster. I'm so sorry!"

"When was all this?"

"Um…about a month ago."

Olivia looked at Matt and mouthed *warrant*? He nodded, taking his cell phone from his pocket and excusing himself. She knew he was calling the Graham's Ford PD to start the ball rolling.

"Why didn't you call the police?" Olivia asked harshly.

"I was going to, but…she seemed fine," Mrs. Hofstedt said, still hiding behind her hands.

"Wait…what?" Olivia shook her head. "Back up."

She finally looked up, mascara streaked down her cheeks. "I went to her apartment to see what was going on. Anna answered the door…she said she was really rushed, trying to pack for her trip. She was *very* brusque with me. Not like her at all."

"Did you actually *see* her, or just talk to her through the door?"

"Uh…she opened the door, but only a crack. I'm sure it was her!" she said, the words tumbling out.

"Let me get this straight," Olivia closed her eyes for a moment, trying to keep the sarcasm out of her tone. "Seamus asks to borrow the carpet steamer and tells you that Anna is out of town; later that morning, you see him throw away a bloody woman's blouse, at which point you go to Anna's apartment to check on her. Someone you perceive as Anna opens the door, but not enough for you to actually see who it is; they act strangely and suspiciously, and you haven't seen Anna since. But you never called the police or thought to mention this to anyone. Does that sound about right?"

"Well, when you put it like that…" Maggie Hofstedt said, disgruntled. "I come off sounding pretty dumb."

"Ma'am, we'll need you and your husband to come down to the station to give official statements," Olivia sighed. "Do you know where Seamus Kiely is?"

Both Hofstedts looked at each other. "I haven't seen him much lately," Maggie admitted.

"We're going to get a warrant to search his apartment, so I'll need a key from you. In the meantime, I'll have a car take you both down to the station," Olivia said, taking her cell phone from her pocket.

"I don't really feel comfortable just *giving* you a master key," Maggie said hesitantly.

"That's fine," Olivia said dismissively, dialing her phone. "We can just break the door in."

The blood ran from George's face. "No, we'll give you the key," he said strongly, giving his wife a look. "No need to start breaking things."

Olivia called the dispatcher and introduced herself, then asked for a uniform and a car to pick up two witnesses, liberally sprinkling

Lieutenant Alvarado's name throughout.

She looked to Matt to check on his progress.

"I'm on hold," he told her quietly, making a face.

"A uni should be here in about ten minutes," she said, nodding towards the Hofstedts. "Did you call the L.T. directly?"

"Uh…no…."

Olivia grimaced. "I think she'd appreciate it. I have her cell number, I'll call her right now."

He shrugged. "Fine."

While they were waiting for the uniform, Olivia went back to Seamus' apartment and took her business card from the ground, where it had apparently fallen. No need to tip him off if he happened to come back. She figured he couldn't stay gone for that long when his cat was wandering around outside; it was clearly well-fed and taken care of. When she walked across the parking lot, she looked down the row and saw the gold Mini Cooper was gone.

The Hofstedts were transported down to the station, but they were told a warrant wouldn't get signed until the morning. As the L.T. said, there was nothing to indicate a need for urgency, so no reason to rouse a judge out of bed.

"It'll just piss them off," she told Olivia on the phone. "But I'll have an unmarked sit on Kiely's apartment in case he comes back during the night. We can at least pick him up while we wait for the warrant. And my best Det-3 is assigned to you, the one I told you about."

"Oh?" Olivia had asked.

"Yeah, Detective Gossett will love her." Olivia could hear the humor in the Lieutenant's voice. "She's a big, brash, opinionated female. She's blunt and never pulls punches. They'll be perfect for each other."

Obviously Matt's reaction upon meeting her hadn't gone unnoticed.

Olivia closed her phone up, noticing the time on the display. Bill still hadn't called her back. That was probably for the best, she thought a little sadly. It wasn't as though they could have pursued a relationship, and she really didn't have time to drive all the way back to Seattle for a late dinner, anyway.

In fact, she was *tired.* Her body was still two hours ahead and it had been a busy couple of days. But, they still had to go back to the station and get the Hofstedts' official statements on record before she could hit the sack.

Hopefully, a long tiring day would mean a dreamless sleep tonight.

Several hours later, Olivia's head finally hit a hotel pillow. The bed was lumpy and the pillow was flat, but the linens were clean and fragrant. She stretched luxuriously, yawning and reveling in being able to close her eyes at last.

Just as she had begun to drift off, her cell phone rang.

"Goddamnit," she muttered. She reached for it blindly, answering without lifting her head from the pillow or even opening her eyes.

"St. George," she sighed groggily.

"Who is this?" A woman's voice asked frostily.

"Olivia St. George, who's this?"

"Why did you call my husband?" Getting even more frosty.

Olivia opened her eyes and lifted onto one elbow. "Who's your husband?"

"William Gustafson, whom you took the liberty of calling *Bill* in your very personal voicemail. I trust he didn't accept your invitation to dinner."

Olivia's heart dropped into her stomach. "I assure you, Ma'am, I was not aware that he was married." She struggled to make the words came out. "We met at the airport-"

"I really don't give a fuck where you met," the woman said coldly. "Stay away from my husband."

Click.

Olivia groaned, tossing her phone onto the side table and falling back onto the pillow. Just her luck – she gets picked up by a good-looking, intelligent, seemingly well-adjusted man and he turns out to be a lying, cheating, asshole. What a *super* end to the day.

CHAPTER 7

Day Four

The next morning's shared ride to the station was tense and silent. Matt grunted good morning, and Olivia replied equally tersely. She was flat-out exhausted, which seemed to have become her normal state of being lately. On arrival they split off, Matt veering towards the restroom and Olivia heading straight for the Crimes Against Persons work area.

Elaine Barstad, the Det-3 assigned to the case, had called both Olivia and Matt earlier that morning to introduce herself. She had arranged to meet them at the station, and when Olivia walked in, she was immediately handed a tall cappuccino straight from Cuppa Joe Espresso, a tiny coffee stand that Olivia had noticed on the corner.

Finally meeting her in person, Olivia was delighted to see she was everything Lieutenant Alvarado had promised. Olivia gauged her as at least six foot but she carried herself with ease. Her sleek brown hair, just a touch of gray beginning along her temples, was pulled back to showcase high cheekbones and a generous mouth. She was dressed in a loose-fitting blue silk blouse with gray linen slacks and matching jacket. It showed off her athletic frame without losing even a hint of professionalism.

"Wow," Olivia said, taking the coffee gratefully. "Already you know me so well."

"You look tired," Detective Barstad said frankly.

"Didn't sleep well," Olivia admitted. She had tossed and turned for an hour after getting that upsetting phone call, and then her sleep had been interrupted by a mishmash of bad dreams. Bill, the redheaded woman in the mirror, and the mysterious frightening voice had all made appearances. She remembered looking at the clock on her cell phone display three times; but at least two of those times must have been in a dream because it always read 3:13 a.m.

"This place is amazing," Olivia said to change the subject. "I've never seen so many little coffee places. It seems like there's one on every block."

"There is!" Barstad said cheerfully. "I know, it's great, right? But don't say coffee, people will laugh at you. It's *espresso.*" She put on a hoity-toity voice as she said it, then laughed at herself. "Personally, as long as it has caffeine I'm happy."

"Amen to that," Olivia agreed, lifting her own espresso in the 'cheers!' salute.

Both women turned as Matt turned the corner from the hallway.

"Hey, it's Liv and Lainy," he said wittily, seeming in much better spirits.

"That's your one," Detective Barstad said, handing him his own cappuccino. "That's all you get."

He looked confused. "That's all right, this one will be enough. Thanks though."

Olivia rolled her eyes. "She means your *comment*, smartass. The attempt at humor."

"Oh." He looked dejected. "Sorry."

"That's all right." Elaine heartily slapped his upper arm, nearly knocking the coffee from his hand. "You'll learn."

Matt leaned over to Olivia. "She's scary," he said in a stage-whisper, pointing his thumb at Detective Barstad.

Elaine chuckled. "Alright, let's get down to business. I ran the vic plus the two names you gave me – Kiely and Thompson. Let's go over the vic first. Anna Taylor, no record, not even any speeding tickets. Local girl, according to her credit report, but doesn't pop up on the internet radar until her early 20's. Her name is listed as a participant on a lot of volunteer events – several Habitat For Humanity builds, Sierra Club trail cleanups, stuff like that. Other than that, she's kind of a ghost, at least in the modern sense. No Facebook account, no Twitter, no MySpace, no social media of any kind."

"Any family?"

"None that I could find."

"Hmm," Olivia looked over the file. "I wonder where her boss got all that stuff about a sneaky Uncle and younger sister."

"Yeah, it is curious," Elaine said. "I called Mrs. Pace yesterday and got pretty much the exact same scenario she gave you – scary boyfriend, sneaky Uncle, the works."

"Did you ask her where she got the info about an Uncle and sister?" Matt asked.

"No, that was before all the data had come back, so I had zip to work with," Elaine admitted. "But now that we know, we can go talk to Mrs. Pace in person later today. On another topic, you'll be happy to know the lab made your girl's bathroom a top priority and found several interesting things last night."

"Yeah?" Matt and Olivia both perked up.

"Yeah. Heavy greasy smoke residue imbedded in the ceiling panels and particles of organic matter, some kind of plant, throughout the crevices in the floor. They also said the melted lines were probably caused by many applications of hot wax poured over the floor. There was still wax residue left behind."

"Many applications of hot wax poured around a body," Olivia said slowly, thinking out loud. "Plant particles in the floor, and greasy smoke residue in the ceiling. Are you guys thinking what I'm thinking?"

"No," said Matt, grumpy at feeling left out. "I have no idea what you are thinking."

"She's studying theology," Olivia prompted. "And she has all kinds of books about demons and stuff…"

"Ah," Elaine said, her eyes lighting up. "Homemade Sacrament! I get it."

"Or some other kind of ceremony," Olivia shrugged. "That's my guess, anyway."

"It's a good guess," Matt said, still grumpy. "It's something to keep in mind."

"Now, your two friends-slash-potential suspects," Elaine continued. "Neither has a record, although they are both so young that so anything before last year would be sealed by Juvy. Both have the same local address."

Oliva frowned. "The same address? Mrs. Hofstedt made no mention of a girl living with Seamus."

"That's the interesting part," Elaine said. "It's the same *fake* address. I Google-mapped it and it's a convenience store off I-5. Nowhere near the apartment building."

"Are they local kids?" Matt asked, sipping his gift coffee.

"Sort of," Barstad replied. "Thompson was born here but I don't have much else on her. As far as the system is concerned, she popped up out of nowhere when she got her Washington driver's license last year. Kiely is actually from out of country. Ireland."

"Illegal?" Olivia asked.

"No, he's legit. Student visa, everything's good except for the fake address. But he was a minor when he came over so his paperwork had to be signed by a relative in the States. Any guesses who sponsored him?"

Elaine looked pleased with herself, holding the closed folder close to her chest.

"Anna Taylor," Matt tried.

"Wrong. Try again."

"Uh…." Olivia hazarded a guess. "Melissa Thompson."

"Wrong again. And she would have been a minor at the time, anyway. How does Maggie Hofstedt sound to you?" She held out the folder, grinning like the Cheshire cat.

"What!" Olivia snatched the folder from her hand, scanning the document inside. "She's his *aunt*," she said amazed. "No wonder she's been covering for him."

Elaine nodded. "Kiely is her maiden name."

Matt shook his head. "I hate it when people lie to me," he growled in his best Clint Eastwood.

"Let's get the warrant and get over there," Barstad urged, growing impatient with the banter. "We'll pick up the Hofstedts, too, since they're obviously still withholding information. We can go talk to the vic's boss at the library later."

The unmarked sitting on Seamus Kiely's apartment had reported no activity during the night. Andrew the cat had eventually mewed a pity-dinner out of the Hofstedts and then disappeared into the woods surrounding the complex.

"Either someone tipped Kiely off, or he got spooked when you two were walking around," Elaine said. "That's all right. We'll go through his apartment and see what there is to see. We'll find him."

Warrant in hand, they went through his apartment with a fine-toothed comb while a tech team checked for blood residue. Seamus had lived like a typical young bachelor; piles of dirty laundry covered the floor of his bedroom closet while a pile of slightly cleaner laundry took up one end of a ratty, threadbare couch. The 'coffee table' – really just a length of plywood balanced on cinder blocks – was covered with empty beer cans. The bathtub had a serious ring of grime and clearly hadn't been cleaned in months, if not years. The kitchen cabinets were empty of dishes; Seamus apparently used the dishwasher as a storage bin, as it held both clean and dirty dishes. A half-empty box of Chex sat on the counter next to a small stack of canned soups. The refrigerator held more beer than food. The only decorations on the walls were framed posters from horror movies and several blown-up covers from gothic graphic novels. The television and sound system were by far the nicest belongings in the place.

"I seriously don't get what Anna would ever have seen in this kid," Olivia commented as she rifled through his dresser drawers. "She was all flowers and ceramic cats, and he's all dirty black T-shirts and scary movies."

"Maybe he made her laugh," Elaine said wryly from the bathroom, where she was going through the medicine cabinet.

"Gag, is more like it," Olivia muttered. "This place stinks like dirty socks and teenage hormones. How does he afford this apartment by himself, anyway?"

"Family discount, no doubt."

After two hours all three Detectives had come up empty-handed, and the tech team had found nothing.

"We'll go sweep the Taylor place now," the tech team told Detective Barstad.

"Thanks," she said. "There's probably not much point but let's get fingerprints, too."

Matt frowned as he took off his latex gloves. "Didn't they already do her place for fingerprints?" he asked Olivia.

"Oh, yeah!" she said, surprised. "That's how we got the ID on our vic in the first place. Well, that and the IUD."

Elaine looked perturbed. "Really? They didn't tell me that."

"Hey…someone *did* clean Anna's place," Olivia realized suddenly, looking at Matt. "Otherwise there would have been fingerprint powder all over it. Did you notice that, Matt?"

He nodded. "You're right. I can't believe we didn't realize it yesterday."

"When did they sweep for prints?" Elaine asked, looking more frustrated.

"Day before yesterday."

"Add it to the list of questions for the Hofstedts," Matt said.

Olivia sighed. "Unless Seamus has a key to Anna's place."

Elaine's face was dark. "Let *me* talk to the Hofstedts. They've twisted this investigation before it even began."

"In the meantime, we still have to find Kiely," Olivia pointed out. "And I want to search Anna's place again."

"If you don't mind, I'd like to do that too," Barstad interjected. "Fresh eyes and all that."

"Uh…I'll help you," Matt offered.

"Have at it." Olivia handed him the master key. "I'm going to talk to the neighbors again, see if anyone's friendly with Kiely."

They split up to their respective tasks. Olivia started knocking on doors, beginning with Seamus' neighbors and working her way back down Anna's way. The only people that knew who Seamus was didn't seem to think much of him. Anna's across-the-way neighbor, the woman who had actually known her by name, scowled when Olivia asked her about the boy in black.

"Oh, *him*," she said, almost spitting. "I could never figure out what she saw in him."

"So they spent a lot of time together?" Olivia asked.

"He was always coming and going from her place," the woman frowned. "And always smelling weird, too."

"What kind of weird?"

"I don't know, like burnt grass or something. Sometimes I'd smell it coming from her apartment while he was in there…and weird noises, too."

"Music?"

"More like chanting. Sometimes with other sounds…screechy instruments noises. But I definitely wouldn't call it music."

"Thank you, Mrs. Woodruff," Olivia said as she wrote in her notebook. "Is there anything else you can think to tell me?"

"It's Ms., actually," she corrected. "I've been a single mom for eight years now. The only other thing is that damn pet."

Olivia looked up. "What about it?"

"Always hanging around my door, trying to beg for food. Anna said it was his but it came over here a lot, I don't mind telling you. And I don't have anything against dogs – but I do get tired of opening my door to see bird guts and feathers scattered all over my front stoop."

"Is it a fat little cat?" Olivia frowned, trying to imagine Andrew the tabby actually catching anything. "Looks like a bowling ball with feet?"

"No, no, a dog," Ms. Woodruff corrected. "A scraggly-looking thing. Looks more like a wild animal than a pet. It killed every pigeon in a two-mile radius, I think. Ugliest black dog I've ever seen."

Olivia found the other two Detectives in the hallway of Anna's apartment, watching the tech guys as they cut pieces of carpet from the bedroom floor.

"Blood residue," Elaine said over her shoulder. "On the wall, too."

"Splatter?" Olivia asked.

Matt nodded. "Yeah, drip pattern and one handprint. Showed up nice and bright with the luminol."

"Uh…I hate to burst your bubble, but may not be Anna's," Olivia pointed out. "She didn't have any major wounds except her face, and the ME said that occurred pretty close to her death, so it probably didn't happen here."

"Could be from her killer," Elaine offered. "Maybe *she* hurt *him*."

"I hope so," Olivia said. "I hope she ripped his fucking balls off."

They both turned to look at her.

"What?" she shrugged innocently. "It's the least he deserved, whoever he is."

Back at the station, Maggie Hofstedt spent the first twenty minutes denying that Seamus could possibly have done anything wrong, then ten more minutes crying before finally drying her eyes, looking resigned. But she still insisted that she didn't know where he might be.

"I don't know who his friends are," she said several times. "He comes and goes as he pleases. He's an adult, after all."

"He's nineteen," Matt pointed out. "And he's *your* nephew, living in a strange place in a strange country. You didn't pay any attention to what he did with his time?"

"I gave him his privacy," she insisted. "The only one of his friends I met was some kid named Mark – another theology student."

"You mean, another theology student like Anna," Matt said.

Maggie Hofstedt frowned. "No, like *Seamus*," she corrected. "He was in the undergrad program at St. Agnes'. That's how he met her in the first place – in fact, I only gave her a discount on rent because he begged me to."

Olivia, watching all this from the observation room behind the one-way mirror, shook her head. "No way was that kid a serious theology student," she said out loud.

"And this Mark – do you have a last name?" Matt asked Mrs. Hofstedt.

"No!" she said. "I only met him one time. I'm surprised I even remember his first name. Why don't you believe me?"

"Probably because you keep lying to us," Matt said, leaning forward across the table. "For all we know, *you* helped him get rid of Anna's body after he killed her."

Mrs. Hofstedt looked shocked. "No!"

"Then help us out," he answered, speaking slowly as if he was growing angry. "*Where – is – Seamus?*"

Olivia watched the drama for another few minutes before leaving the observation room. She knew Matt would get any info there was to get, and in the meantime she wanted to check on Elaine's progress with George Hofstedt.

"He's been pretty talkative," Lieutenant Alvarado commented when Olivia stepped into the other observation room. "Not happy about being forced to lie to you guys yesterday. Doesn't like the boy much, either. But he's standing firm on not knowing where Kiely is hiding."

"His wife wouldn't have told him, I'm sure," Olivia said. "Probably didn't trust him to keep his mouth shut."

"And with good reason." The Lieutenant nodded at the husband. "There he goes again."

"I warned her and warned her!" George Hofstedt pounded his fist on the table. "I told her that kid was no good. But does she listen to me?

Nooo, not about her *sister's* boy." He practically spat as he said it.

"Is he talking about warning Anna or his wife?" Olivia asked.

"Wife," L.T. answered. "Claims he didn't even know Anna and Seamus were seeing each other."

They both turned as Matt opened the door. "Got it," he said cheerfully, waving a piece of paper. "Wife says Seamus likes to hang out with some school bud named Mark Campbell. I ran the name - here's the address of the kid's apartment and a print-out of his driver's license, as well as Seamus'."

"Alright, let's get over there," Lieutenant Alvarado said. "Good work!"

"Thanks," Matt said, looking pleased.

Mark Campbell's apartment building was a free-standing four-story brick building in a run-down part of town. The landscaping consisted of one lonely, stunted tree surrounded by a sea of asphalt and concrete. When they pulled up, Elaine pointed out a green Ford Bronco in the parking lot.

"That's Kiely's truck," she said. "Plates match."

When Elaine knocked on the door, a young man answered immediately.

"That was fast," he said, looking pleased, then confused.

"Police," Elaine said, holding up her badge. Are you Mark Campbell?"

"Uh.....yeah," he answered hesitantly. "I thought you were the pizza guy."

"Afraid not," Elaine said brusquely. "We're looking for Seamus Kiely."

"He's here," Campbell said immediately, and then flushed. "Shit....I wasn't supposed to say."

"Can we come in?" Olivia interrupted, tired of the banter. The boy gulped and stepped back as they walked past. Another boy was sitting on the grungy couch, watching Japanese cartoons on the oversized television. He didn't appear to even notice the visitors, his faze fixated on the bright colors and loud noises emanating from the TV.

"Seamus Kiely?" Olivia asked (although it was more of a statement) as she stepped in front of him. He ignored her, and apparently pained by the gap in conversation, Mark Campbell offered up a "that's him" from the across the room. Seamus spared him one withering glance before going back to staring at the TV, still completely ignoring Olivia and the rest of the officers.

"Mr. Campbell, we're investigating the death of this girl. Do you know her?" Elaine asked, handing him a printout of the ME's facial shot. The boy took one look at the picture of the dead woman and turned green. "Anna," he said faintly. "Anna Taylor. She sort of dated Seamus for awhile."

"We'd like you and Seamus to come in and answer some questions," Elaine continued. "We'd also like to take a look around your apartment. Do we have your permission to do that?"

"Uh….aren't you supposed to have a search warrant?" he answered hesitantly.

"We could wait for a warrant, Mr. Campbell," Elaine acknowledged. "Have you ever seen what someone's home looks like after a search team gets done with it? The mattresses cut open, holes busted in the walls, carpet torn up?"

His eyes were huge and he was getting greener by the moment. "I don't…." he gulped and tried again. "I don't think my landlord would like that very much."

“If you give us permission to take a look around, that’s all we’ll do,” she emphasized, her voice kind. “No mess, no damage. We just want to figure out what happened to Anna.” She held the picture up again and he nodded, looking about ready to faint.

Campbell lived in a grungy apartment with one bedroom the size of a walk-in closet. The bathroom was only accessibly by spider-crawling across the oversized King bed and wedging oneself through the door on the other side. Olivia donned another pair of blue latex gloves and began going through the boy’s things.

After finishing with the bedroom, she reached into the bathroom and flicked the light on. Her stomach immediately dropped into her gut and she let out an involuntary gasp.

Matt heard her. “What’s the matter?” he called from the living room.

“N-nothing,” she managed. Mark Campbell’s bathroom looked exactly like the one she kept dreaming about; same chipped, free-standing porcelain sink, same dirty mirror, same cracked tiles. *It must be a coincidence*, she thought, trying not to freak out. *A lot of bathrooms look like this one.*

She turned off the light and crawled her way back out into the living room. “Uh, I’d like to have the tech team in here,” she said to Elaine, trying to sound normal.

“Are you okay? You look pale,” Barstad frowned.

“I’m fine,” Olivia answered, avoiding her gaze and looking to Seamus. He was in the exact same position he’d been, arms folded, staring holes through the incomprehensible cartoons shrieking from the flat-screen. She dropped to one knee in front of him and waited until the awkwardness of her proximity forced him to look away from the TV.

“I know you had her in here,” she said quietly, staring at the boy coldly. “Did you kill her here, too?”

His dark eyes narrowed and he dropped his chin, resuming staring at the floor. He had yet to say a word.

"Hey, whoa, what…?" Mark Campbell said loudly. "Nobody got killed here!"

"That remains to be seen," Elaine said as she lifted her radio to her mouth. "I need the tech guys up here."

"But – but you said…." The kid stuttered.

"They won't hurt anything," Elaine promised.

The two boys were placed into two separate uniform cars and taken down to the station. The tech team arrived and began going over the apartment with spray bottles of Luminol, black lights, and the other tools of their trade.

As Olivia expected, they found blood spatter on the grout between the tiles in the bathroom floor, as well as on one sofa cushion. When they were all satisfied, she and the other two Detectives finally left to go question Seamus and the other boy.

"There's something I've been wondering," Olivia commented to Matt as they were enroute. "Maggie Hofstedt said that Seamus is a theology student, but he didn't have anything in his apartment to indicate that. Anna at least had textbooks and other religious books. And this kid, Campbell – nothing about him screams 'priest in training' to me."

Matt nodded. "Yeah, same here. But maybe these kids weren't aiming for the priesthood."

"Well, what's the point, then?" Olivia said, frustrated. "They could have majored in anything."

"Hmm…I could see Seamus doing it to appease his family," Matt said thoughtfully. "Maybe that was the only way they'd let him stay in the states – they thought it would keep him out of trouble or something. Maybe Campell's the kind of kid who just does what his friends do."

"I dunno, it's all so weird," Olivia sighed. "In any case, I'd like to go to St. Agnes' tomorrow and see what we can find out."

Seamus and Mark had already been fingerprinted, booked and placed into separate interrogation rooms for questioning.

"I'm gonna let Kiely stew for awhile," Elaine told them. "Do you mind just watching while I talk to Campbell?"

"Of course not," Olivia said, raising an eyebrow.

"I don't want you to feel like I'm taking over your case," Barstad said.

Matt laughed. "Hey, less work for us." He and Olivia stepped into the tiny observation room as Elaine went in to question Campbell.

"Do *you* feel like she's taking over the case?" Matt said quietly to Olivia as they watched from behind the one-way mirror.

She shrugged. "She has to take it over. We don't work here, remember?"

"Yeah, I suppose."

"Why, is it bothering you?"

"No, I just don't like feeling useless."

Olivia looked up at him. "But Matt, you're always useless," she said sweetly.

He grinned, shaking his head. "You always know just what to say."

Elaine sat across from a nervous, shaking Mark Campbell and set a plastic cup of water in front of him. She looked like an oak tree across from a trembling twig.

"Okay, Mark," she said gently. "I know Seamus is your friend, but you can't protect him anymore."

"I didn't know I was protecting him," Campbell said weakly. "He just said he needed a place to stay for awhile."

"What was wrong with his apartment?"

Campbell shrugged. "Um, he said it was being painted or something."

"Mark, I've seen Seamus' apartment. It hasn't been painted since the Reagan administration," Elaine countered.

He looked confused. "Huh? Who?"

"Oh, God," Olivia groaned. "He cannot be that young and that dumb."

"Oh, he can, and he is," Matt said gleefully. "I feel like I'm watching an episode of Jackass."

And it was much like Jackass, only without the rampant destruction of property or angry obese parents. Campbell didn't seem to really know anything about anything, including Seamus' relationship with Anna, where she was, how long she'd been missing, or even that she *was* missing.

"You mean your best friend's girlfriend disappears off the face of the Earth and you *don't notice?*" Elaine said pointedly.

"I didn't even know she was his girlfriend!" he wailed, trying to bury his face between his cuffed hands. "I swear! She was just some girl he brought over a couple of times. And after that last time, I was just as glad to not see her again."

"What happened on that last time, Mark?"

"She – she went nuts! She had blood all over her face. She got my couch all bloody!"

"Did Seamus hurt her?"

"No!" he insisted. "She did it to herself. Girl was a complete loon, I tell you!"

Elaine glanced meaningfully at the one-way mirror.

"Impossible to verify," Olivia commented. "Being that her face was removed and all."

“Explains the blood in the bathroom and sofa, though. We’ll see what Seamus says about it,” Matt said.

“We were just sitting around, watching TV,” Mark continued, “suddenly she gets up and goes to use the bathroom. She was in there forever, then she starts screaming for no reason! We rush in there, of course, I’m thinking she saw a spider or something stupid but she was just standing there with blood running down her face! I’m telling you, she was *nuts*. It was like she tried to tear her own face off.”

“Had she ever done anything like that before?” Elaine asked.

He shook his head, looking down at the table. “No…sometimes she’d kinda zone out, just staring off into the space, but nothing like that.”

“When exactly did that happen?”

“Uh…it was last month, sometime.”

“Before or after Christmas?”

“Right after we went on break. Yeah, I remember ‘cause we were supposed to go skiing the next day but then Seamus said he couldn’t go. So about a week before Christmas.”

“And you never saw her after that.”

“No! But I didn’t think much of it…I figured she was just embarrassed to come around, or maybe Seamus was embarrassed to bring her around. She did get my couch all bloody, y’know,” he reiterated.

“Yeah, Mark, we know. I’m going to go talk to Seamus now. Are you sure there’s nothing you want to tell me before I do?”

N-no…” the kid looked confused again. “Like what?”

“Like anything *you* did that you haven’t mentioned,” Elaine said pointedly.

“But I didn’t do nothin’.” He looked weak. “I swear.”

“Okay, Mark.” She rose to her feet, towering over him.

"She got my couch all bloody," he said mournfully, dropping his head again.

Elaine glanced at the one-way mirror, rolling her eyes and shaking her head. Olivia almost laughed out loud – she could practically see the thought cloud hanging over Barstad's head, the word 'moron!' in big bold letters with an arrow pointing towards the kid.

"Oh goody," Matt said gleefully, rubbing his hands together. "Now we get to see what the other jackass has to say."

"Oh, can you ask Elaine to hold off for a moment?" Olivia asked. "I want to get that background info about Melissa Thompson and check on the registration for the gold Mini Cooper before she goes in to talk to Kiely. I have a feeling I know who answered Anna's door that day."

"Roger that," Matt said, opening the door. "Hey, Barstad! Hold up a minute."

Elaine stepped into the observation room and closed the door behind her.

"What do you think, you guys?" she asked.

"I think that kid needs to go back to high school," Matt said disdainfully. "But besides that? He doesn't know anything."

"I agree." Elaine nodded. "I think Kiely kept him out of the loop. Maybe they aren't as good of friends as Campbell thinks they are."

"I think so too," Olivia agreed. "Kiely just uses him for convenience, like he uses everyone else around him. Hey, Elaine, did we ever get the background checks back on Thompson and Kiely?"

"Oh, yeah, thanks for reminding me," Elaine said. "They're on my desk."

The three Detectives left the observation room, leaving the "Busy" sign on the door so others would know the interrogation room was still in use. Two folders were waiting on Barstad's desk, and they gathered around as she opened them. Olivia noticed Matt trying not to stare at the framed picture of the woman next to Elaine's computer.

The first folder, on Seamus Kiely, was scant. Elaine looked it over, pursing her lips.

"Well, he has no record here in the states," she said, "and any juvy record he might have back in Ireland would take a lot more digging. We'll go without for now. This one on Melissa Thompson…" she opened the second folder. "You're right, Olivia, that was her Mini Cooper."

Olivia looked over her shoulder. "Yup, I thought it might be. Five bucks says she was in Kiely's apartment when we came by the first time. Probably tipped him off and that's why he spent the night at Campbell's."

"Nothing else of note," Elaine continued. "But, again, if she has a juvy record it would be sealed."

"Let's see what Kiely has to tell us," Olivia said. "So far there's nothing to suggest Thompson has done anything besides cover for him. We'll see if that stays the case."

Olivia and Matt again went into the observation room, joining Lt. Alvarado who had been looking in on Seamus. Elaine gave them a few seconds, then opened the door to the interrogation room.

"What's he been doing?" Olivia asked the Lieutenant quietly.

Alvarado shook her head. "Just sitting, staring at the top of the table. No fiddling, twitching, crying, or sleeping."

They watching Barstad walk in, closing the door behind herself, and sit in the chair across from Kiely.

"She'll start out soft," Alvarado told them, "unless he's one of those kids with an attitude."

Although Kiely was taller and more muscular than his friend

Campbell, he was still dwarfed by the Amazon woman seated across the table. Barstad folded her hands, keeping her manner mild and soft-spoken to offset the size difference.

"Alright, Seamus," she began. "You know why we brought you in. Is there anything you want to get off your chest?"

He didn't react; just kept staring at the table eight inches from his nose. His hair was light brown with blond streaks and razor-cut to fall across his face. It looked strange against his all-black getup, like a surfer boy gone Goth.

Barstad waited a moment, then leaned in a little closer.

"Anna was last seen with you," she bluffed, keeping her voice soft but firm. "We have witnesses that saw you behaving angrily and violently towards her. Make it easier on yourself and tell me what happened."

He didn't look up, but all four people watching saw the smirk that passed across his face.

Barstad sighed, sitting up straighter and placing her palms flat on the table.

"Seamus, you are facing a very, very long prison sentence. The more you cooperate, the easier it will be for you."

Still not a word – but she saw him inhale a little deeper, as if he was about to speak. Elaine waited, not wanting to spook him.

Finally, his lips opened.

"Where's the other one," he said quietly and flatly. It was more a statement than a question. His voice was surprisingly deep for his size.

"The other one what, Seamus," she said, just as quietly.

He looked up for the first time. His features were fixed, his dark eyes cold.

"The other woman Detective," he said. "*Olivia.*" He put a lilt on the end, so that it was just shy of sounding like an insult.

At the sound of her name coming off his lips, a river of ice ran down Olivia's spine.

Elaine raised an eyebrow. "If you mean Detective St. George, she is elsewhere at the moment."

Kiely leaned forward, his gaze fixed on Elaine's face. "Don't you want to know how I know her name?" he said jeeringly.

"I'm sure you heard us talking to each other," she replied calmly. "Why don't we talk about Anna."

The one-way mirror was on the side wall, so that the observers could see both parties seated at the table. Olivia watched as Seamus twisted his head to face the wall without moving the rest of his body. He stared at the mirror as if he was looking right through it. His eyes seemed to bore right into her; Olivia felt her heart pounding and willed herself to calm down.

It's an old trick, she reminded herself. *Acting like he can see us. Everybody knows about the mirror now, thanks to TV and movies.*

"I will only speak to *her,*" Seamus said silkily, still staring across the room.

"That's not an option," Elaine replied firmly, leaning forward. "Seamus, look at me. If you don't want to spend the rest of your life in prison, you need to talk to me, *now.*"

Seamus licked his lips, the tip gliding across pink skin like an adder's forked tongue. Then he slowly turned his head so he was once again staring at the table, and was still. His movements seemed so machine-like that Olivia was uncomfortably reminded of a robot.

Elaine tried for another few minutes but he was unresponsive. Finally she rose and left the room.

"Well?" she said, coming into the observation tank.

Lieutenant Alvarado looked at Olivia. “You want to go in there?”

Olivia looked doubtful. “Is that legal?”

“I’m in here, watching,” she replied. “That makes it legal, if you’re up to it.”

“Absolutely,” Olivia said strongly. She gathered herself together, waiting until her heartbeat had slowed to normal and she was composed.

Then she stepped into the interrogation room to meet the monster.

CHAPTER 8

Day Four and a Half

You are now pregnant, and you will give birth to a son; you shall name him Ishmael, for the Lord has heard of your misery. He will be a wild donkey of a man; his hand will be against everyone and everyone's hand against him, and he will live in hostility towards all of his brothers.

- Genesis 16:11-12

Olivia walked into the interrogation room, expecting Seamus Kiely to do something spectacular; projectile-vomit pea soup, perhaps, or spring from his cuffs and cling to the ceiling above. Something dramatic and frightening.

But as she pulled the chair back and sat, waiting quietly for him to make the first move, he did nothing. He just continued to stare at the table.

Finally, she leaned forward. "Mr. Kiely, you asked for me," she said, sounding bored but polite. "Why don't you tell me why."

He twitched at the sound of her voice. Slowly he raised his chin, his eyes traveling across the table and up her chest until they met with her eyes. She felt a shiver run down her spine at the coldness she saw behind his pupils. His eyes were two dark holes in the white canvas of his face.

But his voice was mundane; slightly higher-pitched than when he'd spoken to Barstad, and she thought she even detected a slight tremor in his lips.

"Huh?" he said, his brows furrowing just slightly. "Oh. I didn't hear you come in."

"Mr. Kiely, don't waste my time with these games," she sighed. "Do you have something to tell me or not?"

"About what?" he looked genuinely confused.

Olivia's patience had just about run out. She slapped her palm on the table, making him jump, his eyes going wide.

"About how you murdered Anna Taylor," she hissed, leaning forward. "Now *tell me* what happened!"

She watched as his face morphed; there was no other word for it. His eyes narrowed to slits. He grinned, his mouth growing wider and wider until the ends practically met his ears.

"*Oliv-iaaa*," he whispered in a sing-song voice. Her nose twitched; his breath was putrid and it was wafting right into her face. "*Oliviaaa*," he whispered again, leaning across the table. He didn't seem to notice the handcuffs, still attached to the side of the table, digging into his wrists as his arms were stretched down. His voice descended an octave, then another, as he continued to say her name over and over again until she realized it had become the voice from her dream.

He knew as soon as she recognized it, and began to laugh. It was a hollow, empty sound, and it seemed to reverberate from the walls. It was all around her; it was inside her head, making her skin itch from the inside out.

Shaken, she slid her chair back and stood, not caring how it looked to those watching, and walked from the room as fast as she could. The laughter followed her out, growing louder as she walked away.

After closing the door behind her she just stood for a moment, eyes closed, back of her head resting against the door. Then she took a deep breath and went back in the observation tank.

She had expected the others to be a little freaked out or at least look at her strangely, but they just looked bored.

"Sorry, I guess that was a waste of your time," Barstad said apologetically. The Lieutenant and Matt were discussing batting averages of their favorite ball players, clearly unaffected by the events that had just occurred.

"Um, didn't he seem a little strange to you?" Olivia asked tentatively, looking from one face to the next.

They looked at each other. "Weird how?" Alvarado finally asked.

"Did he say something?" Matt asked, raising an eyebrow.

"Wh- didn't you hear what he said?" Olivia asked, her voice raising just slightly.

"All I heard, and saw, was the two of you sit there quiet," Elaine frowned. "And then you stood up and left."

"No," Olivia stressed, frustrated and a little panicky. "He stood up and – he was *mocking* me. And then his face, his *mouth* – how could it stretch like that?" She realized her voice had risen an octave and the others were staring at her, concerned.

"Look, don't let him freak you out," Matt said soothingly, trying to pat her shoulder. She jerked away, growing angry.

"Weren't you paying attention?" she said loudly, looking from one to the next.

Lieutenant Alvarado frowned. "Detective St. George, if the subject said or did something to make you uncomfortable, I would chalk it up to mind games. He's trying to upset you."

Olivia looked down at the floor. "Well, it worked," she muttered.

Matt cleared his throat. "Why don't we go talk outside for a minute," he said to Olivia, throwing an apologetic glance at the other two.

She jerked her arm out of his hand and stalked out of the observation room, Matt close behind her.

As soon as the door was closed behind them, he yanked on her elbow to keep her from walking away.

"What is with you?" he hissed low, glancing around the squad room to see if anyone was paying attention.

"Matthew, there is something wrong with that boy," she hissed back, knowing he thought she was crazy and not caring.

"Yeah, he's a psychopathic murder," he said sarcastically.

"There are things happening that you don't know about, things I don't even understand," she whispered vehemently, looking up into his reddening face. "People appearing to me in dreams, telling me things I couldn't possibly know…Matt, I saw Anna Taylor standing in Mark Campbell's bathroom with blood running down her face in a dream I had two days ago. I was there, *in his bathroom,* two days before we flew out here."

He stared at her, the vein in his forehead throbbing.

"I know you think I'm stupid," he said slowly, "but this is just so childish, so – so – juvenile. I don't even know what to say to you."

"I'm not making this up to try and make you look bad!" she argued. "Talk to Dr. Johansson. Ask her about things I told her days ago. This isn't a joke, Matt. Everything in me says that boy in there isn't completely human anymore."

An unbelieving laugh burst out of him, and he reined it in as curious eyes looked over.

"Dr. Johansson? What the fuck are you *talking* about?" he hissed, his eyes angry slits in a face growing redder by the minute.

"I'm saying that I honestly believe that boy is possessed, or – or haunted in some way," she said slowly and firmly, looking into his eyes.

"It's finally happened," he said wonderment. "You've gone off the deep end."

"Matthew, I-" she protested.

He held up a hand. "Don't feed me any more of this bullshit, Olivia," he said quietly. "I can see that you don't know what you're saying. For your own sake, you need to go back to the hotel and excuse yourself from this case."

"You have got to be kidding," she said angrily. "I've *made* this case. We wouldn't even know who Anna Taylor was if not for me."

He shook his head. "It doesn't matter," he said, almost sadly. "I have to call Lieutenant Martin and tell him you're returning, and I have to make up an excuse to Lieutenant Alvarado to explain why you're going back."

"I'm not going anywhere," Olivia hissed, giving him a hard poke in the chest with one finger, the other hand on her hip. "You just stay out of my way, Matthew Gossett. You have no idea what you're messing around with."

Barstad poked her head out of the observation tank. "Uh…we okay out here?" she asked hesitantly.

"We're fine," Olivia said loudly, still staring up at Matt. "Just a minor difference of opinion."

Barstad pulled her head back in, leaving the door cracked, and Matt leaned down.

"Pull it together, *or else*," he whispered in her ear. "I'm not covering for you again."

Olivia just walked away.

She plastered a smile on her face and opened the door to the obs tank. "Sorry, just jet lag catching up with me," she lied pleasantly. "I just need a moment to use the ladies' room and then I'll go back in there."

"You sure?" Alvarado said, lifting an eyebrow.

"Oh, yeah, I'm fine," Olivia assured her. "I'll be right back."

In the restroom she ran a wet paper towel over her face and neck. The cold water was soothing, the feel of the scratchy paper on her skin reassuring. *This is reality*, she said to herself, looking in the mirror.

Don't let him fool you. But she couldn't help remembering what dream-Anna had told her; *Just because it's in your head doesn't mean it's not real.*

When she walked back into the interrogation room, the real Seamus Kiely was in there. She saw immediately that he was different than the creature who'd been waiting for her earlier. His skin was still pale but not so pasty, and he shifted in his seat anxiously, his eyes skating around the room. In short, a teenage boy waiting nervously to be questioned by the police.

"Mr. Kiely," she said, ignoring the chair. She stood at the end of the table, her fingertips resting lightly on the scratched wood. "I'm Detective St. George. Do you remember me?"

He looked up at her, trying to appear uninterested and sullen, but she saw the fear behind the act. She saw with interest that his eyes were now the color of summer grass.

"No," he said shortly.

"Do you know why you're here?"

He shrugged. "Dunno."

"We brought you in because you are involved in Anna Taylor's disappearance and murder," she said. "Does that ring any bells?"

He sat up straight. "I didn't have nothin' to do wi' that!" he exclaimed, his brogue so thick she had to mentally translate each word. She suddenly realized that he'd had no accent when he had spoken in their earlier confrontation.

"But you know who killed her," she stated.

He flushed. "I – it's not like that."

"It's not like what?" she asked kindly, treading softly.

"Nobody killed her," he said, looking away.

Olivia sighed. "Anna was murdered," she said, a little less kindly. "I know it's hard to face, Seamus, but if you don't help us, her killer will go unpunished."

His face hardened, changed. "I'm telling you, *nobody killed her*!" The last few words were angry, his tone lowering into a growl, and Olivia unconsciously took a step back.

The other Seamus had returned. He looked up at her, his green eyes gone as cold and black as a moonless night. "You have no idea what's going on," he jeered, his voice as flat and free of accent as it had been earlier.

Olivia stepped forward again, determined not to be frightened. "Then *tell* me what's going on," she said fiercely, leaning over the table. "*Tell me*."

He looked up at her. She saw her reflection in the glassy black marbles that his eyes had become; she looked determined, but scared. As she watched herself in his eyes, a shadow passed across his face. His hands clenched and unclenched, his muscles rigid as he fought against the other that inhabited his space.

She saw, just for a brief moment, his eyes return to green as the boy momentarily pushed the other back.

"Brother Sheridan," he whispered urgently, staring up at her. "He'll tell you."

"Seamus, what-" she began.

"*Ask him*," he said, the words bursting from his lips, and then the shadow returned and the boy was gone. In his place sat the smug, amused creature wearing Seamus' face.

"*Oliv-iaaa*," he sang, then laughed.

She straightened up, looking over at the one-way mirror and shaking her head slightly.

"Okay, Seamus, let us know when you're ready to cooperate," she said solely for the sake of those watching, and left the room.

"He's not talking," she said, walking back in the obs tank. "I think he's protecting someone." She watched the others for any indication that they'd seen what she had seen; but again, nothing.

"We have enough to hold him for tonight," Lieutenant Alvarado said. "What now?"

"We still need to find Melissa Thompson," Olivia said. "We know that was a fake address on her license, but she does work at the school so they might have an accurate one."

"I'm on it," Elaine nodded. She looked pleased to have something to do.

"I'm right behind you," Olivia said. "I need to, uh, check in back home."

Matt was looking at her strangely, but she ignored him and he let it pass.

She found a quiet corner where she could use her cell phone without being overheard. Directory Assistance gave her the number for St. Agnes' switchboard; she was hoping that Brother Sheridan was on the staff there and would be easy to find.

"Enter your party's extension," the pleasant computerized voice instructed, "or enter the first four letters of the last name of the person you wish to speak to."

She typed in 7 – 4 – 3 – 7 and waited.

Pause. "For Tómas Sieroffda, press one," the voice said cheerfully. "For Reginald Sheridan, press two. For Amy-"

Olivia pressed two and heard the buzz-buzz-click as the switchboard processed.

Four rings and it picked up. "You have reached the voicemail of

Brother Reginald Sheridan," an elderly man's voice said, carefully enunciating each word. "I am away from my office. Please leave a message."

It was a start. At least now she knew he was real and he *did* work at St. Agnes'.

"Brother Sheridan, this is Detective Olivia St. George," she said calmly. "It's imperative that I speak with you right away, regarding a student there at the University. Please call me back as soon as you get this message."

She closed her cell phone, debating about what to do next. She knew that Melissa Thompson was an important piece to this puzzle, but she also knew in her gut that there was more going on here than just murder. Brother Sheridan could give her the rest of the story. She glanced at her watch, and realized she probably knew where he was.

She walked back into the squad room. Elaine and Matt were preparing to go to the Personnel office at St. Agnes'.

"Hey, you two go ahead without me," Olivia said, having made her decision. "I've got to go take care of something."

Matt frowned, but Barstad seemed unfazed. "Cool," she said. "We'll keep you updated."

Olivia took the rental car, knowing Matt would be riding with Elaine. She gave them a few minutes' head start, not wanting them to realize she was also going to the University. It was only a few miles to St. Agnes'; once there she followed the signs to the church. The parking lot was full. The board in front of the Church said that afternoon Mass had just begun twenty minutes earlier.

Not wanting to walk in during the middle of services, she decided to look around the grounds for a few minutes. As she walked past the end of the parking lot, she noticed a small foot-trail leading away into the woods that surrounded the church. No doubt a shortcut popular with the students, she thought.

The trail began at the far corner of the parking lot. As she stepped into the woods, the tall trees immediately blocked most of the sun. The remaining light was almost palpably tinged with green.

She walked further, feeling oddly at home. After a few minutes the foot-trail widened into a gravel-covered path, and she realized that the trail from the parking lot was just an offshoot; this was a maintenanced path with a real beginning and end.

The air was heavy with moisture and the musky, vibrant smells of the plant life that burst from every available inch of soil. As Olivia walked, she felt like she had been transported into a National Geographic special. She had no idea what sort of trees these were; most of them had thick, crevassed bark covered with a heavy layer of moss, and they reached higher than any trees she'd ever seen. As she passed one particularly large tree, a small gray squirrel ran down the side of the trunk, stopping about two feet above her head. It chattered at her as she walked by, apparently taking it upon itself to remind the human interloper that this was, in fact, its forest.

"You're a brave one," Olivia commented admiringly, watching the squirrel as it watched her. Its eyes were black and bright, and it twitched its tail rhythmically as it yelled at her in squirrel-speak. About ten feet further down the path she looked back; it was still watching and chattering, but had moved higher on the trunk.

Five more minutes by her watch and she had reached a small stream that bubbled from the undergrowth and flowed next to the path. A set of wooden water-bars had been installed to keep the stream from overtaking the trail, but it had overflowed its banks and washed out a two-foot section. All the rain lately, Olivia thought to herself.

The stream had washed away the layer of gravel, so that even the part of the trail not directly under water was thick with mud. Several deep footprints showed where hardy people had trudged right through, but she took it as a sign that it was time to turn back. Looking around, she couldn't help but wonder – was this the trail from her dream? Surely Anna Taylor would have traveled this path many times as she made her way around campus, or just taken a relaxing walk during lunchtime.

She walked back to the church parking lot, hoping the squirrel would make another appearance, but it did not. Perhaps it already felt her thoroughly chastised and without need of further reminders.

On reaching the church, she eased open the door and took a seat in the last pew. She spent the remaining half-hour of services looking around at the congregation. There were a lot of young people – students, she guessed – with a number of priests sprinkled throughout.

When the service was over, she approached the nearest priest.

"Excuse me," she said, "I'm looking for Brother Sheridan."

"He's right over there," he replied kindly, pointing across the room at a small, wizened man in a brown robe who looked like a strong breeze would blow him away. She realized belatedly that most of these men were probably monks, not priests; St. Agnes' still had a working Abbey, according to the school's website.

He looked up and smiled as she approached.

"Brother Sheridan?" she asked.

"Can I help you?"

"I hope so," she said, speaking low but urgently. "I'm Detective Olivia St. George with the Grand Forks Police Department. Seamus Kiely sent me. I need to ask you some questions." She handed him a business card which he tucked into his voluminous pocket, forgotten.

His face fell at her words. "Oh, dear. He's gotten worse, hasn't he."

"Is there somewhere we can talk?"

"Of course. My office is not far. Follow me."

She trailed beside him as he walked slowly but steadily to a small brick building just down the street. The key was on a cord around his neck, and he left the door unlocked behind them. His office was at the end of a short hallway.

"Please," he gestured to a wooden chair beside the worn desk piled with papers. "Please excuse the mess. I'm perpetually two weeks behind on my paperwork." He smiled and carefully lowered himself into the seat behind the desk.

"Now," he said, folding his hands on the desk. "Tell me about Seamus."

"Actually, Father, I mean Brother, I'm not here about Seamus," Olivia said, leaning forward. "I need to talk to you about Anna Taylor."

His brows furrowed. "Then Seamus is fine?"

"I wouldn't quite say that," she admitted. "Do you know what's wrong with him?"

Brother Sheridan sighed deeply. "I have been treating Seamus for several months, but it's a very long process. It's not like in the movies, you know."

Olivia shook her head. "I don't understand – what are we talking about?"

"I'm sorry, my dear, I get ahead of myself. Seamus is possessed." He was very matter-of-fact about it.

"I – do you mean like by a demon or something?" She couldn't help but sound doubtful, even though she herself had said the same thing to Matt less than an hour earlier.

"Yes. It is more common than you think."

"I do believe you," she assured him, trying to sound sincere. "But I need to know about Anna Taylor."

Brother Sheridan bowed his head for a moment. "You've found her, then," he said sorrowfully.

"Yes," she said quietly.

"When she didn't come back after Christmas, I thought – I hoped she'd gotten help elsewhere," he sighed. "Seamus assured me she was fine, and I had no reason to doubt him, except...except the one within him could be so tricky. It has been part of him for so long that it has become excellent at playing the part."

"Yes, I've experienced that myself," she said. "Had you been, uh, 'treating' Anna as well?"

"Yes, but she didn't respond at all. Her situation was entirely different than anything I've seen before."

"You mean she wasn't possessed?"

"She was, but – I don't know how to explain it." He seemed hesitant. "You must understand that I am bound by certain rules. An exorcism is like a medical procedure for the soul – it's not something you can do on a whim or change to suit your mood."

"I don't understand," she said, frustrated.

"Let me put it another way," he said. "Me performing the Rite of Exorcism on Anna was like prescribing exercise for a broken leg. It wasn't just that it was the wrong treatment entirely – it made her worse."

"So you're saying that the rules you are bound to by the Church wouldn't let you perform a treatment that would actually help?"

"That is part of it, yes," he nodded. "The Church is very strict on when, why, and how the Rite can be performed. It must be not only sanctioned by the Abbot but performed by a properly trained and certified person. Although there are certain allowances for changes depending on the type and severity of the situation, we *must* follow the basic framework that has been approved by Rome."

"I thought only priests could do exorcisms."

"No. Believe or not, there is an actual school for it that is open to many types of religious practitioners. I have been treating people for many years."

"So why didn't it help?"

"The official reason was that she suffered from mental illness," he said slowly. "But she had been thoroughly examined by both a psychiatrist and a medical doctor before even being considered for the Rite. That is also standard practice."

"So what was the unofficial reason?"

He paused, considering his words. She waited patiently as he seemed to debate his next statement.

"You must understand that what I'm about to tell you is solely my opinion," he said finally. "Based entirely on my personal experiences and research, not on Church doctrine."

"I understand," she nodded. "CYA." Giving the shorthand for 'cover your ass.'

"Yes, exactly." A glimmer of a smile passed across his face before turning serious again. "I came to believe that the spirit within Anna was not just a demon – that it was something much, much older."

"Uh…aren't demons supposed to have been around forever?" she asked hesitantly.

"To a degree, yes. However, the demon, *as defined by the Church*, is a relatively new creation as compared to the span of human existence. Although I could never officially say this, in my experience there is much more out there than can be explained by accepted Church doctrine."

"Whoa, Brother," Olivia realized. "You're a liberal!"

He laughed, the tension in the room lifting briefly. "Not exactly. But I have seen many things in my life, and in my old age I have been forced to admit that the Church does not hold the sole answer."

"Isn't that sort of heresy?" she frowned.

"CYA," he reminded her. "As I said, this must remain between us. I tell you only in the hopes it will help you in your search."

She leaned forward intently. "Okay, tell me more about Anna. What was so different about her situation?"

"She believes that she is being visited by an evil presence called *Iblis*, which is attempting to enter her while she slept by taking the form of an incubus. Iblis is a very ancient malevolent spirit that pre-dates Christianity. I believe that this spirit was resistant to a traditional Christian exorcism because it is literally in the wrong category; like treating a virus with an antibacterial."

Olivia raised an eyebrow disbelievingly. "No offense, Brother, but that just sounds ridiculous."

Brother Sheridan nodded. "I understand how you feel. I will just say one thing, and leave it at that; just because something happens entirely in your head doesn't mean it's not real. It's real to her, and that's all that matters."

Olivia reeled back, his words echoing exactly what the dream-Anna had said to her. By instinct she pushed her fright aside to make room for an immediate analysis of the situation.

"Wait – you mean, it *was* real to her," she said, realizing his use of the present tense.

Brother Sheridan looked confused. "I don't understand."

"Oh, Brother, I'm so sorry," Olivia said sympathetically, her fright forgotten in the moment. "I thought you understood. I'm here because

Anna has been murdered."

Face slack in horror, he slowly removed her business card from his pocket with a trembling hand, looking down at it for the first time. His eyes read her duty title – *Detective II, Criminal Investigation Bureau (CIB)* – and the card slipped from his fingers, wafting down to land on his desk.

"Oh, no, no, no." He whispered, wringing his hands. "No, this is terrible." He began to pace back and forth behind his desk; three steps, turn, three steps, turn, his face a mask of pain and worry.

"Brother, please, calm down," Olivia said, standing. "I understand this is a terrible shock."

"You don't understand!" he shouted, turning to face her. "If she wasn't given absolution before she died – if she wasn't given Last Rites – oh, this is the worst thing that could have happened."

"But, isn't being murdered like a straight ticket to Heaven?" Even as the words came out she realized how callous they were.

He shook his head, still pacing, still wringing his hands. "Not necessarily," he said apprehensively. "Please, I must know everything you can tell me about the circumstances surrounding her death."

Olivia shook her head. "I can't tell you details about an ongoing investigation, Brother. I'm sorry."

He stopped and took a deep breath, his wrinkled hands gripping the back of his chair. "I will make you a deal," he said slowly. He looked like he was being tortured. "I will give you Anna's journal if you will tell me everything you know so far."

Olivia was immediately suspicious. "Why do you have her journal?"

"She gave it to me to read as part of her counseling sessions. She often said she could write what was happening to her much easier than explaining it out loud. I was waiting to return it to her when she came back to school."

"Oh. Well, I'm not sure I-"

"Please!" he shouted again before covering his face with his hands. "Please. I am willing to break the most sacred of trusts – that of Confession – by giving you her journal. It details everything she was going through. I do this because I *must* know."

Olivia debated. Having Anna's journal could be exactly what she needed – and she had to admit to herself, she was horribly curious.

"Under one condition," she said finally, reluctantly. "You cannot do anything with the information I give you. You cannot speak to the police, to the press, to anyone here at St. Agnes', to *anyone* about any of this."

He held up a hand. "Yes, yes, absolutely."

"Do you have the journal here?"

"Yes." He walked over to the bookshelf that was built into the side wall of his office. The shelves were full of leather-bound Bibles, textbooks, and manuals. He began to empty one shelf, laying the books on his already-full desk.

"These shelves were not here when I was given the office, so many years ago," he explained. When the shelf was half-clear, he pressed his finger against a small divot in the wood and dragged it to the side, revealing a dark crevice in the wall. "This was simply a wooden box set between the posts – recovered space, as it were. I took it upon myself to cover it with a pocket door, and made no mention of it to the men who built the shelves."

"Clever," she commented.

"It has come in handy." He took out a half-full bottle of Jameson and blew on it, creating a cloud of dust. "I used to quite enjoy a drink after Mass." He set the bottle down and reached back into the hiding place, pulling out a small journal covered in purple silk. As he handed it to her, she realized he had tears running down his cheeks.

"Thank you, Brother," she said quietly. "I will take good care of this."

He nodded, rubbing a hand over his grizzled cheeks. "I know you will. And now, please, will you tell me what you know?"

She looked over the journal before tucking it into the inside pocket of her jacket. "Unfortunately, we don't know very much yet. Anna was found in a ditch a few miles outside of Grand Forks, North Dakota. She had adhesive residue, probably from electrical tape, around her wrists, ankles, and on her chin. Half of her facial skin and muscles had been removed after death with a serrated edge blade." She saw his eyes widen. "She died from freezing. She'd probably been taped to a fence or pole so that she'd remain upright."

"Oh dear." He half-lowered himself, half-fell into his chair. "You say her – her face was…"

"Yes," she nodded. "But that was done after she died, Brother. So she wouldn't have, um…felt it." She cleared her throat, giving him a minute, and then continued. "There was no alcohol in her system. I'm still waiting on the full tox screen to come back from the lab, but her organs showed no obvious indications of poison. There was also no indication of sexual or other trauma, other than…" she paused, debating. How to tell this poor man that the girl had been suffering from some kind of rash, both inside her female area and out? That while it could be an as-yet unidentified STD, it was more likely the result of some kind of trauma?

He didn't seem to notice that she hadn't finished her sentence. "Did she…" his voice was weak. "Did she fight her attacker?"

Olivia shook her head. "All I can say is that she had no defensive wounds, no bruises, and nothing under her fingernails."

He looked up at her, warring emotions passing across his face. "Was she pregnant?"

"Uh, no, Brother, she wasn't." Her voice betrayed her surprise at the question.

"Anna believed that Iblis was trying to impregnate her," he said quietly. "It's all in her journal. Had she *been* pregnant and then lost it, or maybe, um…gotten rid of it?"

"I don't know," Olivia said. "I can call back home and ask the medical examiner, if it would make you feel better."

"No," he said faintly. "I suppose it no longer matters."

"I suppose not."

He seemed to be gathering himself together. "Do you have any idea why she was in North Dakota?" he asked, sighing.

"No, I was going to ask you the same question," Olivia admitted. "We don't yet know where she was killed. We're still working on that."

"But you seem to think that Seamus may have had something to do with it," he said flatly.

She shrugged. "It is a possibility. There is also another girl, Melissa Thompson, that we believe was involved. My partner is out looking for her right now."

He looked up, surprised. "Melissa? But that's….how odd."

"What?"

"Melissa was the daughter of a staff member here. But I wasn't aware that she even knew Anna."

Olivia sat back down. "They worked in the library together. You say *was* the daughter – meaning her parent is no longer on staff?"

He sighed. "Yes. Her father was a professor. He was terminated some years ago."

"He was fired? Why?"

The monk frowned. "He had become obsessed with what he saw as 'correcting' some misperceptions about witchcraft. The Church teaches that anything having to do with magic is potentially opening a door to Satan. Some of the teachings are a little overboard, even I must admit – for instance, I don't honestly think that reading Harry Potter is making oneself open to demonic attack. But Albert – her father – went completely overboard."

"How so?" Olivia belatedly took her notebook from her pocket, opening it to a fresh page.

"He claimed that he'd been visited by a spirit who was guiding him. He started dressing strangely, he stopped coming to Mass, he even started smelling odd. The students began complaining and finally he was fired. It was quite a scandal at the time."

"When was this?" she asked, scribbling notes.

"Oh….Melissa was a little girl at the time, so it was at least ten years ago. I was quite surprised when I saw her on campus last year – I would not have thought she would want to attend school here after what happened. But I suppose bygones are bygones."

"I suppose," Olivia said absently, still writing away. "You were friends with her father?"

"Yes, we were quite close before he started changing. I urged him to seek professional help for what was clearly a mental disorder of some kind. But I don't know if he ever did."

"Did something happen before he started acting that way? A catalyst of some kind?"

Brother Sheridan frowned. "All I knew was that he left suddenly to go on a trip somewhere, and when he came back he was different. He went downhill very rapidly after that – by the middle of the following semester he'd been fired."

"Did you keep in touch afterwards?"

He looked down. "He wouldn't return my phone calls, and finally I stopped trying. The last I heard, he had moved out of state."

"What about her mother?"

"She passed away when Melissa was very young, I believe. Her father – Albert – didn't talk about it, and I never pressed the issue."

"Thank you, Brother." She finished writing and put the notebook back in her pocket. "I will probably have more questions for you later, if that's alright."

"Yes, of course." He waved his hand. "Anytime."

Olivia stood, handing him a business card. "This has my cell number on it. Please call me if you need to, Brother."

"Thank you." His face was sorrowful as he took the card. He stared at it for a long moment, lost in thought, before putting it in the desk drawer. "May I ask you a personal question, Detective?"

"Yes, although if it's *too* personal I may not answer." She smiled to lighten her reply.

"Have you..." he hesitated. "Have you ever been through an exorcism?"

Olivia was startled into laughter. "Well, no. Why do you ask?"

"I just sense something about you...something I can't put my finger on. I had thought perhaps that was it. The Rite sometimes leaves a spiritual mark on people, a kind of glow."

"I've been through a lot in my life," she admitted, "but being possessed is not one of those things, thank God."

He smiled. "Indeed."

She held out a hand. "Thank you for your help, Brother." His palm was warm and dry and his skin felt like tissue paper.

"You are very welcome, my dear." He smiled again, his face momentarily joyful. "There *is* a glow about you...perhaps someday I will be privileged enough to know what it is."

"That makes two of us," she said, raising an eyebrow. "One last thing, Brother. What kind of person was Anna?"

The momentary joy on his face brightened, even as sadness hooded his eyes. "Anna was the most beautiful soul I've ever met."

"Were you attracted to her?"

He shook his head. "I don't mean beautiful in that sense, although she was an attractive woman. I mean her being, her inner self. Her soul."

"What made her so beautiful?"

"She was the only person I've ever met who was completely, entirely selfless. She always put others before herself, but not in any kind of martyred way. She truly and simply thought of others first. She was – an angel."

"What about her family?"

"She doesn't have any that I know of. She alluded to growing up in an orphanage, but I never pressed for details."

"Thank you, Brother. I'll let myself out."

As she was shutting his office door, she saw his hand hesitate over the bottle of Jameson for just a moment before closing around it. She felt the old familiar thirst rising up from her gut and forced it back down. This was no time to let her demons out of their pen; she had better things to do.

CHAPTER 9

Day Four and Three Quarters

Behind your image, below your words, above your thoughts, the silence of another world waits.
- *Anam Ċara* (John O'Donohue)

As much as she wanted to dive right into Anna's journal, other duties beckoned. As she walked back to her car, Olivia flipped open her cell phone and dialed Matt.

"Hey," she said shortly. "What's the status?"

"The school has the same address on file," he told her, his words clipped. "The fake one. We're headed back to the station to try again with Kiely."

"Copy that. I'll meet you there," she replied, hanging up.

She beat them back by ten minutes. She wanted to use the time to observe Seamus; she was curious to see how he behaved when he was alone.

But as Schrödinger said, the observer cannot watch without affecting the outcome of what she observes; Seamus either had incredible ears or was simply very intuitive, because when she stepped into the obs room his head immediately turned towards the mirror. His lips moved just slightly but there was no sound. She realized that the volume control on the in-room mic was off; had it been off all along? That would explain the lack of reaction from the other three. She twisted the knob, hearing the brief buzz as the speakers woke up, and then the sound caught up to his lips.

"*I seeeee you,*" he was singing. "*Oliviaaa I seee you...I seee you... Oliviaaa....*"

How could he know it was her? *Just mind games,* she told herself firmly. He's just guessing. He'd say that no matter who was in here.

He started laughing, a deep coughing laugh like a sick dog barking. The sound made bile rise into her throat.

"*I know it's you, Oliviaaa,*" he sang, and laughed again, throwing his head back in a fit of insane merriment.

"*Did you go see him,*" he whispered, turning his head back towards the mirror and staring right into her. "*Did you did you did you did you?*"

She couldn't help it; she nodded. He immediately laughed again.

"*I knew you would,*" he whispered with glee. "*Now you know you know you know you KNOW!*" His voice got louder with each word until the final *know* was shouted, his eyes huge and dark in his skull-like face. A small line of spittle ran down from the corner of his mouth.

"Oh my God," she whispered, covering her mouth with one shaking hand. Had he *seen* her nod? How was that possible?

His body snapped around, both arms straining against the cuffs that still held up to the table. His wrists were purple, the skin puffy around the metal that bit into his flesh. He strained towards the mirror, his face as white as a corpse.

"*I SEE YOU!*" he shouted angrily, spit flying in a cloud. "*Don't you call for* Him *because I SEE YOU!*"

She couldn't take any more. She twisted the speaker volume to Off, nearly breaking the knob, and walked out of the room as fast as she could. Her legs barely held her and she had to grab the wall for support as she made her way to the restroom.

Luckily all the stalls were empty because she charged into the nearest one, falling to her knees on the cold tile, and threw up until there was nothing but yellow bile coming from her stomach.

When she finally emerged from the bathroom, Elaine was already in with Seamus and Matt was in the observation room.

"How's it going," Olivia asked him faintly, digging in her pocket for a piece of gum.

He didn't seem to notice her wan face. "She just started," he said, turning back to the window.

Olivia leaned against the back wall, chewing the peppermint gum and wishing for a chair. Her head hurt and her legs were still shaky.

From where she stood, Kiely looked perfectly normal. He sat hunched over the table, sweat rings growing under his arms, one foot tapping the floor nervously. There was no indication of the ranting, demonic creature he'd been earlier.

Elaine seemed to be making some headway. Kiely was answering her questions – albeit mostly with single-syllable grunts – as she quizzed him about his background and his family. It was just a warm-up to get him comfortable, before she tried bringing up Anna again.

Finally, Elaine pushed back from the table, her face turning serious.

"Okay, Seamus," she said quietly. "Tell me about Anna."

He shrugged. "Whaddya wanna know?" The accent was in full swing.

"Tell me about your relationship."

"We were friends."

"Just friends? That's not what everyone else tells us."

He looked down. "People can think wha' they want. She was a nice girl."

"How did you meet?"

"Saw 'er at the library one day."

Olivia was growing impatient. She knew Elaine wouldn't get any information that really mattered, and the journal was burning a hole in her coat pocket.

"Hey, Matt," she said.

"Huh," he grunted without turning.

"I'm not feeling well. I think I'm gonna go back to the hotel."

"Okay."

She waited a long moment for him to say anything else or even turn around, but he ignored her. Finally she pushed herself off the wall and left the room.

Her stomach was growling, and combined with the journal in her pocket, it seemed a good time to kill two birds with one stone. Leaving the rental car where it was, she jogged across the street to an IHOP she had spotted earlier. The restaurant had only a few patrons so early in the day, so she had no difficulty getting a corner booth. It was habit to sit with the wall at her back and an eye on the exit; and it was private, so she would be able to read Anna's journal without anyone staring over her shoulder.

She waited until the waitress had taken her order and then pulled the small book from her coat pocket. The cover was thick purple silk, with Anna's name sewed into the spine in gold thread. Olivia ran her thumb over the letters. It looked homemade, the letters sewed by hand; the stitches were just inconsistent enough to rule out a machine.

She opened the cover and saw that underneath the fabric was a piece of balsa wood. The journal itself was clearly handmade, the pages glued at the edge and then sewn together with twine, the two sections of balsa wood connected with a leather strap. The paper was light tan with bits of wood throughout; recycled, probably, or homemade.

There was a little scrap of paper tucked underneath the fabric cover, where it folded over the corner of the wood. Olivia used her thumbnail to pull it out, unfolding it carefully.

Merry Christmas! To Anna from Melissa, it read in purple ink.

Olivia gazed at it for a moment before refolding it and putting it back.

She had maintained for the last hour a crazy hope that the journal would magically contain all of the answers they'd need for a swift resolution to the case. A murderer's name written in Anna's blood, perhaps, scrawled by Anna's own dying hand; or, barring that extreme solution, perhaps a very pointed journal entry where Anna would just tell them she was being stalked/threatened/ harassed by a named assailant.

There was to be no such luck. A considerable number of pages had been forcibly torn out, and the rest were blank. Olivia thumbed through, disappointed even as she was unsurprised. Sadly, it seemed, there was to be no quick and easy "CSI" ending to this story.

Suddenly feeling a loss of appetite, she sighed, tucking the journal back into her coat pocket and rising from her seat. The waitress was just approaching and Olivia waved her off, shrugging her coat back on as she thought.

I need to talk to Brother Sheridan again, she decided, frustrated. *Why would he give me a blank journal?* The restaurant felt suddenly constrictive, like the walls were leaning in and sucking the air out before she could get a decent breath.

She hurried across the street and to the rental car, throwing it in gear and screeching out of the parking lot.

She was almost to the hotel when she realized she'd also forgotten to ask Brother Sheridan about the cross.

"Shit," she mumbled, pulling the car over. "No time like the present." She dialed the school's number again, wishing she'd thought to ask for his direct number, and finally made it through the switchboard.

Why am I so forgetful lately?

It went to voicemail again. Perhaps the good monk had decided the

Jameson was a fine idea after all; it was what *she* would have voted for, under the circumstances.

"Brother, this is Detective St. George again," she said urgently. "Please call me as soon as you get this. Thank you."

Okay. Get yourself together. She pulled back out into traffic. Five more minutes and she was walking down the hallway to her room, pulling the keycard from her wallet.

She was still three rooms down when she smelled it. She stopped dead in her tracks, lifting her nose like a hound tracking its prey. A charged memory passed through her mind of Darren looming over her, reeking of that scent; a vision brought unbidden and unwelcome by the all-too-familiar odor.

Coincidence, she told herself. *Lots of men wear that cologne.*

But as she got closer to her room she knew something was wrong. Her hotel room door was open just *ever* so slightly; it was barely noticeable. A slight breeze, perhaps, emanated from the open door because the smell only got stronger as she approached. Her heart suddenly quickened and she flattened against the wall, reaching for her duty weapon before remembering it was still in the room safe. She hesitated for a long moment before her stubbornness and anger got the better of her.

She eased up next to the door, feeling the slightest hint of draft pushing from the opening that was inches from her face. It was only open a hair; most people would never have realized it. She remembered when she first walked into this room; underneath a thick layer of cheap paint the door was heavy steel, meant to protect against fire, and when she swiped the key card that first time and the lock disengaged it had almost broken her nose. Whether by design or by accident, the door was hung so that it wanted to be open. The substantial metal leaned outwards, pulled by gravity towards a halfway-open position.

So she knew someone had to be holding the door to keep it from swinging further open. They were probably waiting for her to walk up, her shadow blocking the light as she swiped the keycard and turned the handle. Her mind's eye saw it perfectly, the details all too clear, brought forth in a flood from memories long buried; a heavyset white guy, six foot tall, brown hair, breathing heavily as his heart raced from anticipation. She saw the pistol he held, the killing end trained at where he guessed her heart would be as she stood there unaware. She even smelled the cheap whiskey in each exhalation of breath.

She knew she should just retreat; call the local PD, have them sweep the room. But what would she tell them? *Hi, this is Detective St. George, I'd like to report that my dead husband is in my hotel room.* Yeah, right.

She tried to take a deep breath to clear her head, like a diver preparing to head to the bottom, but the smell of whiskey mixed with the cloying cologne made her gag. All the memories of that night so long ago were rushing back into her mind, washing away the interim thirteen years as if they'd never happened.

She couldn't take it anymore. Throwing caution to the wind, she rushed the door, grabbing the handle as she went by, and pulling it open with all her weight. After a brief resistance the door flung outward, her hand still grasping the handle, and she slammed against the wall on the other side.

Heart hammering with fear, she saw Darren clearly as he spilled in slow motion out onto the floor, the gun dropping from his grip as his hands splayed out to catch his fall, his mouth open in a moue of surprise.

And then, in mid-fall, he was gone. She stood alone in an empty hotel hallway, feeling like a fool, staring at the spot where he should have been laying. She heard Whitney's voice in her head; *Smells are the strongest trigger of memories, Liv. The cologne brought it all back and your imagination did the rest.*

She released the door handle and it swung back into the hallway, settling into its desired half-open position with a slight screech of hinges. The hallway was quiet. She carefully slid over one step, peering into her dark hotel room, ready to move at any sign of danger. There was no sign that anyone was within.

Olivia carefully slipped into the room, sliding along the wall with her heart racing. The room was quiet, dark, and just as she had left it, with one exception.

When she had first checked into the room she had unplugged the clock radio, as she always did. The displays were always grotesquely bright, and she'd learned the hard way over the years that the alarms were invariably set to go off at top volume at a ridiculously early time of the morning. Rather than mess around with resetting the alarm, turning the display to the wall, or turning down the volume, she always just unplugged the clock and left it at that.

But the clock radio on the bedside table now blinked twelve o'clock, and as she got closer she heard the muttering of a deejay. Someone had plugged the clock back in and turned on the radio.

She turned up the volume, expecting to hear the slightly rounded, lengthened vowels of a local Washington deejay, and was shocked to instead hear the familiar nasalized tones of her home-town Native radio.

"…and that was the Bear Springs Singers doing a traditional called 'The Grandmother.' You're listening to KILI 90.1 in Porcupine, South Dakota," the voice said pleasantly. "And now for the weather. A low tonight of minus fourteen, with winds of…."

This wasn't possible. A clock radio was simply not capable of pulling in a radio station from five states away. Olivia sat heavily on the bed, listening to what had been one of her favorite stations as a teenager when she was still trying to connect to what she believed was her Lakota heritage.

As she stared at the radio in shock, her phone rang, making her jump. She hit the Off button so hard she almost knocked the gadget to the floor as her other hand fumbled for her cell.

"St. George," she said dully, her mind still on the radio.

"Detective, this is Brother Sheridan," his tremulous voice said.

"Oh…oh! Yes, Brother, thank you for calling me back." She turned the radio towards the wall, forcing her mind back to reality, and stood up. She liked to pace while talking on the phone. "I forgot to ask you about something. Did Anna commonly wear a cross on a chain?"

"Yes, she did," he answered. "A little gold cross."

"We found it on her," she said. "There was an engraving on the back; I'm hoping you can tell me what importance it had to her."

"I will certainly try," he said. She thought she could hear the slightest slurr in his speech.

"I understand the use of one; it's the other I'm not sure of. It's a Bible reference, Luke 7:21."

"Ah, yes," the monk said. "I am very familiar with that one. *'And in that same hour, he cured many of their diseases, and hurts, and evil spirits.'* It refers to Jesus performing the first exorcism, among other things."

"So those two inscriptions on the cross were for protection?" Olivia guessed. "Sort of a good-luck charm?"

"Oh, much more than a charm," the Brother protested, sounding anxious. "An important extension of the Rite."

"But you said the Rite made Anna worse," Olivia reminded him. "Why would she wear that cross?"

He sighed, his voice heavy with sadness. "I believe she was desperate, grasping at straws," he said. "Anna was suffering terribly. She was ready to try anything that might give her some relief. Have you looked at her journal yet?"

"Yes, as a matter of fact." Olivia was glad he'd brought it up first. "It's empty – pages torn out, the rest blank."

He was silent for a moment. "This isn't possible," he said finally. "I've read it myself, and I'm positive that no pages were torn out when she gave it to me."

"Then either you were mistaken, or someone knew where you kept it," she pointed out. "I'm going to hang on to it, in any case. I do have another question. Anna had a tattoo, a Latin phrase-"

"*Vocatus o non vocatus, Deus aderit*," he interrupted. "Yes, I know. She asked me about the Latin to make sure it was correct."

"But what does it mean?"

"It means, Called or not called, God is there," he said almost wistfully. "I do not really understand the thrill in tattoos, but I know it gave her comfort to have that on her."

Olivia kept her comments on that subject to herself. "Thank you so much," she said. "I'll come by tomorrow to get an official statement from you."

After closing her cell phone, her eyes were drawn back to the clock radio. Before she knew was she was doing, her hand reached out and clicked the radio to On. She flinched as a voice filled the room; but there was no hint of a nasalized vowel in this man's voice. It was pure Seattle.

"…and we're gonna keep you rockin' all night long on 99.9," he was promising. "We'll start off another long set with this one from Temple of the Dog." She recognized the opening strains of *Hunger Strike* and lay back on the bed, exhaling loudly.

Maybe it was a hint. She hadn't eaten all day, running on nothing but caffeine and adrenalin. Her last trip to get food had been cut short by disappointment; maybe a good hearty meal would make everything better.

Yeah, right, her cynical side offered up. *Good luck with that one.*

It was worth a try, she decided. At least it would get her out of the hotel room for another hour or two. She remembered there was a Denny's across the street. It was as good an option as any.

As she was sopping up the last bit of gravy with her dinner roll, her cell phone rang, displaying Brother Sheridan's office number once more. She answered, only to be greeted with fuzzy silence.

"Brother?" she asked, listening intently. There was a thump and just before the connection was broken, she thought she heard a moan of pain.

Throwing money on the table, Olivia sprinted back to the rental car, peeling out of a parking lot for the second time that day. She made it back to the University at speeds a NASCAR driver would have envied.

The monk's office was still lit. *Please let him be in there,* she prayed silently as she hurried up the sidewalk. The front door was unlocked so she let herself in.

"Hello," she called down the dark hallway. "Brother Sheridan?" A triangle of light emanated from his office window, and as she got close enough to look in, she saw that he was slumped face-down on his desk, the bottle of Jameson on its side between two stacks of papers. It looked empty.

"Aw, shit," she muttered, opening the door. "Brother Sheridan? Reginald!"

He didn't reply.

She took him by the shoulders and eased him upwards. Ink had smeared onto his grizzled cheek in a parody of some student's essay. His eyes were shut and his breathing was labored, the smell of good Irish whiskey pouring off him in waves.

"Reginald," Olivia said urgently, shaking him gently. His head lolled forwards and for a moment she thought he stopped breathing.

She debated for a moment what to do. He was an old man; she couldn't just leave him and trust that he'd recover. A dozen terrible fates passed through her thoughts; alcohol poisoning, dangerously low blood pressure, stroke….

Gritting her teeth and trying to hold him up with one hand, she lifted his office phone and dialed 911 with her pinky. She cradled the phone between her shoulder and ear, freeing her other hand to keep the sodden priest from crashing face-first back onto his desk.

"911, what is your emergency," the dispatcher asked.

"This is Detective St. George," Olivia said urgently, forgetting that she wasn't part of the force here. "I need an ambo at 214 Heritage Drive, St. Agnes' University, building C. White male, approximately eighty years of age, toxic alcohol levels. Pulse thready, breathing shallow."

She heard fingers tapping. "A unit is on the way, Detective," the dispatcher replied, her voice efficient and calm. "ETA two minutes."

The paramedics were right on time. Olivia stayed on the phone with the dispatcher to guide them in – she was afraid to leave the monk alone. They got him on a stretcher, an IV of saline bringing cleanliness to his poisoned blood.

She watched the ambulance pulling away, thinking that she should probably tell someone at the University, but decided against it. There was time enough to worry about that later.

Heaving a sigh, she glanced at her watch again. She needed to find out what was going on back at the station – with any luck they'd tracked down Melissa Thompson or gotten more from Seamus Kiely than garble.

She walked back to the rental car, trying to enjoy the pleasant night air despite everything that had happened. It was forty degrees with just a touch of a breeze – a warm evening for wintertime. Back home it was at least forty degrees colder, she knew.

As she drove the few miles to the station, she thought about Matt. As much as it pained her to acknowledge it, she needed him on her side. Even if he refused to believe that ghosts and demons were a possible truth, he needed to understand that *Anna* believed it, and perhaps more importantly, her murderer may very well have believed it too.

Matt and Elaine had already left the station. The desk sergeant checked his computer and told her that Seamus and Campbell were in holding; the Hofstedts had been released with instructions to stay local. No news on Melissa Thompson.

Olivia was irritated that no one had bothered to call her, and then remembered that she was supposed to be in her hotel room. Matt had probably tried calling her room and then, when she didn't answer, figured she was already asleep.

She drove back to the hotel, feeling like she could have made the trip with her eyes closed, and headed towards Matt's room. He was two floors above her; she'd wanted no illusions of intimacy between them.

For some reason, that thought reminded Olivia to call and check on Brother Sheridan. Information was happy to connect her with the hospital, and the duty nurse seemed glad she'd called.

"I hoped someone would check on him," the nurse admitted. "Such a sweet old man. It's a shame when the elderly come in and have no one to care about them."

"How's he doing?" Olivia asked, sitting on a stair while they talked.

"He's fine," the nurse assured her. "He's on his second bag of saline and his tox levels have gone down significantly. He's resting comfortably."

"Thank goodness," Olivia sighed, closing her eyes for a moment. She felt somewhat responsible for what had happened to the monk – obviously their conversation had upset him so badly that he turned to drink to ease the pain. She knew from experience what a tempting but futile solution *that* was.

"Are you his granddaughter, Miss…?"

"St. George. No, just a friend. What time can I pick him up tomorrow?"

"He can be released after eight."

Nice and early. Looked like she had something to do in the morning.

She finished her journey to Matt's room. He answered the door wearing nothing but basketball shorts, giving her a momentary pang before she remembered who she was looking at. But damn, he *did* have a nice body; too bad he was so aware of it.

"I thought you were sleeping," he said, surprised to see her.

"Uh, a minor white lie," she admitted. "Can I come in? We need to talk."

He hesitated for a moment, finally shrugging and stepping aside. "Sure."

"I need to show you something," she said, stepping inside and unbuttoning her coat.

"Whoa," he said, holding up his hands. "Thanks but I've already seen it."

Olivia stared at him in shock, frozen in mid-button. He dropped his hands, giving her a rueful grin.

"Just joking," he said weakly.

She felt such a wave of anger rush over her that it actually made her hands tremble. “If you ever – *ever* – mention that again I will slit your throat,” she hissed, meaning every word.

He took a step back, startled by the forcefulness in her voice.

“God, what’s with you?” he said defensively. “I was just kidding.”

Olivia felt angry tears prickling her eyes and willed them away.

“I may be a joke to you but I deserve more respect than that,” she said furiously, finally giving voice to what most angered her about that night. “How dare you treat me like some *whore?*”

Matt’s eyes widened. “I never…” he tried, his voice fading. “I didn’t. I don’t!”

She buttoned her coat back up, forgetting why she’d come upstairs and everything else in her anger.

“Fuck you!” she snarled as she rushed for the door.

He jumped up and caught her by the arm just as she reached for the handle.

“Wait,” he pleaded. “Just let me explain-”

Without looking behind her, Olivia stiffened her arm into a battering ram and shoved her elbow backwards, catching him just below the solar plexus. He half-fell backwards, letting out all his air in one painful burst, his fingers sliding off her arm.

He groaned painfully, falling into the little wooden chair across from the bed.

“Jesus, that wasn’t necessary,” he moaned, massaging his chest. “I just want to talk to you, for God’s sake!”

She paused, already feeling guilty. That was her biggest personality defect; an overabundance of guilt. Slowly she turned, reaching for the other chair and dragging it to a comfortable distance away. She lowered herself into it, trying to be calm, but her heart was pounding wildly. A bruise was already blossoming at the center of his very white skin. She felt a little proud, despite her guilt; that was a pretty good move.

"You've got a hell of an arm," he said, echoing her thoughts.

"Thanks," she said reluctantly.

He looked away for a moment, obviously gathering his courage.

"Look, uh, there's something I need to tell you," he said slowly. "But you're gonna think I'm such a complete asshole…"

She raised one eyebrow. "More than I already do?" she said pointedly.

He chuckled weakly. "Good point. Um, the thing is, what you think happened that night isn't exactly what *did* happen."

She felt the heat as blood rose to her face. "Look, this isn't a conversation either one of us want to have," she said harshly. "So why don't you cut the bullshit and just say what you need to say."

He looked down for a minute, still massaging his chest. She was surprised to see that he was blushing furiously. "The thing is…" he repeated, "uh…we didn't actually – that is to say, we've never…"

She bit the bullet. "Are you trying to tell me that we did not have sex?" she asked warily, her voice devoid of emotion despite the heat in her face.

He nodded, still looking down. She waited for him to fill in the rest, but he was silent.

"So?" she prodded finally. "What did happen?"

He looked up. "What do you remember?" he asked.

Very little, she started to say, but that wasn't strictly true. That night was vague and fuzzy, but she distinctly remembered trying to drink away a terrible sadness. Something had happened, something that now seemed so far way it was just out of fingertip's reach. She tried to place that night in a mental timeline; the best she could get was about a year had passed.

She also knew that even just a year ago, she'd still been trying desperately to fill the terrible void in her heart with booze and men; ironic, since that was part of what she'd tried to escape by leaving Darren. But as her shrink assured her, promiscuity was a common reaction to sexual trauma. *You need to feel in control of your own body,* he'd said. *But perhaps we can work on finding a better way to do that, shall we?*

Feeling no desire to go into all that with Matt, she hedged. "Very little. We all went to Buck's for drinks. I was still, uh, drinking pretty heavily back then so I don't really remember much."

He nodded. "I guess I figured that. I hoped you wouldn't remember anything, truthfully."

She hugged herself, the words bursting out of her in a rush. "Damnit, Matt, if we really didn't sleep together, why did you let me think it all this time? Why did you *tell* everyone that we did if we didn't?"

"Because it was better than the truth!" he yelled furiously, suddenly angry with her. "Shit, Olivia, do you have any idea what you were doing at Buck's, what the whole Department saw you doing? I *saved* your reputation by making everyone think you only slept with *me* instead – instead of…" the words faded as he lost courage.

She swallowed heavily, flashes of buried memories bursting across her vision. Her mouth was dry, the old familiar thirst scratching at the walls of her throat. "What did everyone see? What did *you* see?"

He looked down again. "I went out to have a smoke. I saw you walking out with these four guys….guys you'd been dancing with all night, practically making out with right there on the dance floor. You were so goddamn wasted, you could barely walk! Two of them were holding you up….they were just about to put you in the back of their van. So I….I yelled, ran up to them, told them you were my girlfriend and if they didn't drop you I would shoot. I actually pulled my gun on them," he admitted, shaking his head at the memory. "They dropped you right on your drunk ass and peeled out in their van. I took you back inside, made sure everyone saw us together, and then took you home."

"But you took me to *your* home," she pointed out, her voice still faint.

He sighed. "I kept asking you where you lived but you were so far gone…you couldn't even tell me your own address. So I took you home, put you in my bed, and crashed. I *never* touched you." He looked up and gazed into her eyes, his face earnest. "I'm telling you the truth. I never touched you."

"But I woke up with no clothes on," she said sadly. She wanted so badly to believe him, to believe that he had actually been there for her rather than taken advantage of her, to think that there was *one* person in the whole wide wicked world who actually cared.

"I didn't do that," he said softly. "When I woke up you were gone. I only crashed in the bed because my couch is way too short for me to sleep on. Didn't you notice I was still fully clothed?"

She looked away, shaking her head. "I didn't even look," she admitted. "You had the covers pulled up almost over your head. I was too horrified at being…being naked and waking up next to you. I was only interested in getting out without waking you up."

He looked sad. "I'm sorry you thought that," he said. "And just for the record, I didn't actually tell anyone that we slept together. I just didn't correct them when they assumed it."

"But all this time…why didn't you tell me?" she pleaded, her guilt at all the anger she'd felt for him washing over her. "Why would you *joke* about it, if it didn't happen?"

He shrugged. "I don't know. I was going to tell you but…time went by…I didn't know how to bring it up."

"Wait a minute," she said suspiciously, her natural cynicism rising. "How do I know this isn't just another load of crap?"

He looked helpless. "How am I supposed to prove something I didn't do? I don't know. You just have to believe me."

She looked at him for a long moment. "How many tattoos do I have?" she said suddenly, wanting to catch him off guard.

He certainly did look startled. "Huh? I didn't know you had any."

He was either an excellent liar and actor or he was telling the truth. "So, what…you were protecting me?" she said. It was more a statement than a question.

He nodded, shrugged. He looked helpless. "I guess."

She was quiet for a moment. "Did you know I quit drinking after that?" she said finally.

He looked away. "I wasn't sure, but I…I hoped," he admitted. "You seemed better."

"It's taken me a long time, but I am better," she said quietly. "I did a lot of terrible, stupid things when I was drinking. I guess I have to thank you for not letting me do one more."

He didn't say anything.

Olivia chewed her lip, gazing at him thoughtfully, then stood up. "Can we start over?" she said hopefully, holding out a hand.

He stood up and stepped forward, taking her hand uncertainly.

"Hi, I'm Olivia St. George," she smiled, shaking his hand. "Nice to meet you."

He grinned ruefully. "Hi, I'm Matt Gossett. It's very nice to meet you too."

"Can I ask a favor, now that we've met?" she asked, still holding his hand.

"Sure, of course."

"Can you put a shirt on?"

He looked down, flushed, and dropped her hand. "Sorry," he mumbled.

"Hey, I'm not entirely complaining," she admitted cautiously, holding up both hands. "But, you know, professionalism and all that."

He smiled as he pulled a white T over his head. She could tell he was flattered.

"Now!" she said, clapping her hands together and clearing the awkward tension from the air. "Matt Gossett, how about we talk about why I came up here in the first place?"

"Oh, you mean there was a reason?" he quipped.

"Yes, actually. Remember our victim? The dead woman?"

He smirked. "Yeah."

"Well, I had a pretty involved conversation with one of the monks at the University, Brother Sheridan. Both Anna Taylor and Seamus Kiely were being treated for demonic possession – I know, I know." She waved off his protests before they could start, seeing the skeptical look on his face. "It doesn't matter if we believe in that stuff or not because they clearly do. Did. Anyway, the monk also gave me Anna's journal, that she had given him for safekeeping." Olivia took it from her coat pocket and handed it over. "All the pages that aren't blank have been torn out, but he swears it wasn't like that when he put it away in his office."

Matt thumbed through it, noticing the little slip of paper in the front just as she had.

"To Anna, from Melissa," he read. "So they were close, then."

Olivia nodded. "Close enough for a nice hand-made gift, anyway."

"Who would have had access to the monk's office, and motivation to tear out the pages? And why not just take the whole journal?" he asked, getting immediately to the heart of the issue.

"I haven't gotten that far yet," she admitted. "Just a few of the questions I'd like to ask Melissa Thompson when we bring her in."

Handing over the empty journal, Matt leaned back against the chair and crossed his arms. Olivia realized with surprise that he had an Airborne Rangers tattoo on his left bicep. Somehow she'd missed it when faced with his half-nakedness. She couldn't picture him in a military uniform.

"That's going to be a problem, then," he said, and she brought herself back to the conversation. "Thompson appears to be missing."

"What? Since when?"

"After you left the station, Lieutenant Alvarado got a call from some lady at St. Agnes'. She said she was Melissa's boss."

"Lauren Pace?" Olivia suggested.

"Yeah, that was it. Anyway, she said Thompson hasn't been to work for three days. She tried calling the girl's cell phone but it went straight to voicemail every time. Then she tried calling you at the home office but they told her you were here, so – she called here."

"Did you guys ask Kiely or Campbell about her?"

"Of course," Matt responded. "Campbell didn't recognize the name, or so he said, but when we showed him a picture he knew her. Said Kiely had brought her around a few times, but not for months."

"That feeds into the unrequited love triangle I've been positing this whole time," Olivia said. "Anna finally gives in to Seamus, so he drops Thompson like a hot potato. What did he say about her missing?"

"He claims he hasn't talked to her in over a month. But here's the interesting part; *he* says that Thompson and Anna left for vacation together right before Christmas, and that was the last time he saw either one of them."

"Oh yeah?" Olivia raised an eyebrow. "And where did they go?"

Matt grinned wickedly. “I couldn’t wait to spring this on you. Guess.”

Olivia groaned. “Don’t do this to me!”

“I’ll give you one hint,” Matt said, leaning forward intently. “It’s a Mecca for fashion-conscious shopaholics, and it’s only a few hours from Grand Forks. Oh, wait, that’s two hints.”

Olivia sat up straight. “Are you shitting me!”

He laughed, slapping his knee. “Nope. They went on vacation to-”

“Mall of America! Oh, for Heaven’s sake.” Olivia couldn’t believe it. The Mall of America was the largest indoor shopping mall in the country, and it was just over in central Minnesota. And Matt was right – it was a huge tourist draw for those who saw shopping as a recreational activity. But going specifically *to* the mall on vacation?

“How very suburban of them,” she said dryly. And then something occurred to her. “Wait, there’s something else I forgot to tell you. Melissa Thompson’s father used to be a professor at St. Agnes’-”

“How do you know this?”

She waved him off. “More info from the monk, I’ll tell you in a minute. Anyway, they moved out of state about ten years ago. What do you bet they moved to Minnesota?”

“Possible,” he agreed. “It would be a much more affordable trip if they were staying with her family, especially for two college students.”

“Did Kiely say anything else of interest?” Olivia asked. Half of her hoped to hear that the boy had begun spouting flames from his mouth and, as Mel Gibson had put it, ‘lightening bolts from his arse.’ Or was it thunder bolts? Either way that would certainly have convinced Matt.

But he only shrugged. “Not really. He did give me a message for you, though.”

A chill ran down her spine. “Oh?” she said casually. “That’s strange.”

“I guess you made quite an impression on him. He said – wait, I wrote it down." Matt walked over to the closet and fished a folded-over piece of paper from his coat pocket. "He said, 'Darren is in here with us now. Did you enjoy his visit?' " Matt looked up. "Does that mean anything to you?"

She shrugged, trying to smile despite the ripple of fear running across her skin. "No. He's just trying to mess with me," she said, playing it off.

"Who's Darren?" Matt asked, sitting back down. He handed her the slip of paper and she took it without looking at it.

"I don't know," she lied. "Maybe he's confused me with someone else."

"Probably. He didn't seem entirely with it," Matt shrugged. "So anyway, what direction do you want to take on this Thompson angle?"

"Let's check out her dad," Olivia suggested. "We'll go from there. Brother Sheridan can give us a first name and description."

"Sounds good," he nodded. "In the meantime, you should get some sleep."

It was a logical suggestion and probably said with the best of intentions, but for some reason Olivia's hackles immediately rose.

"Are you giving me an order?" she said jokingly, trying to play it off.

He raised an eyebrow. "Well, I didn't mean it like that, but it has been pretty obvious that you need to get some rest."

Let it go, her instincts said, but she just couldn't help it.

"What's that supposed to mean?" she asked, her voice stiff.

His face tightening, Matt took the bait. "You told me earlier today that you're seeing things, having these weird dreams," he pointed out. "You keep talking about Dr. Johansson, for God's sake, as if she's here with us. You're obviously losing it, just like-"

Like you did before. He left it unsaid, but she knew immediately where he was going and lost whatever bit of cool she had left.

"You have no right to bring that up," she hissed. "That was a long time ago, and Lord knows I don't rub it in your face every time you have a problem. And as far as Dr. Johansson goes, I don't know what in the world you're talking about. And I *have* been having these weird dreams, and I *did* see weird stuff happening back at the station today."

"That Kiely kid changing his face around? So what!" he charged. "It doesn't mean he's possessed by demons!"

She gasped in shock. "You *asshole!* You saw it too!"

"Of course I saw it," he huffed. "So he can do a good Jim Carrey. *Who cares?*"

She poked his chest with one finger. "You liar!" she seethed. "You said you didn't see anything!"

He leaned down until they were almost eye-to-eye. "All I saw is a manipulative psychopath who knows exactly what buttons to push, and he's got you running around believing this shit," he said furiously. "Goddamn it, Olivia, you are a *cop.* Start acting like one!"

She turned away without a word, her mouth set stubbornly, and stalked towards the door.

"Oh, fine!" Matt shouted, throwing up his hands in defeat. "Just walk away. That's really going to help."

She swiveled on her heels. "What color were his eyes?" she asked point-blank, her eyes narrow and cold.

"Whose eyes? What are you talking about?"

"Seamus Kiely. *What color were his eyes?*" she demanded.

He lifted his arms again. "I don't know! Black, brown, who gives a shit?"

She walked forward until they were face-to-face again. "When I talked to that boy, I *saw* his eyes go from completely black to bright green and back again. Now you explain to me how that's possible without contact lenses?"

"Some trick of the light," he challenged. "He leaned in and out of a shadow. I don't know. *I don't care.*"

"I can see that," she said flatly before turning away. "The problem is, I *do* care, and if you had any sense at all, you would too."

He just stared at her retreating back as she walked away, not saying a word. The door to his room slammed shut behind her with the satisfying crash of heavy steel.

BOOK TWO
UNLIKELY PROBABLES

In a tribal camp there lived a girl who was very beautiful and greatly loved, as well as being kind and virtuous; but she was also somewhat contrary, and did not want to marry. One day, a young man from somewhere came to pay her court; he was very handsome. Whereas before she did not want such attention, now she was pleased, and promised to marry him. But she didn't confide in her parents that she agreed to go with him, and she got ready secretly, preparing pemmican and moccasins for the journey which she carried in her belt as she waited for him.

In the twilight of evening, he came for her. They traveled fast until they came to a deep river. The man said, "I will swim across; you shall sit on my back." She didn't care to do that and immediately he became very angry, saying "Do what I tell you, or I shall throw you in the river!" Because she now feared him greatly, and because she could not swim, she did as he said. As she sat on his back while he swam along she looked at the back of his head and on that side also was a face. Now she knew that this was not the handsome young man she loved; this man was what is known as Double-Face.

- Excerpted from *Double-Face Tricks the Girl,* as translated from the Dakota by Ella Deloria, published in *Dakota Texts*, 1932

CHAPTER 10

Day Four, late, and into Day Five

Sometimes, being a bitch is all a woman has to hold on to.
- *Dolores Claiborn* (Stephen King)

With each step down the stairs she only got more furious. How dare he speak to her like that? How dare he *treat* her like that?

What a fucking asshole! she thought furiously. *Just like a man. Just when you think they've got your back, they turn on you. How could I* ever *have thought that Darren would underst-*

Olivia paused in mid-step, realizing what her mind had just done. She closed her eyes, focusing her energy on the organ that had just betrayed her; the Freudian slip was startling in its obviousness.

Not Darren, she thought fiercely. *Matt. Matt.* Matt, *not Darren.*

All of the recent reminders about her ex-husband were making her slide back into a place she didn't want to be; a chaotic, frightening place where she had to constantly fight against slipping over the precipitous edge of insanity. She'd spent nearly a year in that place, back in her mid-twenties; it was a trip down memory lane that she had no desire to repeat.

But as Olivia stood in the middle of the stair, one hand still on the rail, eyes open but staring at nothing, she knew in her heart that her current state of mind was attributable to more than just Darren's sudden death bringing him back to the forefront of her mind. Even Seamus' odd and frightening behavior wasn't entirely to blame.

When Brother Sheridan had related the tale of Anna's attacks by the spirit she called 'Iblis,' Olivia had experienced a wave of recognition; a wave so unwelcome that she'd immediately snuffed it. Whether she wanted to admit it or not, Olivia knew all too well what Anna had gone through, because she herself had suffered through a terribly similar experience.

Before finally making up her mind to leave Darren, she had spent over ten months being afraid to sleep, barely getting through each day, barely getting through life at all. A shrink would (and had, in fact) say it had been brought on by the stress of an abusive marriage, and that was certainly true; but at the time it hadn't felt like stress. It had literally felt like an outside force was attempting to invade her very being, night after sleepless night. Certain that she was teetering on the edge of a complete nervous breakdown, she had been afraid to say anything to anyone. Every single night, she could feel a very real physical presence touching her with unseen fingers; attempting to penetrate her mind and body, filling her thoughts with evil, lustful and violent thoughts. It was all she could do, every night, not to scream in horror and painful agony until the unseen presence would finally give up for the evening and leave her to shiver herself to an uneasy sleep. Alcohol had become her closest friend because it sometimes allowed her to fall into a dreamless, empty blackness of sleep.

She understood now, after years of self-therapy and psychiatric discussion, that those experiences had been her mind trying to fight against the terribly invasive actions of her husband. Because she hadn't been able to mentally cope with the fact that her "loving spouse" was actually a cold, manipulative abuser, her subconscious had manufactured an "outside force" separate from the evil man who was her husband.

Or so she had come to believe; for how could it be anything else? Even back then, she hadn't been lying there telling herself "I'm being invaded by a demon!" The idea was laughable. But still, there was no denying how real the "presence" had felt.

The memory of that time still made her stomach clench painfully. The bullets that had finally ended it had been almost a let-down in comparison; they had damaged only her physical self, whereas her soul still felt tattered after everything she had gone through in the months and years leading up to that final, terrible night.

She slowly continued down the stairs, her anger at Matt forgotten. *He's probably right,* she thought sadly. *I need to excuse myself from this case. I'm turning it into something it's not.*

Olivia slowly walked down the hallway back to her room, her emotions a turmoil of self-doubt and confusion.

She remembered one particular day as a little girl on the playground at school. That morning was her first day back at the Catholic elementary school that serviced the orphanage, after yet another short-lived stay at a foster home in Rapid City. This one had been particularly bad (although, in retrospect, not as bad as some that would come later); the foster parents were young, new, and hadn't even made the pretense of wanting to provide a good home for an orphaned child. They thought fostering an 'Indian child' would be an easy way to get state money for doing basically nothing. When they discovered that she was not the quiet, shy little red-skinned girl they had pictured getting – that in fact she was *quite* willful and stubborn – they decided she was more work than the money was worth.

She had been sitting in a swing, just sitting, staring at the end of one shoe as it made a figure-eight in the dirt. She hadn't been aware of Sister Theresa as she walked up, not until the young nun had sat in the swing beside her. Young Kaya, as her name had still been at the time, looked up, startled to see one of the nuns actually in a swing.

Sister Theresa hadn't said anything for a long time. She had just sat quietly, ignoring the bell that marked the end of recess, waiting for little Kaya to say what was on her mind.

Finally, the nun had spoken first. “Did you know that if you turn the figure eight on its side, it becomes the symbol for infinity?” she had said companionably, as if they were two friends sitting in any coffee shop in America.

Little Kaya had wrinkled up her brow. “What’s infinity?” she had asked, not really interested but momentarily distracted from her sorrow.

Sister Theresa had knelt down and in the dirt, drawn a figure-eight lying on its side. She had traced it over several times, showing the watching child how it made an endless loop.

“We have trouble seeing infinity, because we live one day at a time,” the nun had said gently to the little girl. “It is both a blessing and a curse. A blessing because a momentary joy is so deep, but a curse because a momentary pain is so sharp.”

The child just nodded, still not understanding. Sister Theresa had smiled gently and patted little Kaya on the back.

“No matter what happens, the world continues on,” she said softly. “When you have sorrow, just remember that this, too, shall pass. Tomorrow will always be a new day.”

The child’s eyes had welled up with tears, her sadness finally brimming over. The kind nun had patted her back as she cried, until finally the little girl wiped her eyes on her sleeve.

“Sister,” she had asked, her voice choked with emotion. “Is it a sin to think that I was meant to be somebody else?”

Sister Theresa had looked thoughtful. “If who you are being doesn’t feel right, then it is up to you to discover why,” she had replied. “God set you on a path when He made you, but life is full of distractions. We must always strive to be the best we can be and to not forget that we are made in God’s image.” Then she had smiled, and said something that might, back then, have gotten her fired or worse had her higher-ups overheard.

"Never forget to walk the red road, and you can't go wrong."

It was the last line that had caught little Kaya's attention, because walking the red road was a Native concept; it meant to be a good person, to fulfill your true purpose and not get distracted by greed, vanity, or other shallow needs. For a Catholic nun to reference it was like the sun turning purple or rain being dry. It was because of this that the little girl missed the unusual distinction of the nun saying 'who you are *being*,' rather than the standard 'who you are.'

The conversation came back to Olivia now as she stepped into her hotel room, and the nun's words seemed full of portent. She had been struggling since the first moment of life to figure out who she was. There had been many distractions along the way, and too often she had listened to people like Darren who would have her believe that her path was *his* to choose. She had learned the hard way that trying to be someone she wasn't, trying to be the wife that *he* wanted, was frighteningly akin to dying a slow, painful death. She had to fight to be free, to live, to be who and what she really was. She had indeed forgotten about the red road.

Anna Taylor had suffered through struggles of her own. Someone had chosen a drastic and permanent way to end the woman's problems; but Olivia knew that the woman's fight hadn't ended with her death. Maybe it was high time that she tried to understand what Anna was still fighting for.

The next morning she was at the hospital at quarter to eight. She found Brother Sheridan, looking somewhat the worse for wear, but dressed and ready to go.

"Ah, my savior, so to speak," he said dryly as she knocked on the door. "I understand that I have you to thank for all this."

She didn't miss either of the double *entendres*. "Actually, you have yourself to thank for at least half of it," she said cheerfully but pointedly as she handed him a tall coffee. "Jameson might not have been the best choice."

"True," he sighed, taking the coffee thankfully. "Long gone are the days when I can drink away my sorrows, apparently." He gazed at her, scrutinizing. "You look like you had a pretty rough night yourself."

Olivia rubbed her face ruefully. "Yeah. Didn't sleep too good."

"Oh?" he said as he put on his shoes. "Anything I can help with?"

She hesitated for a moment. "Would you think I'm crazy if I told you that Anna has been visiting me in my dreams?" she said finally. She saw no reason to tell him that the demons, if that's what they were, as well as her murderous ex-husband were visiting in her sleep as well.

The priest looked up. "Crazy? No. Not unless you said she was telling you to climb a tower with a rifle in hand, like that what's-his-name."

"Uh, no, definitely not," Olivia replied, eyebrows raised. "But what if I said she keeps asking me for help?"

He smiled. "I would say she made a good choice. You are obviously the right one for the job."

"You have more faith in me than I do," Olivia muttered as they walked down the hallway.

He let it pass. "Would it be alright if I came with you to see Seamus?" he asked. "I would very much like to see how he's doing."

"You can come with me," Olivia allowed, "but I don't know if they'll let you in as a visitor since you aren't a relative. But we can find out."

"I would appreciate that." He patted her arm. "You're a good egg."

Olivia chuckled. "I'll tell the mother hen you said so."

To say that she hadn't slept well was like saying the Empire State Building was sort of tall. From the moment she'd closed her eyes she had been plagued by unhappy thoughts. Some of them were just run of the mill bad dreams; Bill from the airport was there with his arm around his young, beautiful wife (who eerily resembled Cynthia Miller from high school, for some reason); then Bill turned into Darren and he was chasing her down the dark path behind their trailer, the ditch waiting to gobble her up.

But some of the dreams were not just dreams; they were too clear and she was too lucid to say they were 'only' nightmares.

It had begun with a repeat of the first night. She was on the same trail in a place she now realized was western Washington. This time, she was ready for the rain shower, taking shelter under the arms of a huge ancient cedar the size of a medieval castle.

Then the forest went away and she was standing in darkness. A window hung in front of her, apparently attached to nothing. When the room on the other side of the window lit up, she realized that she was looking into Mark Campbell's bathroom, and not through a window – through the mirror that hung over his sink.

The bathroom was lit by the glare of a single fluorescent bulb. She heard the sound of a television blaring and young men's laughter, then the *snik* of a door closing.

A moment later a lovely redheaded woman came into view. It was Anna Taylor. Her face was drawn and pale, but whole. The glint of a thin golden chain was just visible around her neck, although the cross that she surely wore was hidden inside her shirt.

Olivia watched as Anna leaned over the sink, splashing cold water over her face. She seemed unaware that she was being watched.

After drying her face on a hand towel, the redheaded woman leaned forward, examining herself in the mirror. Fascinated, Olivia leaned closer as well, looking deep into the eyes of a woman that she had only met as a corpse. Anna's eyes were a nearly incandescent shade of blue, but as Olivia watched, they began to darken, overtaken by a shadow that swam up from behind Anna and swarmed over her. It was a darkness that came from nowhere and everything, leeching out of the very air that surrounded her. It enveloped her, was drawn into her skin, and reappeared as a blackness that turned her lively blue eyes into those of a dead animal.

Anna continued to stare into the mirror, seeing not Olivia on the other side, but herself transformed. The expression on her face was one of sadness and resignation, but then it changed; she seemed to suddenly awaken to what had been done to her. Eyes wide with anguish, she raised her hands to her face and, as the Detective watched in horror, the lovely redheaded woman scraped her fingernails down her skin, pulling the nails against her flesh until her forehead and cheeks were running with blood.

Mark Campbell saw part of this, the sleeping Olivia thought, *but he had no idea. No idea at all.*

Anna began to scream. Olivia heard a door burst open and the two boys appeared, both their faces a mask of shock. Seamus wrestled Anna's arms to her sides, both boys yelling at her to stop, then they pulled her to the side and out of view, presumably out of the bathroom and into the living room as Mark had described.

Olivia wanted to cry. She pressed her hands against the cold glass, wanting to reach through and pull Anna back into a better place, but the bathroom was empty. She seemed to stand there for an eternity until the finally the fluorescent light was turned off and she stood alone in the darkness.

After that she had a nightmare that was all too familiar. It was one she had had quite often after leaving Darren. It was simply a replaying of her married life, but in the present, as if she had never gotten away from him at all. In this nightmare, real life was just a dream of wishful thinking, a lovely dream she'd woken from to find herself still trapped in the all-consuming hopelessness of her life with him. Her despair was as palpable as the smell of mildew and cheap liquor that permeated the small trailer.

It seemed to last forever, but as Sister Theresa had said, this too shall pass. Eventually she woke for real, struggling out of the sheet that had gotten twisted around her, swearing as she hit her hand on the nightstand. The pain brought her back to reality better than anything else could have.

Her relief washed away the horrible feeling imbued in her by the nightmare. She sat up and turned on the light, checking the time on the clock radio by habit.

She saw that the time was three-thirteen in the morning, but it was another long moment before she remembered that she had never set the clock. She had forgotten to unplug it again before falling asleep and she knew for a fact that it had still blinked 12:00 when she closed her eyes.

Even as she realized all that, she smelled again the cloying odor of his cologne and bottom-shelf whiskey. It wafted over her as strongly as if he was laying right there in the bed.

Her stomach immediately rose into her throat and she had to race for the bathroom. She only just made it to the toilet before her chicken-fried steak and side salad made their reappearance, throwing up until her stomach was wracked by spasms of pain and emptiness.

After that she didn't even try to sleep. She spent the remainder of the night researching the malevolent spirit that Brother Sheridan had mentioned, thankful that the ancient laptop she'd checked out from work was still capable of an Ethernet connection, basking in the glow of every light in the room burning brightly.

When she and Brother Sheridan walked into the station, the desk sergeant gave them a strange look. Olivia supposed they were an odd-looking pair; the monk still wore his brown robe, now slightly rumpled, and Olivia knew they both looked like hell.

"Is Seamus Kiely still in holding?" she asked. The desk sergeant nodded and pressed the buzzer to release the door.

"Yeah, go on back," he replied.

She opened the door for the monk. "Brother, if you don't mind, I need to go see someone. Can you go it alone?"

"Yes, I'll be fine." He patted her shoulder as he went by. "Thank you, dear."

She found Matt and Elaine at Barstad's desk.

"Feeling better?" Elaine asked kindly.

"Yes, thanks," Olivia said, ignoring Matt's look. "Any luck on the Thompson thing?"

"Yeah, I think we've found her dad," Elaine replied. "He's teaching at a community college in western Minnesota. We were just debating about whether to call him directly, or call the local PD to go talk to him."

Olivia pulled up a chair. "What's the name of the town?"

"Uh....Crookston."

"Crookston!" Olivia looked up in surprise. "That's half an hour from Grand Forks. Why don't we call home?"

"Because they don't have any jurisdiction in Minnesota," Matt pointed out.

"And we don't have any here," Olivia retorted. "Yet, here we are. They can go *talk* to the guy. I'd rather ask them to do it than some local PD I've never met."

Matt sighed. "Fine. But you get to call Lieutenant Martin and ask."

"Whatever," she shrugged. "No skin off my nose. Elaine, you mind?"

she asked, holding out her hand.

"Be my guest." She handed her desk phone to Olivia.

Lt. Martin was, for once, glad to hear from her.

"We got a break," he said, jumping right in. "Not ten minutes ago, Crookston PD called me that they had a walk-in off the street. Guy comes in, dumps a bag of bloody clothes on the desk sergeant's counter, and leaves."

"What!" Olivia was surprised. "That's a new one. Did he even fill out a statement?"

"Nah, just grunted something about finding it in his trash can. He literally threw it at the Sarge and ran. No chain of evidence, obviously, but the state lab will run DNA and see if matches it with the girl. Crookston PD didn't have any other ongoing cases that they thought it might be related to. Desk Sergeant followed the guy out and got a license plate number as the guy was peeling out. We traced it to this address." He read the info to her and Olivia scribbled it down, then stared at it, her brow wrinkled. "L.T., hang on a sec." She set the phone down and gestured to Matt.

"Hey, gimme that printout on Melissa Thompson's father." He handed her the sheet of paper and she read the info, then picked the phone back up.

"L.T., you won't believe this," she said, excited. "We just tracked down the father of one of our main suspects, and he literally lives next door to your walk-in."

"Well hot dog," L.T. said. "Sounds like y'all better get on back."

"We've got a few more people to talk to here, then we're on our way." She hung up, looking to Matt. "We've got something," she grinned. "Time to go home."

"And here I was enjoying our little vacation," Matt groused.

"I know, I'm not ready to go back to real winter either," Olivia admitted. "And we still have work to do here. But this is a real lead!"

Elaine spoke up for the first time. "Maybe I can come with you," she suggested, looking from one to the other.

Olivia was surprised to see Matt perk up. "Really?" he asked. "You can swing that?"

Elaine shrugged. "I can try. It is my case now too, sort of."

A grin spread across his face. "That would be awesome."

Olivia was surprised at the tiny flicker of jealousy she felt; it was so brief she couldn't even be sure which person she was jealous of. "That would be very cool," she agreed. "Should we wait here while you go talk to Alvarado?"

Barstad pushed away from her desk, standing up with an *oof.* "Yeah, let me go see if she's in her office. You guys just hang out for a minute."

After Elaine walked away, Olivia looked back at Matt and gave him a mischievous grin. "So you *do* like her," she joked.

He flushed. "Hey, she's pretty cool. And we can always use another brain on this case."

"Uh-huh," Olivia said, still teasing. "Whatever you say, macho man. I think you just want a woman who's big enough to kick your butt."

He grinned. "Maybe."

They were still laughing when Elaine walked back up.

"We're good!" she said, giving a thumb's-up. "But I only get 48 hours, so we better make the most of them."

While they worked the plane tickets back to Grand Forks, Olivia went to check on Brother Sheridan. She found him sitting on a chair outside Kiely's cell.

He looked up as she approached. "The Sergeant was nice enough to bring me a chair," he smiled.

"Oh, good. How's everything?" She looked into the cell. Seamus was cross-legged on the narrow mattress, head leaned back against the concrete wall. His eyes were closed. He looked like a perfectly normal incarcerated teenage boy.

"We're making progress," the monk said. "The one in him is very strong, though. Stronger than I had hoped."

Olivia had decided that no matter what Seamus – or the creature masquerading as Seamus – did or said, she would react as she would to any other murder suspect. She couldn't let him get under her skin.

So she looked into the cell, leaning against the bars next to Brother Sheridan. "And who might that one 'in him' be?" she asked conversationally, the tone of her voice giving neither disbelief nor support to the idea that he was possessed.

"I have yet to get a name," Brother Sheridan admitted. "It varies from case to case. Sometimes they are eager to boast of who they are, sometimes they guard their name very hard. This one is extremely guarded."

Without opening his eyes, Seamus spoke. His voice sounded perfectly normal despite the topic. "*She* knows who one of us is," he said, then fell silent again.

The monk looked to Olivia, the question in his eyes.

She shrugged. "He's been trying to psych me out, to make me think that the ghost of my dead ex-husband is hanging out with whoever else is in there."

Brother Sheridan frowned. "Oh?"

"It's just mind games," she assured him. "I'm not worried about it."

Seamus sniggered. "You should be," he said silkily.

She ignored him. "Can you come out with me a minute?" she asked the Brother. "I want to talk real quick."

"Of course." He carefully levered himself upright, straightening his back with a painful wince, then followed her down the hallway and out of the lobby. She had thought to sit on the bench out front, sparing them both the pain of standing, but the rain had kicked up several notches so they stayed under the eaves.

"Thanks," she said. "I want to limit what we say in front of him."

"Good idea," he agreed. "How are you?"

"I'm okay," she nodded. "I haven't been sleeping well but that's neither here nor there. I wanted to tell you that I'm flying back home tonight. Detective Barstad will be taking on the local aspects of this case."

"Does she know about Anna's treatment?"

"Not yet," Olivia admitted. "But she'll have to soon."

"But she won't understand it the way you do," he said shrewdly.

"No. She will take it as proof that Anna was suffering from some kind of mental illness. I actually tried to talk to my partner about it last night, and it didn't go well."

Brother Sheridan was quiet for a minute. "I suppose it doesn't really matter if they believe or not," he said finally. "As long as they – you - find who killed her."

Olivia saw no reason to cause him more pain by telling him that she doubted anyone else would ever believe that Anna had been possessed. "I need to tell you something else," she said hesitantly. "Anna's body is still in our morgue. If no family steps forward to claim her, she will either be donated to the medical school for study or cremated."

The color washed from his face. "Oh….oh, dear. That won't do at all. She must have a proper burial."

"Does she have any family? Anyone who will be willing to pay the cost of having her body brought back here?"

"She had no one," he said sadly. "I will talk to our Abbot. Perhaps there are church funds that can be used for that purpose."

"Just let me know," Olivia said gently. "I'll help as much as I can. Can I give you a lift back to your office?"

"No, thank you, dear," the elderly monk said. "I am going to visit with Seamus a bit more, and after that I think a walk will do me good."

"I did want to ask you – if we are agreeing that both Seamus and Anna are possessed, are you able to tell me how it happened?"

He shook his head. "These things aren't like the movies, Detective. No one put a voodoo curse on Seamus or anything like that. All he knows is that things began to happen to him several years ago – he could never pinpoint a date or an event. As for Anna, she was always hesitant to talk about how it started; I got the feeling it was a very difficult topic for her."

"Alright, then," Olivia said, opening the front door for him. She walked back to Elaine's desk to check on the progress of their plane tickets.

"Hey," she said to the two Detectives, lifting her chin in greeting. "What time we leaving?"

"We don't fly out until six tonight," Elaine answered as she logged into her email. "So we've got plenty of time to go talk to the lady at the library."

"Good. What time is it now? She doesn't get in to work until ten."

Matt checked his watch. "It's quarter after nine. Why don't you and I go check out of the hotel so they don't charge us for an extra day."

"Good idea," Olivia nodded. "See how smart he is, Elaine?"

"Uh, sure," Barstad replied, not really paying attention. She was busy scrolling through a long list of unread emails. "When you guys get back we'll head over to the school."

Matt gave Olivia a dirty look as they walked to the rental car. "What was that all about?" he said, irritated.

Olivia shrugged innocently. "What?"

"Playing matchmaker. I don't need your help, you know."

"Hardly!" Olivia was startled into laughter. "Even if you were interested, she would *not* be, as I'm sure you've figured out."

"Sure," he muttered. Olivia, seeing that his mood had shifted, kept her mouth shut.

Matt was silent until they were pulling into a space at the hotel parking lot.

"All that shit you were talking about gave me bad dreams," he burst out suddenly. "As if I haven't been sleeping bad enough already."

"I'm sorry!" Olivia said honestly. "That was certainly not my intention."

"I know. But Jesus, Liv…this case sucks enough without making it into some kind of paranormal freak show."

"I agree," she replied, "but I can't help what is. I'm only passing on information."

He just shook his head grumpily.

"Uh…do you want to tell me about the dreams you had?" she asked hesitantly as they stepped into the hotel lobby.

"No," he said shortly. "I'll meet you at the front desk in ten." Without looking at her, he opened the door to the stairs and charged through.

"Okay then," she called to his retreating back, feeling like an idiot talking to herself. "I'll just, uh…yeah."

She had never unpacked, so repacking was just a matter of throwing her bathroom items back in the suitcase, zipping it up, and giving the room a once-over to make sure nothing had been forgotten. She was back at the front desk in five minutes. They checked out of the hotel, drove back to the station, and walked to Barstad's desk all without speaking.

As they approached, Elaine lifted her eyes from the computer screen and looked at their faces suspiciously.

"Did you two have a fight?" she asked shrewdly. "You have the same look my parents have had for the last twenty years."

"Not at all," Olivia said lightly. "Just being our usual cheery selves." But as Matt sat down, she gestured at him from behind, rolling her eyes and making a face.

Elaine grinned. "Glad to hear it. Let's go talk to Mrs. Pace, shall we?"

St. Agnes' University Library was a marvel of architectural engineering; proof of what can be accomplished if enough funding is available. Although the plaque next to the front doors said 1993, it was built from gray stone to match its much older compatriots, the Abbey and Church. The front doors were solid oak wrapped with bronze banding, and they met at the top to form two halves of a rounded pinnacle. The doorway itself spanned nearly seven feet wide, the top a sweeping arch of rough-hewn tightly pressed stone blocks. The building looked like nothing less than a medieval castle, complete with a tower that rose several stories above the rest of the building.

"That must be where they put the bad students," Olivia joked, pointing to the tower as they walked across the wet, squishy lawn.

"What kind of school is this, anyway?" Matt asked, looking curiously at the medieval-looking building.

"St. Agnes' began as a Roman Catholic nunnery in 1885," Olivia recited from memory, having researched the school several days earlier. "It was the women's side of a larger monastery. The nuns opened a school for local youth which eventually became the University. There is still a small monastery on the back of the grounds, but the monks took over the running of the school when the nunnery shut down some decades ago. They kept the original name, though, in honor of the nuns."

The front desk was manned by a petite brunette wearing the thickest reading glasses Olivia had ever seen. When the girl looked up at their approach, her eyes were magnified to those of the Kelvin nurse in Star Trek 2009.

"We're here to see Lauren Pace," Elaine said curtly, showing her badge before the girl had even spoken. She blinked her huge eyes and pointed to an open door across the room.

Mrs. Pace must have just gotten to work because she was in process of shrugging out of her coat as they walked up to the doorway. She was a tiny woman, barely five foot, and wouldn't have weighed a hundred pounds sopping weight. Her silver hair was in a tight bun and pince-nez glasses hung around her neck.

She turned when she heard footsteps. "Hello?" she said, seeing they were obviously not students.

Elaine lifted her badge again. "Mrs. Pace, I'm Detective Barstad, this is Detectives Gossett and St. George."

Olivia stepped forward and lifted her hand. "Olivia St. George. We spoke on the phone, Ma'am."

"Uh....yes," Mrs. Pace said, looking confused. "Is this about Anna?"

"May we step inside your office?" Elaine suggested politely.

"I'm sorry. Yes, of course, please come in." Mrs. Pace closed the door behind them and gestured in front of her desk. "I'm afraid there are only two extra chairs."

"No worries," Matt said easily, leaning against the wall.

"Mrs. Pace," Elaine began, flipping open her notepad, "when you spoke to Detective St. George you mentioned that Anna has an uncle and a sister. Do you have contact information for either of them, or for anyone else in her family?"

"I'm afraid not," she replied, still looking confused. "I don't maintain any files here – you'll have to ask the Registrar or the Student Employment Office."

Elaine nodded. "Okay. Can you tell us what you know about her family? Anything she's said in the time you've worked together?"

Mrs. Pace played with the glasses that hung on a chain around her neck. "She didn't say much, to be honest. Much of what I know was inferred from little comments she made. Let's see…" she thought for a moment. "I asked her once if she was ill, because she frequently looked so exhausted when she came in to work. She said that her sister was going through a personal issue and had been keeping her on the phone until very late each night."

"And the uncle?" Elaine asked.

"Oh, dear. That came up because…well, apparently a male student had come up behind her while she was reshelving books in a back aisle. He didn't mean to startle her, I'm sure, but she was taken by surprise when she realized he was standing right behind her. She was quite hysterical. I had to bring her in my office until she calmed down."

"And she explained this by saying she had been abused?" Olivia probed.

"Yes," Mrs. Pace nodded. "She very reluctantly told me that her uncle had done things to her as a child, and that she was still having a difficult time with it."

"Did she give you any details? The uncle's name, dates, anything like that?" Elaine asked.

"Oh, no," Mrs. Pace put a hand to her throat. "No, I didn't ask her for details and she didn't volunteer any. I got the impression that the uncle was a minister but I don't recall why I thought that."

"When did that occur – with the male student frightening her?"

She thought for a long moment. "I'm not sure exactly. Sometime in early November, is all I can say."

"And this sister – did she mention a name?"

Mrs. Pace shook her head. "I'm afraid not. Anna really didn't talk about her personal life at all."

"Alright, Ma'am, thank you," Elaine scribbled in her notebook. "Also, I understand that another of your employees has gone missing?"

"Yes, Melissa Thompson." Mrs. Pace looked upset. "Do you think that whoever hurt Anna – that they -"

"We have no reason to believe that Melissa has been hurt," Elaine said soothingly. "At this time, it looks like she may have gone to stay with family. Did she seem worried to you when Anna disappeared?"

Mrs. Pace raised an eyebrow. "She hasn't come back from Christmas vacation, either. Luckily this is a slow time of the semester for us, or it could have been a disaster. Apparently Betty has been running the desk practically by herself."

"Is Melissa a theology student as well?" Matt piped up.

"No. Ironically enough, she's studying library science with an emphasis in book repair and restoration," Mrs. Pace sighed. "I can't imagine that girl having the patience to repair a Dr. Seuss book, much less a hundred-year-old text."

Olivia leaned forward. "Lauren," she said, "did Anna ever mention to you that she was considering becoming a nun?"

"Not in so many words, no. But I wouldn't have been surprised. She was very religious, very spiritual. Very strong in her faith."

"Did she ever mention that she was having any sort of mental or emotional problems?"

Elaine was giving her an odd look – no doubt wondering where this line of questioning was coming from. But Mrs. Pace just shook her head.

"No, nothing like that. She seemed fine, other than being tired all the time. Well, and, you know – the lasting effects of abuse. But otherwise, no."

"Did you notice any changes in how she dressed or behaved over the last few months?" Olivia stressed.

The librarian wrinkled her brow. "Actually, now that you mention it, she *did* seem distracted, and she began dressing somewhat strangely. Sort of – mannish."

Olivia was beginning to get an odd feeling about the librarian. She didn't seem anything like the woman on the phone three days ago – so much more reserved and proper.

"Mrs. Pace, when I spoke with you on the phone, you specifically mentioned that Anna had changed quite a bit after she started going with her boyfriend," she frowned. "Do you recall our conversation?"

Mrs. Pace looked startled. "Boyfriend? Anna didn't have a boyfriend, Detective. I'm sure of that. And I'm so embarrassed to admit this, dear, but I don't remember talking to you. My memory must be getting worse than I thought."

"Ma'am," Elaine broke in. "What's your office number?"

"Why, it's extension two," she said. "Why?"

"So when we call, uh, 555-3060," Olivia said, reading from her notes, "it doesn't go directly to you?"

Mrs. Pace looked confused. "No. It rings the front desk and they have to connect you. If I don't answer, it goes right back to the front desk. They have to stay on the line for it to connect with my voicemail. It's quite a pain, I must say – some kind of glitch in the phone system."

Elaine and Olivia looked at each other, realization dawning.

"Ma'am, I believe someone has been talking to us and pretending to be you," Elaine said.

"But….to what end?" Mrs. Pace frowned.

They avoided the question. "Who is that girl at the front desk? The one with the thick glasses?" Olivia asked, rising from her seat.

"That's Betty," the librarian said, rising too.

"Please stay here, Ma'am," Elaine said, giving Olivia a meaningful glance.

"Yeah, me and Matt will go," Olivia answered her unvoiced question.

"Matt and I," Mrs. Pace corrected automatically. "This is terribly distressing. I don't understand what's going on."

Olivia and Matt walked back towards the front desk. They tried to look casual, but it was hard – the enormously tall blond man and the tiny olive-skinned woman, dressed in business casual, walking with a purposeful gait side-by-side. In other words, they looked like cops on a mission.

The girl with the magnified eyes was still behind the desk. Olivia had half-expected her to bolt.

The girl looked up, up, and up at Matt and then back at Olivia, gulping visibly.

"Betty," Olivia said, showing her Grand Forks badge. "We need to talk."

Betty turned out to be Beatrice Huntsman, twenty years old, of Fife, Washington when she wasn't attending school. She broke down and cried almost immediately, taking off her glasses when the tears began to flow. Without them, she was a lovely girl, with completely normal non-alien-sized eyes.

"I didn't mean to do anything wrong," she sobbed as a pile of tissues grew on the counter in front of her. "It was just supposed to be for practice."

"Practice for what?" Olivia asked as Matt stared down at the tops of their heads.

"For acting," Betty weeped. "I'm going to go to California as soon as I can afford Lasik. Can't be an actress with these Coke-bottle lenses, you know." She held up her glasses for display.

Ever thought about contact lenses? Olivia thought uncharitably.

"Did you know you were talking to real police officers?" Matt asked – overly kindly, as far as Olivia was concerned.

Betty shook her head. "Melissa said they were other students," she said in a tiny voice. "She was helping me practice for auditions and stuff. She told me what to say and everything."

"I hate to break it to you, but one of those 'other students' was me," Olivia said gruffly. "We may have to arrest you for hampering a murder investigation."

Betty cried harder. "Please don't arrest me!" she sobbed. "I swear, I had no idea. I really, really, really-"

"We get it," Olivia interrupted, sighing. She looked up at Matt, twisting her lips.

He shrugged and turned back to the girl. "Betty, where is Melissa?" he asked.

She pulled another Kleenex from the box, still weeping uncontrollably. "She's sick at home," she cried. "I haven't seen her in days. I've been taking her shifts."

Matt leaned down to mutter in Olivia's ear. "I don't see any point in arresting her," he said low.

"It's Barstad's call," Olivia said pointedly. "Not ours." She had no desire to arrest the soggy Beatrice Huntsman but she was irritated that he was being so easy on the girl.

"Betty, did Melissa write a script for your 'practice' sessions or did she just give you an idea of what to say?" Matt asked, leaning one arm on the counter.

"Um, sort of a script," Betty answered. "Not really lines, but like info, you know? Like, what to say if the other person said this or that."

Olivia did have to admit the girl was an excellent actress, at least on the phone. In person she was a pile of weeping goo.

"And do you still have the paper with the 'info' on it?" Matt continued.

Betty nodded. "She told me to shred it but I didn't," she admitted. "I liked to, um, sort of practice in my room at night." She reached behind the counter and brought up a back-pack. She shuffled through it, then pulled out two sheets of computer paper folded in half. "Here."

"Oh, look, Detective St. George," Matt said pointedly. "Melissa was nice enough to add a hand-written note reminding little Betty here to shred these after the phone calls. Wasn't that sweet of her?"

Olivia glared at him. She knew what he was doing – rubbing it in that they shouldn't arrest 'little Betty' since she was apparently so innocent.

"So sweet it makes my teeth hurt," she growled, still glaring. Betty was staring at them in confusion.

"Um, do you want me to call Melissa's cell phone?" Betty offered, lifting the phone hesitantly.

Matt looked at Olivia, his expression one of saccharin delight. "Why yes, Betty, why don't you call her," he replied, still looking at Olivia. His eyes sparkled with mischievous glee. "But don't mention that we're here. That would spoil all the fun. Just ask her if she'll be coming in for her next shift."

"Okay." Betty put the phone to her ear and dialed ten digits. She waited for a moment, then gave the two Detectives a thumbs-up, indicating that Melissa had answered.

"Hey, Mel, it's Betty," the girl said casually, then cleared her throat. Olivia had to give her props for a quick recovery – or maybe she was just a really good bald-faced liar.

"I was just wondering if you still need me to take your shift tomorrow, 'cause I was gonna go out with Kevin tonight and-" she paused and seemed to be listening. "Oh, you're still sick. Can I bring you anything?" she chirped helpfully. Olivia noticed her tears had dried. "I make a mean chicken soup….oh, okay. Well, I hope you feel better."

Betty slowly lowered the phone. She looked simultaneously happy and defeated.

"Gee, I guess she's really sick," she said. "Did I do good, though? I don't usually do improv."

"We'll go check on her for you, Betty," Matt said. "And yes, you did great. Where does Melissa live?"

Smooth, Gossett, Olivia thought. He obviously had this well in hand.

"Oh, she's in the Whispering Pines Apartments right down the street," Betty turned and pointed as if they could see through the walls. "Same as me, only she's in 341 in the back and I'm up front in 118."

Matt fished a business card from his coat pocket. "Thank you so much, Miss Huntsman," he said as he handed her the card. She looked starry-eyed as she took it.

Olivia waited until they were a decent distance away before commenting to Matt. "Is it just me, or are all these kids mentally challenged?" she said.

He chuckled. "She's just young. You were young once too, you know."

Olivia thought back to when she was twenty; already married to an abusive husband for over two years, every day a struggle just to be allowed to exist in her own skin.

"No," she said, but low. He didn't hear her. "Not like that I wasn't."

Olivia unconsciously turned and looked back at the girl as she and Matt rounded the corner. She was startled to see the girl staring back at her with a look of bare hostility plastered across her young face. As soon as she saw Olivia looking, the girl turned away, but not before Olivia saw her glance at Matthew, lustful hunger obvious in her demeanor.

Strange, Olivia thought, disturbed. *Stranger and stranger.*

CHAPTER 11

Day Five, midday

“Move ye,” said he; “prepare to move.” We were unwilling. Said I, “I’ve come back weary. Every one of us is unwilling to move.” “No,” said he, “the Great Father wishes you to remove at once and you must move to the Indian Territory.”

- White Eagle’s Narrative [Ponca Tribe] (*Bury My Heart at Wounded Knee*, Dee Brown 1970)

Detective Barstad was more than enthused at the idea of visiting Melissa Thompson’s apartment. Not being as gullible as poor Betty, none of the Detectives bought the ‘at home sick’ story. More likely, they agreed, Melissa was holed up at her dad’s house in Crookston, Minnesota, and was using the alibi to buy herself time.

The problem was getting a warrant. They had no evidence that suggested her apartment was a crime scene, and so far, everything linking Melissa to Anna was based on the shaky testimony of other shady characters.

So the Detectives decided to go with the Landlord method; believing that Melissa could be injured or in danger, the Landlord would be able to give them entrance.

“And no one’s seen Melissa for three days,” Olivia said. “Theoretically, she could be dead on the floor for all we know.”

“Theoretically means we did not overhear her talking to Betty,” Matt pointed out.

“Theoretically, we don’t have any proof that that was actually Melissa Thompson,” Olivia countered as Elaine watched the back-and-forth. "There could be more than one girl in on the fake-movie-scene action."

"True," he shrugged. "Hell, it's all whatever to me."

Elaine grinned. "Are you sure you two aren't married?"

"Ha ha," Matt said stiffly. "*Not* funny."

As they walked to Whispering Pines – there was no point driving since it was only a block away – Olivia brought up something that had been bothering her.

"Why do you think Thompson called me?" she asked, only slightly rhetorically. "If she had done nothing, we likely wouldn't even have gotten this far, at least not so quickly."

"I've wondered about that too," Matt agreed. "Didn't you say she made a point of saying she was calling from Washington, and that she'd seen something about Anna's death on TV?"

"Sure did," Olivia nodded.

"Alibi," Elaine suggested. "For whatever reason she felt she needed to establish that she was here when you found the body."

"And now we know she wasn't," Matt pointed out, "assuming we are correct that she's been in Crookston this whole time."

"But again, if she'd just laid low…" Olivia said, frustrated.

Elaine shrugged. "Too many movies, no real understanding of forensics or criminal investigation. That's all."

"I agree," Matt said. "Just another dumb kid."

"I do have to say, she didn't seem all that bright when we talked, especially for someone who worked in a library," Olivia admitted. "Or at the least her vocabulary was pretty limited."

"I actually majored in library science for almost a whole semester," Elaine confessed. "My experience with it was that it's one of those majors that people think will be super-easy, a way to float through college without having to work."

"And was it?" Olivia grinned.

"Hell no! You don't see me working in a library, do you?" Elaine chuckled.

"Not to mention a librarian is supposed to be kind, and gentle, and helpful, and friendly…" Matt teased.

"Watch it, Gossett," Elaine pretend-growled. "I have a black belt in Who Flung Poo and I'm not afraid to use it."

They were still laughing as they walked into the Whispering Pines Management Office. The young man at the front desk smiled as they approached.

"Good morning! May I help you?" he asked very perkily. His hair was tinted purple and his face was a display case for decorative piercings. The two in his lip waggled as he talked.

"Why yes you can, Justin," Elaine said, reading the name plate on the counter. "I'm Detective Barstad, these are my colleagues. We're here to check on one of your tenants, Melissa Thompson in 341. She hasn't been to work in several days and her employer is very concerned about her."

"Uh-oh," Justin said, looking quite worried. "I'll take you over there at once."

He took off speed-walking across the complex. The Tall Twins had no difficulty keeping up, but Olivia trailed behind, huffing and puffing with exertion.

"Geez, it's not a race," she muttered.

Melissa Thompson's apartment was in the last building at the rear, tucked away from sight of the street or parking lot. A grove of strange-looking trees with peeling, papery red bark encircled the building.

"Who do you suppose has been driving her car?" Olivia muttered to

Matt as Justin the Speedy knocked on the door. "The gold Mini Cooper, remember?"

Matt just shook his head.

Hearing no answer, Justin fished out the master key, turning it in the lock and swinging the door open. He gasped, startled by what he saw.

"Oh shit," he said, dismayed. "Mrs. Morgan will not be happy about this. Not at *all*."

The apartment had been emptied of furniture and personal belongings, but piles of trash littered the floor. Melissa had obviously left in a hurry and made no effort to clean up after herself.

"I take it she didn't give notice," Elaine said dryly, stepping into the apartment.

Justin shook his head. "Um, I need to go call my boss," he said, stepping back. "Are you…?"

"We'll be fine," Matt assured him.

"Thanks," Justin gulped. He almost ran back across the complex, disappearing around the corner of the front row of buildings.

"Poor kid almost had a stroke," Matt commented, following Barstad through the door.

"Do you think she lived like this?" Elaine said as she stepped over a mound of empty beer cans, some of which still trickled pungent amber liquid onto the carpet.

"Ugh." Olivia wrinkled up her nose. "It smells even worse than Kiely's place."

"There's still food in the fridge," Matt reported, "but it's all growing something. Cupboards are empty, though."

"What's that children's rhyme?" Olivia said absently as she used her toe to sift through a drifted stack of school papers. She was afraid to touch them for fear something might be hiding underneath. "Something about, the cupboard's all empty, not even a bone…"

"That's 'Mother Hubbard,' " Barstad called from the hallway. "The bedroom's cleaned out, too, if you can call this 'clean.' "

"There's nothing here," Matt announced after about twenty minutes. "I don't see any point in sifting through all this shit any further."

"I think I have to agree," Olivia sighed. "Not to mention this is just *nasty*."

"Okay children, let's clear out." Barstad headed for the door. "It's time for a coffee break, anyway."

"Didn't you just get a cup when you got in this morning?" Matt commented, holding the door open for the ladies.

"He hasn't learned yet," Olivia said to Elaine, gesturing with her lips at the offending officer. "It's *always* time for a coffee break."

When they returned to the station, Barstad put out an APB for the gold Mini Cooper. After that she did paperwork, finishing her report to bring Lieutenant Alvarado up to speed, while Olivia and Matt sat and waited.

"This is the life," Matt sighed, leaning back in his chair and lacing his hands behind his head.

"What are you talking about, this is exactly what you do at home," Olivia said ironically.

"Ah, I may not *seem* to be doing anything," he replied loftily, "but my brain is always working."

She chuckled. "That explains why your head is so big, then." She leaned back, yawning and stretching. "Damn, I'm tired. Hey, what's going on with the Kiely kid?"

"He's being processed for release," Elaine answered without turning from her computer. "I put in a call to the locals back in his hometown, but being that Ireland is eight hours ahead of us, I don't expect to hear back until long after the 24-hour window is up."

"You think he's got a record?" Matt asked.

She shrugged. "Just covering the bases."

"Well, I'm going to go talk to him again," Olivia said, rising to her feet.

Matt gave her a strange look. "What about?"

She gave him a sardonic smile and echoed Elaine's justification. "Just covering the bases."

Kiely was sitting just as she'd seen him last. He barely glanced up when she walked in and sat on the chair that was still against the wall.

Olivia watched him for a long minute, trying to gauge which "him" she was seeing. He looked normal; no growling, twitching, or strange voices. But with his hair hanging in front of his face, it was hard to tell.

Finally, she leaned forward and clasped her hands together. "Seamus, I know you're in there," she said quietly. "I know you want and need help. I want to help you."

He shook his head almost imperceptibly. "No one can help me," he answered, his voice faint.

"Even Brother Sheridan?" she questioned.

"He tries." His voice was still faint. "But he's too weak. It's just been too long."

"How long have you been this way?"

He sighed, a sound of such despair and anguish that her heart clenched. "As long as I can remember," he said sadly, hanging his head even further. "Anna tried to help, too. Nothing works." He coughed into his hand, curling around himself as if in pain. "Nothing works. Nothing."

She could see he was becoming distressed and took a different tack. "Tell me about Melissa," she suggested.

"She wanted to help too," he shrugged. "She thought that because of her dad, she could handle it. But it didn't work that way."

"Did she like you?"

He glanced up, just for a moment, but Olivia was relieved to see that his eyes were green. "I guess," he said dully.

"I mean, did she *like* you," Olivia stressed. "Was she jealous of Anna?"

She was startled when he laughed. "The only one Melissa was jealous of was God," he answered wryly.

"I don't understand," she said. "Help me understand, Seamus. What was going on between the three of you?"

He shook his head. "Nothing. Absolutely nothing." He turned away from her and lay on his side, curling up and facing the wall.

Olivia sighed. He was obviously done talking. She stood and took a card from her pocket, writing her number on the back. "This is my cell number and my direct number at the office. Please call me anytime, okay?"

He didn't respond, and she left the card sitting between two bars of his cell.

They left for the airport early, and were glad they did. Traffic was so heavy they spent almost two hours creeping up I-5 before finally reaching the exit for SeaTac.

"What is all this?" Matt asked grumpily. He had stretched out in the back seat, leaving the driving to Olivia. Barstad had opted to ride with them in the rental car rather than pay airport parking fees for her own vehicle.

"Ah, combination of factors," Elaine sighed from the passenger seat, resting her head against the window. "There's a big concert tonight, along with some kind of demonstration over in the business district. Plus it's late afternoon."

"All this excitement and they're letting you fly off to North Dakota," Matt joked. "The land of snow-covered emptiness. Aren't you lucky."

Barstad chuckled. "Next you'll tell me that it's still Indian country and I'm out of luck because I can't ride a horse."

An uncomfortable silence ensued. After a very long, awkward pause, Elaine looked at her riding companions.

"Oh-uh....what'd I say?"

Olivia was silent, but Matt cleared his throat meaningfully, casting his eyes towards the driver's seat.

"Oh, shit," Barstad gulped, looking at Olivia. "I just shoved my big 'ol foot right down my throat, didn't I."

"It's okay," Olivia said easily. "Actually, I can't ride a horse either, so I think you'll be fine. And it *is* still Indian country, thank you very much!"

"Sorry," Elaine said whole-heartedly. "I've been told I speak without thinking. I also don't pay much attention to what people look like. It can be a dangerous combination."

Olivia took her eyes off the traffic long enough to give Elaine a little pat on the shoulder. "Really, it's okay," she assured her. "Only a fool would assume they knew somebody's ancestry just from looking at them."

"Is it bad to say Indian?" Elaine half-whispered, clearly embarrassed to be asking.

Olivia smiled. "Like anything else, it can be neutral, positive, or negative depending on who's saying it, who you say it to, and how you use it. I prefer the term 'Native,' myself, but everybody has their own personal preference."

“Gotchya,” Barstad nodded. “I’ll remember that.”

“Uh, back to what Matt said, though,” Olivia said, “you did bring lots of cold weather gear, right?”

“Yeah, I’ll be fine,” Elaine assured her. “Don’t worry! I have no desire to be a popsicle.”

There was little conversation over the next few hours until they were finally boarding the plane. Once again they would have to fly to Chicago, then get on a smaller flight to Grand Forks.

Since Olivia hadn’t been there when they booked the tickets, she didn’t know what to expect for their seat assignments. She was relieved when her section in the rear was called and Matt remained seated.

“I’m in the first row,” he said, waving her off. “For once I’ll actually have enough leg room.”

“What about you?” she asked Elaine who had also stood up to board the same section.

“I’m right next to you,” she explained, grinning. “You get to fight me for elbow room for the next four hours.”

“Better you than a stranger,” Olivia responded.

The flight left on time and it didn’t take long until they both had a drink in front of them. Olivia had asked for orange juice while Elaine had opted for tomato juice.

“Cheers,” she said, raising the tiny red can. They clinked drinks together, then Olivia turned to watch the lights below disappearing as they moved away from populated land. She was glad they’d gotten her a window seat, since she hadn’t thought to ask beforehand.

“Say, uh, there’s something I want to ask but I’m afraid it’s going to be horribly offensive,” Elaine said hesitantly after the land below had turned mostly dark.

“You want to ask me what tribe I am,” Olivia guessed shrewdly. She was surprised to see the other Detective flush.

"Is that bad?"

Olivia laughed. "You worry too much. It's no different than asking about anybody's lineage, if you are genuinely interested in learning about them."

"Oh. Cool. Okay, so?"

"Uh…unfortunately, I don't actually know what I am," Olivia admitted. It felt strange to say it out loud in a terrible, cathartic way. "I was abandoned as an infant."

Elaine flushed darker. "Oh geez, I'm so sorry. I've done it again."

Olivia waved her off. "No, no, you couldn't have known. I wound up at a Catholic orphanage in Sioux Falls, and so went to a Catholic school that serviced the orphanage through most of my childhood." *Excepting the few months here and there that I was at a foster home,* she thought, but felt no need to say. "But, I naturally always assumed I was Lakota and so did everyone else, although they didn't call it that, of course. South Dakota has a bunch of reservations, you know."

"Sioux? Is that the common term?"

Olivia nodded, although that was only partially correct. *Sioux, redskin, squaw, apple*….the list went on and on, especially when considering that "common term" really meant "what white people say."

"It was a rough way to grow up. I, uh, I got in trouble a lot, especially as a teenager." She couldn't help but laugh, though it had a hint of sadness. "Once I punched a girl in the face because she called me a bad name."

"You?!?" Elaine looked impressed. "Was she bigger than you?"

Olivia nodded. "She was indeed. She liked a boy that I was seeing, my ex-husband actually, and called me, er….well, a pretty bad name." Olivia, who was still Kaya back then, and Darren had been enjoying the teenage ritual of snuggling in the hallway before splitting to go to their separate classes. Cynthia Miller was a girl from the other side of the tracks who knew exactly how to wear makeup, how to expertly curl her platinum locks every morning, how to make the poor kids on scholarship and the kids from the orphanage feel like crap without even trying. Olivia's second-hand school uniform, her unfashionable straight black hair, and her un-makeuped face were often topics of derision from Cynthia Miller and her cronies. Darren was no rich kid or jock, but he was a good-looking boy and they couldn't begin to understand what he saw in Kaya/Olivia.

Olivia could still hear the girl's mocking voice echoing off the metal lockers that lined the hallway as she walked by the locked-lip couple. *Race traitor!* the taller girl had snarled, as if a white girl would know anything about such things. *Fucking prairie nigger slut!*

Olivia had spun on her heels, her plaid skirt swishing, and decked Cynthia Miller with all the force in her five-foot body. She had not really meant to break the girl's nose but that had mattered little to the girl's parents, to the nuns that had rushed to the girl's aid, and to the principal who had threatened to have Olivia arrested. The only bright spot in that day – or so it had seemed at the time – was how impressed Darren had been with her willingness to fight to keep him. What he couldn't begin to comprehend was that she hadn't done it for him. She loved him, yes, but the reasons she had punched Cynthia Miller were entirely for herself. It was hard enough to be an orphan, to not know her own family or where she came from, to lay claim to a culture that she wasn't entirely sure she actually belonged to; but to have some uppity yellow-haired *wašíču* bitch talk to her that way? She wouldn't stand for it, then or ever.

The other part was that she did *feel* like a race traitor, a little bit. In retrospect she wasn't even sure how she had ended up with Darren; she knew that he had chased after her, calling her "exotic," but as for why she'd fallen in love? Who knew. Love was a funny thing, especially when you were seventeen and lonely. She realized now that his "love" for her was really just his fascination for all things interracial; it didn't have anything to do with her as an actual person. She was just an icon to him, a symbol, a red-skinned black-haired girl to stand in for all of his fantasies. As a teenager, though, his desire for her had seemed like the most romantic thing in the world.

For breaking Cynthia Miller's nose, they had suspended her for a week. Being that it was November, she thought she'd make use of her extra time and trek into town for some holiday shopping. No family to buy for, but plenty of friends....she'd been a fairly popular girl back in those days, at least with her own group of fellow outcasts. She wasn't the only Native at the party, either; the High School served three counties and there had been a few handfuls of other red-skinned kids, some like her from the orphanage, some from town, some from out in the rural lands, all of them clinging to one another like life-rafts in a sea of white people. Five or six of them had piled into someone's car and trundled over to the mall for the afternoon, her friends happy to support her during her suspension by playing hooky to go shopping. It was supposed to be a fun and relaxing outing, but had turned into something much darker – at least for Olivia.

Remembering that day, she couldn't help but grit her teeth. "So, here's something I've never told anyone about," she said to Elaine, surprising herself with a sudden need to unburden. She paused for a long moment, remembering, while Elaine waited expectantly.

"You really don't have to tell me," Elaine said, "if it makes you uncomfortable."

"It's just that I've never talked about this before," Olivia admitted. "I have to think about how to explain it. I guess the best way is to say that I accidentally found my doppelgänger and it made me rethink the assumptions I'd made about who I was." She took a sip of her orange juice. "A couple of my friends and I went into the city to go Christmas shopping. I was in this little candy shop looking at the maple sugar leaves, and I noticed a little black-haired girl walk in. She was probably about ten years old, and I swear to you, Elaine, I felt like I was looking at a younger version of myself." She shook her head, bemused at the memory. "In retrospect I realize now that the resemblance was probably slight; at that time in my young life, I'd seen so few non-whites. But you can't imagine how excited I was. I honestly thought she had to be my little sister. I followed her when she left the candy store – I wanted to see her mom and dad, you know? But then she walked up to this white guy and I thought, oh, she was abandoned too, that's her foster dad or whatever. But then…." Olivia took another sip of the orange juice, her gaze on a faraway time and place. "Then this tiny, dainty, black-haired woman walked up, and it was so obvious that she was the girl's mother. The resemblance was unmistakable. And you know what?"

She looked at Elaine, both horrified and amused by that long-ago event. "The woman was Asian. I mean, *definitely* Asian. She even spoke to the girl in what I thought at the time was Japanese, although that was just a wild guess. I looked again at the dad – his haircut, his build, his demeanor - and realized he looked military. He had probably met her while stationed overseas. And somehow, that Asian woman and her white husband's genes had conspired to create a child who looked just like me, or so it seemed at the time. In thinking back, I can't even remember what that little girl actually looked like. All I can see is my own face in my elementary-school graduation picture - the only picture that I had ever had of myself."

Elaine's eyes were wide, yet sympathetic.

"Anyway, to put it plainly, that completely fucked up my head," Olivia continued. "Suddenly I doubted everything I had thought was a known fact. I actually felt betrayed all over again…as if my mother, whoever she was, had dumped me all over again." *And everything I thought I knew about myself, about who I was, got ripped away in a heartbeat.*

"Did you say anything to that family?" Elaine asked.

Olivia shook her head. "Nah, I was too busy being horrified and shocked. I told my friends I was sick and went and sat in the car for the rest of the afternoon while they shopped. And I've never said a word about that day to anyone, until now."

She had wanted so bad to tell them, to be comforted by them; back then, her friends were everything to her, and that had been the worst part. In that one moment she had lost not just herself but her connection to the only family she had. Every one of them, orphaned or not, knew exactly where they came from, who they were, who their parents were. Would they still accept her if her Nativeness was no longer such a surety? Would they still love her? Or would she be cast out of yet another family, to walk alone forever?

It had been too much to bear and so she had said nothing, running to Darren that night for unspoken comfort that he was more than happy to give, because for him it was just sex. It didn't matter why they had it, as long as he got his. Slowly over the next few months, she had begun to drift away from her friends, constantly questioning her own motives and reasons for clinging to them so tightly.

And finally, school had ended; she had married Darren and moved to the next county to become the only red girl in a white-trash trailer park while he apprenticed in his Uncle's plumbing business. Her friends had become a happy memory, something left over from an earlier and nicer world. In her new world was nothing but disappointment and the slow death of her soul slowly being sucked away.

"So why now?" Elaine asked gently. "Why me?"

"Why you? I'm not sure. You seem to have a good ear, and the fact that we don't actually work together is sort of comforting for a confession like this one. And as for why now....a lot of that is this case, actually. It's been making me think about things... like how I've been running away from myself for the last seventeen years, how I tried to find a sense of identity by running into the arms of a man who turned around and treated me like shit. I've been lost for a long time. But I understand a lot more now about genetics than I did on that day in Sioux Falls, and I finally realize that seeing that girl and her multiracial parents doesn't change anything about *my* life. Coincidences happen."

"That's very true," Elaine said thoughtfully. "Genetics can play a lot of tricks when it comes to the way people look. I have a friend who is half Irish, a quarter Syrian, and a quarter Egyptian, but she lives in Texas and everybody always assumes she's Hispanic."

"Yeah, exactly!" Olivia perked up. "We see what we expect to see, I guess – with human faces just like everything else."

"Have you ever considered getting a DNA test done?" Elaine asked. "A mitochondrial DNA test will map your maternal ancestral heritage. They'll be able to tell you just about anything you want to know about your lineage, at least on your mother's side."

"I've thought about it," Olivia admitted, "but for some reason, I've been scared to. I think I'm afraid of what the results might be."

"Well, it's just a thought," Elaine suggested. "But another way to look at it is to ask what's more important to you – genes from parents you've never met, or the culture that you grew up in? A culture that I can see was very important to you."

Olivia just nodded, agreeing with the statement even though it was half-false; she had not grown up in any culture except that of the Catholic church. Back then, everything she knew about the Lakota people had been learned from her friends. They had been her singular connection to a world she desperately wanted for her own, a world she knew only through their few experiences and Hollywood movies. What few facts she knew had been cobbled together from the rare history books she could find – books always written by white historians or missionaries, not by Native authors. The little language skills she had were, sadly, learned from watching Dances With Wolves five hundred times and from hanging out at the houses of her few red friends whose parents still used a few Lakota greetings and words.

As an adult, especially once the internet was in full bloom, she was able to access so much more. But even that was dry, lacking in human interaction and any exposure to the real, well-rounded culture of a living people. When she had happened to read the short story *The San Francisco Indians* by Acoma author Simon Ortiz, it had made her laugh out loud. In that story, set in late-1960's San Francisco, a group of white flower-child hippies had wandered around San Francisco trying to find an "Indian" to "show them the way." Despite San Francisco being packed full of Native people from all across the country, the white kids had been completely oblivious to the very presence of the actual people they were looking for because they were so intent on their own selfish and preconceived notion of what it meant to be Indian.

That's me, she had realized humorously and then sadly. Wandering through life, trying to figure out what it meant to be "Native." But she couldn't figure out any other way, not in her current situation. She had fled to Grand Forks originally because she thought it was the last place

Darren would think to look for her. He probably assumed she would go to one of the reservations to be with "her people." But in even considering such a move, she kept visualizing herself driving on to a vague and unnamed reservation, getting out of the car and announcing "Okay! I'm here!" as if there would be a welcome wagon just waiting for her arrival. The mere thought of it made her laugh at her own naiveté and shallowness. And now, after being in Grand Forks for so long, she had made a life for herself, such as it was. If she truly wanted to "find herself," she wouldn't even know where or how to start.

Bringing Olivia back to the conversation, Elaine smiled and quipped, "In the end, you are who you are, as a very wise sailor once suggested."

"Let me guess....Popeye?" Olivia said, her eyes twinkling.

"Very good."

"What about, be all that you can be?"

Elaine chuckled. "If we're still talking cartoon characters than I'd have to go with G.I. Joe. Simper Flexi?"

Olivia couldn't help but laugh out loud. "Gumby!"

"All very good advice, of course."

"Alright, enough of all that," Olivia waved her hand in the air. "Make me laugh too hard and I'll snort this orange juice right out my nose. Tell me about you."

"Me? I'm just an ordinary supercop. Stronger than steel, faster than light, and more loyal than a puppy dog."

Oliva was still laughing. "Stop that! I'm serious."

"Okay, okay. Nothing too exciting, I'm afraid. Farm girl from Indiana, left to become a teacher and wound up a cop instead."

"Hmm...I sense an untold story in the ginormous gap you left."

Elaine scrunched up her eyebrows. "We-ell....yeah, okay. For one thing, it took me seven years to get through college 'cause I kept changing my major. Started out in Education, then to Library Science, then I was an Art major for almost a whole year, and finally on to Criminal Justice."

"And what precipitated each change? And why the huge jump to Criminal Justice?"

"Honestly, this makes me sound terrible, but I just kept getting bored. I finally realized I needed a career that would keep me on my toes, one where there's always something new to learn, new techniques, new technologies, new bad guys. Etcetera."

"I can understand that," Olivia nodded. "But you said 'for one thing.' Is there a second?"

"Well," Elaine said, playing it light. "I assume you probably figured out that I'm gay."

Olivia flashed a smile. "I *did* notice the picture of the woman, being a Detective and all that. Girlfriend?"

"Wife, actually," Elaine said proudly. "We were some of the first in line once it became legal in Washington. But in college, I was still trying to figure out who I was supposed to be. I was still trying to come out of the closet, get comfortable in my own skin, and none of the careers I was contemplating really seemed to fit. Ironically, cops aren't really supposed to have personal lives, you know, which strangely is part of what attracted me to the field in the first place. I'd just had a really bad breakup – she was in the Art program too – and our school happened to have Career Day right after that. There was this woman cop representing the local force and she was so fucking *cool,* she seemed to have it so together, but she was saying how it's hard to have much of a personal life because of the long hours, etcetera. Right then that sounded pretty damn awesome to me."

"I can understand," Olivia nodded. For some odd reason she

suddenly remembered one of her last days with Darren. She'd woken up early to make him pancakes before work, trying to be thoughtful, not realizing until it was too late that she'd forgotten to get syrup during her last trip to the market. He had walked into the kitchen, looked at the syrup-less stack of pancakes on his plate, and shaken his head mournfully.

"You're such a shitty wife," he had sighed matter-of-factly, then grabbed his lunchbox and left. Olivia had been left standing alone, still holding the spatula, his statement resounding in her ears where it remained all that day and for many days to come.

"When I was working back in Indiana, I felt like no matter what I did, being the 'lesbian cop' just made me into a stereotype," Elaine frowned. "At some point, while still chasing that never-ending road of 'what am I supposed to be?' I finally realized I'm not *supposed to be* anything. I just am who I am. Two weeks later I was in Washington, applying for the job in Graham's Ford. Never looked back and sure as hell never regretted it – in fact, I met Meagan only a few months later."

"That's really admirable," Olivia said, heartfelt. "I've rarely had the guts to just make a big change like that."

"It wasn't necessarily easy," Elaine admitted. "Before that I'd never even been out of Indiana. My family is still extremely unhappy about all of it, but that's just too bad."

Olivia raised her eyebrows. "I take it they don't approve of your decisions?"

"Yeah, well, some things still haven't made it out to Indiana farm country, and open sexuality is one of them. My dad equates being gay with being a Communist, for God's sake."

"How sad for the Communists," Olivia quipped, twisting her mouth to show she was joking.

"Yeah, really. At least we get our own bars," Elaine said. "And we get to claim a lot of awesome people as our own. All the Communists get are despots and tyrants. Well – and Che Gueverra, but no one ever remembers what he was trying to do."

"Really, though," Olivia said, "I am impressed. Thank you."

"Thank *you.*" Elaine raised her nearly-empty can of tomato juice. "To baring our souls."

Olivia grinned, clinking the little can with her own plastic cup. They talked of other things for the rest of the plane ride, and by time it landed in Chicago and they boarded the smaller plane for North Dakota, it was just as if they were old friends who had finally met after many years apart. Olivia couldn't wait to introduce Elaine to Whitney; together, the three of them would create a trifecta of female power, a virtual tornado of brains and beauty that would take the Midwest by storm. They might even solve this case while they were at it.

CHAPTER 12

Day Five, Evening

On a cold, wet afternoon, in a room full of emptiness, by a freeway I confess; I was lost in the pages of a book full of death, reading how we'll die alone and if we're good, we'll lay to rest anywhere we want to go.
- *Like a Stone* (Audioslave)

One of the blessings of a small town is a small airport. After debarking the commuter plane in Grand Forks and picking up their few pieces of luggage, it was a thirty-second walk to the airport exit. When the automatic doors slid open and the burst of frigid winter air flowed over them, it was clear from Elaine's expression that whatever she had thought she was prepared for, this wasn't it. She quickly backtracked, taking a sweatshirt from her bag and throwing it on over her long-sleeved silk blouse before putting her coat back on. Olivia could see right off that what the visiting Detective had brought just wasn't going to cut it. The sun had long since set and the temperature was already five below. With wind chill, probably closer to fifteen.

"If you can suffer through about fifteen minutes, I've got plenty of spare warm stuff at my apartment. You're welcome to whatever you need," she told the shivering Detective Barstad.

"Thanks," Elaine said through clattering teeth, pulling her plush felt cap down further over her ears with one hand while gripping her bag with the other. They rushed across the parking lot, giving Matt a quick wave good-bye while dodging small mounds of snow that the wind had piled against anything that rose more than six inches from the ground. Olivia got Elaine into the passenger seat, starting the car and pulling from the space without wasting any time. The car could heat up during the drive, she figured.

"Here," she said, reaching into the back without looking. Her hand found the blanket that she kept folded on the back seat and brought it up front. "It's cold, but it'll keep you warmer than nothing until the car heater gets going."

"Thank you," Elaine said gratefully as she spread the blanket over her legs and torso. "I'm embarrassed at how ill-prepared I am. You guys warned me. I'm even from Indiana, for God's sake. I've been gone too long, I guess."

"Don't be embarrassed," Olivia said honestly. "We'll get you set up, don't worry."

The CD player started back up, launching into the middle of a very loud "*...same old shit, different day....gotta get up, gotta get up!*" until Olivia stabbed the Off button.

"That would make a good alarm tone," Elaine chuckled through her chattering teeth, clutching the blanket close.

"Do you like Puddle of Mudd?" Olivia asked curiously. Elaine had struck her as more of an indy-bluegrass chick, but maybe she was making a terrible assumption.

"I only know that one song," Elaine admitted. "You know, 'she fucking hates me?' Every time I hear it I think, hey, I dated that same girl!"

They both got a laugh over that and for a brief moment, even felt warm.

Elaine had made reservations at the Holiday Inn, over in the newer section of Grand Forks. From the airport it was a straight-shot to stop at Olivia's apartment and then continue on to the hotel. Elaine had asked if she ought to reserve a rental car but Matt and Olivia both suggested that it would be an unnecessary cost. One of them would always be going anywhere she needed to go, they figured, so she could just ride with them.

There was very little traffic on the road, which was not unusual considering the time of night. In less than fifteen minutes Olivia was pulling into her own assigned parking space.

"I'll leave the car running," she said. "We won't be that long." They ran up the stairs and down the hallway, laughing like schoolgirls as the door banged shut behind them.

"Oh, Lord," Elaine gasped, leaning against the wall and pulling off her gloves. "How do you stand it? I left the Midwest for a reason!"

Olivia chuckled as she opened the hallway closet, pulling out a heavy, sheepskin-lined canvas parka and handing it to Elaine. "This is old but it'll keep you comfortable. Do you have any other shoes but those?"

"There's no way you have shoes in my size," Barstad said bluntly. "And why do you have this parka? This thing must be a tent on you."

"Actually, I snagged this from the Lost and Found at work, after it sat there for a year," Olivia explained. "I'm a terrible pack rat when it comes to cold weather stuff. You can never have too much."

"Geez, I see why. This thing is awesome."

"As for shoes, no, I don't, you're right. But I *do* have a pair of rubber overshoes that will keep your feet dry, and they should have enough room that you can wear the heavy woolen socks I'm about to go get for you."

"Wow. You must host visiting Amazon-sized cops all the time."

Olivia laughed. "I'll get those socks."

Before long she had filled a shopping bag full of good warm things for Elaine to wear while she was in town, and they were off to the hotel.

Elaine tumbled out of the car and ran, arms full of bags and luggage, in to the hotel lobby.

"I'll pick you up at seven!" Olivia called, waving goodbye. They planned to get an early start and go straight to Crookston to do interviews and canvas the Thompson's neighbors.

After dropping her off, Olivia called the lab to see if Whitney was still working. There was no answer, so she sent a quick text to her cell phone; *I'm back, call if ur still up ☺*.

When she finally got back home, she collapsed into bed – or rather, "onto mattress" – and fell straight into a deep sleep. Thanks to having just gained back two hours of time difference, morning was going to come far too soon.

In retrospect, she should have expected to dream and perhaps taken steps in advance. A sleeping pill, maybe, or left a lamp burning. But after the plane ride and running around town, her mind had been on other things.

So when her mind's eye opened to see a familiar bathroom mirror staring back at her, she was unexpectedly shocked.

But I've already done this! she shouted in surprise and fury, banging a dream-hand on the sink. It hurt, and she sucked on the side of her palm to ease the stinging.

She sighed in resignation. *Alright, bring it on,* she said aloud (or thought she did), taking a step back to lean against the wall behind her. The mirror didn't answer, but perhaps it didn't need to, because when she leaned back there was no wall to catch her. The lean turned into a fall, and her arms flew up in surprise as she landed in a very cold, very wet patch of mud and moss.

It was raining, and all around her the forest dripped steadily. She looked up at what sky wasn't blocked by trees. A very grey, overcast day was overhead, and she wasn't at all surprised when a fat drop of cold rain landed directly in her left eye.

Goddamnit. She rubbed her eye ruefully. *Didn't your mother ever tell you not to stare up at the sky when it's raining?*

No, actually, her mother had never said any such thing, because her mother had been long gone by the time Olivia/Kaya had understood even the littlest bit of human speech.

These dreams are getting really, really old, she said out loud – or thought she did – and then became aware of an uncomfortable squishy feeling underneath her nether regions. *Oh, for God's sake. Am I* naked?!?

And her dream-self looked down to see that yes, indeed, she had sprung into being in this forest in nothing but her birthday suit. When she had landed in the patch of wet, muddy moss, some of it had gotten squelched up between her legs and, unfortunately, between the two parts of herself that were meant to provide padding when she sat.

I've got mud in my buttcrack, she sighed to herself. *That's just great.*

With some difficulty she got to her feet, feeling strangely warm despite being naked in a cold wet rainy forest, and especially despite having mud in her buttcrack (in fact, all up her backside and even in her hair). The mud between her toes felt pretty nice. The moss was soft and spongy underneath her feet as she took a few steps forward.

Should be a trail around here somewhere. The forest looked familiar, not that she could claim to recognize any landmarks. At least, it was the same type of forest she'd been to in the past dreams, and looked pretty much like the one near St. Agnes' when she'd gone trail-exploring.

As she walked forwards, from behind her she heard the crack of a small branch being stepped on. Olivia whirled around, the hairs on the back of her neck standing up.

A figure stood in the forest. Shadowed by the trees around it, she could only make out that it was human-shaped and seemed vaguely male.

"Hey!" she shouted, trying to scare it/him off before it came any closer. "I see you there!"

As her voice died away, she realized she had finally spoken out loud and not just in her head. The figure didn't move. She stood still, waiting for it/him to move, speak, anything that would give her a clue as to how to react. Around them, the forest continued to drip as the rain made its way through the trees and off the tips of branches. Olivia felt herself sinking ever so slightly into the mud, and she shifted her weight from foot to foot to loosen the hold.

The figure just stood, and even without being able to see a face, she could feel its eyes boring into her.

Finally, a faint, mocking voice floated through the air. It came from all around her, drifting from leaf to leaf and landing on her ears like a moldy brown moth.

Oliviaaaa

The sound of it made her head hurt.

She didn't respond. She just stood and waited, shifting her weight back and forth to keep her feet free of the treacherous, sucking mud.

Oliviaaaa, it came again. Her gun-hand twitched towards her waist, and she belatedly realized again that she was naked.

"What do you want?" she yelled, spooked into responding, but as soon as the words left her lips she knew it was a mistake. The figure laughed, no, it *tittered*, taking her back to the very worst days of junior and high school.

"You sound like a teenage girl," she called out contemptuously, trying to sound firm and brave and everything she wasn't actually feeling.

Whether it was her words or the feeling behind them, the figure finally moved. She didn't see it actually take a step, but she heard the bushes rustling and *felt* its presence get closer.

Don't run, she told herself determinedly. *Don't run. Don't run. Don't –*

The figure came closer. Now she could see the bushes moving as it pushed through them, and she could just begin to make out the features of its face.

And as it came yet closer, she realized it *was* an "it." This was no he, no man, no human of any kind. It may have taken on a basic human form, but that was where the resemblance ended.

"What do you want?" she asked again, her lips trembling.

It pushed closer, the waist-high salal bushes parting reluctantly to give it space, and she saw now that its facial features bore a passing resemblance to Seamus Kiely. It was like looking at a poorly-made clay version of the boy.

"I know who you are," she tried bravely. "You are the one she called Iblis."

It chuckled, a deep ripping sound that scraped across her bones.

Be careful what you wish for, it hissed, and two small pitfires glowed red, deep in its pretend-Seamus eye sockets.

"But I didn't wish for anything," Olivia demurred, and despite her best efforts she took a step backwards. The figure was only a few yards away now.

Oh but you did, it disagreed heartily. *For when you name me, you wish to know me. Would you like to know me, Oliviaaaa?*

"No thank you," she said faintly, taking another two steps back.

The figure advanced again, startling her, and she *jumped* backwards. Betrayed by the mud, her feet slid out from under her and she landed on her rear end with an *oomph.*

Sitting in the mud, she was now hidden from the figure – and it from her – by the abundant, enthusiastically growing salal bushes and ferns that covered the forest floor. Olivia dug her feet into the mud, preparing to stand, and was propelled another few inches backwards into something cold and very hard.

She felt behind her with one hand, fingernails scraping painfully against rough stone. She braced herself, using the whatever-it-was to pull herself upright, looking around frantically for the figure.

It was nowhere to be seen. The forest was, for all appearances, empty and peaceful.

Olivia looked behind her to see the whatever-it-was. It appeared to be some kind of statuary, built from natural stone and mortar roughly in the shape of a cross, with a space built into the join of the "t" that she guessed might once have held some kind of religious artifact. Most of the stone was covered in moss.

Putting the stone cross at her back, she once again turned to survey the forest. She gasped when the bushes moved just a few feet away and out trotted a wet, mangy black dog.

The dog stunk like, well, wet dog. She could smell it from where she was. It paused and sat in the mud, regarding her solemnly. She couldn't help but notice that its eyes were the color of summer grass, but even as she watched, they turned the color of a moonless night sky.

The dog's tongue came out and swiped across its nose, and as its eyes swirled with darkness, it laughed at her.

"You did not just laugh," Olivia whispered, pressing back against the stone.

The edges of the dog's mouth turned up at the corners as its tongue lolled. Its eyes swirled and danced, a few red sparks chasing across the dark skies of its pupils. She was hypnotized by the dance of those sparks, and felt herself relaxing into the stone.

The dog winked, and spoke. "Darren says hello," it chortled, its red tongue wagging.

"No," she said, jerking upright. "No. I want to wake up now. I want to wake *up!*" And she slammed her arm back, hitting the stone statuary square on her funny bone.

"Owwww *fuck!*" she swore, holding her elbow and sitting bolt upright on the mattress. She kicked off the blankets furiously, jumping to her feet and striding to the bathroom.

"I am so goddamn sick of this!" she hollered, not caring that it was the middle of the night or that she had neighbors on every side. She slammed open the bathroom door, flicking the light switch and stepping up to the sink.

And gasped, when the woman she saw in the mirror was Anna Taylor.

"No," Olivia said between clenched teeth. "This is too much. *Leave me alone.*"

Anna shook her head and shrugged. She seemed bemused, lifting her shoulders and dropping them as if to say, *Nothing I can do about it.*

Olivia looked down at herself. The mud was gone, but she was still naked. Her elbow hurt like a son of a bitch with a big red spot where she'd banged it on the stone.

"Is this what they put you through?" she said, mostly rhetorically. "Is this what killed you?"

Anna didn't answer. She just stared back at Olivia, one hand playing with the golden cross she wore around her neck.

"How do I end it?" Olivia leaned forward, putting both hands on the cold glass. "*Tell me how to end this.*"

Anna seemed to think for a long moment, but finally she just frowned, shrugging again, her face falling in sadness.

"You don't know. Just great." Olivia started to step back and then, remembering what had happened last time she did that, looked behind her. Nope, just a bathroom wall.

Sighing in relief and exhaustion, she started to turn back towards the mirror and the ghost it held.

"Can you at least-"

Anna wasn't there, but something else was. Olivia was blinded by a painfully bright light shining right in her eyes, surrounded by pitch-black dark. A noise rumbled out of the blackness, shaking her to her core, and she instinctively jumped to the side as a *woosh* of cold air was pushed out of the night.

She landed in a snow bank, rolling down into a ditch half-full of dirty ice and random wind-driven debris. The cold hit her all at once, and she was overtaken by uncontrollable shivering as a mound of disturbed snow crystals washed over her bare skin.

Another noise broke the night, and under better circumstances she would have recognized it as screeching tires.

The sound of a metallic door slamming; a car door, then, or truck.

"*What the hell is wrong with you?!?*" A voice boomed, cracking in the middle from emotion. *"Goddamn woman I coulda killed you!"*

Olivia's teeth were chattering so hard against one another that she was surprised they hadn't yet broken. She struggled to see the owner of the voice, but it was so dark; her eyes couldn't make out anything but the dim shape of a large vehicle.

She slowly realized that the light coming at her had been headlights, and the noise a horn.

“Holy shit!” the voice said, and a figure loomed out of the dark, sliding down the side of the ditch towards her. She blinked as a fresh cloud of snow was thrown up and over her. “You’re barely wearing anything!”

Olivia couldn’t answer, couldn’t nod, couldn’t do anything but hold herself as her bones tried to rattle their way out of her skin.

Two hands grasped her arms, pulling her out of the snow. The pressure on her frozen skin was unbearable; she tried to scream, but the air in her throat was a block of ice, her tongue a prisoner in the jail of her mouth behind bars of teeth.

The figure continued to pull her up, yelling as it did so.

“Jenny! Get that blanket outta the back! And crank the heat up!” It hollered.

Olivia was half-dragged, half-carried to the waiting vehicle. She thought vaguely that her feet should probably be hurting from being dragged across the rough asphalt, but she couldn’t feel them at all.

The last thing she noticed before the night finally claimed her was that the back seat of the mystery vehicle was very, very comfortable. And then her eyes closed for good, and she let the dark take her away.

CHAPTER 13

Day Six, Late Morning

The life and passion of a person leave an imprint on the ether of a place.
- *Anam Ċara* (John O'Donohue)

Olivia hated soap operas. But if she had ever watched them, she would have immediately recognized the scene that met her eyes the next morning.

Anxious faces peered down at her, offset by a background of not-quite-white walls. Soothing music played somewhere far-off in the distance, punctuated by blasts from a PA system. Someone in heels was tapping their way down a linoleum hallway nearby, and the air was redolent of cleaning products and bleach, with a vague undertone of vomit. Everything came together in her mind, and only two possible answers popped up; she was either in a hospital or a psych ward.

While she debated these two options, the faces staring at her all seemed to be waiting for her to say something. She wanted to be witty or at least comforting, as in general they seemed to be upset, but nothing particularly great came to mind so she said the first thing that did.

"Am I dead, or just crazy?" she finally said.

The faces looked startled, and a few of them glanced at each other.

"Was that wrong?" she said anxiously. "It sounded better in my head."

Out of the crowd that surrounded her, an older white-haired man stepped forward. He took a small penlight from his pocket and clicked it on, flashing it across her face.

"Ow," Olivia said, blinking and turning away.

"Now, young lady, I need to examine you," the doctor said only slightly condescendingly.

"My eyes are fine," she retorted, trying to put a hand up to shade her eyes. That was when she realized that both wrists were bound in restraints.

"Hey, whoa," Olivia said, alarmed. "What's going on?"

"You can let her out now," the doctor said over his shoulder before returning the penlight to her face. A nurse (or so Olivia assumed) reached out and undid the restraints.

"You were acting very upset," the nurse said soothingly. "It was for your own protection."

"Yeah, right," Olivia muttered. "Will you *please* stop shining that light in my eyes?"

"Yes, I'm done now," the doctor put the penlight back in his pocket. "How are you feeling? Any headache, blurriness of vision? Any aches or pains?"

"I feel fine, other than being on display," Olivia groused.

"Ah, but you are quite the miracle case." The doctor patted her hand. "We had to show you off."

"That's awesome, but I'm not a trophy," she said pointedly.

"Okay everyone, let's give the patient some rest time," the doctor said like it was all his idea. The crowd turned to go just as Olivia belatedly realized that she knew one of them.

"Whitney!" she said, pleased and startled.

The redhead turned to the elderly doctor. "Can I stay?" she asked.

"Yes, but just for a few minutes. The patient needs her rest," he warned, as if he hadn't just been showing Olivia off like she was the bearded woman in a sideshow carnival.

Whitney waited until the room had cleared, closing the door gently behind the last person. She then turned and sagged against the door, wiping imaginary sweat from her brow with the back of one hand and shaking it off in an exaggerated pose of exhaustion.

"Well now that *they're* gone," she heaved a sigh, rolling her eyes.

Olivia laughed. "Thank God you're here," she said wholeheartedly. "What the hell is going on?"

"Really? You don't remember?" Whitney frowned, taking a seat by the hospital bed.

"I don't know what I remember," Olivia said honestly. "I was having this crazy dream, and everything's all jumbled up with reality."

"You almost got plowed over by a farmer and his wife on their way home from Fargo," Whitney said. "They think you were sleepwalking."

Olivia waited, cocking one eyebrow. "But?" she prompted finally.

"*But….*" Whitney blew out her breath. "You were wearing only thin pajamas, and yet somehow managed to sleepwalk all the way out to County Road 3 without getting even a smidgeon of frostbite or hypothermia."

"Well, duh, I didn't sleepwalk out there," Olivia said dismissively. "I just woke up there."

"But you did *get* there somehow," Whitney pointed out. "And where, my dear, were your clothes? Is this a trendy new thing you've neglected to tell me about?"

"I don't know about trendy," Olivia shrugged. "Cold, though, definitely."

Whitney sat back against the plastic chair. "So?"

"So? What?"

"So, are you going to explain all this, or do I have to make up my own story?"

"Honestly? You might have to," Olivia said sheepishly. "Because, geez, I don't think I really know."

“Oh, for – Liv, tell me *something*, for Pete’s sake!” Whitney huffed.

“You won’t believe me,” Olivia warned.

“Try me,” the petite doctor challenged.

Olivia heaved a massive sigh. “Okay. So, you know those dreams I’ve been having?”

Whitney narrowed her eyes. “No, not really. You’ve haven’t mentioned anything about dreams.”

That gave Olivia pause. “Really? Hmm. Coulda sworn. Well anyway, I’ve been having these very detailed dreams, more like nightmares though, and Anna Taylor keeps showing up along with that kid Seamus, and the black dog, and I keep getting moved around between the forest and the bathroom,” she rambled. “And so anyway, I think the demon or spirit or whatever it is just plopped me in the middle of that road.”

Whitney, in her usual level-headed way, took all this in without blinking an eye. But that wasn’t to say she simply took it all as fact. “To what end?” she questioned logically. “Why would it spirit you, in your pajamas, into the middle of a rural road in the middle of the night?”

“Uh….hmm.” Olivia was momentarily stumped. “I really have no idea. Maybe it wants to kill me. Maybe it just wants to drive me mad, like it did Anna.”

“Is that what you think happened to her?” Whitney asked intently. “She was driven mad?”

“Shit, I don’t know,” Olivia admitted, suddenly tired. She slumped down into the bed. “I have no idea what’s going on, Whit. All I know is this crap is ‘bout to drive *me* to the loony bin.”

“Well, we can’t have that,” Whitney said brightly. “Or I’ll have no one to hang out with. What say we get you checked out of here?”

“Really?” Olivia perked up. “That would be *super* awesome.”

"They'll complain, but I think I can swing it," Whitney winked. "Go ahead and get dressed. I brought you clothes, since you neglected to bring your own." She lifted a brown shopping bag and set it on the end of the bed.

Olivia chuckled weakly. "Gee, thanks. I would have hated to have to walk out of here in my soggy pj's."

"It's okay," Whitney teased. "Everyone already saw you bare-assed when you came in."

"Great," Olivia grumbled. But she gratefully pulled clothes from the bag, sliding into the pants and socks before shrugging off the paper gown they'd dressed her in. There was no bra or underwear – not that Olivia would want to borrow either of those from Whitney – and the shoes were tight on her feet. But she was glad to be clothed, especially after all the barely-dressed traipsing around she'd done the night before.

"So how are you going to 'swing' getting me out of here?" she asked curiously as she buttoned up an almost-too-small flannel shirt.

Whitney chuckled. "I'm basically their on-call Dr. Death. See, hospitals mess up way more than they want anyone to realize, so having their own pet pathologist to come in and assist with determining cause of death is always to their benefit, especially if I can certify that it wasn't due to their error."

"And what do you get out of it?" Olivia wondered.

Whitney shrugged. "An exchange of services. They run lab tests for me when I don't feel like waiting for the State to get around to it. Look, you wait here a minute and I'll go talk to the attending physician."

Olivia complied, sitting on the edge of the hospital bed like a good child as Whitney closed the door behind her. She was already wondering how she'd get into her apartment. No clothes meant no pockets, and no pockets meant no keys. Her building had no superintendent, and the only "landlord" was the bank that owned the whole block.

Well, she'd cross that bridge when it arrived, and so forth. If worse came to worse, she'd just call the emergency maintenance number.

After a long while, tired of waiting, she walked out into the hallway, trying not to wince in the too-small shoes. She saw Whitney standing at the nurses' station, arguing with the doctor.

"You can release her to my care," Whitney was saying emphatically, her hands on her petite hips.

"You are not capable of caring for a patient in this condition!" the white-haired doctor insisted. He towered over the short redhead, but she stared up at him with the fierceness of a mother lion.

"I am fully capable of caring for *any* patient in *any* condition," Whitney blasted back.

The doctor, desperate to regain lost status points with the nurses who were watching bemusedly, pulled out all the stops.

"My dear, you are a pathologist, not a *real* doctor," he said condescendingly, straightening to his full height.

Up to that moment, Olivia had been happy with the turn of events. Sure, getting spirited in front of a moving vehicle had been not so great, but she had come out whole and unharmed.

What happened next changed her mind entirely.

As she watched in awe and horror, Whitney's mouth widened and lengthened, becoming unhinged like some crazed children's toy. The hinges opened and the top of her head flipped back, hanging down with her red hair touching her neck and back.

Then the pathologist *leaned*, grabbing the still-arguing doctor by his arms and pulling him down into the maw of her open throat. He went head-first, his voice fading as he was swallowed down the dark tunnel between Whitney's voracious lips.

Whitney put a hand up, pushing on the back of her head. It flopped over and plopped back on top of her lower jaw with a squishy *thunk*. She turned to face Olivia, winking widely.

"There!" She said brightly. "Problem solved. Let's go!"

"Uh-uh," Olivia said emphatically through stiff lips, shaking her head and putting her arms out in front of her. "No way, Jose."

"Oh but Liv," Whitney said slyly, licking her lips as she advanced on the backpedaling Detective. "It would be *so fun*!"

"Whatever the hell is happening, I refuse to believe it," Olivia pronounced firmly. A childhood habit, long unused, took over in the stress of the moment and she made the sign of the cross; forehead, chest, shoulder, shoulder.

Whitney laughed loudly. Her mouth was far too large and dark, her tongue far too red and lolling. "Do you think that stupid little superstition will help you?" she hissed, her eyes narrowing. Her red hair was beginning to smoke.

Olivia continued to backpedal with her arms held out in front of her. "Um – I think you're on fire," she pointed out helpfully as she scooted backwards down the linoleum hallway.

Whitney glanced up, patting her charring hair with one clawed hand. "Pardon me, while I burst into flames," she purred demurely.

"You aren't seriously quoting Incubus at me, are you?" Olivia challenged. "Well, pardon *me*, but this is the stupidest dream I've had yet. You are not Whitney."

"What makes you think it's a dream?" Demon-Whitney asked, long red tongue swiping across her face.

"Because the real Whitney doesn't do *that*," Olivia pointed out. "So let me out of here because I refuse to play your games."

"She's had enough of the world, and its people's mindless games,"

Demon-Whitney agreed helpfully. Olivia groaned as she realized she'd fallen right into that trap.

"I'm serious!" she shouted. "Let me OUT!"

The creature with Whitney's face suddenly stopped advancing, putting both hands on her hips and leaning forward aggressively.

"*FINE!*" she shouted, spittle flying. "*But you won't like it!*"

And Olivia opened her eyes.

She looked around warily. Same hospital room, but no crowd of onlookers; just one, sitting in the chair next to the bed.

Olivia saw that it was Whitney and flinched reflexively, putting up one hand to ward her off.

"Crap," she said succinctly.

"What's wrong?" Whitney asked, leaning forward in alarm.

"Is it really you?" Olivia peered closely. No lolling tongue, no red eyes, no clawed hands – but only time would really tell.

"As far as I know," Whitney played along, looking down at her arm and giving the skin a generous pinch.

"Okay, 'cause I'm getting real tired of being jerked around," Olivia sighed. "Fucking nightmares are driving me nuts. Was there a crowd of doctors and nurses in here earlier?"

Whitney frowned. "Not that I know of. Liv, what the heck is going on?"

"I don't know," Olivia said, pulling the thin hospital blanket off vehemently, "but I'm getting out of here."

"Um…okay," Whitney said, standing up and moving aside. "Are you sure you're up to it?"

"I'm fine," Olivia responded absently, looking around for some clothes. "Was I dressed when they brought me in?"

“Somewhat. They put your things over there.” She pointed to a small pile of folded-up pajamas, a pair of dirty fuzzy slippers setting on top like two dead but very cozy little animals.

“Wait a minute.” Olivia stopped in mid-dress, straightening to face Whitney and looking at her closely. “You know the dreams I told you about?”

Whitney’s brow furrowed. “Um…”

Olivia shook her head. “Never mind. I’ve gotta get out of here.”

She couldn’t help but stay wary as they left the hospital, but nothing out of the ordinary happened, other than seeing a few of the same nurses that had appeared in her dream / nightmare. They gave her a stapled stack of paperwork when she checked out and she rifled through it in the back of the cab.

“So…” Olivia said, reading the top sheet. “I was found wandering in the snow?”

Whitney glanced at her. “Yeah, you don’t remember the truck almost running you over?”

Olivia shook her head. “The last thing I remember – other than the stupid dreams I had – was falling into bed last night after dropping Detective Barstad off at her hotel.”

“Hey lady, are you okay?” The cab driver asked, glancing at her in his rear-view mirror.

“I’m fine,” she responded, thinking, *weird question to ask someone you picked up from a hospital!*

“Well, we’re here,” he said, and she looked up from her paperwork to realize the cab was sitting in front of her apartment building.

“Oh,” she said, embarrassed. “I’m sorry, I could have sworn I asked you to take me downtown.”

"Nope, this is the address you gave me."

Weird, she thought again, gathering her things. She looked to Whitney questioningly, hoping the doctor would volunteer to pay the fare, and she just grinned, shaking her head.

Olivia sighed. "I'll have to run up and get my purse."

The cabdriver shrugged. "I'll be here."

When Olivia had apparently decided to go wander outside in her sleep, she had thoughtfully brought her keys with her, locking the apartment and putting the keys in the pocket of her pajama bottoms, where she found them while getting dressed at the hospital. She had not taken her wallet, however, apparently deciding she wouldn't need money while sleepwalking. She rushed up the stairs and back down again, handing the cabdriver her credit card and waiting as he swiped it and wrote her out a receipt. Oddly, when she looked in the back of the cab, she saw Whitney was gone.

"Where'd she go?" Olivia asked the driver, gesturing towards the empty bench seat.

He looked in his rear-view mirror and looked back at her. "Where'd who go?"

She frowned. "The other woman, the one I rode here with."

He looked even more concerned, and answered hesitantly. "I really couldn't say. Maybe I should take you back to the hospital?"

She shook her head, grabbing the receipt from his outstretched hand and stepping back. "No…no, thank you." Her head was pounding and she was suddenly freezing, standing in the cold air in nothing but her pajamas and slippers.

She watched as the empty cab drove away, rubbing her aching temples with one shaking hand and holding the receipt in the other.

I'm going mad, she thought sadly, wondering why it had taken so long for her to notice. *That's been it all along. The dreams, the visions, Whitney eating people – it's all in my head 'cause I've gone completely nuts.*

She climbed back up the stairs slowly, ignoring her shivering, closing the door softly behind herself. The apartment was cold and bleak and depressing, but that didn't seem to matter anymore.

Standing in the kitchen, waiting for the microwave to turn a mug of water into hot tea, she cast her thoughts back across the days since this investigation had begun. She remembered once more dream-Anna's words to her; *Just because something is in your mind doesn't mean it isn't real.* Those words now seemed ridiculous; of course it wasn't real if it was all in her head. No wonder Matt didn't believe her – he was right not to.

She felt herself slipping down into a black despair, and it was an oddly soothing feeling. It was like lying down on an old couch that had been the centerpiece of the living room for decades, a couch that despite its lumpy uncomfortable cushions and splintery wooden armrests was still an old and dear piece of furniture. The despair felt as much a part of her as her skin; it had been with her always, following her from foster home to foster home, hiding behind the face of every pseudo-parent and waiting to greet her behind the door of every one of 'her' bedrooms.

She had been foolish to think she could ever escape it, she thought, and she let the despair take her down into its dark, comfortable arms.

But Olivia was not one to wallow in self-pity, and it didn't take long before anger shoved the despair aside. She would never have survived her childhood, much less her marriage, if she let trials and tribulation rule her life.

Alright then. No more internalizing; no more pushing down

emotions and memories; no more ridiculous, tumbling, frightening forays into the dream world, urged on by whatever the malevolent spirits could dig up out of her subconscious. It was worrisome that this morning's events were nowhere in her memory, but she refused to let it drag her down. Call it a momentary slip, rather than a full-scale slide backwards.

Olivia shook her fist at the microwave. "I hereby announce this life to be my own!" she declared loudly to the four walls, ceiling and floor. They didn't answer.

"I am who I am!" she tried again. *Just like Popeye the Sailor Man.* Geez, this was idiotic. She glanced at her watch. She had just enough time to get a quick shower before she had to leave for her promised appointment with the Department shrink.

Carrying the finally-hot mug, she took two steps into the living room and stopped short as her eyes fell upon the mattress. A puddle of tea began to gather on the floor next to her as she stood, hand trembling, her whole body beginning to shake. A buzzing noise filled her ears as the blood rushed from her face, and she heard herself moaning softly, off in the vague distance.

No. No. *No.*

The blankets were in a twist at the bottom of the mattress, her night-clothes in a heap on the floor, but what had drawn her eye was the person-sized splat of dark brown mud that covered most of the bed. Muddy footprints led from the dirty mattress, across the living room and into the bedroom that she never used. Halfway across the living room, the human footprints turned into hand-sized paw prints. The door was still closed, one paw print tantalizingly halfway under the door, leaving her to only imagine what could possibly be on the other side.

No. They were *dreams*, for Pete's sake, and this was just outright ridiculous.

“This isn’t real,” she whispered aloud, admitting defeat. “Something’s wrong with me.”

Good thing I already have an appointment with a shrink, her smart-ass side couldn’t help but add.

Forget the shower, forget the tea. She was changing her clothes and getting the hell out of Dodge, and if she was really lucky, maybe when she finally returned the dream-detritus would be gone.

CHAPTER 14

Day Six, Afternoon

In [regards to] Indian civilization, I am a Baptist because I believe in immersing the Indians in our civilization and when we get them under, holding them there until they are thoroughly soaked.

- Capt. Richard Henry Pratt, Superintendent of Carlisle Indian Industrial School 1879 – 1904

Dr. Henry Kennedy was short, plump, and balding, and as always, his hand was sweating just slightly as Olivia shook it. He seemed perpetually to have just rushed from somewhere and always looked slightly out of sorts, even when all he'd done was sit and listen to a patient for the last hour.

Perhaps it was having to bear the burden of other's problems, Olivia had always thought. It made him seem stressed and disheveled, regardless of what menial task he'd been attending to.

Although she had not visited him in nearly six months, out of habit she sat in the same middle cushion on the patient couch.

"So? How are you doing?" he asked after settling into his own cushioned office chair.

Olivia thought for a moment; thought of all the things she could say, all the recent events she could describe, and how he would react to each of them.

"Fine," she said finally.

Dr. Kennedy sighed. "Verbose as always, I see. Am I going to have to yank each word out of you, like I used to?"

"Only if you really want to," she offered. The banter, while more light-hearted on her end than on his, was comforting and familiar.

But it seemed that his patience had grown as thin as his hair.

"Olivia, let me set you straight," he said plainly. "After what happened last night, you can't go back to work until I clear you to do so. Eventually you will be fired, placed on some sort of disability, and/or encouraged to quit. Basically, either you play nice or they will make you go away. So let's cut the crap, okay?"

"Geez," she said, raising an eyebrow. "I didn't know you cared."

He frowned. "Alright. I can see that this is just fun and games to you. Why don't you go on home and I'll let Lt. Martin know that you don't have any interest in going back to work."

"Well, I-" she started, and stopped. What could she say? Telling the truth would be much more likely to land her in an institution than back at her desk. So she sighed, shrugged, stood up, and put her coat back on. Dr. Kennedy gazed at her balefully as she stood there for a long minute, shifting from foot to foot, until she finally turned to leave.

"Olivia," he said, as her hand touched the doorknob. She dropped her arm and let it fall to her side, turning to face him.

He sighed and stood. "Look," he said. "If you don't feel like you can talk to me, we can make other arrangements."

She frowned. "Really?" He had never made that an option before.

"I don't want to see a good cop get booted," he responded. "And you and I have never exactly, uh, bonded, have we?"

"But Doc," she quipped. She couldn't help it. "I *like* you."

He rolled his eyes. "I'm sure. But for both our sakes, I'm going to do something I've never done before and make a deal with you. I'll go ahead and clear you for duty beginning tomorrow morning, but you are on probation, do you understand?'

"And what do I have to do?" Olivia asked cautiously.

"Just keep your appointments with whatever provider you've chosen. They will keep me up to date on your progress. But - and I emphasize this, just so you understand – only I can make the final evaluation to put you back on duty permanently. *And* you take the rest of today off - no excuses."

"Okay," she shrugged. "Cool." Why did being in his office always turn her into a petulant thirteen-year-old? Or maybe it was just her nature and she only noticed it around him.

"My secretary will give you the list of approved providers on your way out," he said.

She took the dismissal for what it was and left.

She got back in her car, buckled up, started the ignition, and sat there for a moment. Then it dawned on her that she really had nowhere to go, and she turned the ignition off, unbuckled her seatbelt and leaned against the back of the seat.

"Damn, I wish I smoked," she said wryly. "At least then I could pretend to be sitting here for a reason."

Her legs began to get cold as she sat there, so she turned the car back on and flipped the heater switch all the way to the right. Hmm, what to do with herself? At least she could still *call* work, even if she couldn't go there or actually do anything. She flipped open her cell phone, scrolling through the contacts until she found Matt's cell number.

He answered on the second ring. "Gossett," he barked in her ear.

"It's me," she stated the obvious. "So what's the scoop?"

There was a long pause. She knew him well enough to realize he was debating what to tell her.

"You're still allowed to talk to me, you know," she pointed out.

"Oh….right," he said finally. "I just didn't want to, uh, upset you or anything."

Olivia heaved a sigh. "Matthew, look. I have no idea what happened last night. I don't even remember last night. But I'm not delicate, I'm not fragile, I'm not going to crumble to pieces. So, please, just tell me what's going on with our case?"

He started to respond, then she heard a brief scuffle in the background, Matt's protestations, and then Elaine was on the line.

"Hey, Liv," she said cheerfully. "Sorry, I had to wrestle the phone away from Günter over here."

"Thank God," Olivia said wholeheartedly. "Please tell me, for God's sake, what happened, other than me sleepwalking? I've been kicked off the island and I don't even know why."

"Lucky for you, I had a front-row seat," Elaine chirped. "When you didn't show up, I called Gossett here, who picked me up. You didn't come in to work and you weren't answering your phone, and then your Lieutenant got a call from the hospital saying you'd been admitted. I don't know how they figured out who you were, with no I.D.; someone must have eventually recognized you, I don't know. You were apparently sleepwalking, out in the cold with nothing on but your PJ's. Gosh but your L.T. was pissed!"

"Wow." Olivia was taken aback. "What the hell for?"

Elaine laughed from deep in her chest. Olivia could hear Matt grumbling in the background, and traffic noises; they must be driving somewhere. "Beats the heck out of me," she replied. "You'd probably have to ask Günter over here."

Olivia *harrumphed*. "Yeah right, that's a conversation that's never going to happen."

"I worked with a narcoleptic once," Elaine mused. "We had an on-going pool as to when and where he'd crash out. But he never wandered around in the snow."

"Sounds like a fun coworker. So where are you and Matt off to?"

"Ah, your keen Detective skills are at work again. We are, at present, driving to the home of one Albert Thompson, father of Melissa Thompson, to bring her in for interrogation. Oh, and Anna's car was still parked at his house; we had to go back to the station house to do the paperwork to have it towed. Your L.T. is really a stickler for protocol. He wouldn't let us just call it in since it was a different jurisdiction."

"What happened with the neighbors?"

"The one who brought in the clothes finally made a statement, but otherwise canvassing came up empty. No one saw anything. DNA test is gonna take a couple days at least, so we don't even know yet if the clothes belonged to Anna Taylor. Your L.T. said we had enough to bring Thompson in, though, although at this point we don't have enough to actually arrest him."

"Okay. Hopefully he'll be a squealer. Keep me posted, okay? I'm going loony with nothing to do." She paused. "So to speak."

Elaine chuckled. "So to speak. Don't worry, Günter and I will keep you in the loop."

Olivia heard Matt grumbling again; "Don't call me Günter!" and then they were gone. She sighed, put her phone away, and decided to fill the remainder of the afternoon with grocery shopping. If she was going to be an outcast, at least she could be a well-fed outcast.

Olivia was not usually much of a shopper. She'd rush in, grab a box of macaroni and cheese and a bag of apples, maybe a roasted chicken from the hot deli, and rush out again. She certainly was not, as her Home Ec teacher had urged them all to be, a "comparison shopper."

So it felt a little strange to actually take off her coat, get a cart, and trundle her way up the first aisle. She realized she didn't even know where most of the items in the store were kept. So she took it slow, eyeing this and that, reading ingredients, and in general trying to pretend that she was any other stay-at-home wife getting a little shopping done before the kiddos and hubby got home for the day.

Maybe it was her uncertainty, maybe it was the gun on her hip, but the other shoppers weren't fooled by the pretension. They gave her wide leeway as she slowly meandered through the store.

As she was reading the back of a box of instant oatmeal, impressed by the amount of fiber, her hip buzzed. Expecting it to be Matt or Elaine, she didn't even look at the display.

"Hey, what's up?" she answered casually, setting down the box of oatmeal and trundling down the aisle.

There was a long pause. "Olivia?" a male voice said finally.

She cleared her throat. Oops. "Yes, this is Olivia."

"Uh, this is Bill. Gustafson? We met at the airport the other day?"

"Oh, right….Bill." Her voice was frosty.

"I'm sorry, did I catch you at a bad time?"

"Bill, why are you calling me?" she said, cutting right to the chase.

"Well, I – we hit it off so well, or so I thought, but you never called, and I…" his voice meandered to a halt.

Olivia sighed. He wasn't going to make this easy. "Look, your wife clued me in on your game, so let's just leave it at that, shall we?"

"I don't understand." He sounded truly confused. "I'm not married."

"Bill, I did call you that very night. And, an angry woman called me back from *your* number and told me in no uncertain terms that you are very much married."

"Oh, geez," he sighed mightily. "Look, it was probably my sister-in-law. My wife passed away two years ago. She's having some trouble, uh, moving on, I guess you could say."

"Why would your ex-sister-in-law care who you are dating?" Olivia asked reasonably, then winced at her use of the d-word.

"It's a long story," he replied. "If you met her, I'm sure you'd understand. But at least now I know why I never heard from you – I'm sure she erased your message from my phone. Um, I'd still really like to get together with you sometime, if you....maybe...."

"I don't live in Chicago," she reminded him – but had she told him that before? She couldn't remember.

"I don't either." He sounded surprised. "You're somewhere around Grand Forks, right?"

"Ye-eah...did I tell you that?"

"I was on the same flight as you to Chicago. I didn't tell you before because I didn't want you to think I was stalking you or something."

"Hmm. That would have been very suspicious." She felt herself being involuntarily drawn in to the conversation and opened her mouth to accept his invitation. As she did so, she felt an odd, sudden flash of anger. It was so surprising that it made her feel ill. "Uh, look, can I call you back? I've got to take another call," she lied.

"Of course."

As she slowly put her phone away, she cast her mind out, trying to feel what it was that had brought on such a disconcerting and unexpected emotion. Her nose tickled and she rubbed it absent-mindedly. Suddenly she sneezed, and she realized it was because she was standing in the laundry aisle; the overwhelming fumes and scents of all of the detergents and soaps had brought on the sneeze.

As she registered all of the smells, she recognized one in particular. It was the heavily-perfumed detergent that Darren had favored, the one she had always bought back then because of that. It was far too strong for her; she had always hated the smell of it on her clothes, but the one time she got something else he had thrown an enormous fit. *You can't even do the smallest things for me,* he had accused as if he was mortally wounded. *I don't ask for much, why is it so hard for you to just make me happy?*

Surely that was what her mind had reacted to that had brought the flash of anger; the memory of being so controlled that she couldn't even buy a laundry detergent that she actually liked. She had bought nothing but the perfume-free, unscented detergent ever since, and the smell of "his" brand now was making her want to vomit.

I feel manipulated, she realized. *Whether Bill Gustafson is really married or not, I feel controlled and manipulated by what happened.* Such big personal insights were rare for her, and she cheered up immediately, leaving the laundry aisle and the vomit-inducing smells behind.

But the insight also gave her a determination and a self-confidence that she rarely felt when it came to her inner life. *I don't want to go out with Bill Gustafson,* she decided firmly. *I don't need drama right now. I don't have the time or the energy to devote to becoming involved with someone. Someone new*, her mind amended, involuntarily going back to the image of Matt, shirtless.

No, anyone! She thought savagely, stubbornly yanking her mind away from thoughts of romance with someone who was not only a coworker, but a man she swore she didn't even like. *Much*, her mind amended again.

"Damnit!" she swore out loud, drawing strange looks from other nearby shoppers.

After filling her back seat with full-to-the-brim brown paper bags, Olivia steered the car through the parking lot and on to the main road. Traffic was just beginning to be heavy as the lunchtime crowd hit the streets.

Thinking about men and relationships past kept her mind so occupied that she opened the door to her apartment without hesitation. Her arms were full of shopping bags, and it wasn't until the third trip back up the stairs that she remembered the mud and the footprints.

Setting the last bag on the kitchen floor, one hand on her holster, she cautiously peered around the half-wall and into the living room.

Her bed was in order; if anything, it was neater than she usually left it. There was no mud, no dirt, no footprints. No signs of her previous night's struggles remained to taunt her.

"Well," she sighed, taking her hand off her holster. "I guess I am just going nuts, then." It wasn't an especially comforting thought.

Reminding herself that she was still a cop, she decided to do a full sweep of the apartment. It didn't take very long to satisfy herself that no red-eyed intruders were waiting in closets, cupboards, or behind closed doors. All she found were a few dust bunnies and a very large, very dead, spider.

The evening stretched in front of her like a long, empty runway. Sighing, she set herself to the task of putting groceries away, tidying up, and generally just keeping herself occupied. She couldn't help but glance at her phone every few minutes just to make sure she hadn't missed any calls. What in the world were Matt and Elaine doing? They could have driven to Crookston and back three times by now.

The gears in her mind turned as she suddenly thought back to the conversation in the library with Melissa's boss, Mrs. Pace.

"She's studying library science with an emphasis in book repair and restoration, but I wouldn't trust that girl to repair a Dr. Seuss book," the librarian had said, referring to her least favorite student employee – Melissa Thompson, the girl who had hand-made Anna's journal; the

same journal with multiple pages that had been inexpertly removed.

Thinking about Mrs. Pace led her mind to Betty, the alien-eyed library aid. Olivia was suddenly struck by a memory of Betty on her cell phone; a memory of such clarity that for a moment, she was back in the library, surrounded by the smell of books and college-student hormones.

"Hey Mel, it's Betty," the girl had said, and then cleared her throat.

At the time Olivia had thought nothing of it, but now she wondered; why would the girl clear her throat? Before that her voice had seemed perfectly clear.

Unless she was warning Melissa that someone was listing, Olivia thought, sitting straight up in her recliner. The Thompson girl wasn't pretending to be sick so that Betty would cover for her; Betty *was* her cover.

Is that who's been driving her Mini Cooper around? Olivia wondered to herself.

At that moment, Olivia's phone finally rang, jarring her thoughts. She snatched it up and saw by the display that it was a 360 area code – hopefully Elaine.

"St. George," she answered.

"Yo." It was Barstad. "Tow truck finally came to get Anna's car. Matt asks if you can meet the tech guys over at the lot."

"Hell yeah," she said with heartfelt enthusiasm. "Oh, but…ugh. I think L.T. would have my head if I came in tonight. I'm supposed to be out until tomorrow."

"We won't tell if you don't." Elaine's voice was full of good cheer. "It's just standing there while they work, after all."

"Outstanding. Did you get the Thompsons?"

"Just the girl."

"Alright. I'll be at the lot in ten."

The tech guys were already at the impound lot when she arrived. Olivia introduced herself to the tech team, shaking hands all around.

"I sure appreciate you guys coming in on a Saturday," she said whole-heartedly. "Can I get you anything? Coffee? Donuts? Lunch?"

"How about a six-pack?" suggested Chad, the Team Leader, only half-kidding.

"Absolutely."

The tow truck arrived twenty minutes later. It took them several hours to go over the car. Olivia watched anxiously, trying not to hover like a mother hen, wanting to see what they were doing without getting in the way.

Their first step was to remove all of Anna's personal belongings from the car. Like many college kids, she had apparently lived in her automobile, and by the end of fifteen minutes the tech team had filled a large plastic bag with papers, clothes, and various debris. All of it would have to be analyzed separately, but Olivia slipped on a pair of gloves and did a pre-emptive pick-through. She didn't really expect to find the "one big clue" that would wrap up the entire investigation, but hope springs eternal, as the saying goes.

"Any luck?" Chad asked as he opened a fresh bottle of Luminol.

Olivia shook her head and settled back on her heels. "Nah," she sighed. "Just college kid stuff."

After three hours it was obvious that they hadn't found anything because there was nothing to find. Anna's car, while dirty, had not been a crime scene. There were no foreign fingerprints or bodily fluids, and while it was still possible that the vacuum sample would reveal hairs or something else of note, Olivia had a feeling that it wasn't going to happen. The car was just a car, a sad hulk of metal left behind by its owner's untimely demise.

As the tech team was wrapping up, her cell rang. She saw it was Elaine and flipped it open eagerly.

"Hey," she answered.

"Any luck?"

"Nothing yet. They have some other tests to do at the lab, but the car was clean."

"Damn. Uh, I hate to be the bearer of bad news, but L.T. wants you two in his office pronto."

Olivia grimaced. "Crap. Why?"

Elaine sighed. "Thompson girl lawyered up. We had nothing to hold her on so she's walking."

"Shit. Alright, I'm on my way."

Olivia pulled up to the station house just in time to see a stony-faced young brunette jump into the passenger seat of a green Ford sedan. The car screeched off like its wheels were on fire.

"Was that Melissa Thompson?" Olivia asked Matt as she walked by his desk, cocking her thumb at the door behind her. "Who was that picking her up?"

"I don't know, and I don't care," he said shortly as he stood up. "This case was fucked from the beginning."

Olivia felt the blood beginning to rise to her face. "I suppose that's my fault?" she retorted.

"Not at all," he said straight-faced. "I blame the ghosts and demons."

She just stood there as he walked by, her face hot with embarrassment.

Matt walked up to L.T.'s open doorway, and seeing that he was on the phone, waited with arms crossed.

“Gossett! Get in here,” Lt. Martin barked as he hung up. “And bring St. George with you.”

Feeling like a puppy who was about to have its face rubbed in its own peed-on rug, Olivia hustled herself into his office.

Lt. Martin was more upset than she’d ever seen him. He couldn’t stay sitting, but paced behind his desk like a caged lion.

“Explain to me why your only suspect just walked out our front door,” he said furiously. The vein in his left temple was throbbing, Olivia saw.

“Lou-” Matt began.

Olivia cleared her throat. “We’re-”

Lt. Martin waved one meaty hand in the air, as if clearing the stink. “It was a rhetorical question!” he bellowed. “It’s been a week, you’ve been jumping all over creation, and you have *nothing*.” He slapped his open hand on the desk in emphasis. “That was Captain Logsdon chewing my ear off just now. He wants me to pull both of you off this case.”

“What!” Olivia and Matt protested in unison.

“Someone leaked to the T.V. stations,” L.T.’s teeth were gritted as he held up a screen-shot printed from his computer. “In *both* states. I’ve gotten twelve phone calls in the last half-hour, asking why we don’t have someone in custody. One goddamn reporter is calling your vic the ‘Snow Angel.’”

He threw the print-out down on his desk and it slid forwards where Olivia and Matt could see it. She saw it was from a news station in Olympia – Lt. Martin must be able to get streaming television on his computer, she mused. The joys of internet. The screen shot showed a perky brunette in a low-cut green blouse, with an image of a smiling Anna Taylor on the display behind her. Olivia could only imagine what the brunette was saying; the look on her face was one of eager raptness as she no doubt discoursed about the recent tragedy that had befallen a local college girl.

"Tell me you're at least close to a breakthrough," Lt. Martin fumed.

"We're trying," Olivia said helplessly. "The lab-"

"Speaking of which," L.T. interrupted, "have you gotten *anything* back from them?"

"Well, there were some hairs on her clothes, but they haven't analyzed them yet-" she tried.

"Why the hell are you just waiting for them?" Lt. Martin fumed. "You should be riding their asses like- like-" he sputtered to a halt as a comparison failed to come to mind.

"Like a monkey on a circus dog?" Olivia offered helpfully.

"Don't even get me started," L.T. glared, vein throbbing. "And you!" He turned on Matt. "I barely see you. Some days I'm not even sure you work here."

"That's not fair." Matt's face was the color of a ripe beet.

"Fair?" L.T. leaned on the desk. "This isn't kindergarten, *Detective*. Fair's got nothing to do with it. The only time I hear from you is when you're bitching about *her*." He gestured towards Olivia. "Here's what's going to happen," he said slowly, emphatically. "You are going back to the beginning, *both* of you. You will go over every detail, every moment, of this case with a fine-toothed comb. And you will work together with smiles on your faces or so help me God…" he shook his head dangerously. "In the meantime, I've got a Crookston uni sitting on the Thompson house. You have twenty-four hours until I give this case to another team."

CHAPTER 15

Day Six, Late

When demons dance upon my head, my body their temple, bathed in furious glory, shall I join in? Take hands and waltz to the sound of my own screaming? I too can leap as high as the flames, the heat scourging the land from within. When demons dance, should I then succumb, my tears a joyful exclamation of the abandon?

- *From the journal of Anna Taylor*

Olivia and Matt walked back to their desks, both feeling a little shell-shocked. Matt flopped down in his chair and slowly tapped the keys to log in to his computer, a hangdog look on his face. Elaine, sympathetic, ostensibly got up to use the restroom, but really was just giving them a little space.

Olivia, sighing, pulled her chair up to the end of Matt's desk, a stack of files in her arms.

"Back to the beginning," she said morosely.

Matt ran one hand over his head and face, his eyes closed wearily. Olivia suddenly realized that the blond hair perpetually hanging in his eyes was now the length of her pinkie nail.

"When'd you cut your hair?" she asked curiously.

"Look," he said, ignoring her question. "No matter what L.T. wants us to do, I just don't have it in me to go over the entire file again right now. I'm goddamn exhausted."

Olivia gritted her teeth and tried again. "Why don't you and me and Elaine go get some dinner," she suggested. "We can bring all this," hefting the pile high, "with us and hash this out over some hot coffee and food."

"Actually, that does sound good," he said, softening. "But I'm driving. I don't trust you to operate a car with me in it."

Olivia shrugged. "Whatever."

They spread out in a corner booth at Perkins, photos and files everywhere. The waitress, realizing who they were and what they were doing, didn't even ask if they wanted coffee; she just left the carafe on the table.

"And extra cream and sugar, please," Olivia called as she walked away after taking their orders.

Elaine opened her notebook to a fresh page and took out a pencil. "Okay," she said. "Why don't we do it this way; since I wasn't with you guys in the beginning, you talk me through it all from moment one. I'll take notes, and I'll bet you we figure out some new stuff along the way."

"Okay," Olivia nodded. "Well, for starters, she was found here." She pulled the map from the file and opened it, showing Elaine the circled area. "She was found by a farmer's dog…"

By the time they had finished eating, Barstad felt brought up to speed. Elaine frowned as she flipped through her notes, reading them over again.

"Here's what doesn't add up for me," she said. "One, Melissa Thompson calling you about Anna. Two, her being in Minnesota while her Mini Cooper is being driven around Graham's Ford. Who's driving Melissa's car? And three, a motive for killing the girl in the first place."

"Crap." Olivia slapped her forehead. "I had a thought about that earlier today and in the excitement I completely forgot to run it by you guys. What about Betty?"

Matt and Elaine looked at each other.

"Who's Betty?"

"You know." Olivia circled her two thumb and forefingers and put them in front of her eyes like glasses. "Miss Bug-Eyes from the library at the girl's school."

"Oh yeah," Matt remembered. "The actress."

"I was thinking about the phone call she made while we were there," Olivia explained. "The way she cleared her throat and then paused. What if she was signaling Melissa that someone was listening?"

Matt frowned. "Pretty far-fetched."

"True," Olivia acknowledged. "But we already know she was making false phone calls. What if *she* was the one that called me, not Melissa?"

"Why would she want to implicate her friend?" Elaine pointed out.

"Maybe she didn't realize she was," Olivia said. "She thought she was establishing an alibi for the girl."

"And she's been driving around the gold Mini Cooper?" Matt asked, one eyebrow raised.

Olivia nodded. "Again, thinking she was establishing an alibi."

"I can see it," Elaine said. "Melissa must have realized we found the body. She's obviously been hanging out at her dad's place for a reason. Maybe she even asked the girl to call on her behalf."

"Okay, but what about the clothes?" Matt piped up. "If she was so sloppy as to leave a bag of bloody clothes in the next-door-neighbor's trash, why haven't we found anything else?"

"That's assuming those clothes belonged to Anna," Olivia reminded him, reaching for the coffee. "DNA hasn't come back yet."

"Oh, c'mon," Matt said disgustedly. "Who the hell else would it be?"

Olivia shrugged. "I'm just sayin'. Can't make an arrest based on 'might be.'"

Matt sighed. "Whatever. I still vote for the lover's triangle, as far as motive goes."

"I'm starting to doubt the whole lover's triangle angle. But speaking of motive..." Olivia took the journal from her coat pocket. "There are pages missing from Anna's journal, and I'm fairly certain that Melissa was the one who removed them."

Elaine frowned, taking the journal from her hand. "Why didn't I know about this?"

"Uh, Matt didn't feel it was relevant," Olivia replied meaningfully. Elaine glared at him as she flipped through pages.

"There's nothing in there," Matt protested.

"The missing pages could very well talk about the motive behind this murder." Olivia reminded him forcefully.

"Well, without the missing pages, it's all supposition anyway," Barstad reminded them both, handing the journal back to Olivia. "But it gives us something to start with."

"What about the hairs you said were on her clothes?" Matt said, changing the subject.

"Without a suspect to compare them to, it doesn't matter if they were Anna's or not," Olivia shrugged. "And right now, I don't see either of the Thompsons willingly giving up hair for analyzing without a warrant."

"What we *need* is a witness," Matt jumped in. "I think we should recanvass, plus we need to look deeper into both of the Thompsons."

"Well, I don't mind recanvassing the neighbors," Olivia offered.

"Thanks," Matt said, looking surprised. "We can do interviews at the father's work, talk to his friends, so forth."

"By the way, I forgot to ask - how'd you swing bringing the Thompson girl over the state line?" Olivia wondered.

"Didn't have to," Matt grunted. "She was at the mall."

"How nice of her."

"Yeah, but we drove all over creation to find her," Elaine grumped.

"You didn't enjoy your tour of western Minnesota and eastern North Dakota?" Olivia raised an eyebrow sarcastically.

"No, really, it's great," Barstad said wryly. "The giant metal moose was the best part." The Blue Moose, a popular restaurant and bar in East Grand Forks, MN, was famous for the life-sized blue metal moose statue in front of their building.

"Wait until this case ends and we celebrate," Matt slapped her on the shoulder. "You get to drink some real Moose Drool."

Elaine, clearly taken aback, looked to Olivia for help.

"It's a beer," Olivia offered helpfully.

"How nice," Elaine said faintly.

"It's good, you'll like it. Look, I'm gonna make a few phone calls, call in some favors I don't really have, and see if we can at least get the hairs from both sets of clothes analyzed," Olivia said. "I'm thinking tomorrow morning first thing would be an ideal time to recanvass."

"Early Sunday morning? Yeah, probably have better luck than late on a Saturday night," Elaine agreed wryly. "What can I do to help?"

Olivia gestured with her lips at Matt. "Just keep him in line."

"Hey," he frowned indignantly.

Olivia chuckled. "Alright, I'm outta here. Don't stay up too late, you two."

After all the events of the week, Olivia was more than a little reluctant to lie down on the mattress and close her eyes. But she knew that *not* sleeping wasn't an option, and after her trip to Washington she realized the dreams would come regardless of her location. So there was no point in spending the money on a hotel room; if she was going to sleep badly, she might as well do it for free in her own bed.

She did, however, make preparations. The first thing she did was open the hall closet door and lash the door handle to that of the refrigerator, a few feet away inside the kitchen; effectively blocking off the path to the front door. If she *was* sleepwalking, hopefully her sleeping-self would be stymied by the blockade.

Secondly, she took a sleeping pill. She debated for a long moment before swallowing it, standing at the bathroom sink with the pill in her hand and thinking over the ramifications. What if she needed to wake up and couldn't? Was this really a good idea?

But the part of her that was desperate for decent sleep overrode her reservations. *I'll be sleeping too deeply to dream,* that part of her reasoned.

She considered handcuffing herself to the radiator; but that seemed a bit extreme. So she put on her night-clothes, pulled the blankets up over her face, and let the sleeping pill do its magic.

Some hours later, it was the scratching that got her attention. Olivia blearily opened her eyes, raising her head just enough to look around the apartment. Everything was just as she'd left it. The only light was the moonlight sneaking through the crack in the curtains, falling on her holstered gun slung across the recliner arm. She could just make out the closet door still blocking the hallway. She picked up her cell phone and saw from the display that she'd been asleep for less than four hours.

She heard again the sound of a paw scratching at a door, and this time recognized it as coming from the bedroom side of the apartment.

Aaagh, she mentally groaned, flopping her head back down on the pillow. *Neighbor must've gotten a dog.*

Wait a minute. There *was* no neighbor on that side; her empty bedroom was on an outside wall.

The noise came again and she stiffened as a low whining resonated through the dark living room.

There was something in her bedroom – something that wanted out.

"I'm dreaming," she said out loud in a sing-song voice. "La la la, just dreaming." *Maybe if I lay here it'll go away*. Like a child, she pulled the blanket entirely over her head and shut her eyes tightly, hoping the monsters would overlook her in the dark.

The scratching came again, louder, and then a *bang* as something hit the door. The whining deepened into a mumbling growl, the pitch going up and down, up and down like a signal fading in and out.

Bang. Bang.

Olivia gritted her teeth and in one movement, threw back the blanket and lunged for her gun. Her feet tangled in the covers and she fell, smacking her chin on the carpeted floor, but her fingers snagged the edge of the holster and pulled it down with her. It landed next to her head and she scrabbled at the snap, pulling it open and sliding her gun out in a furious rush of adrenaline.

She kicked the covers away and jumped to her feet. She made it to the wall switch in two large bounds, jamming her hand underneath it to bring the comfort and civilization of electric light.

But there was no comfort, because the light wouldn't come on. She wiggled it up and down several times before acknowledging that it was no use.

Alright, then. She might have to play by the rules of this game, but that didn't mean she had to play fair. With her thumb, she clicked the gun safety to Off, holding the weapon in front of her in the smooth motion given by years of experience. She slid along the wall towards the bedroom, trying to ignore the way the growling vibrated in her bones, the way the banging and scratching was getting louder and louder.

BANG. BANG.

The noise was shaking the whole apartment. How in hell were the neighbors not awake?

BANG.

The kitchen cupboards, jarred open by the steady shaking, let loose their contents and a cascade of plates and bowls spilled in a crash onto the floor.

Someone'll call the cops, she thought, not knowing if that would be a good thing or a bad thing. And then she remembered that her neighbors all knew she *was* the cops, and would likely assume she was taking care of the problem.

Even if someone kicked her door in and tried to charge to her rescue, they'd find the closet door barring their way.

It's up to me, then, she realized. *The lone Indian, facing down the cavalry.* She almost laughed at the mental image that arose, then squelched the urge; hysterical laughter was not what she needed right now.

She was halfway through the living room; the moonlight was behind her and only darkness lay ahead.

BANG.

From the corner of her eye she saw the toaster, having spider-walked to the edge of the counter, tip over the edge in a shower of crumbs.

Damn. I knew I should've cleaned that thing out. She was past the kitchen now, easing into the central hallway with her eyes impossibly wide, her nerves as frayed as a kitten's yarn toy.

BANG.

A thunderous crash right in front of her pulled a startled scream from between her lips. Her trigger-finger twitched and for a split second she saw a dark shape rushing at her; then it was gone, and Olivia realized she was directly in front of the open bathroom door. Cursing wildly, she thrashed inside the doorway for the light switch.

Miraculously, this one worked. Towels, cleaning supplies, and rolls of toilet paper were scattered all over the floor, and she realized the crash had been the wall cupboard that now lay in a splintered mess, partially covering the toilet. It had been jarred right off its drywall screws. The mirror had shattered into a thousand pieces and bits of glass were everywhere.

BANGBANG

The light went out as two more, in quick succession, shook the light bulb loose from its seat.

BANGBANGBANGBANG

Olivia felt the floor roiling beneath her feet, and it was the last straw. Screaming wildly, she rushed at the bedroom door, kicking it solidly with the bottom of one bare foot. It flew open and stuck, the inside handle wedged into the drywall opposite the door.

"*FUUUUUCKYOUUUU*!" she screamed, leaping into the open doorway, her gun pointed straight ahead. She was ready to take down King Kong himself should it come to that.

The blinds that normally covered the bedroom window lay in a heap on the floor, and a square of bright moonlight fell in the center of the room. She kept the gun pointed in front of herself as she turned to the side, sweeping the room for monsters and boogiemen, looking for anything worth shooting. Quickly she turned from side to side, clearing the room as if it was any new and dangerous crime scene, ready for anything that might jump out to grab her.

Feeling the openness of the room at her back, she swiveled on one heel, sure that something was standing right behind her. The corner was empty. In fact, the whole room was empty. Slowly she lowered the gun, keeping her trigger-finger ready and the safety off, just in case.

A low moan came from behind her. Gasping, Olivia jumped and

turned in midair, gun raised, her eyes wide with fright.

The closet, you idiot. Feeling like the worst cop ever, she slowly eased up to the door, putting one finger in the metal divot and gently pulling it to one side. Keeping the wall at her back, the gun up and ready, she quickly ducked her head in and out of the open doorway.

The image that was left on her retinas was of a large bundle lying on the floor of the dark closet. Cursing the architect who had decided that bedrooms just didn't need ceiling lights anymore, cursing herself for not leaving a lamp in this room, and cursing herself twice for not grabbing her duty flashlight from the kitchen counter, Olivia realized her only option for light was to leave this room and then come back.

Would she have the nerve to do this twice? She certainly didn't have the nerve to feel around in the dark and try to ascertain the nature of the dark bundle using nothing but her bare hands.

But it doesn't really matter, she reasoned, *because clearly I've just gone completely insane so none of this is real anyway.*

Deciding that, insane or not, she was going for the flashlight, she let out the breath she'd been unconsciously holding in a huge sigh. Immediately the lump on the floor moved and turned. It moaned again, sounding – of all things – in pain.

"*Help*," the lump moaned.

"Shit," Olivia said, then jumped as the words came out of her mouth.

Startled anew by this turn of developments, Olivia gritted her teeth and made a dash for the bedroom door. She was back with the flashlight in seconds flat, and didn't even let herself think about what might be waiting for her in the closet.

Was it a trick? Probably. Nonetheless, she clicked the button on the Maglight and focused the beam on whatever creature had landed inside her delusion.

CHAPTER 16

Day Seven, Very Early

All life is given, all hope wasted, when upon my soul the demons dance.
- *From the journal of Anna Taylor*

The flashlight beam was startlingly bright, and for a painfully long moment her retinas were washed out by the stimuli. Finally they adjusted, and Olivia blinked her eyes to clear away the tears.

There was a body on her closet floor. A dirty, muddy, scratched-up man's body, wearing nothing but a pair of grungy boxers. He was curled in the fetal position, his back to her, his arms clenched around a torso rocked by violent trembling. He was so covered in dirt and mud that she couldn't even make out his skin or hair color.

His legs moved slightly and her trigger-finger twitched reflexively.

"Don't move," Olivia said coldly, keeping both the gun and the flashlight trained on him. Delusion or not, she was still a cop, her instincts jumping to the foreground to adjust for splintered nerves.

"Please help me," the man said plaintively.

"How did you get in here?" Olivia asked, her voice strong and firm.

"I don't know." His voice cracked and she heard the beginnings of hysteria creeping through the words.

"Calm down," she replied. "I need you to *very slowly* sit up and turn around. Do you understand?"

He was silent for so long that if not for his shaking, she would have thought he'd died. When he finally responded, it wasn't at all what she expected.

"Olivia?" he questioned, the single word full of wonderment and confusion.

Shocked, her gun hand began to drift down. Then her nerves, overloaded by the night, screamed in her ear, *it's a trick!* and the gun drifted back up.

"Sit up and turn around," she ordered again. "*Slowly.*"

The man, grunting in pain, carefully raised himself up onto his right arm, then used his legs to lever his body around. He kept one hand raised in front of his face as he turned towards the front. His whole body was wracked by shivers, and she saw what looked like fresh blood mixed with the mud on his arms and legs.

"Lower your hand," she commanded harshly.

Slowly he lowered his hand, blinking against the glare of the flashlight in his eyes. Olivia swallowed hard, her gun hand beginning to tremble violently.

"Matt?" she asked tentatively.

"It's me," he said, not sounding entirely sure. "Is that you?"

"Yes, it's me, Olivia." Her breath rattled in her throat as her chest tightened. *This isn't fair*, she thought fiercely. *They can't get me by using him. I won't allow it.*

"Why are you here?" she asked again, keeping the gun and flashlight trained on him.

"I don't know," he said, teeth chattering, his hand trembling as he raised it to block the light. "Please, can I have a blanket or something? I'm freezing."

She hesitated for a long moment, but finally sighed in defeat, lowering the gun and moving the beam of the flashlight away from his eyes.

"How about a hot shower?" she suggested. "No way am I giving you one of my blankets in your condition."

He looked down at himself as if noticing the mud for the first time.

"Yeah, a hot shower sounds great," he admitted.

"C'mon." She offered a hand. He took it gratefully, wincing as he got to his feet.

"I feel like I got run over by a truck."

She raised an eyebrow, recalling what she'd been told of her own experience from the other night.

"Maybe you did," she said wryly. She helped him walk to the bathroom, and then as she fumbled for the light switch she remembered.

"Shit," she groaned. "Hang on." She leaned him against the wall and fetched her broom and dustpan from the kitchen. She tightened the bulb, got the light back on, and then cleaned up the mess and broken glass as best as she could.

"Be careful," she warned as she laid a thick towel over the bathmat. "I might've missed some glass." She hung a fresh towel on the rack and turned the water on for him.

"There ya go." She helped him off the wall and into the bathroom. Just as she was closing the door, he reached out and gripped her arm.

"Olivia," he said, looking at her intently. "Thank you."

"Uh – you're welcome," she said, taken aback. "I'll find something for you to wear." She closed the door awkwardly and backed away, a strange feeling in the pit of her stomach.

It could still be a trick, she reminded herself. *Or the strangest delusion yet.*

"Yeah, I know," she said out loud, and then went to see what she had that a six-foot-six, 280-pound man could possibly fit into.

After intensive digging, she found a pair of oversized sweatpants left over from her "I really hate myself" phase years before. She figured with his lack of hips and butt, they might just fit, albeit as long shorts rather than actual pants. She folded the sweatpants and set them just outside the bathroom door, then settled into her recliner to wait.

Twenty minutes later, she was still waiting. She stared at the clock on the wall impatiently, wondering just how long of a shower he was going to take.

Damn, I know he was muddy, but this is ridiculous, she griped mentally, her brain already calculating the effects on this month's water and electric bill.

After another ten minutes, she sighed and got to her feet.

"Matt!" she called, knocking on the bathroom door. "You okay in there?"

He didn't answer. She knocked again, starting to wonder if he'd passed out in her shower. Finally she eased the door open and stuck her head in.

"Matt, answer me or I'm coming in there!" she warned. The only sound was the continual thrum of water pouring from the showerhead.

"Alright, I told ya so," she grumbled, opening the door all the way and stepping in to the hot, humid bathroom. Without peeking, she reached in to the shower and turned the water off. The sudden quiet was deafening.

"Matt?" she asked again, steeling herself for the inevitable.

I do not want to see this man naked, she told herself. *Okay, maybe I do, but not like this.*

Nerves properly girded, she pulled the shower curtain back, expecting to see him sprawled across the white enamel.

The bathtub was empty.

"What the fuck…" Olivia groaned. She looked at the towel that covered the floor; dirty footprints led in to the tub, but the towel was dry. No wet feet had walked on it since she'd laid it down.

The towel she'd left for him was still neatly folded and likewise dry and unused. His muddy boxers were in a heap on the floor right where he'd left them. He was just….gone.

Olivia collapsed against the wall. *This can't all have been a dream.* She felt like Bill Murray in *Groundhog Day*, living the same bad day over and over again with no end in sight and no escape back to her normal life.

She walked in to work the next morning bright and early – *very* early, having never gone back to bed. She was immediately concerned when she saw Matt's car already in the parking lot. But a peek into the station revealed no Günter, and so she kept on track and went straight down to the lab.

Whitney was at her desk reading over a document, and looked up when Olivia opened the door.

"Damn, woman," the redhead said bluntly. "You look cracked out."

Olivia sighed, collapsing into a chair. "I *feel* cracked out," she replied honestly.

"Still having bad dreams?"

"They aren't even dreams anymore," Olivia said in a daze. Just sitting down was making her eyes start to glaze over. "They keep being real."

Whitney narrowed her eyes. "What do you mean?" she asked, concerned.

"Last night Matt appeared on my closet floor, covered in mud. So I put him in a hot shower 'cause, y'know, he was all dirty, and he vanished. Left the water running and everything."

"Whoa, back up." Whitney put a hand up. "You mean, you *dreamed* that Matt appeared and so forth."

"Nah, that's the crazy part," Olivia said in amazement. "There's mud all over the floor, my apartment is still trashed from the shaking – oh, I forgot to tell you that part – and he even left his boxers behind."

"Matt's boxers are in your apartment?"

Olivia couldn't help but laugh. It figured that Whitney would focus on that part of the story and ignore the rest. "Yes, they are. I even took pictures with my phone to convince myself that I'm not completely delusional." She took her cell from her pocket and held it up, showing the pathologist the evidence.

Whitney, shaking her head in amazement, peered closely. "I have to ask this," she said bluntly, "as your friend and all. Are you drinking again?"

"Wish I was," Olivia said honestly. "But nope, haven't had a drop."

"Damn. So you didn't, like, just forget that you brought him home?"

"Are you fucking kidding me?" Olivia sat straight up. "This is *Matthew Gossett* we're talking about here, give me a break," she said, protesting even as she flashed back to her thought of the previous evening: *I would like to see him naked, but not like this.* "Plus, what about the mud and my trashed kitchen?"

"Sorry, sorry. Had to ask. Have you seen him this morning?"

"No, why?"

"Honestly?" Whitney half-grinned. "If he looks half as shitty as you do, then I'll know for sure that it was real."

Olivia rolled her eyes, already starting to feel silly about the conversation. "I already know it was real. Look, I probably fell asleep while he was in the shower and didn't realize it. Then when he came out, he didn't want to wake me up, so he snuck out."

Whitney raised an eyebrow. "I thought you said the water was still running."

"I don't know, you'd have to ask him," Olivia grumbled. "I've got to get upstairs."

"Okay, sorry." Whitney raised her hands in submission.

Olivia sighed, contrite. "Sorry. I'm just exhausted." She leaned forward to hug her friend and was startled when Whitney flinched away.

"Uh, I'm getting a cold, I don't want to give it to you," Whitney hedged.

"Sure. I've got to get to work." Olivia stood awkwardly. "Give me a call later and we can hang out."

"Of course."

That was so weird, Olivia thought as she made her way back upstairs. She realized belatedly that her once very huggy friend had long-since changed. How long had it been since Whitney had initiated a hug or a joking slap on the back?

Since the accident, she realized, mentally counting back the months.

Well, it was no wonder. A person couldn't very well go through an experience like that and not be changed; and Whitney might very well still be experiencing physical pain after her terrible trauma. She *had* been in the Intensive Care Unit for almost three weeks, for goodness' sake; and although she had seem to rebound amazingly well, she had never been one to talk about her difficulties.

But she doesn't talk about any of that, Olivia thought suddenly, one hand on the stair railing, one foot on the landing. *Not her husband, not what happened....not anything.*

Her thoughts were interrupted by Matt and Elaine coming through the front door.

"Hey, guys," Olivia said almost gratefully. Perhaps today would actually be a normal day, such as there was in the life of a homicide detective.

Her hopes were dashed immediately as Matt grunted hello, avoiding her eyes as he brushed past her. He looked absolutely terrible; the bags under his eyes were nearly big enough to soak a tea-bag in, and his usual quasi-metrosexual, well thought-out ensemble had been replaced by threadbare jeans and a pair of scuffed Reeboks.

"We're a mite grumpy this morning," Elaine stage-whispered to Olivia with a conciliatory pat on the shoulder.

"What's going on?" Olivia asked.

She shook her head. "Not sure. He called me and said he'd left his car here last night and had to take a cab in, and did I want to share the cab. I tried to get details out of him but he is like an f-ing Fort Knox today."

"Hmm."

As they walked into the CIB work area, she saw Matt was already bent over paperwork at his desk. She tentatively came up next to him.

"So, uh," she said hesitantly. "I wonder if we should maybe talk about last-"

"No," he interrupted, still not looking at her. "We don't need to talk about last night, or any other night. *Ever*."

His tone left no argument and so she left him alone, stepping back to fall into her own chair.

"Is everything okay?" Elaine asked, concerned. She had stopped at the restroom and so missed Matt's reaction.

"It's fine," Olivia said brightly. "Hey, there's someone I've been wanting to introduce you to. Dr. Johannsson, our Medical Examiner? She's pretty cool." She saw Matt twitch at the mention of Whitney's name, but dismissed it as more of his odd grumpiness.

"Sure," Elaine nodded, relieved to have the tension broken. "That'd be great."

They trouped all the way back downstairs, only to be greeted with an empty ME's office.

"That's weird," Olivia frowned. "She was just here. She must have stepped out for a minute."

"No worries," Elaine said easily.

On their way back out of the lab, Olivia saw one of the new student techs just coming in the door.

"Hey, did you see Dr. Johannsson leaving?" she asked the girl.

"Um, I'm not sure who that is," the girl replied nervously, as if she was being tested. "I only know Dr. Jennings."

"Who?" Olivia was startled. "Never mind, I'll track her down later."

Letting long-legged Elaine practically sprint ahead, Olivia slowly climbed the stairs to her own floor. She felt so damn feeble – it was amazing how a few days without decent sleep could turn a healthy human being into a lump of wasted clay.

As she approached her desk by way of the coffee machine, she casually looked around for Matt. His chair was empty, the top of his desk clean and uncluttered. His computer was already asleep.

Shaking her head, she glanced at her watch and realized they had almost an hour until their shift officially began.

Crap. Well, she had a lot of emails and paperwork to catch up on. There were travel vouchers to be filled out, receipts to be copied, time logs to be signed…enough to keep her busy for the morning.

Taking a swig of coffee, she set to work.

CHAPTER 17

Day Seven, Late Morning

There was something soothing and calming in the repetition of nearly-meaningless paperwork, and although she still struggled to keep her eyes open, the morning passed quickly. By eight she had a stack of forms ready to turn in and her desk was cleaner and neater than it had been in a long time.

Olivia sighed and pushed her chair back. She was more than ready for another tall coffee, which was ironic because the bathroom was also calling her name.

As she stood up, she realized with alarm that Matt's chair was still empty.

On her way to the ladies' room, she belatedly remembered that she'd promised to recanvass the Thompson's neighborhood, as well as make phone calls to get the ball rolling on the DNA analysis. *Shit.* Well, it was only eight – she still had plenty of time.

Deep in thought, she opened the bathroom door too exuberantly and nearly clipped Elaine right in the face.

"Damn!" Elaine said, catching the edge of the door with one hand. "Calm down, there, turbo."

"Sorry," Olivia said sheepishly. "Do you have any idea where Matt has gotten off to?"

The tall borrowed Detective shrugged. "Got me. He wasn't exactly verbose this morning."

"True. On that note, want to come with me to the crime lab? I need to prod them along for those DNA tests, see if they found anything on any of the clothing."

"Sure. Sounds more exciting than sitting around here, watching the paint on the walls."

Another ten minutes and they had reached the front lobby of the Crime Lab. Olivia signed in Elaine as a guest and they walked down the hallway towards Forensics 2.

"Why are these places always painted puce?" Elaine complained, looking around.

"What the hell is puce?"

"You know, vomit colored."

"Wouldn't that be puke?"

Elaine laughed as Olivia rang the buzzer at the door of Forensics 2.

"Just a minute," the buzzerish voice came through the intercom. "I'm finishing a vac job."

A 'vac job' was when the tech went over a piece of clothing with a high-powered vacuum hose to collect any trace evidence. At some point the Lab had learned that the opening of the room's door while the vac was running created a vortex effect, wherein any loose items in a two-foot radius of the end of the hose was promptly eaten by the machine. The Tech working at the time had had to explain to the D.A. how the button of her own lab coat had managed to find its way into an evidence bag. The electronic lock on the door and the intercom system had followed shortly thereafter.

Finally the electronic lock clicked and Olivia was able to push the door open.

"I hope your vac job wasn't something from our case," she commented to the Tech as they walked in.

"Nah, yours have been done for a bit. In fact, I have something to show you." Allen, the Tech on duty, walked over to a locker and removed several large plastic bags. Each piece of clothing had been individually vacuumed, analyzed for blood and other fluids, and then sealed into an airlocked plastic bag. He spread the pile out on the table. Olivia recognized them immediately.

"These are what Anna Taylor was wearing when we found her," she said to Elaine.

"Yes, and this," Allen the Tech held up a small bag, "is the piece of fabric the farmer's dog brought home. I had expected to find a match in your victim's clothing."

"So did we," frowned Olivia. "Are you saying it didn't come from Anna Taylor?"

"Definitely not," Allen confirmed. "At first I thought it was a random piece of debris – unrelated, and just by happenstance led the farmer to your victim. But that was before Lt. Martin brought us these." He walked over to another locker and brought out another pile of bags. "These are the clothes turned in by the neighbor."

"The ones found in the garbage?"

"The very same. And look here – the tear on the cuff of this shirt?"

Olivia and Elaine both bent to look. "Certainly looks like a match," Olivia agreed.

Allen nodded. "We did a fiber-by-fiber comparison. Definitely the missing piece. Most likely got caught on the barbed-wire fence near where the victim was found."

"Was there blood on the torn piece?" Elaine asked.

"Yes. Probably what attracted the dog to it. The blood stain continues up the arm of the shirt, and the DNA is a match to your victim."

"Anything that points to who was wearing it at the time?"

"I found a lot of cat hairs, as well as several human hairs on both sets of clothing. I DNA typed them but don't have anything to match them to. At this point all I can tell you is they are all head hairs from two Caucasians, one male and one female, not related to each other."

Olivia wrinkled her brow. "Are you saying that both people left hair on both sets of clothing?"

"Yes."

"Anything else?"

"Yes," Allen confirmed. "I also found a very small amount of blood in the crotch of these pants that were thrown away. It was old and has been washed several times. I'm guessing menstrual blood."

"Could you tell if it was Anna's?" Olivia asked.

He shook his head. "No. There's nothing salvageable to do a DNA test."

Olivia sighed. "Okay, so human hair from two white people. And a cat." She turned to look at Elaine. "Maybe Albert Thompson and someone else?"

"Maybe so."

"Let's go check in at the office and then we can go question the Thompson neighbors again. Maybe we'll get really lucky and get enough for a Judge to order a DNA test on Mr. Thompson."

Back at the office, Olivia told Lt. Martin everything they'd learned at the Lab. He was more than ecstatic to hear that for the first time, they had actual hard evidence leading to several someones; now they just had to nail down who the 'someones' were.

"Are you ready to head back out to Crookston?" Olivia asked Barstad as they stood in the hallway.

Elaine looked happy to have something useful to do. "I'm all yours."

"What about me?" A voice said behind her.

Elaine turned, Olivia leaning to look around her, to see Matt finally coming down the hallway.

"Ah, the prodigal son returns," Elaine said in a wise voice. "And where have *you* been all morning?"

He frowned, his eyes shifting away. "I wasn't feeling well." His face was wan and pale.

Olivia felt herself staring at him. Was it even possible that he'd simply appeared in her bedroom closet, almost naked and covered in mud, and then vanished just as suddenly?

"Both of you had a rough night?" Elaine looked from one to another. "You two have got to stop hanging out together."

Olivia opened her mouth to ask him how his scratched-up arms and legs were doing, and then closed it just as quick. She just wasn't feeling brave enough to venture there.

"I didn't think you wanted to recanvass," she said instead.

He shrugged. "Might as well. The more of us, the faster it goes, right?"

"True. Alright then, you get to drive."

Crookston, Minnesota was a 30-minute drive across the Red River and down Highway 2. They started at the mobile home park where the Thompsons lived, Matt pulling in to an empty space in front of a dingy blue trailer at the front of the park. The parking space was marked with a large sign that cheerily proclaimed it was *Reserved For Future Resident!* and Olivia realized this must be the park office. She and Elaine waited while Matt called in their location and time of arrival to dispatch.

"Okay," he said, hanging up. "So do you guys wanna split up? How do you wanna do this?"

Oliva and Elaine looked at each other and shrugged. "Just split up, I guess," they both said. "It's faster."

Olivia took the west side of the park, examining it on the map Matt handed her before setting out. Three streets branched off from the main, each of them dead-ending in a small cul-de-sac. She estimated about thirty trailers lined the three roads.

She walked down the first road, keeping her eyes open all the while. Some of the trailers were in disrepair, their yards dirty and cluttered with abandoned belongings, but most of them were obviously well-loved by their inhabitants. Multiple trailers had decks built from scavenged materials, tarps had been turned into awnings, and short rock-walls were made from piles of field stones. She could tell people were doing the best they could with the little they had; the rock-walls were well-made, the tarp awnings were clean and free of holes, and the decks were decorated with lights, wind chimes, bird feeders, and potted trees, all presently covered in a thin layer of snow.

The first two streets went quickly, as no one had any information or at least none that they wanted to volunteer. About halfway down the third street, Olivia noted from her map that the Thompson's trailer was directly across the common area behind the next resident she had to interview. It was a double-wide with green trim, a stack of plastic tubs of Kleen Kitty litter stacked underneath the deck. Some of them were lidless and clearly empty, but others still had the plastic band that secured top to bottom.

Olivia climbed the front steps and knocked on the door. When it opened she was nearly knocked backwards by a wave of pungent odors.

"Detective St. George," she said, her voice strangled by the smell. The elderly woman holding the door eyed her badge closely, then slowly backed up to give her room to enter.

"C'mon in," she said in a surprisingly strong voice.

Olivia stepped up, endeavoring mightily to stay in the open doorway, but the woman shooed her inside.

"C'mon, c'mon," she said impatiently, using her foot to keep several cats from fleeing out the open door as she closed it behind Olivia.

The entire living room appeared to be made of moving, breathing, fur-covered objects. Olivia could barely make out an inch of furniture for the sleeping, squirming, and playing felines that covered everything. The air seemed to be pure ammonia, and she tried mightily to take shallow breaths. It didn't help.

The elderly woman shuffled to the sofa, shooing away several cats before taking a seat. The animals she had just disrupted immediately draped themselves across her lap.

"Ma'am, we're investigating the death of a young woman," Olivia began, raising her voice in case the woman was hard of hearing. "Have you noticed any strange activity in the area, especially in the last month or so?"

She shrugged and shook her head, one hand petting the nearest feline mechanically. "Don' s'pose."

Olivia stepped forward and handed her a picture of Anna Taylor. It was actually a print-out from the internet; the same picture the television stations were using. She would have preferred to use a different one but they hadn't had much success finding anything decent.

"Have you seen this woman?" Olivia asked as she handed the picture to the elderly resident.

The woman pursed her wrinkled lips, peering at the picture. "Ayuh," she said slowly. "She looks like the one had been visiting with the Thompsons. Ain't seen her in some time, though."

"Do you remember when you saw her last?"

"Oh, woulda been sometime 'round Christmas," she shrugged. "Cain't 'member exactly. Not since they had that big fight out front."

"They had a fight?" Olivia was trying and failing to keep from getting excited.

"Surely. Right out front a' their place, too. Lots a' screamin' and yellin'. Then they got in a car an' drove away. Hadn't seen none of 'em since. Ain't seen the car neither, come to think of it."

"What kind of car was it?"

"It were Melissa's car – a gold Mini Cooper. Always wondered how she afforded such a fancy thing, her bein' in school an' all."

"Can you show me where you were when you saw the girls?"

Mrs. McCready heaved a mighty sigh, then stood up and shuffled off down a hallway, beckoning for Olivia to follow. She stopped halfway down in front of a small window.

"That tan one there, that's the Thompsons' trailer." Mrs. McCready tapped on the window glass with one yellowed fingernail.

Olivia peered through and saw that the window had a perfect view of a tan trailer across the way. Thanks to the way the street curved and the placement of the other mobile homes, the window looked directly between two trailers, straight at the front of the Thompson's.

She made a mental note to measure the distance between Mrs. McCready's and the Thompsons, but from eyeballing it, she didn't think it was more than twenty yards.

"Did you see them when they drove past your house?" Olivia was betting that Mrs. McCready had scrambled to get out to her living-room window to see them go by.

"Ayuh," she nodded. "I saw th'redheaded girl's face perfectly cause she were pressed up to her window, lookin' right in my direction. That's how I knowed it was that girl in the picture you showed me, even though her face had bandages on it."

"Bandages?" Olivia raised an eyebrow.

"Yup," she nodded again. "She had a big ol' white bandage covering most of her cheek." She rubbed her own face to indicate the size of said bandage, and Olivia remembered Mark Campbell's description of Anna trying to tear her own face off. "The other side of her face was kinda scratched up, too, but she was still a pretty girl."

"Ma'am, would you be willing to sign a statement about everything you saw?" Olivia asked.

The elderly woman shrugged noncommittally. "I s'pose."

"Thank you, we'd appreciate that."

"If there's nothin' else, I need t'be feedin' m'cats now," Mrs. McCready said.

"Of course. Thank you so much for your help. I can see myself out." Olivia was only too happy to leave the smell of a thousand cats all living in a small space.

"Whew!" she breathed a huge sigh of relief as she closed the door behind herself, taking a deep breath of blissfully clean, cold air. Just as she was stepping off the porch, she realized something.

"Shit," she muttered, turning right around. She knocked on the door again, waiting a long time before Mrs. McCready answered.

"Yes?" the old woman asked impatiently.

"I'm so sorry, Ma'am, but when you talked about the girls having a fight, you said you hadn't seen *none* of them again. Were you saying there were more than two girls?"

"Ayuh, was three of 'em," she sighed, looking hassled. "Melissa, that redheaded one you showed me th' picture of, an' some other girl."

"What did the other girl look like?"

Mrs. McCready shrugged. "Couldn't see much of her. All I really noticed were the huge glasses she had on. Girl musta been blind as a bat."

CHAPTER 18

Day Seven, Afternoon

When Elaine called home to have her people pick up Betty, she discovered they already had the girl in custody.

"She was picked up twenty minutes ago in Melissa's Mini Cooper," Barstad related, one hand over the speaker of her phone as she talked. "It's been impounded for parking illegally, and they ran the plates and saw she wasn't the owner."

"Have them run it through all the lab tests," Olivia instructed. "We know the car was here; it's possible Anna was transported in it after she was killed."

Elaine nodded and spoke into the phone, then listened for a moment. "Lt. Alvarado's going to question her," she told them. "I told her everything we've found out."

"Meanwhile, we need to somehow convince *our* L.T. that we need an interstate warrant to search the Thompson's trailer," Olivia sighed.

"I'll ask," Matt volunteered, to her surprise. "I think I can convince him."

Elaine slapped him on the arm. "Go get 'em, tiger!"

Olivia never heard how Matt did it, but somehow he worked magic. Only two hours later, they were all meeting at the Crookston PD building. Lt. Martin was already there, talking shop with his Crookston counterpart, Lt. Vepp. They both turned as Matt's car rolled up to the curb and the three Detectives piled out.

Lt. Martin waved them over and introduced them to Lt. Vepp, a short heavyset man with an impressive unibrow.

"Here's how it's gonna go," Vepp jumped right in. "We'll go in first and take out the girl and her father. Then you three can go in, under supervision of my guy, and do your search."

Olivia, Matt, and Elaine nodded. "Great."

"I understand you've had a car sitting on their place?" Olivia asked.

Vepp nodded. "Sorta. Watching from afar, anyway. Last word is, both girl and father are inside. No movement. Probably sleeping, being Sunday morning and all."

"Oh yeah," Matt mused aloud as they got back in his car. "It *is* Sunday."

"I know, I'm so ready for a day off," Olivia agreed. "It's been a long week."

The two Lieutenants were the head of the caravan that snaked its way across Crookston and into the trailer park. The Crookston uniform car met them partway down the street from the Thompson's place, then the Grand Forks PD waited patiently as the Crookston guys went up to the front door and several unis covered the back and sides.

Olivia watched as Lt. Vepp personally knocked on the door, presenting a bleary-eyed Melissa with the warrant. She was brought out, stone-faced and angry, and put in the back of a car while they went in to get the father.

The wait seemed interminably long. Finally, Albert Thompson stumbled out between Lt. Vepp and his Detective, looking confused and lost. He was put in a different car from his daughter, and then Vepp waved to the three GF Detectives to go on in.

The Crookston Detective met them at the front door. "Michael Huff," he said as they all shook hands. "Good ta meetchya."

"Likewise."

The Thompson's trailer was clean and tidy, and a refreshing change from Mrs. McCready's acrid Dungeon of Cats. The four Detectives split into two teams.

Olivia hated doing searches, only because of the necessity of being destructive. She knew how invasive it was for the people that lived there; but it was the only way to be sure no evidence was being overlooked or hidden. It wasn't so bad when they were searching the home of a known meth dealer, or something similar, as she knew that person's family knew all too well what their "loved one" was up to. But when the family had no idea that one of their own was being investigated for criminal activity, Olivia found it hard to not keep apologizing to them for ransacking their home.

She and Elaine took the back bedroom while the men took the front. When she opened the door, the two women were confronted by what looked like the aftermath of a tornado.

"Uh, crap," Olivia said disgustedly, stepping into the mess. "Apparently their cleaning habits don't extend past the doorjamb."

"Probably the daughter's been cleaning the rest of the house." Elaine wrinkled her nose. "What's that smell?"

Olivia shook her head as she tried to breathe shallow through her mouth. *At least it's not cats,* she told herself firmly, trying to look on the bright side. But the aroma – a mix of old man body odor, sweat, dirty laundry, with a heavy layer of cologne over top - wasn't much better than the ammonia fumes of Mrs. McCready's feline haven.

"I'll take the dressers if you take the closet," she suggested in a strangled voice. Elaine, her face still wrinkled in a moue of disgust, nodded in agreement.

They were about twenty minutes in when Elaine made the discovery.

"Hey," she called to Olivia. "Lookit this." She held up a small brown leather-covered Bible.

"Yeah?" Olivia stopped what she was doing and walked over.

"It's Anna's." Elaine pointed out the name embossed in gold inside the front cover.

"Great." Olivia took out an evidence bag and plopped the Bible inside. "Where was it?"

"Inside this trunk, right on top of all the other books." Elaine showed her a rusted metal trunk at the end of the closet. They pulled the trunk out and went through the rest of the books, then emptied the trunk out and went over the inside and outside carefully. The books were mostly old textbooks, presumably from classes Albert Thompson had once taught; Olivia noticed the St. Agnes emblem stamped inside many of them. The trunk, disappointingly, did not have any hidden catches or secret spaces as part of its construction.

The rest of the search was unproductive. Finally the team called it quits, packed up, and headed back to the station. Lt. Vepp was kind enough to let the Grand Forks crew take care of all the paperwork, as Lt. Martin noted wryly when they regrouped.

Melissa and Albert Thompson had been split into separate interrogation rooms. On the drive back from Crookston, Elaine had called back to Graham's Ford PD and arranged for the video from their earlier questioning of bug-eyed Betty to be sent to Lt. Martin's email. He had suggested, and they all agreed, that it would be a good idea to watch it before speaking to the Thompsons; maybe Betty said something that could be used.

Once he'd received the file, the IT guy patched it over to the conference room computer.

"I don't know what the quality will be," Lt. Martin warned as the digital projector warmed up. "Lt. Acevedo said they'd have to downsize the file quite a bit in order to make it small enough to email."

"As long as we can tell who's who, I think that's all that really matters," Olivia quipped.

"Your L.T. also included her impressions of the girl," Lt. Martin said, nodding at Elaine as he pulled several sheets of paper off the printer. "Here's her notes." He gave one sheet to each Detective and they settled down to watch the video. The quality *was* terrible; grainy and so washed-out from being downgraded that it was nearly black-and-white. But it was easy enough to tell which one was Betty, as even now her glasses were the most obvious part of her.

"That's Detective Haines," Elaine pointed as a man walked into view and sat across from Betty. "I can tell by the shine off his bald spot."

"Hey now," Lt. Martin said mildly. He was sensitive about his own quickly-growing bald spot.

"And that's Detective Yoshihara," she continued as another figure entered and leaned against the back wall. "He never sits down. He likes to just observe for awhile before jumping in."

The audio was not bad, although Olivia found herself straining to hear inflections in the girl's voice. It wasn't easy to pick up subtleties in tone when the girl was so hard to see. She hadn't realized before how much of talking was actually body language.

They watched for nearly twenty minutes, glancing occasionally at Lt. Acevedo's notes, before anything really interesting happened. Lt. Haines had just asked Betty for the tenth time why she was driving Melissa's Mini Cooper, and Betty had answered yet again that Melissa had told her to keep it visible while she was in Minnesota. But this time, for the first time since the questioning had begun, she added more.

All those watching leaned in and then gasped.

"Did she just say what I think she said?" Olivia said in amazement.

"Back it up, let's see that again."

They all listened intently and then looked at each other.

Matt was the first to speak. "I think we got her."

CHAPTER 19

Day Seven, Evening

…it is in giving that we receive; it is in pardoning that we are pardoned; it is in dying that we are born to eternal life.

- The Prayer of St. Francis

Someone found a laptop and brought it to Olivia while Lt. Martin transferred the file onto a thumb drive. By this time, Melissa Thompson had been sitting alone in the interrogation room for several hours. The uni who'd been watching her reported that she seemed relaxed, but impatient.

Matt went in first, since the girl already knew who he was. His job was to warm her up for Olivia's entrance.

"Hi, Melissa," he said casually as he entered. "Do you remember me? I'm Detective-"

"Yeah, yeah, I remember," she said shortly, crossing her arms. "Didn't we play this game last time?"

"Actually, if you recall, we didn't get very far last time," he said easily.

"Well, I don't know why you think this time's going to be any different," she snapped back. The look on her face was one of stony indifference. "We didn't do anything."

Matt raised one eyebrow. "We?"

Melissa flushed and clamped her mouth shut.

In the observation room, Olivia and Elaine looked at each other. "Which 'we' is she talking about?" Elaine wondered out loud.

"Good question," Olivia responded. "I guess we'll find out pretty quick."

Olivia's cue to enter was Matt tapping on the table. After several more minutes of attempted banter with the girl, all of which she ignored to stare stonily off into space, Matt's right hand did a tap-tap on the table. Olivia hefted the laptop under her arm and gave Elaine a high-five.

"Wish me luck."

"Luck!" Elaine said agreeably.

Olivia entered the interrogation room with the laptop in tow. Without looking at the girl, she set it on the table and plugged it in.

"We just got some new evidence in," she said to Matt, still ignoring Melissa. "The Graham's Ford PD sent a video over."

"Oh yeah?" he said, as if he didn't know what was on it. "Let's have a look."

Olivia sat next to him and they both stared at the screen as if it was the most interesting thing they'd ever seen. The computer was turned away from Melissa, but the audio was purposefully turned up. She didn't react until she heard Betty's voice and then she jumped like someone had stuck her with a cattle-prod.

"What the hell is this!" she asked angrily, finally uncrossing her arms.

Olivia looked up like she had just realized the girl was sitting there. "Oh, your friend had an interesting chat with *our* friends back in Washington," she said calmly. "I think you'll really want to hear this part coming up." She fast-forwarded the video and turned the laptop to face Melissa just in time for Betty to speak again.

"It was Melissa!" Betty was saying eagerly. "I didn't have anything to do with Anna. It was all her."

Melissa's face was crimson. "Why that lying stupid little bitch-"

"Wait, this is the best part," Olivia leaned forward.

"Melissa wanted Seamus all for herself," Betty said. "That's why she killed Anna."

Melissa's mouth was hanging open, her face the color of a ripe plum. Olivia hit the Pause button and slid the laptop aside.

"But I know something Betty doesn't know," Olivia said calmly. She had only figured this part out while standing in the observation room. The journal, hand-made with love for a much older classmate; Seamus' comment that had suddenly come back to Olivia - *the only one Melissa is jealous of is God;* the missing pages from the journal, expertly removed. Suddenly, it all made sense.

"Betty doesn't know you're gay, does she, Melissa?" Olivia said quietly. "You loved Anna. You would never have hurt her."

The effect was instantaneous. The color drained from the girl's face as if a plug had been pulled.

"How did you-"she stuttered.

"Seamus figured it out," Olivia said. Matt was staring at her strangely; this wasn't anything like what they had discussed, but when she realized the truth, she knew bringing it out would be the only way to get Melissa to talk.

Melissa gulped hard, looking like someone had just punched her in the gut. She finally nodded, slowly, looking down at the table.

"Yes, I did love her," she said almost under her breath. Her face twisted and she let out a sob. She laid her head in her arms as she began to cry heart-wrenching, wracking tears of pain.

Olivia and Matt waited patiently as Melissa cried. Elaine stepped in briefly and set a box of Kleenex on the table. Finally, her tears slowing, Melissa raised her head and reached for a tissue as Olivia pushed the box to her.

"Thanks," she said gratefully, drying her face.

"Is that the first time you cried for her?" Olivia asked kindly.

Melissa nodded. “I couldn’t – before. I couldn’t let anyone know.”

“Who are you protecting, Melissa?” Olivia asked. She was loath to dive right in, but she had to catch the girl while she was still off-guard and emotional.

“I don’t know,” the girl answered. She sounded like she meant it.

Olivia pursed her lips. “Who did you *think* you were protecting?” she rephrased.

The girl looked down at the table again. “I – I thought…..my dad. I wasn’t sure but….I don’t know.”

“You thought your father killed her?”

She nodded, still looking at the table. “He has….problems. He hurt someone once before, a long time ago. I thought he might have….when Anna didn’t come back that night, I didn’t know what to think.”

“Does your father know about you?” Olivia asked gently.

Melissa shook her head, leaning forward and burying her face again in her folded arms. “He thinks…” her voice caught and she had to pause. “He says that, um, homosexuality is unnatural, that it’s a sign of possession.” She could barely force the words from her mouth. “If he knew, he would try to fix me.”

“Like he might have tried to fix Anna?” Matt asked quietly. The girl nodded again.

“Why don’t I take this out,” he suggested, folding up the laptop. Olivia smiled gratefully and gave him a nod.

“Can you start at the beginning?” Olivia said to the girl after Matt had left the room. “Tell me everything that happened.”

She sighed deeply. “I’m not even sure anymore what the beginning is.”

“Start with the trip over Christmas break,” Olivia amended.

“It was supposed to be – relaxing. I don’t know why but I thought

Anna would be better here."

"That she'd get a break from what was plaguing her?"

"Yes." Melissa looked at her hard. "You know about that?"

Olivia smiled sympathetically. "I've talked to Brother Sheridan."

"Ah. Yes. You do know, then. Well, I had this crazy idea that they would leave her alone if we went on vacation. Stupid, I know, but I just wanted to spend some time alone with her."

"Did Anna know how you felt about her?"

Melissa's face colored. "I hope not. I tried so hard to just be – friends. I mean, she almost became a nun. She couldn't possibly have…"

"Loved you back?"

The girl nodded, her face a mask of pain. "Yeah. And I'm not….I mean, no one knew about me, anyway. I pretended that I liked Seamus so that I could hang out with the two of them." She laughed sadly. "I was on such cloud nine when he said he didn't want to come on the trip. Finally, it would be just me and Anna."

"Why did you and Seamus use the same fake address for your drivers' licenses?"

The girl looked embarrassed. "That was so stupid. Seamus didn't want to use his real address because his aunt owns the complex – I don't know why that matters, but he was really insistent about it. He convinced me to do it too – he said it would be more believable if we seemed to be a couple. I just played along because I was supposed to be having a crush on him."

"So he was helping you with your pretense of being straight."

She seemed surprised. "Yes, I guess so. I never thought about it that way."

"When did Betty join you here?"

Melissa rolled her eyes. "*She* flew in to Minneapolis the day after we got here. Called me totally out of the blue, wanted me to come pick her up. How inconsiderate can a person be, y'know? She knew I didn't want her here. But she knew I wouldn't just leave her at the airport, either."

"You two didn't get along?"

"Betty is such a…" Melissa shook her head, at a momentary loss for words. "I don't know how to put it. You never knew who she really was because everything was a movie to her. She was always acting, especially when boys were around. That girl thought every man wanted her, and she sure as hell wanted every guy. It's sick."

"Why did she fly in to Minneapolis?"

"She had begged me to bring her on the trip, and I said no. She said it was because of the Mall of America; but I think that was just her excuse. She was sure that Seamus was going to be here, even though she was there when he backed out of going. She couldn't stand the thought of the three of us being together without her."

"She wanted Seamus for herself?" Olivia guessed shrewdly.

Melissa nodded. "It was so stupid. If she'd stayed in Washington, she would have *had* him all to herself! Except that he didn't want anything to do with her. And, she already has a boyfriend. But one man was never enough for her."

"Why did you and Anna drive separate cars?" Olivia asked. This detail had been bugging her since they learned of it. "Why drive separately? Or why drive at all, why not fly?"

Melissa wiped an eye, sniffling. "Anna was leaving afterwards. When I said I could ride with her and fly back, she said she needed the practice of driving alone. I got the feeling that she had never been on a long drive before and was nervous about it. So I said I'd drive too, and that way if she had any problems she knew I wasn't far behind."

This was new to Olivia. "Where was she going?"

"She'd heard about some guy down in Flagstaff who had helped people like her. Some kind of ceremony or something. It sounded like bullshit to me, just another guy running a scam. But she was desperate."

"Had she been taken by these 'scams' before?"

Melissa nodded again. "She gave a grand to this guy down in Portland. He sold her a little glass jar of some disgusting brown goop. She was supposed to use it every day and night for a month and it would 'scare the demons away,' or some such crap." She rolled her eyes. "She did it for a week, but she said it burned, and I finally made her stop."

Olivia raised an eyebrow. "Was she supposed to rub it on her face or something?"

Melissa wrinkled her face angrily. "She was supposed to dip a tampon in it and put it in her – you know. The guy said it would 'ward off' the demons because that was how they were entering her. Can you believe what people will do for money? As if her head wasn't fucked up enough when it came to her sexuality." She seemed oblivious to the irony of that statement.

"When did she stop using it?"

"After the first night of our trip. We stopped at a motel in Billings. She was putting lotion on her legs and I saw that the insides of her thighs were all red. She said it was from sitting in the car all day with that nasty thing inside of her. I made her stop using it right then." She wiped her eyes again. "She said it had hurt her inside." She bowed her head, throat clenching as the tears began to flow anew. "And that fucking asshole charged her a grand for that, can you imagine?" A choking, ironic laugh burst out and then died as she heaved a tremendous sigh.

"What happened when Betty arrived?"

"It was horrible. She ruined everything. I'd been so careful not to tell my dad too much, because of how he gets, and the first thing she did was open her big fat mouth. Before that, Anna had actually been starting to relax a little bit."

"Why didn't you want to tell your dad?" Olivia asked.

Melissa looked down at the table. "Like I said, my dad hurt someone, a long time ago. I just figured it was better if he didn't know what Anna was going through."

"Why did Betty tell him?"

"I don't know."

Olivia leaned it. "Melissa, did you tell Betty to call me, pretending to be you?"

The girl looked up, startled. "What? No. Why would I do that?"

"How about calling me, pretending to be Mrs. Pace?"

She shook her head. "No, that's stupid. Why would I do that? I don't even know you."

"What were the dates of your trip?" Olivia asked.

"Um, we left on December seventeenth, and we were supposed to be here until January fifth."

"But Anna was found early on the fourth," Olivia pointed out. "What happened before that?"

"When Betty got here, she acted like she owned my house. She made herself all comfortable, cozied up to my dad, and told him every single one of Anna's secrets. I figured she was trying to ruin the trip as much as she possibly could. Poor Anna was mortified. My dad started asking her all kinds of questions, trying to analyze her problems, telling her that she'd been dealing with it all wrong. It was horrible."

"And then?"

Melissa sighed. "We all got into this huge fight. I was trying to defend Anna, make Betty shut the hell up, make my dad shut the hell up. Everyone was pissed off except Anna because she didn't *get* mad. About anything. She was actually too *nice* to get mad." She shook her head. "But even she had had enough and she told me she was going to take off for Flagstaff early."

"One of the neighbors saw you three girls having a fight outside," Olivia said. "Can you tell me about that?"

"It had to be the last night. January first. Anna was trying to pack so she could leave, and I told Betty she wasn't welcome anymore. I was packing up *her* stuff, told her I was going to take her to the airport and leave her there. She started screaming at me, grabbing stuff out of my hands, throwing it all over the living room. My dad just stood there staring at this madness. I started throwing Betty's shit outside. I didn't care if it was all over our lawn, I just wanted her out of our house. She went outside, still screaming, started picking it up. Anna was trying to play peacemaker even as she was getting ready to leave. God, it was such insanity." She shook her head at the memory. "Finally, Anna suggested we all just calm down, go get some dinner, get a breather so we could talk rationally. We went to RBJ's, just the three of us."

"You took your car?" Olivia asked, remembering Mrs. McCready's statement about the Mini Cooper.

Melissa nodded. "While we were there, my dad came in. He said Anna had gotten an emergency phone call at the house. She stepped out to talk to him about it, and.....that was the last time I saw her."

"Was she expecting a phone call?"

"I didn't think so, but I don't know." Melissa shrugged helplessly.

"Did she own a cell phone?"

"Yeah, so that was even more weird that anyone would have called our house."

"What did your dad say?"

"When she didn't come back in to the restaurant, I went out to look for her. They were both gone, and I assumed she had gone with him back to the house. Betty and I got back, but only my dad was there. He said Anna had gotten a message, told him she had to leave, and taken off." She let out a sob. "But her *car* was still here."

"How did he explain that?" Olivia asked gently.

"He said someone had picked her up at the house, but he didn't know who or why. It just didn't make any sense. She didn't even know anyone here except for me."

"You thought he killed her?"

She nodded tearfully.

"Why would your dad kill Anna, Melissa?"

She sniffled. "He has some mental issues. He thinks he can do things that he really can't do."

"Like heal people who are possessed?"

"Yes. He hears voices. He says they are the ghosts of witches who were burned at the stake, that they've taught him 'real' magic."

"You said he hurt someone once before. What happened?"

"When I was little, when we still lived in Washington, he was teaching at St. Agnes'. He went on a research trip to England, and when he came back he started getting....weird. There was a little girl down the street who had some kind of disability. I think she was probably autistic or something. My dad told her mother she was possessed by demons, that's why she had problems, but that he could 'fix' her. He fed her a bunch of weird herbs or something, did this big ceremony, and she....I guess she had a bad reaction because she died. He went away for awhile after that. I had to go live with my grandparents until he came back."

"Did you ever perform an exorcism on Anna?"

"Um..." she bowed her head again, reluctant to keep going. "Not exactly."

Olivia waited patiently as the girl struggled. Finally Melissa heaved another tremendous sigh.

"It's my fault," she said sadly. "I thought we could help Seamus. God, I was so naïve!"

"The ceremonies in Anna's bathroom," Olivia realized suddenly. "They were for Seamus?"

Melissa nodded sadly. "Anna was fine before that. She was so good, so selfless...she honestly thought she could take some of the bad away from him and that it would just.....dissipate, I guess, into her goodness." She laughed a thoroughly unhappy laugh. "And me, stupid little girl that I was, I thought I knew everything about everything. I set up the ceremonies, ordering everyone around like it was a play or something and I was the director."

Olivia belatedly realized what Melissa meant; that they had attempted some kind of reverse exorcism, where Anna was to 'siphon' demons from Seamus to make him better. "After that is when she began suffering?" she clarified.

"Yes. Almost right away, but it took us awhile to make the connection. Even then she wanted to keep going, as pointless as that would have been, but neither Seamus or I would have any part of it anymore."

"Why don't we take a break," Olivia suggested. "Are you hungry? Thirsty?"

"I could use some water," the girl agreed, her face wan and tired.

"I'll be right back," Olivia promised as she stepped out. She immediately went into the observation room.

"What do you think?" she asked the three observers.

"I pulled her dad's record while you were talking," Matt reported, handing her a file folder. "The girl's mother didn't press charges, but he was involuntarily committed for three years after the daughter died. Diagnosed with schizophrenia and delusions of grandeur. After he got out, he kept his weekly appointments for two months, then disappeared."

"Moved here, I'm guessing," Olivia said, looking through the folder.

"Yup. I'm betting his employers have no idea of his past. He started as a fill-in adjunct professor, so part-time, on call. By time he got hired full-time he had been there long enough that they probably didn't feel the need to check his references."

Olivia turned to Lt. Martin. "Can we get a warrant to pull Betty's phone records? And those for both Melissa's cell phone and Albert Thompson's home phone? Oh, and they should do a search of Betty's apartment, too."

The L.T. nodded. "I'll make the call if you one of you gets the paperwork going."

"I'll do it," Matt volunteered. "You're doing a great job in there."

"Thanks!" Olivia said, surprised and oddly touched. "I appreciate that."

"Yeah, well, don't get used to it," he grumbled as he left the room.

Elaine chuckled and gave Olivia a wink. "He's trying so hard to still be mad at you, but I don't think that boy could hold a grudge if his life depended on it. Plus, I'm pretty sure he kinda likes you."

"Eew, cooties," Olivia joked, ignoring any implications of what she'd just heard. "Okay, I'm going to get Melissa a glass of water and get back in there."

She found a clean glass, filled it to the top and brought it in to the interrogation room. Melissa drank it gratefully, draining nearly half in one long gulp before setting it down.

"Thanks," she said, wiping her mouth.

"No problem. Melissa, can you tell me how and why Betty has your car?"

"Oh, that," Melissa sighed tiredly. "When Anna left – or we thought she left, or whatever – Betty turned into a whole different person. It was bizarre. She got all light and bubbly, acted like we were the best friends in the whole world. She just wouldn't leave, no matter how much I hinted or flat-out asked when she was going home. I had already decided I needed to stick around and keep an eye on my dad, just in case – you know….and finally I asked her if she'd drive my car back to Washington for me. It was the only way I could get rid of her."

"Did you ask her to drive it around town and make it look like you were still around?"

Melissa frowned. "Hell no. She was supposed to park it in my space and put the keys in my mailbox. Obviously she didn't."

Olivia cleared her throat. "I, uh, hate to bring this up, but when we checked your apartment – when we still thought you were in Graham's Ford – it was pretty much cleaned out. Well, not cleaned so much as emptied."

The girl's eyes widened and her face went crimson. "Are you fucking kidding me? Are you saying Betty-"

"The Graham's Ford PD will do a search of her apartment, but since she had your keys, she's our first suspect," Olivia confirmed. "Is there anyone else that would have a key to your apartment?"

"No. God, I can't believe her. I guess she figured I was never coming back. I'm pretty sure she stole my phone, too – I haven't been able to find it since she left."

"Do you have a key to Seamus' apartment?" Olivia asked, guessing shrewdly, if after the fact, that Betty had likely been in the boy's apartment when she and Matthew had been canvassing that night. That explained why the business card had been on the ground and the Mini

Cooper had been gone when Olivia returned; Betty had left in the interim.

"Yes, he gave me a spare," Melissa confirmed. "I fed his cat sometimes when he wasn't doing too good."

"One more thing," Olivia said, deciding to try and get an answer to a question that had been bugging her; namely, why a self-professed virgin and near-nun would have a birth control device implanted in her body. "Do you know why Anna decided to get an IUD?"

"Oh." Melissa turned crimson. "That was my fault. I told her it would make her less scared to lose her virginity, because she wouldn't have to worry about getting pregnant. When she gave up on being a nun she got really embarrassed about being a thirty-something year old virgin."

Olivia opened her mouth to respond when the door opened and Lt. Martin stuck his head in. "St. George, I need you for a moment," he said and shut the door.

Olivia patted Melissa's arm. "I'll be right back."

"What's up?" Olivia said curiously as she stepped out in the hallway.

"I'm about to go talk to Albert Thompson," Lt. Martin said. "Also, we'll need to get blood and hair samples from both Thompsons to compare to what was found on the clothes."

Olivia nodded. "Okay. And from Betty?"

"We don't have enough evidence yet to get that without her consent, unlike these other two. But the Graham's Ford PD are going over to search her apartment right now, so hopefully they'll find something to implicate her further so we can get the blood sample. We need something besides Melissa's story."

"Have they found anything in the Mini Cooper?"

"There was blood on the back seat. Probably Anna's, but it's being tested right now. It's Melissa's car so we've really got to nail down the timeline to absolve her, if indeed she's innocent."

"Okay. Do you know if Dr. Johansson is still downstairs? She can get the blood sample from both Thompsons."

His brow furrowed. "I'll call downstairs," he hedged. "And, St. George," he added as she turned away. "Don't forget to keep that appointment." He tapped the side of his head and she realized he was trying to refer to a 'head shrinker' – a psychiatrist – without declaring it in front of everyone.

"Uh, sure will," she agreed, thinking, *weird time to bring that up!*

Melissa was happy to give up a small tube of her blood and a couple of hairs to help prove her innocence. When pressed, she admitted that she didn't believe her father was capable of purposefully murdering Anna in cold blood, but just couldn't imagine what else had happened to her friend.

After the technician left, samples in hand, Olivia opened her bag. "Okay, Melissa, I need you to help me account for everyone's movements those last few days," she said, sliding a tablet of paper and a pencil across the table. "Please write down everything you can remember, times as best as you can possibly remember, and what everyone did. We need as much description as possible, right up until Betty left in your car."

"I'll try," the girl promised, taking the paper and pencil.

"Also," Olivia continued. "Is there anyone else that had interactions with you, Betty and Anna? Anyone that might have seen something, heard something? Anyone that can verify when she had your car and you didn't?"

Melissa thought for a long minute. "We ran into a couple people I knew at RBJ's. We actually ran into someone that Betty knew, too. That was weird. And I took my car in to get an oil change right before she left. Does that help?"

"Yes, definitely. Include all that on the timeline – everything you can remember. Names, dates, times, everything."

While Melissa was working on that, Olivia took another opportunity to check in with her coworkers.

"If she's telling the truth," Olivia said to Elaine in the observation room, "then not only was she not the one Betty called while we were standing there in the library, but at least one other person is helping Betty. Someone had to be on the other end of that phone."

"And Melissa said that they ran into someone that *Betty* knew at RBJ's," Elaine pointed out. "Maybe she didn't fly into Minneapolis by herself."

Olivia nodded. "Let's see if we can find out her flight information and get the passenger manifest for that flight."

"I'll take care of it."

"Thanks. Do you know how Matt's coming on the warrant paperwork for all the phone records?"

"They're pushing it through. I think your L.T. already talked to the judge."

"Great. Hey, I'm going to order a pizza. Are you particular about your toppings?"

"No, I'm good with anything."

After putting the call in to Domino's, Olivia realized she needed to make a pit stop at the restroom. When she opened the bathroom door, the room was dark.

"That's weird," she muttered, flipping the switch up and down. Normally the light was on a motion-sensor, turning on automatically when the door opened. "The bulb must be burned out." As she fussed with it, the hallway behind her went black, surrounding her with a pressing darkness.

Did the power go out? She felt a lump forming in the pit of her stomach. Taking the cell phone from her pocket, she opened it and tried to shine it down the hallway. The weak light from her screen couldn't begin to make a dent in the blackness, but she thought she saw movement at the peripherals of the light.

"Hey, what happened?" she called out, struggling to see who it was. "Did the power go out?"

The figure didn't answer.

"Hey!" she called again, and was rewarded with a tittering laugh that sent fear stabbing straight through her gut.

"Oliviaaaaaa," the figure called, moving back and forth just at the edge of the light.

She shook her head mutely, taking a step back and keeping her cell phone up with a shaking hand. "Stay back," she said weakly, feeling for the wall behind her with the other hand. "I mean it."

"Oh I know you do," the figure answered. *"You always did."* It tittered again, and a memory jumped to the front of her mind of Darren, looming over her with his gun in hand. She had her back against the wall in their tiny bathroom, both hands raised in defense; her voice, dripping with fear, telling him to *stay back. I mean it!* Darren laughing, raising the gun, his finger slowly tightening on the trigger as she cringed against the wall. The *BOOMBOOM* of the gun, deafening in that small space, and a feeling of being punched in her shoulder, then hip. Then nothing but darkness.

Olivia shook her head, forcing the memory back into the depths.

"No," she said shakily, trying to make her voice sound stronger than she felt.

"But Kaya," Darren's voice came out of the darkness, the figure still keeping just beyond the edge of her meager light. "I love you."

"You're not him," she whispered. *"You're not him."*

"But Kaya," it said again, and she felt her hair begin to move as a cold wind touched her face. "I *love YOU.*" The wind pushed against her as the figure rushed forward. She caught a glimpse of a face contorted with anger, its mouth grotesquely large and filled with razor-sharp teeth, coming into the small circle of light. The image was burned into her retinas just as her cell phone's screen turned off. Then there were only eyes in the darkness, two red eyes burning in twin fires, coming straight at her like a speeding freight train. She opened her mouth to scream and a hand fell on her shoulder.

"Liv, you okay?"

Olivia blinked, the sudden light from the bathroom shocking her eyes. She was standing in the open doorway, one hand holding the door open, the other hand on the light switch. She looked behind her and saw Elaine's concerned face.

"Are you okay?" Barstad asked again, taking her hand off Olivia's shoulder.

"I'm – yeah, I'm okay," Olivia answered. "I think."

"What happened?"

She shook her head. "I don't know."

Elaine looked at her steadily. "Well, the pizza's here. I got worried when you were gone for so long."

How long was I standing here? Olivia wondered, frightened. "Um, I'll be right there. I just need to use the restroom."

"Okay." Elaine walked away, giving her one last wondering look, and Olivia took a deep breath as she stepped into the restroom. She did her business as quickly as she could, eager to get back to the company of people.

She ate two slices of pizza in silence, listening to Matt and Elaine's banter, Darren's voice still ringing in her ears. *I really am crazy,* she kept thinking, over and over again. *It's the only explanation. Demons aren't real. Ghosts aren't real. I'm losing my mind.*

But the image still sizzling against her retinas belied this explanation.

CHAPTER 20

Day Seven, Very Late

Melissa labored away at the timeline for the better part of an hour, stopping occasionally to fill in more gaps as Olivia continued to ask questions about the events of those last few days.

Finally, clearly exhausted, the girl asked if she could take a break. Olivia brought her pizza and more water then took the notepad away so she could look it over with the other Detectives.

Matt and Elaine were still sitting around his desk. Olivia pulled up a chair just as the Desk Sergeant walked up.

"Hey, got a message for you," he said, handing a slip of paper to Olivia. "Your landlord called and said the neighbors are complaining about your dog whining and scratching at the door. He wants you to call and let him know when you're going to go home and take care of it."

Elaine raised an eyebrow. "I didn't know you had a dog."

Olivia took the paper, laughing weakly. "I don't," she said. "Must be a prank call."

"That's weird."

"Yeah, I have some weird neighbors," Olivia lied, thinking of the muddy prints leading to her unused bedroom door. She realized now that she should have been more concerned about the fact that there were no prints leading *out* of the apartment. Something had been in her apartment that night, and her gut instinct was telling her it was still there.

Olivia forced herself to shake it off. Paranoia wasn't going to help.

"Okay, about this timeline," she said, forcing a cheerful tone from her lips. "Let's see if we can nail down what happened between the afternoon of January first, when Anna disappeared, and January fourth, when she was found."

"When did Betty leave Melissa's?" Matt asked, still chewing on a slice of now-cold pizza.

"The afternoon of the third."

"So she would have had the Mini Cooper," Elaine pointed out. "She could have dumped Anna before leaving town."

"But where would she have hid the body for the two days in between?" Olivia said, frustrated. "It bothers me that we still haven't found an actual crime scene. Where was Anna killed? And another thing – Betty's tiny. How could she possibly have forced Anna to be duct-taped to a fence or whatever it was, and then carried around her frozen body?"

"She had to have help," Matt concluded. "Melissa said they ran into someone Betty knew at RBJ's. Did she remember who that was?"

"Uh…" Olivia checked the notepad. "Kevin, no last name. Roughly six foot tall, sandy blond hair, looked like a linebacker, she says. Must have made quite an impression."

"That has to be it," Matt nodded. "A guy that size would have had no problem moving Anna around, living or dead."

"Why does the name Kevin sound familiar," Elaine wondered out loud, her brows wrinkling. "Kevin….Kevin…oh yeah," she remembered, her face clearing. "When Betty made that phone call that was supposedly to Melissa, while we were at the library-"

"She said she had a date with Kevin!" Olivia joined in, her mind clicking into place.

"Maybe that part wasn't improv," Matt suggested.

Elaine shrugged. "They say the most convincing lies are based on the truth."

“We’ve got to get the plane manifest. What’s the status on that?” Olivia said to Matt, her frustration growing. They were so close to wrapping up this case, if only all the tiny little pieces that were hanging out on the edges would fall into place.

“It’s in the works. These things take time. But, hey, uh, I have a question,” Matt said hesitantly, chewing on his lip. He seemed to be thinking hard.

Olivia and Elaine both waited. “Yes?” Elaine finally prompted helpfully.

“Well, it’s just….why are we assuming that she froze to death outside?” He asked. “It seems like it would have been a lot riskier to tape her to a fence than to just stick her in a freezer.”

“But the doc said she was upright when she died,” Olivia reminded him impatiently.

“Yeah, but….I’m just saying, we’re making an assumption.”

“He’s right,” Elaine nodded. “Did you look into commercial freezers?”

“No,” Olivia admitted reluctantly. “I guess I figured, the whole outdoors is one giant freezer right now. Why make it more complicated? Besides, Betty’s not from here. How would she have gotten access to a commercial freezer?”

“I don’t know, I just think it’s an angle that we should look into,” Matt shrugged.

Olivia sighed. “Okay. Well, let’s see, there’s Zane Refrigeration, Harris’ Commercial Supply, and any number of restaurants with large freezers right here in Grand Forks. Where do you want to start?”

“I was thinking the meat plant,” Matt answered.

Olivia frowned. “The processing plant over on 4th? Why?”

His eyes shifted. “Uh, I just have a hunch, I guess.”

Olivia leaned forward, raising an eyebrow. "A hunch? Do you get those?"

"Hey, I get hunches!" he said, offended. "I *am* a Detective, y'know."

"Okay," she shrugged. "I'm game. Let's go over there right now."

"Now? It's the middle of the night."

"Yeah, but I have a *hunch* there will at least be a security guard on duty," she teased.

"Fine," he grumbled, standing and grabbing his coat from the back of the chair. "But I'm driving."

"What is this thing he has about driving?" Olivia griped to Elaine as they walked out the door.

Geir Processing, Inc. was a massive 2-story red brick building on the edge of the industrial side of Grand Forks. Dating from the early 1900's, the building was originally on the end of a massive yard that had been used to contain the thousands of heads of cattle driven in off the plains by cowboys on horses. Eventually the train company, once running only a single line on the edge of the yard, bought out the space to expand as more industries relied on shipping by train. The days of running cattle across the prairie were no more. Mooing heads of beef now arrived by train or semi instead of on foot, and all that remained of the original yard was the intake area between the train tracks and the building.

Matt parked next to the loading dock, where a sign advised them to Ring For Service. Although it was, as he had pointed out, the middle of the night, there were other cars in the parking lot and the hum of machinery was leaking out into the cold night air.

Matt rang the bell and after a few minutes, a door next to the loading dock opened. A harried-looking woman wearing a plastic hair net and holding a clipboard peered out at them.

"Nothing scheduled until tomorrow," she said. "What's your – oh." Matt was holding up his badge. She sighed, straightened up, and opened the door wider. "Whadya want?"

"We just need to have a look around," Matt said. "Are you the manager?"

"Close enough," she shrugged. "Katy Geir."

"The business is still in the family?" Olivia asked as Katy led them through the loading area. The cement floor was stained a deep burgundy from a century of cows dying above it, despite the area being hosed down even as the three Detectives walked past it.

"They're still partial owners," Ms. Geir answered. "I'm just another employee, though. I actually married into the Geirs, and was blessed with all of this as well." She opened another door and gestured at a room filled with noisy machinery and lines of plastic-clad workers cutting and trimming various pieces of meat. Her tone was sarcastic, but not without humor.

"Oh? What's your maiden name?" Olivia asked casually, her pen raised to make a note.

"Uh…" she seemed reluctant to say. "Why do you need to know that?"

"It's standard protocol," Olivia answered truthfully.

Mrs. Geir chewed her lip hesitantly. "I'm a Murdoch," she said finally. "So what did you need to look at?" she turned and asked, raising her voice to be heard over the clamor.

"I'd like to ask you some questions while they look around," Olivia answered, nodding her head at Matt and Elaine.

"I can't let you walk around without an escort," Katy warned. "USDA and OSHA and all that. Hey, Bruce!" she yelled across the room at yet another plastic-wrapped employee with a clipboard, who seemed to be examining the results of one of the line workers. He looked up and walked over to the door, dodging piles of trimmings along the way.

"This is my husband, Bruce Geir," Katy introduced. "These Detectives want to have a look around."

"What for?" he asked, much less friendly than his wife had been.

"It's just a lead in an ongoing investigation," Olivia answered, keeping her tone friendly but noncommittal.

He looked at each of them in turn. "Alright," he said finally, grudgingly. "I'll walk you around. But only the open areas. I have work to do and I can't spend all night opening every janitor's closet for your amusement."

"Of course not, and we appreciate your time," Elaine said smoothly.

Katy took Olivia to a small office off the main hallway where the noise was reduced to a background hum.

"Do you know any of these people?" Olivia asked, taking a picture out of her notebook. It was a group shot from the library that Melissa had printed from her Facebook account. All of the library workers were in it, including Anna, Betty, and Melissa in the front row, looking fresh-faced and young. Mrs. Pace was on one side, and various other workers formed a second back row. Even Seamus was there; he'd been volunteering at the time, Melissa had explained.

Mrs. Geir took the photo and looked closely, pursing her lips. "Um, this girl in the front looks vaguely familiar," she said finally, handing it back. "But maybe she just looks like someone I know."

"Which girl in the front?" Olivia asked, showing her the picture again.

"That one," she said, a finger on Betty's head. "But like I said, she just seems familiar. I wouldn't say that I know her."

"Okay," Olivia said pleasantly, putting the picture away. "Can you tell me about your security procedures?"

When the three Detectives met up outside, Olivia had in hand a map of the processing facility and an employee list. Katy had been eager to help, and seemed reluctant to get back to work.

"Did you guys get anything?" Olivia asked Matt and Elaine as they bundled back into the warm car, her breath steaming into the frigid night air.

"We did indeed," Elaine confirmed. She opened her notebook and scanned a page. "There's an unused area in the far back, in the oldest section of the building. It's basically an empty concrete room with two big thick steel doors, one that opens directly to the outside and one to the rest of the building. Close those doors, and you could do anything in there – no one would ever hear you."

"So if the door to the outside were left open, someone could quite easily freeze to death," Olivia nodded. "Seems rational."

"And we found these on the floor." Matt held up two small evidence bags. "It's a button, and a little piled of burnt paper. There's a few readable bits left on the edges of the paper, I'm guessing these are the missing pages from your girl's journal. The lab techs can run a comparison."

"Mrs. Geir thought she recognized Betty in the photograph, but she wasn't too certain," Olivia told them. "Who has access to that concrete room?"

Matt shrugged. "Anyone. Apparently since this place is operating twenty-four seven, they never have a need to lock the doors. Bruce Geir admitted that he doesn't even know where his keys are. Slip in through the back, avoid the processing room in the front, and you'd be home-free."

"What about security cameras?" Olivia asked.

Matt shook his head. “None back there. They only have cameras in the main processing room and in the loading area.”

“So the question we have to answer is, what connection does Betty have to this place, if any?” Elaine wondered aloud. “Because Melissa is looking like a much likelier candidate at this point.”

When they got back to the station, it was the wee hours of the morning. Lt. Martin had released Melissa Thompson and had himself gone home to get some rest. A note on Olivia’s desk said that Albert Thompson was in holding, pending a psychological evaluation in the morning. The station was quiet and partially dark, with only a few officers at their desks or in one of the offices.

“Ooh, spooky,” Elaine teased, elbowing Olivia as they walked into the half-lit CIB area.

“Ha ha,” Olivia said dryly. She was still jumpy from earlier, although she’d never admit that out loud. “Hey, what’s this?” She picked up a folder from her desk and opened it, sitting down as she read.

“Well?” Elaine prompted her.

“It’s the plane manifest,” Olivia said distantly, “but I don’t even see Betty on here, much less that Kevin kid….crap. What day did Betty fly in?”

“Uh….” Matt pulled out his notes. “Anna and Melissa arrived on December 19th, Betty came in the next day.”

“Shit,” Olivia sighed, throwing the folder down on her desk. “They sent the wrong manifest. It’s the right flight number, right airline, but from December thirtieth, not the twentieth. Back to square one.”

“Geez, why don’t we call it a night?” Matt asked tiredly, falling into his chair. “We’ve been working forever and I’m trashed.”

“Can we go back over the case?” Olivia hedged. “There’s a lot to talk about." She was in no hurry to go back to her cold, dark, and probably haunted apartment.

Matt yawned and stretched. "For God's sake, St. George. It can wait a few hours, can't it?"

"I guess," she replied grumpily, although not without affection. "Lazy bones."

"Yeah, right," he muttered, rolling his eyes. But Elaine, sitting at an angle from both of them, saw the corners of his mouth wanting to turn up and smiled to herself.

After dropping Elaine at her motel, Olivia returned to her apartment building, parking in her numbered spot. She trudged up the stairs, dreading what she might find behind her front door. Her mind kept rehashing the case, over and over again; a broken record stuck between songs. Betty or Melissa? Betty *and* Melissa? Melissa and her father?

Standing at her door, one hand on the knob, she shook off thoughts of the case. It didn't matter; at the moment, all that mattered was what might be waiting for her when she turned that knob. What would it be this time? A slavering black beast of a dog, sitting in its own puddle of drool as it waited to tear her face off? She hesitated, leaning closer to the door and trying to listen.

After a long moment, hearing nothing from within, she put the key in the lock and slowly turned it until the mechanism clicked. Grasping the knob in her other hand, she turned it ever so slightly, a fraction at a time, trying to make as little noise as possible. As adrenalin rushed through her veins, she started to feel a little silly; an overgrown teenager, being quiet so as to not wake Mom and Dad.

Heaving a sigh and simultaneously laughing at her own fears, Olivia gave the knob a solid turn and felt the bolt slide free of the door, making a slight grating noise (as it always did) as it passed the strike plate. She was granted a half-breath of peace, just long enough to decide that nothing bad was going to happen, when the door flew open with a *whoosh* of wind. The knob was ripped from her hand as the door was quite literally sucked open by the whirling vortex that was her apartment.

Olivia cried out in surprise, throwing her arms out reflexively as she was pulled towards the maw. She caught the doorjamb with the tips of her fingers, her hair streaming past her face, her coat and bag straining towards the blackness that was inches away. She clung to the doorjamb with every bit of strength she had, her feet sliding towards the blackness as the storm within pulled at her body with all the force of a hurricane.

She groaned in pain as her arms were bent backwards; her feet were a mere fraction from the edge, and she was losing her grip. *Please God don't let me get sucked into that!* She cried out with all of her being, having a brief flash of déjà-vu as her mind took her back to that long-ago night of desperate prayer. The noise of the whirling storm was a freight-train in her ears, the swirling clouds within the room ink stains on an otherwise pitch-black canvas. *There's no hope,* she thought desperately, crying out to someone, anyone, to answer her plea. *Please help me!*

Olivia opened her mouth to scream for help, *real* help, and the words were sucked from her throat before her lips had a chance to form them. She felt the very air being pulled from her lungs, and she gasped for one last breath as her arms and hands spasmed in agony. The old injury in her shoulder was a screaming red-hot poker stabbing into an exhausted body. The storm roared with a fresh burst of intensity, and she strained to hold on, to pull back, to just *get a breath* so she could keep fighting. But the doorjamb slid away underneath numb fingertips, the freight-train screamed into her face with a sound startlingly like fury, and she closed her eyes just as her toes crossed into the darkness.

And she was gone.

The door slammed shut like a sound-bubble bursting. When a sleepy-eyed neighbor peeked out a few moments later, wondering what that strange noise had been, he saw nothing but a vacant hallway and a closed apartment door, a set of keys still dangling from the lock.

CHAPTER 21

Day Seven, Very Very Late

And then she saw that there was a light ahead of her; not a few inches away where the back of the wardrobe ought to have been, but a long way off.

- *The Lion, the Witch and the Wardrobe* (C.S. Lewis)

Olivia opened her eyes, but there was nothing to see so she closed them again. She couldn't feel her body. *Am I dead?*

She gradually became aware that she was curled up in a ball on a semi-hard surface. Pins and needles struck as feeling began to come back into her limbs, and without meaning to, she cried out in pain. She suddenly realized she was cold; terribly cold to her very core. Too cold to even shiver. She wet her lips, trying to form words, but the air caught in her lungs and only a mere squeak escaped.

After a moment, a light appeared somewhere off to the side. She curled up tighter, reflexively frightened by what the light might bode.

"Who's there?" a voice called out. It sounded strangely echoey. Olivia tried to respond and could only manage a grunt. *I sound like a pig,* she thought to herself, close to hysteria.

"Who's there!" it said again, more demanding this time. Olivia just curled up tighter into herself, too exhausted and cold to even try answering.

The sound of a sliding door and light poured over her. She turned her face into her arm, shielding aching eyes from the painful glare that reached even through her closed lids.

A long silence followed the light. Finally, the voice spoke again.

"Olivia?" it asked hesitantly.

She thought about this question for a good while, finally grunting in the positive.

"Uh-huh."

"Well," the voice sighed. "I guess it's only fair."

At this revelation Olivia moved her arm just enough to look up. A figure was standing above her, brandishing a baseball bat in one hand and a gun in the other. The light silhouetting him made it hard to make out a face, but the few spoken words had been enough.

"Matt?" she asked tentatively.

"Yes, it's me," he said, crouching down next to her. "And I'm not going to ask why you are in my closet, because I already know. Let's get some warm clothes on you, okay?"

"Why am I almost naked?" Olivia asked, suddenly realizing she was wearing only her bra and underwear.

"Same reason I was," he said gently with no hint of sarcasm. "Just stay here. I'll bring you a robe." He left the room and returned shortly with a plaid terrycloth robe. He laid it over her, helping her stand up into it with his face turned away discreetly.

"This is the most comorftable thing I've ever worn," Olivia said honestly. She felt drunk – a feeling she had not experienced in some years, but one she still missed from time to time.

Matt laughed. "Yes, I think it's very 'comorftable' too." He walked her through the room that she belatedly realized must be his bedroom. She had only been in his apartment the one time; a time that she'd tried hard to forget, impossible as it was. Even now knowing that they hadn't actually had sex in this room (so he said), seeing it made her stomach clench painfully.

He walked her out of the bedroom, gently leading with one arm under her elbow, and into his living room. It was nearly as austere as hers, with only a few scattered items of furniture and a single picture on the wall.

"I like what you've done with the place," she croaked. Her throat felt raw and angry but she couldn't remember why. He sat her on one end of his black leather sofa, thoughtfully pulling over an ottoman for her feet before taking the other end of the couch. He sat and just looked at her for a long moment. She took the opportunity to look him over as well. It was the first time she could recall seeing him in his own environment; like a lion at home on the savannah, she thought, he seemed much more relaxed than he ever did at the office.

"Why do you have that look on your face?" she asked finally, when she'd gotten tired of just staring at him.

"I'm not crazy," he responded. It seemed nonsensical to her confused ears.

"I think I might be," she mused, relaxing back into the soft leather.

"But you're not," he smiled, leaning over and taking her hand. His palm felt so warm on her cold fingers. "I really thought I was going crazy, Liv. All the dreams, all the things I keep seeing, the things that keep happening....popping into your apartment like I did, it was almost the last straw for me. But now you're here, and you're *real* and I'm not crazy at all."

"I'm sorry, Matt," she sighed, closing her eyes and laying her head back. "I'm just so tired. I don't know if I'm really here or not. I have no idea what's real anymore. I just want to sleep."

"I know you're exhausted," he said sympathetically. "I am too." He stood and took a blanket from a chest next to the couch, laying it over her carefully.

"Look, Olivia..." he sat next to her again, and she was forced to open her eyes again or be rude. "I don't know if you'll still be here when

I wake up," he said carefully, searching her face – for what, she didn't know. "But either way, we'll figure this out together, okay?"

"Okay," she agreed, closing her eyes again. Most of what he had said was lost on her at the moment. Her entire body was slowly warming, the pins and needles having receded as the blessed warmth of his apartment seeped through her. She was overtaken by such exhaustion that even yawning seemed like an exertion.

She fell asleep so quickly that she missed it when he stopped at the end of the living room, turning and planting a kiss on her forehead before turning out the lights and returning to his own bedroom, the door closing behind him.

BOOK THREE
THE BOOK OF SHADOWS

Enough, I am still alive; and life has not been devised by morality: it *wants* deception, it *lives* on deception -- but wouldn't you know it? Here I am, beginning again, doing what I have always done, the old immoralist and birdcatcher, I am speaking immorally, extra-morally, “beyond good and evil.”

- Friedrich Nietzsche
From *Human, All Too Human*

There is no death. Only a change of worlds.

- Chief Seattle [Seatlh]
Suquamish Chief

CHAPTER 22

Day Eight, Early

As she lay listening, soon someone entered; and when she looked at him, she saw a very handsome man and as he started towards the place of honor she looked again and saw an elk, with its horns branching out and filling the center of the tipi. Again he turned into a man, and then she saw that he had transformed himself.

- Excerpted from *The Boy with Buffalo Power*, as translated from the Dakota by Ella Deloria, published in *Dakota Texts*, 1932

It was the smell of coffee that woke her; the delicious, sensuous aroma of freshly ground quality beans being percolated with cool clean water. Olivia stretched, unconsciously twisting her left arm to avoid banging her wrist on the radiator (which she still managed to do at least once a week). She was surprised when her left elbow contacted a cushy surface that shouldn't be there, and opened her eyes to see an unfamiliar ceiling.

I'm warm, she realized. She couldn't remember the last time she hadn't woken up shivering in a frigid room. Her radiator never seemed to last the whole night; it started up enthusiastically enough, but somewhere around the wee hours of the morn it invariably gave up and turned itself off.

She turned her head and saw that the cushy surface against her arm was a brown leather couch. A thick fleece blanket lay over her, and she was deliciously comfortable from head to toes. It was still dark, but enough ambient light came through the windows for her to remember where she was. So this was Matt's living room. She hadn't even noticed it last time; she'd been too busy running out like a dog with its tail between its legs. Despite the austerity, it had a cozy feel that her own apartment couldn't quite manage. Perhaps it was the honey-brown wooden planking on the floor, or the woven rug underneath the coffee table. The single tapestry on the wall made her think of the beach and reggae music, although she couldn't quite pinpoint why. Her first thought, as bad as it made her feel, was to wonder how he afforded this place on his cop's salary; and then she remembered the tattoo on his bicep and thought, *ah – a pension, probably.*

Glancing around the living room, she realized the clock on the DVD player read 4:45. *Is that AM?* she wondered. *Jesus Christ, what the hell?*

She was so busy looking around, she didn't realize Matt was standing directly behind the sofa until a hand, holding a coffee mug, appeared next to her face.

"Crap!" she jumped, startled, pulling the terrycloth robe firmly closed. "Geez, good morning to you too."

"I thought you could use this," he said, putting the mug in her hand as she sat up.

"Thanks," she said, taking a sip. The coffee was hot and sweet, with just the right amount of cream and a hint of cinnamon. "Damn, this is good. I thought you never made coffee at home?"

"Only when I have time to really do it right," he said proudly. "Besides, the Starbucks doesn't open until six."

"Um, yeah about that," Olivia said wryly. "Why the hell are we up so early?"

He sat on the opposite end of the couch, his own coffee mug in hand. "I know we have a lot to go over with the case," he said, diving right into it. "But there's someone I want to take you to see, and I think it's best if we go sooner rather than later."

"Who?"

"It's hard to explain," he hedged.

"Whoa." Olivia put up a hand. "If you're talking about a shrink, I already have one of those."

"No, I'm not talking about a shrink," he rolled his eyes. "Besides, I think last night established that neither of us is crazy."

"So, what are we talking about?" she insisted.

"You'll see when we get there," he said, standing up.

"I haven't agreed yet!" she shouted after him as he walked away. He just shook his head, but returned moments later with an armful of clothes.

"These belonged to, uh, a friend," he said, dropping them next to her. "They should fit."

"A *friend*, huh?" she groused, eyeing the women's clothing he'd just laid next to her. "I don't want to know."

After leaving a message for Lieutenant Martin with the Desk Sergeant, Olivia and Matt piled into his sedan.

"Where are we going?" she asked again.

"We're going to visit a friend of mine in Devil's Lake," he answered finally.

"Matt, for goodness's sake," she said, frustrated. "We don't have time to drive all the way to Devil's Lake and back today. We have way too much to do."

"Oh, we're not driving," he answered, his eyes twinkling, and that was all he would say.

They headed north on Highway 29, and drove in silence until they reached the entrance to Grand Forks International Airport.

"There's a private plane waiting for us," he explained as they walked into the airport and straight out the back door. "I called in a favor from a friend."

Seeing the plane – a small but gleaming turboprop with freshly painted red and blue stripes - Olivia whistled admiringly. “Some friend.”

“Beautiful, isn’t it?” Matt agreed. “It’s a Cessna 185. She runs a business flying hunters and fisherman into the backcountry.”

“She?”

“Jill Hennessy. You’ll meet her in a minute.”

The plane’s door opened as they approached and a short, buxomly blond stuck her head out the door.

“Hurry your asses up!” she yelled cheerfully. “It’s fucking cold out here!”

Matt and Olivia broke into a run, Olivia almost laughing hysterically at the bizarre, amazing morning she was having.

“You must be Olivia,” Jill Hennessey said, sticking her hand out as Olivia jumped in the plane. “I’ve heard so much about you.”

“You have?”

“Absolutely. Most of it at four o’clock this morning, but that’s neither here nor there. Grab a seat, please, we take off in five minutes.”

Ten minutes later, Olivia gazed down at the frozen landscape from her seat just behind Jill. The sun was just beginning to rise on the eastern horizon, and the first pink and red rays cast a soft glow across the fields and dirt roads that stretched across the prairie. The rolling hills of the North Dakota Badlands could be seen far to the west, just beginning to be lit by the dawn.

“It’s incredible!” she blurted, unconsciously raising her voice to be heard over the roar of the prop.

“Isn’t it?” Jill agreed from the pilot’s seat. “Every time I come up here I fall in love with the prairie all over again.”

The Cessna flew lower than a commercial jet liner, and Olivia was able to see details that were usually impossible to see from the air. In those areas where the prairie had not been cut down for farming, the tall grass could be seen gently blowing in the light morning breeze. Olivia was suddenly struck with a memory that had not visited in decades; a quick flash of looking out a car window at tall waving grass, her eyeline barely high enough to see above the edge of the window frame. The tops of the blowing grass seemed to be waving at her. *Mommy! Look at the happy plants!* And the reply from the front seat; *I see, Kaya, it makes them happy to see you smile.*

She shook off the memory. It couldn't be real; she was far too young when abandoned to remember anything before it.

She looked down again at the view, trying to bring herself back to the present.

"So tell me why we're going all the way to Devil's Lake?" she shouted over the noise of the plane.

"Because it's easier for us to go to him, than for him to come to us," Matt said, and that was all he would tell her.

It seemed to take only minutes before they began to descend. They landed on a dirt airstrip just outside of town where Matt had arranged for a vehicle to be waiting.

"Another friend?" Olivia asked as they got into a green Bronco.

"Yup," he said happily. "Boy, you are gonna love this guy. He's probably my best friend, if I have to use such a girly term."

"You sure have a lot of those," she grumbled, meaning 'friends' and wondering why that made her feel so crappy.

Matt turned right off Highway 20 and into a fairly new-looking housing development. At each turn, Olivia expected them to arrive somewhere, but they drove through the development and out the other side. He followed the road out the back of the development through open farmland and after a few more minutes, pulled up in front of a small white farm house. An ancient red Ford pickup truck was parked in front.

Matt, still silent, got out of the Bronco but Olivia didn't follow. She was staring at the little white house, her mind spinning in confusion.

I know this place. Why do I know this place?

She watched through the window, but it was as if she were a thousand miles away as Matt climbed the steps and knocked on the door. Moments later a tall, lanky man was standing there with a huge grin as Matt threw up a mocking salute.

"Sir, reporting as ordered, Sir!" Matt bellowed out.

"Knock that off, ya dumb bastard!" the other fellow laughed uproariously, folding Matt into a hug. "Where's this Olivia you keep telling me about?"

Matt turned as if to introduce her and realized she was still sitting in the Bronco. He waved to her impatiently, and she slowly opened the door and lowered herself to the ground, staring at the man as she did so. His pitch-black hair, streaked with gray at the temples, was pulled back into a long ponytail. His eyes, just slightly turned up at the outer corners, twinkled with mirth.

As she walked towards them, she saw the exact moment he looked towards her and his jaw dropped. The look on his face mirrored the shock and confusion that was still rolling over her in waves.

"W-Winchy?" he whispered.

"No, this is my partner, Olivia…." Matt began, his voice trailing off as he saw both their faces and realized something was happening. The other man walked down the steps and towards her, his arms rising as if to embrace her.

"Winchy, can it really be you?" he asked, the blood draining from his face as if he was seeing a ghost. She shook her head numbly.

"No, name's….livia…" she mumbled. Her tongue felt swollen in her mouth, her lips fat and useless.

At the sound of her voice, his eyes widened. "Oh….my Lord…" his whispered. "*Khéya?*"

She shook her head again. The word he had just spoken barely registered, but she had enough sense left to force out, "Kaya. It used to be Kaya."

"No," he said softly, taking her by the shoulders. "No, that's not right. She named you *Khéya.* I can't believe how much you look like your mother."

Olivia/Kaya/Khéya was staring up at him in growing distress. "I know you," she mumbled, panicking in her confusion. "*Why do I know you*?"

"*Tȟuŋžáŋ*, it's me," he said urgently, almost shaking her. "Uncle John. Lekší."

"Lekšíla?" she said, and then realized that she had automatically used the possessive. Suddenly it all came rushing back, and the bit of memory she'd had earlier came back full force, in vivid and almost overwhelming clarity.

Riding in the back of the car. She must have been about four or five years old; it was her first time in the car without being in a booster seat, as she'd finally gotten too big for it. She felt like such a big girl, except that now she sat lower and was just barely high enough to see out the window. Everyone had been so happy that day, almost giddy; they were going somewhere important and exciting, and none of it made sense to her but she couldn't be happier. Mommy had been so smiley that day, and looking out the car window at the tall prairie-grass going by, it had seemed that the whole world was waving hello.

Mommy, look at the happy grass! She'd said, waving back at the blowing plants.

I see, Khéya, had come the reply, her mother's sweet voice like a warm hug every time she heard it. *It makes them happy to see you smile.* Uncle John had been in the front passenger seat and he had looked back at her, laughing aloud with joy when he saw her waving at the grass.

"That was the last time I saw either of you," Olivia realized, speaking aloud before she knew it. With tears in her eyes, she looked up at the man she now knew to be her mother's older brother, her dear *Lekšíla* who, other than her mother, had been her most beloved and trusted relative. "I remember," she said, beginning to cry. *"I remember!"*

He folded her in his arms as she sobbed into his shirt, crying for the little girl she suddenly remembered being, crying for the mother and the childhood that she had lost. She cried for being angry at her mother all these years, the mother she didn't even remember until this moment. She cried for believing that she'd been abandoned, for believing everything the orphanage staff had told her about her life before arriving there.

"Š!" he said. The interjection probably would have seemed harsh to an outsider but it was exactly what she needed, taking her immediately back to a childhood of learning to be strong. "Š, now," he said again, a little softer.

She leaned back, wiping tears from her eyes, looking way up into his kind face. He was more than a foot taller than her, and she had to crank her neck just to look at him directly.

"You haven't grown much," he teased, his brown eyes twinkling even as they rimmed with joyful tears.

"I guess not," she agreed, her face plastered with a smile so big her face was starting to hurt.

"Come," he urged, turning back towards the house. "Your grandfather is inside."

"My…?" It was almost too much. After a lifetime of being completely alone, suddenly she had not just a kind uncle, but a grandfather. Matt, still waiting on the porch, looked almost as stunned as she felt.

"All this time," he kept saying as they walked into the house. "All this time, who knew?"

An elderly man was seated at the kitchen table, running his fingertips over the pages of a book. His eyes were white and cloudy, and he looked unseeingly through them as they walked in.

"You won't believe who I found outside!" John said excitedly, his voice booming in the small kitchen. Olivia tried to hang back, nervous, but he ushered her forward as her grandfather, a polite smile on his face, was rising to greet them.

"Hello," he said. "Who do we have here?"

"Hello," she almost whispered, trying not to stutter in her nervousness. "G-grandfather."

The effect was instantaneous, and for a horrifying moment she thought she'd killed him as his face went sheet-white and he sat down heavily.

"Khéya?" he whispered. "Is it….how…?" Having just sat down, he struggled to get up, to come to her, and she impulsively stepped forward and reached out to him. Feeling her hand on his arm, he reached up to touch her face, tracing the lines of a visage he hadn't seen in thirty years. Tears poured from his eyes and she couldn't help but begin to cry all over again, leaning over as he brought her into a hug so tight she could barely breathe.

It took quite a bit of crying and hugging and crying some more, but finally everyone was able to sit calmly around the kitchen table, faces beaming and eyes more or less dry. Matt looked like he'd been hit by a train.

“They say it’s a small world, but this is too much,” he kept saying, looking back and forth between the three of them. “I can’t believe I never noticed the resemblance.”

“We all look the same to you white folk,” Olivia teased. She couldn’t resist, and laughter kept bubbling up inside as she thought to herself, *I am. I really am, and I didn’t even need a DNA test to tell me so.*

“Now, that’s just not fair,” he pouted, faking a wounded look, and she laughed.

“Son, how about some coffee?” Grandfather asked, and Olivia realized she didn’t even know his name, or her own last name, for that matter.

But John probably realized that too, and preempted her having to awkwardly ask.

“So, I’m sure you have a million question,” he said, squeezing her hand as he got up to make coffee for everyone. “Let us give you the basics and then you can fire away.”

She nodded gratefully and then had to laugh at herself as she realized she was getting out her notebook. *Habits,* she thought almost hysterically, and then, *couldn’t hurt.*

“We are *Húŋkpathi* - Lower Yanktonai Dakota. This is Robert Dead Horse, and I am John Dead Horse,” he said as he opened the cupboard. “You are Khéya Dead Horse.”

“Khéya Dead Horse,” she repeated, wrapping her tongue around the sounds that were so much like, and yet so different than, the Kaya she had been for most of her life. *I am Dakota,* she marveled. It had never even occurred to her that she could be something other than Lakota, despite the abundance of both Dakota and Nakota peoples in the larger Dakota/Minnesota area. “Húŋkpathi.”

"Your mother was Anna Dead Horse," he went on, and it was as if she'd been slapped in the face. *Anna. Of all the names it could have been....* "But I called her Winchy," he chuckled. "When she was born I was so mad she came out a girl! I was determined to have a brother, and so I refused to call her by her name. I just called her *wiĉhíŋĉala*, for 'girl,' and it stuck and eventually became just Winchy. She wanted you to have a more traditional name, and so she named you after her favorite little animal."

"Khéya the turtle," she realized. "I must be the stupidest person in the world. All these years I went by 'Kaya,' never even realizing."

"Don't say that," her grandfather scolded lovingly, reaching out and patting her shoulder. "You were a child. I can't imagine what it must have been like for you."

John chuckled, remembering something. "She used to call you her *bloskúya*," he smiled, laughing at the memory. Olivia looked at him questioningly and he smiled wider. "*Bloskúya*, her 'sweet potato.' When you were born she said you looked just like a round little sweet potato."

Olivia smiled at his joy. "I wish I could remember that."

"Outside, you said something about the last time you saw us," John asked. "You must have remembered something?"

She nodded. "We were in the car…we were going somewhere important, the three of us, and everyone was excited and happy."

"And that's the last thing you remember?" he probed.

She nodded again. "After that…nothing until a long time later. I remember being at the orphanage, but not how I got there or what happened in between." *My first memory had always been being told that I was left in a dumpster,* she choked back. *Until now. Now I have a new first memory.*

At the word 'orphanage' both her uncle and grandfather looked ill.

"Where?" John asked. "Where was this place?"

"South Dakota," she said. "Just outside of Sioux Falls. It wasn't too bad," she hastened to say, feeling like she needed to ease their anxiety. "It was Catholic....the nuns were mostly nice, I guess." The 'mostly' was painting a sweet picture that hadn't really existed, but the past was past and she didn't see a point in distressing them further.

"You were stolen from us," Robert, her grandfather, said mournfully. "I don't understand why."

"What last name did they give you?" John asked, seeming to understand how the orphanage system worked.

She smiled a sad, ironic smile. "Thomas, after Saint Thomas. I'm sure I told them my name but it fell on deaf ears."

"I doubt they would have let you keep your real name, even had you been old enough to put up a fight," Robert pointed out unhappily. His clouded eyes seemed to be looking back in time, remembering the desperate plight of another brown child trapped in a white man's world. "Once....once I was known by another name, a name I had been proud to carry. By time I was able to escape the boarding schools we were sent to, I couldn't even remember what it was." Olivia squeezed his hand, wishing she could undo all those years of sadness. At the feel of her hand he smiled, brought back to the joy of the moment.

"Where's my mother?" she asked eagerly. "Does she still live here? Can you call her?"

"Oh....oh, honey," Robert said mournfully, and she could feel his hands trembling. "You were *both* stolen from us. Your mother was...." He couldn't finish. John stepped over, putting a hand on each of their shoulders in an attempt to comfort.

But there could be no comforting with what he had to say. "She was murdered," John said softly. "We were at a rally....that's the car ride you remember. It was supposed to be a peaceful protest, a sit-in, at the capitol building down in Bismarck. Something happened….it turned violent. I got separated from the two of you, and when I couldn't find your mother I hoped she had taken you and gotten the hell out of there. But our car was still parked where we left it." He had to stop for a moment. "I looked for both of you all day. We finally found her – her body," he had to force the word out. "Down by the river, but we never found you. We looked for you for days, hoping you'd run and hidden somewhere. Finally, we gave you up for dead." He began to sob but choked it back. "Whoever….whoever did that to her, they must have taken you down south, figuring you were too young to remember what happened."

"They were right," Olivia said, but even as she spoke she wondered; was that why she'd blanked out her first six years of life? Were the final memories of her mother's life just too terrible for her young mind to comprehend? She wouldn't be the first person to tuck away traumatic childhood memories, only to dig them up years later. "I was told that I was abandoned as an infant, and I always took that as true." *And I was so angry about it,* she thought sadly, but didn't say.

Robert gripped her hands fiercely, the combination of joy and rage momentarily giving him the look of a much younger man. "Never," he said vehemently. "*Never* would your mother have abandoned you. She loved you more than the earth loves the sun. More than the trees love the rain. She loved you more than life itself."

Olivia bowed her head, feeling a strange and terrible weight lifted from her shoulders; a weight she had always known was there, but taken as simply part of being alive. Having it suddenly gone was like taking off shoes she'd been forced to wear, and having no other choice, had trained herself to ignore how painful they were. Now that they were gone, she was free to examine the bruises and blisters left behind and marvel at how she'd suffered for so long.

"And my father?" she asked softly, somehow feeling that she already knew the answer to this one.

John squeezed her shoulder. "Gone, as well, I'm afraid," he said sadly. "He was a good man, but allowed his personal demons to get the better of him. Even when you were an infant he was already too deep in the bottle to be a good father to you."

"*You* were like a father," she remembered, thinking again of that day in the car. She hadn't felt any sadness that day, no empty hole left by an absent parent. There had been no void in her life, and she wouldn't let there be one now.

John nodded. "She was my little sister. I wasn't going to let her do it alone." He squeezed her shoulder again and heaved a deep sigh. "Coffee?" he asked, looking around.

"Oh, yes please," Olivia said gratefully.

"You were in South Dakota," Robert asked, seeming eager for the rest of the story. "How did you come back here?"

"I married young," she said, "but he wasn't a good man." *Understatement of the century,* she thought. "He…hurt me." She saw from the corner of her eye Matt's hand tighten around his coffee mug until the veins stood out. "When I left him, I didn't know where to go. For some reason I felt like I'd be safest if I came north. Ironically," she smiled, "I actually almost came to Devil's Lake. I was going to enroll in the peace officer program at Lake Region State College. Somehow I got side-tracked in my decision making and went to Grand Forks instead."

"You're here now," Robert said simply and factually. "We finally found each other. The rest is just holes in the road, behind you now."

"And you're a Detective!" John said, impressed. "Your mom would be so proud."

"R-really?" she asked hesitantly. From everything she'd read, she had always felt that she had joined the "other side" by being a non-tribal law enforcement officer.

"Yes," Robert said firmly, seeming to understand what she was thinking. "It must have been very confusing to grow up like that, not even remembering who you were or where you came from. You made a good life for yourself. There can never be shame in that."

"And I would imagine," John continued, "that being a Detective must require you to be very thorough, very aware of your surroundings, to be mindful of all that people leave unspoken."

"Well…yes," she agreed. Matt was nodding as well.

"Those are excellent traits to have," John said. "And they are attributes that we encourage in our young people. They are traits that good leaders must have." He smiled sadly. "Your mother had those qualities, also. She was a true *wiwáŝte*, already working to be a leader in our community even as a young woman."

"She helped organize that rally," Robert remembered, nodding to himself. "Not everyone was pleased with the idea of our people marching around with signs, getting in front of the cameras, but she knew the power of our voices."

Several hours later, Olivia finally felt ready to discuss other topics.

"Matt mentioned that you might be able to help us with our problem," she said hesitantly, feeling awkward about bringing it up. Now that she was discussing it as a granddaughter with her relatives, not a Detective using available resources, she was nervous about even bringing it up.

But Robert nodded his understanding, pulling over and opening a large, flat tome that had been left on the side of the kitchen table. She realized it was the book he'd been reading when they arrived; the printed text had been translated into Braille, added at the bottom of each page. The book itself was bound in black leather and the pages were thick, made of some kind of linen or handmade paper.

"What I'm about to tell you can be hard to understand," the elderly man explained, getting right to the point. He spoke as if he stood in front of a room of many listeners, his voice changing in timbre from a sad and shaky old man's voice into the booming tones of a strong and confident instructor. "Many people find it easier with some kind of picture to look at. Makes it easier to wrap your mind around the idea."

"Your grandfather is an expert on the mythology of the spiritual world from cultures around the globe," John said proudly as he refilled his coffee cup. "He published this book himself when he was a young Professor at the University. It has received many acclaims from other schools."

Mr. Dead Horse waved away the compliment. "That was a long time ago," he said. "But this book has come in handy many times." He ran his hands over the bottom corner of each page as he turned it, reading the Braille until he found the page he was looking for. He stopped in the middle of the book and turned it to face Olivia, Matt stepping over to look over her shoulder.

"Now, young lady, take a look at this page," he instructed. "Does any of this look familiar?"

Olivia's mouth dropped as she gazed on a frighteningly familiar sight. The entire right page was almost pitch-black, except for a figure in the middle. It was vague, amorphous; its only distinct characteristics were its hulking man-shape and the huge maw filled with razor-sharp teeth that encompassed most of the face. As Olivia leaned in closer, she saw there were two red eyes shining just above the open mouth.

"Those should be bigger, brighter," she said vaguely, tapping the eyes. "Oh! I'm sorry." She looked up at her grandfather. "I shouldn't be correcting you. The likeness is amazing."

"Please don't apologize," he smiled. "I painted it from description, not from memory. So this is what plagues you?"

"Yes," she nodded. "The girl in our case – she called it Iblis."

"Also called the Black Demon or the Devil Dog because it is said to appear as a large black dog," Robert said grimly. "The ancient texts talk about Iblis granting wishes, being pleasant, even. But it seems to have taken a darker turn in the last thousand years or so."

"Granting wishes? What, like a Genie?" Matt frowned.

"Yes, Iblis has been connected with the original tales of the *Jinn*," Robert confirmed. "But much of those tales have been softened for today's fairytale palate. *Jinn* was not the round, bearded jolly man that appears in Disney movies. There was always an unexpected – and usually tragic - result from the wishes."

"Be careful what you wish for," Olivia whispered, unable to tear her eyes from the image. The red eyes, even static on the paper as they were, seemed to stare into her soul. "But why….what does Iblis want with us?"

"The girl in your case – she is an innocent?" Robert asked. "Gentle, kind, even saintly in her manner?"

"Um - was, yes, by all accounts," Olivia confirmed.

"And she had no family?" Robert continued. "She was alone in this world?"

"Yes."

Robert sighed and closed the book. The sudden absence of the image was like a veil of evil being lifted away, and Olivia found herself able to raise her head.

Robert leaned forward, his manner growing more serious. "Iblis seeks a way back into this mortal world. A woman like the one you describe is to him only a gateway, but a very important one. She must be, if you will, like the Virgin Mary. Innocent, pure, a woman as close to her God, or Gods, as can be attained. It is through the ruination of an innocent that he creates the way through."

"She – she almost became a nun," Olivia remembered. "Something made her change her mind. Why wouldn't this demon, or whatever, just find a woman who actually *was* a nun?"

Robert twisted his lips ironically. "Becoming a nun is not the same as being an innocent, or pure, or saintly in one's manner. It's not just the actions of the moment – but a whole being, past, present, and future. A very rare thing to find."

Olivia nodded, remembering the behaviors and manner of some of the not so saintly nuns from her orphanage and Catholic school days. "She told her confessor that an evil spirit was attempting to enter her thoughts as a way into her body," she said, hoping it sounded nonchalant despite her pounding heart. "Are you saying that was real?"

"Yes," Robert said simply.

"And he – it – wanted to make a baby?"

"So it thinks. That child would have been a vessel for the spirit of Iblis. A way back onto this earthly plain – a place he has been denied for a very long time. But this is an impossible thing that this particular spirit has been working on for centuries. The inevitable result is always the same." He paused for a moment, saddened, seeming to remember past events. "It is death for the woman, if she cannot be freed in time, as Iblis tears her apart from the inside out."

Olivia looked to Matt. He was still leaning against the kitchen counter, but now the counter seemed to be giving him more support than would have ever been necessary under normal circumstances. His face was white as a sheet, his jaw clenched as he listened. His mug of coffee sat next to his hand, ignored.

"What does this Iblis want with us?" Matt asked, his voice stiff.

"He was denied access to the woman's womb," Robert explained. "Somehow she escaped him, at least temporarily. But she is not gone, and now he is trapped in between life and death, just as the woman is. As long as the woman remains in limbo, so too will Iblis. Their spirits are conjoined as long as she is connected to this world. His only access to her now is through you. And so he fights."

"He fights by torturing us?" Olivia asked in a strangled voice.

"That is all he knows," Robert said sadly. "Anger, manipulation, fear. Those are his only tools."

"What do we do? How do we fight back?"

"You must free the woman," Robert said simply. His milky white eyes seemed to stare through Olivia, past her to a world beyond their own. "How she became trapped, I cannot explain. But I can tell you that none of you will be free until she is."

"Can you help us?" Olivia asked hesitantly.

"I'm afraid not," Robert said apologetically. "I only see. I have no experience in how to fix. You will need to find someone who can help this woman find her way to the other side." He frowned, staring off into space. "I have heard of this happening before. The girl's spirit is waiting for something."

"It was mentioned to me that she should have been given Last Rites," Olivia mused, thinking of how upset Brother Sheridan had gotten over the subject. "Could that be it?"

"I cannot say for certain," Olivia's grandfather shook his head. "Every religion has important ceremonies, tasks that open and close doors to the other side. That may be what she is waiting for."

"What will help us in the meantime?" Matt asked. "I can't speak for Olivia, but I'm exhausted. If I don't get some decent sleep I'm going to end up crashing my car or something."

Robert sighed heavily. "Unfortunately, that is far outside my sphere of expertise," he reiterated. "I can recommend ceremonies in alignment with our Native spirituality, but I cannot really say what the result or reaction would be, in this case."

"Anything that might help us would be much appreciated," Olivia said gratefully, putting out her hand before realizing he couldn't see it. She pulled her hand back and set back down, feeling awkward.

"Anna's death is keeping Iblis here," Olivia mused, thinking how ironic that was. The final act that had been meant to free the woman, whatever good or bad motivations were behind it, had instead trapped both her and her tormentor in purgatory.

"Yes," Robert nodded. "It can feel her presence, so close to his own. If you think of our world as a house, the afterlife is akin to the yard that surrounds it. Right now, it's as if she were in the garage – not quite in the house, but not quite outside in the yard - and the spirit is peering in through the windows into her world. Her nearness is torture to him, and so it turns on you two to vent his rage."

"Do you know why she's stopped appearing in my dreams?" Olivia asked, suddenly terribly worried by the image of Anna Taylor trapped in a cold, dark garage with a venomous spirit hungry to get at her.

"She's run out of energy," he answered. "An evil spirit is fueled by the fear of those it torments, but she is fueled only by her own life force. She has just enough left to remain in her in-between existence for a time, but eventually, if she is not released, Iblis will reach her, and he will consume her until her soul is ripped to shreds."

"Poor girl," Olivia's uncle said, shaking his head sadly. "I wonder how she became open to such an evil spirit in the first place."

"Something may have happened to give Iblis access – something that made the woman particularly vulnerable," Robert answered. "Although, sometimes there is no real answer. It just happens."

"They were conducting ceremonies to try to help a friend," Olivia said. "Anna apparently thought that her 'goodness' was enough to overcome the evil of the spirit that is imbued within their friend. I don't think any of them had any idea what they were dealing with."

"Poor Seamus," Matt said to Olivia, his face sorrowful. "I hope he doesn't realize that trying to help him is what probably made Anna vulnerable."

"I can tell you this," Robert continued. "If you two can stand together against this demon, the girl's spirit has a good chance to be free, and so do both of you."

"Us?" Matt said, surprised. "Why us?"

"The same reason the victim was brought to you," he said simply. "The same reason you feel yourselves drawn to each other. You are both guardians of our world; it is an intrinsic part of your being."

Matt and Olivia glanced at each other uncomfortably.

"Uh....like spirit guardians?" Olivia asked finally. "That seems a little...um..."

"I know what it sounds like," Robert said humorously. "Trust me, young lady, I know exactly what you're thinking. But I see what you are. There is a reason you both chose the lives you did. And I see the connection between you two; even in my blindness, it is clear as day."

Olivia and Matt shared a brief, awkward glance before looking away.

"But Sir..." Matt said hesitantly. "Some of the things I did in the Army..."

"I know," Robert nodded. "You were called on to do things that you never would have done otherwise, and you are still trying to live with your actions. You spend every day trying to make up for the young man you were asked to be."

Matt flushed. "Better than I could have put it."

"And you, *oíyokišilya*," Robert continued, finding Olivia even with his clouded eyes. "You think the things that were done to you, and the things you were forced into doing, have changed who and what you are. But they did not. Your character and your life are your own, and no one can change that."

Olivia was close to tears again. *How could he know any of that?* "Thank you," she whispered finally, sadness and confusion spiraling within her.

Again they all sat in silence for a long moment, contemplating their own personal experiences. Finally Olivia pushed back, sighing.

"I guess we'd better get back to the office," she said. Turning to her uncle, she was suddenly shy. "After we wrap up this case, maybe….maybe I can come back and visit?" she asked hesitantly.

Both her uncle and grandfather were surprised into sudden laughter.

"Dear, you can come back whenever you like, for as long as you like," John said kindly, folding her into a long hug.

"There is so much more for you to see," Robert promised. "Whole boxes of your mother's things, journals and photo albums and artwork. We'll get them out for you."

Back in Matt's borrowed Bronco, both Detectives sat quietly for a long moment, thinking over their individual thoughts.

"St. Agnes," Olivia said suddenly. "Patron saint of young women, especially those who remain pure."

"How do you know that?"

“Catholic school,” she reminded him. “It just came back to me all of the sudden.”

“So St. Agnes would be your patron saint, then?” Matt teased as he put the truck into gear.

“Oh, heavens.” Olivia was surprised into laughter. “I am neither young nor pure, that is for certain. ‘

“By the way,” Matt said suddenly, “I made arrangements for Last Rites for the victim.”

“Really?” Olivia was surprisingly touched. “When did you do that?”

“Right before we left. I called while you were in the restroom.”

“That’s fantastic. Thanks so much.”

It was mid-afternoon by the time they pulled into the station parking lot. Elaine was waiting for them anxiously, and Olivia was surprised to see Lt. Martin also parked in a chair by Matt’s desk.

“What’s up?” she asked.

“Finally got all the tox screenings back,” L.T. answered, holding up a manila envelope. “And there were some very surprising results. We figured you two were gone for good, so I was just filling in your friend here.”

“Sorry, Sir.” Olivia was immediately contrite, and astonished when he actually chuckled.

“No worries, Gossett there said you two were checking out a lead. You can fill me in, in a minute. Okay, so I know you had the Lab check her for everything possible. Narcotics, opiates, toxins, you name it. If there’s a test for it, they ran it. It came back with five positives.” He took several sheets of paper from the envelope.

“First up is tetrahydrocannabinol – THC, or marijuana to the layman. Low levels in her hair and very high levels in her blood suggest she was an infrequent user who had last used not long before death. Not a big deal for a college kid, but here's where it starts getting weird; she had high levels of quercetin, a naturally occurring plant flavanoid that can induce insulin secretion in humans. High levels of sesquiterpene lactones, which are also commonly found in many plants used for medicinal purposes but can cause allergic or toxic reactions. High levels of diterpene, another natural plant compound. Lastly, high levels of a particular diterpene called salvinorin A that is known to cause hallucinations."

"Please tell me we can make sense of all this," Matt said.

"Yes, actually, amazingly," Lt. Martin responded. "I did an internet search combining the three plant compounds – quercetin, sesquiterpene, and diterpene – and discovered they are all found in an herb called boneset. It's traditionally been used to treat dengue fever and other illnesses but is also used in darker rituals for casting curses."

"Ooh, curses," Elaine raised an eyebrow. "And what about that last one you mentioned?"

"The salvinorin A is found in an herb called Diviner's Sage – used in rituals due to its psychoactive effects."

"So....someone gets her stoned, puts a curse on her, and gives her a drug that will cause hallucinations?" Olivia summed up.

"That's what I'm coming up with," Lt. Martin agreed. "Of course, I can only tell you what's in her body. The rest is simply guesswork on my part."

"Could any of these compounds, or the combination of them, been what killed her?" Matt asked.

L.T. shook his head. "Not according to the Medical Examiner. They said all this might have caused a problem for her eventually, but she was dead from hypothermic shock before anything in her blood stream had a chance to really do much. In fact, the exposure to the cold would have slowed down her metabolizing the chemicals. At the most, she would have been a little high."

"Matt, do you remember the particles of organic matter we found on Anna's bathroom floor?" Olivia asked. "Did we ever find out what that was?"

Matt turned to Elaine. "That was all turned in to your lab. Can you give them a call?"

"I'll do it right now." She nodded and stepped out into the hallway.

"What are you thinking?" Lt. Martin asked Olivia.

"I'm wondering if these are the plants that they used in their home ceremonies," she explained.

"And maybe this was a final attempt that went too far?"

"Maybe."

"But why use something that is for casting curses?"

"Maybe they were trying to curse the demons out of her," Olivia guessed helplessly. "I have no idea. These kids obviously didn't have any idea what they were doing, either."

"Boneset is also used for treating illnesses," Elaine contributed. "Maybe they were trying it as a medicine. The curse thing could be coincidental."

"True," Olivia allowed. "We haven't found anything to suggest that any of them are into black magic."

"I'm still not sure I believe Melissa Thompson," Matt mused. "What if she *did* bring Anna home for her father to perform an exorcism?"

"And it went wrong, just like before," Olivia nodded, following his line of thought. "You still think she's protecting him?"

"At this point, it's just as strong a lead as the idea that Betty and some guy named 'Kevin' did it," Matt shrugged. "I say follow 'em both."

"Works for me," Lt. Martin agreed. "We're still waiting on the tests from the Thompsons' blood and hair samples, and from the blood in the back of the Mini Cooper. So in the meantime just continue working both angles."

"You've got it, L.T."

CHAPTER 23

Day Eight, Late Afternoon

Olivia was happy to see that the correct passenger manifests were waiting on her desk.

"Here's Betty, exactly when Melissa said she arrived," she told Matt, looking over the long list. "There are several Kevins on here, none of them seated next to Betty. We'll have to cross-reference against any possible Kevins from the Graham's Ford area."

"And that's assuming the guy didn't just fly in on a different day," sighed Matt.

"Or lives here," Olivia added.

Matt suddenly looked perplexed, his forehead wrinkling in a way Olivia had rarely seen. "Wasn't there a Kevin that lived in Anna's apartment complex?" he asked slowly, obviously straining to remember.

"Oh....hold on." Olivia got out her notebook and flipped through pages. "You are correct. Kevin Murdoch, Apartment 7-C."

"And on the manifest."

She looked again. "Yes, there is a Kevin Murdoch listed. Hey, wait...." Something was pinging her memory. "Why does Murdoch seem familiar?" She flipped back her notebook pages to near the beginning. "Holy crap," she realized, looking up. "Remember Katy Geir, at the processing plant?"

"Yeah?"

"Her maiden name is Murdoch."

All three Detectives looked at each other, bells and whistles going off in everyone's mind.

"What do you think?" Elaine said finally.

"It's got to be," Olivia and Matt said almost simultaneously.

"I'll call St. Agnes' about Kevin Murdoch," Olivia continued, "if someone gets a team over to the processing plant to scrub that room."

"I'm on it," Matt said instantly, picking up the phone.

"I'll run the checks on the Geirs, if I can use your computer," Elaine volunteered.

Twenty minutes later, Olivia hung up the phone and turned around to face Matt.

"Kevin Murdoch dropped out of St. Agnes' last year," she told him. "Actually, he was 'encouraged to leave,' according to the Dean. Poor attitude, plummeting grades, obvious drug use."

"He only moved in to Anna's apartment complex last year, from what Maggie Hofstedt just told me," Matt said, hanging up his own phone.

"He had been in the dorms," Olivia confirmed. "He would have had to find a new place."

"Interesting," Matt mused. "He told Mrs. Hofstedt that he works as an electricians' apprentice. I'm about to start making calls to see if I can locate his employer."

"Didn't the lab report mention electrical tape?" Elaine piped up from behind Olivia's computer.

"That was their suggestion," Olivia agreed, "although they couldn't confirm for certain that the murderer had specifically used electrical tape."

She turned back to her own desk. The calls she needed to make weren't exactly private, but she felt uncomfortable, nonetheless.

The first call was to Brother Sheridan. "Have you had any luck making arrangements for the transport of the bo- for Anna?" she asked, correcting herself at the last second.

He sounded miserable. "No. I had no idea it would cost so much to bring her home. We've only raised about half of what we need."

"I'll see what I can do on this end," she told him. "In the meantime, I wanted to let you know we've got someone coming in to do Last Rites."

"Oh, thank God," he breathed a heavy sigh of relief. "Thank you so much."

"No problem, Brother. You just keep me posted."

As Olivia turned around, she saw Elaine coming down the hallway, cell phone in hand.

"Any luck with the Lab?" she called.

"Yes and no," Elaine answered. "The fragments of plants were too small for them to identify by sight. I asked them to do a chemical analysis that the lab can compare with Anna's tox results."

"Great, thanks. Have they finished searching her apartment?"

"Lt. Acevedo is sending a list of items and photographs to Lt. Martin. Betty's still in custody, too. She's being charged with grand theft auto plus whatever else they can throw at her while we keep investigating her part in Anna's death."

"What about the blood in the bathroom and in the Mini Cooper?"

"There wasn't enough blood in Anna's bathroom to do a DNA test, but my L.T. said there was no reason to think it was from a crime, anyway. She said from the splatter pattern and from the fact that it's a small trail between the shower and the toilet, that it's most likely menstrual blood."

"Eew."

"Yeah. And we don't necessarily know that it's Anna's – blood in grout lasts for years."

"True. Okay, what about the Mini Cooper?"

"They've got DNA results and are forwarding them to your lab for comparison."

"Wow!" Olivia said, impressed. "That's great."

"Well…." Elaine hesitated. "It might not be necessary."

"What do you mean?"

"She said when they treated it with the luminal, the pattern was unmistakable. She's emailing a digital file to Lt. Martin."

"I don't understand. Pattern of what?"

Even the usually stoic Elaine looked sickened. "The pattern of blood on the back seat of the Mini Cooper. It's a picture of a face – or at least, half of one. The missing side of Anna Taylor's face."

Olivia was shocked for a long moment until it all sunk in. "That explains the bone fractures," she said hollowly.

Elaine looked confused. "The what?"

Olivia sighed. "Anna sustained multiple postmortem fractures throughout her torso and lower body. We couldn't figure out why or from what, so it got put on the back burner."

"Why wasn't this mentioned before?"

"I *did* mention it, and it's all in the lab report," Olivia protested.

Elaine was obviously frustrated. "Well, fuck. I guess I'll go back and read the lab report again."

"I'm sorry," Olivia said contritely. "I would have brought it up again if I thought it was important."

"It's fine," Elaine said flatly, looking away. "So what were you saying about how it explains the bone fractures?"

"Oh, right. Um, the back seat of a Mini Cooper is pretty small; it would have been difficult to put a dead body back there, especially if she was already partially frozen. The bone fractures would have happened from the body being forced into the back of the car, probably in a folded position."

"I see. But the funny thing is, Detective, if I had known about the fractures, it would have told me how the body was transported. That's a pretty important clue, don't you think?"

"It's all in the lab report," Olivia said again, weakly.

"Right. I understand now why no one wants to work with you. With your lone-wolf mentality, what's the point of having a partner?" Elaine walked away, leaving Olivia standing alone with her mouth hanging open.

CHAPTER 24

Day Eight, Evening

Several hours later, Lt. Martin had received all of the emails they were told to expect, and called everyone in to his office to go over the materials together.

"Here are printouts of everything," he said, handing a thick packet to Olivia. "Please share, I didn't feel like killing an entire forest just to make a copy for each of you."

Tension still thick in the air, Olivia sat next to Matt to share her packet while Elaine looked over Lt. Martin's shoulder. They flipped through page after page of itemized possessions found in Betty's apartment, many accompanied by a photograph of said items. After the first thirty pages, Olivia felt her eyes cramping up.

"Good Lord, did this girl have enough crap?" she complained tiredly.

"Half of this was probably Melissa's," Elaine reminded her.

"Oh yeah. Hey, wait – go back one page. What's that bottle?"

They all peered at the picture that had caught her eye. "It's just a little glass bottle," Matt shrugged.

"But it fits the description of the one Melissa had mentioned," Olivia pointed out. "The one with the nasty brown goop in it, that Anna bought from the guy in Portland?"

"Good catch," Lt. Martin approved. "I'll make sure they dust it for fingerprints."

"If Anna had that in her possession when she disappeared, then it's exactly what we need to implicate Betty," Matt nodded.

"Unfortunately, we need outside corroboration," Lt. Martin said.

"Betty could simply say that it was in the Mini Cooper when she took it. It's not enough hard evidence to get her on murder."

"Can they tell how long the blood was in the car?" Olivia asked.

He shook his head. "Not to the minute. It's just estimation."

"What about the rest of Anna's possessions?" Elaine asked.

"Good call. We'll see what we can place as being Anna's." He looked to Olivia. "Go back through all the Facebook photo printouts you got from the Thompson girl. See if there are any pictures that show Anna's clothes, her purse, any jewelry, and so forth."

Olivia nodded. "I'm on it."

They finished looking through the packet but nothing else jumped out at anyone. Olivia took hers to compare to the photos while Matt called the Crime Lab to if they had completed the DNA comparison.

"I'm going to take this down to your buddy downstairs," Elaine said, waving the printout of the bloody face from the back seat of Melissa's gold Mini Cooper. "See how it compares to the real thing."

Matt looked up, alarmed. "Uh, I don't think Dr. Johansson is working today," he said urgently. "Better ask for Dr. Jennings instead."

"Um, okay," Elaine said mildly. "Gosh, so worried."

"No, it's just…" his eyes flickered to Olivia. "Never mind."

Olivia spent the next forty minutes looking through pictures and comparing what Anna was wearing to the clothes listed on the inventory. Nothing jumped out at her until she got frustrated enough to stop comparing item-by-item. When she simply looked at Anna as a person, rather than as a mannequin wearing clothing, she realized what she was missing. In every picture where Anna's right hand was visible, there was a silver ring on her right index finger. Olivia peered closer and decided the ring was some kind of celtic knotwork. She quickly flipped back through the inventory of Betty's belongings and immediately spotted a lovely silver ring, complete with celtic knotwork, listed.

Informing Lt. Martin took only moments. As she was sitting back down, Matt pulled his chair up next to her.

"DNA was a match. *And*, we'll be getting all the requested phone records by the end of the day." He looked very proud of himself.

"Well, Detective Gossett, that's very impressive!" Olivia said, surprised. "You've really been on the ball lately."

"Well thank you, Detective St. George," he replied, bending in a mocking half-bow. "Having a beautiful woman magicked into my apartment in the middle of the night does wonders for my deductive powers."

Olivia was surprised enough to blurt out, "You think I'm beautiful?"

Matt's eyes widened as he realized what he'd said, and his mouth was opening to reply as Elaine walked up.

"Hey now," she said mildly. "Not to interrupt, which I obviously am, but Lt. Martin asked to see you both down in his office."

Olivia raised an eyebrow. "Why do I feel like I'm in trouble?" she asked rhetorically.

"We're not in trouble," Elaine replied. "There's another body."

CHAPTER 25

Day Eight, Late Evening

Lieutenant Martin wasted no time. "Graham's Ford PD has arrested Betty," he said immediately upon the three Detectives arriving in his doorway. "She's being charged with the murder of Anna Taylor."

"That's great-" Matt started.

"However," L.T. continued, cutting him off, "that's not really why I brought you all in here. We've got another body. It's Seamus Kiely."

"What!" Olivia exclaimed. "They found Seamus dead?"

"Yes, and it's officially Graham's Ford jurisdiction. But they notified us due to his connection to our case."

Olivia's heart sank, and looking around the room she saw the same emotion on the faces of the other Detectives. "Has it been declared a homicide?"

"Yes. He was strangled and left in his apartment. His Aunt found him."

"Then how....why was Betty arrested?" Elaine asked, sinking into a chair. "She wouldn't have the strength or size to kill him like that."

"Well, that's the interesting part. Hold on." He turned his computer monitor and they saw Lieutenant Acevedo's concerned face, with Detectives Yoshihara and Haines standing behind her.

"I'm going to fill everyone in at once," Lt. Acevedo said via the video chat. "Seamus Kiely was found by his aunt, dead in his apartment." She held up a photo of an obviously dead Seamus, his head on his pillow.

"That poor boy," Olivia said sadly, thinking of the few brief moments when she'd spoken with the real Seamus. He'd had to fight so hard for those tiny bits of freedom – she couldn't imagine what his daily life must have been like.

"He'd been dead about two hours. At this point we think he took, or was given, several sleeping pills – we found a half-full container of Ambien by his bed – but tox screens and autopsy are being done now to determine exact amount. Here's close-ups of the strangle marks." Lt. Acevedo held up another image clearing her throat before continuing.

"As you can see, pretty clear marks of strangulation. Deep bruising, large handprints, force to the point of breaking the hyoid bone. This was an angry, angry man that did this." Lt. Acevedo put the photo down.

"I'm guessing the boyfriend?" Olivia suggested.

"That's exactly what we're thinking," Lt. Acevedo nodded. "We're trying to locate Kevin Murdoch now, as our prime suspect."

"Is there any way Betty could have contacted Kevin while in custody?" Lt. Martin asked.

"Yes," Detective Yoshihara nodded. "She had her cell phone on her until she was formally arrested, about fifteen minutes ago."

"So she could have called or texted Kevin at some point. Is there any way to get an update to the phone records we've already received?" Olivia asked, looking to Matt.

"Let me check the warrant and see the exact language," he nodded. "We may need to go back to the judge if the language is too specific."

"Thank you," Lt. Acevedo said. "And let us know. We're going over what you already sent us right now, and Lieutenant Martin has updated on us the other evidence you identified." She clicked a button and disappeared from view.

"So," Lt. Martin so, turning his monitor back around, "what do you think?"

"I'm betting that Betty either put Kevin up to it, or told him something that got him so angry at Seamus that he went over there and murdered him," Olivia sighed. "Hopefully they'll find him soon."

As they were all leaving, Elaine pulled Olivia off to the side of the hallway. Her face was slightly red and she shifted from foot to foot uncomfortably as she spoke.

"Hey, uh, I'm really sorry I blew up at you," she admitted. "I wasn't even really mad at *you*, just in general, and you happened to be standing there."

"It's okay," Olivia said, as easily as she could muster. "Is there anything I can help with?"

Elaine shook her head. "Just shit from home. I got a text from my mom, nothing I want to go into. It put me on edge, I'm really sorry. All these years and she still knows exactly what to say to set me off."

"No worries," Olivia said, easier than before.

"I have to fly back tonight," Elaine told her. "I didn't want to leave things badly."

"Can I drive you?"

"If you don't mind. I know you have a lot to do."

"Oh, I could use a break to clear my head," Olivia patted her shoulder. "Besides, I couldn't let you leave without seeing you off!"

"What's that all about?" Matt asked curiously as she slumped down at her desk.

"Nothing, just drama," Olivia replied, digging into the pile of papers in front of her.

"You're a female, don't you like drama?" he teased, leaning back in his chair.

Olivia rolled her eyes. "Only the kind that resolves itself in forty-two minutes or less."

He frowned, confused. "Beg pardon?"

"Television drama," Olivia grinned, flicking a pen-cap at him. "Not real drama."

He laughed and threw the cap back. Olivia reached to catch it and her elbow hit the pile of papers, causing a cascade of documents across her desk and onto the floor.

"Crap," she sighed, reaching to collect the errant papers. As she did so, something on one of the documents on the floor caught her eye. Olivia grabbed up the piece of paper and looked closer, her mouth dropping in surprise as she realized what she was seeing.

"What's up?" Matt asked, seeing the expression on her face.

"I can't believe I missed this," Olivia said in amazement, handing him the document. "This is the first passenger manifest they sent – the one from the wrong day? Look about halfway down."

Matt squinted, reading the names. "What am I looking for?"

"In the M's," Olivia said impatiently.

His eyes widened as he was struck by the same realization she had been. "Murdoch, Magdalena – you think that's Maggie Hofstedt?"

Olivia nodded, excited.

"It has to be a coincidence," he continued. "It doesn't make any sense."

"No way," Olivia charged, jumping from her chair and grabbing the paper out of his hand. "She lied from the moment we met her. Ten bucks says her maiden name is Murdoch and that Kevin Murdoch is another relative of hers – there's just too many Murdochs in this game for it to be a coincidence."

"Where are you going?" Matt yelled after her as she dashed away, but Olivia's brain was working so furiously she never heard him.

CHAPTER 26

Day Fifteen, Lunchtime

"I don't believe this wood is a world at all. I think it's just a sort of an in-between place."
- *The Magician's Nephew* (C.S. Lewis)

A week later, Olivia was finishing up her section of the final report when Lieutenant Martin walked up with her coat in hand.

"C'mon," he ordered. "I'm taking you to lunch. You too, Gossett."

"What?" Olivia said, looking up in amazement. "Lunch? Since when do you take people to lunch, L.T.?"

"Since *people* did a spectacular job on this case," he answered. "Your friend Elaine is being taken to lunch at this very moment, and we are going to join them, in a manner of speaking."

"I'm game," Matt agreed cheerfully as he shrugged on his jacket.

Lt. Martin drove them to the Green Mill, a popular lunch and dinner restaurant. Olivia immediately began salivating – their butternut squash ravioli was near and dear to her heart, but a treat she rarely indulged in.

Lt. Martin had reserved a large corner booth in the back of the dining area. After being seated, the waitress brought over a small black wifi device and plugged it into the wall. She then handed a small slip of paper to Lt. Martin.

"Here's the password, Georgie," she said sweetly, giving the Lieutenant a wink as she handed him the paper.

Olivia and Matt looked at one another and broke into wide grins.

"*Georgie*, huh?" Matt teased.

"Yeah, I didn't know you had a first name," Olivia joined in.

"She's my wife's cousin," the Lieutenant growled, reddening. "She likes to flirt. *Anyway*, let me get this set up and we can get started." He took a tablet from his briefcase and signed in to the restaurant's internet. Within moments, the video chat was up and running.

"And here we go," he said with a flourish as another restaurant dining room appeared on the screen, with the three Washington Detectives and Lt. Acevedo in the foreground. Elaine waved enthusiastically as soon as she saw Olivia and Matt, who both waved back happily.

"Some of you I know, some of you I'm meeting for the first time," Matt intoned in an exaggerated voice, and Olivia burst into laughter as she realized he was doing a Dr. Evil bit from Austin Powers. She felt almost hysterically happy; the case was solved, she'd gotten reasonably decent sleep for the past few nights, and with the help of several local churches, Anna Taylor had not only received Last Rites but her body was being prepared for the trip home. Life had more or less gone back to normal, with Whitney still acting weird and Matt mostly avoiding her. She still hadn't called Bill Gustafson back; she dreaded the conversation, and she felt terrible about putting it off for so long. She was not usually one to just blow someone off, and she knew that at some point she would need to call and apologize.

"So, to get this ball rolling," Lt. Acevedo began, "we have a few presentations to make." She and Lt. Martin both took several small packages from their briefcases while the Detectives looked on curiously. "We received very sincere thanks from St. Agnes' and they wanted to show their gratitude to all of you." She handed her paper-wrapped package to Elaine as Lt. Martin gave one to each of Olivia and Matt. Olivia was still delicately opening hers while Matt ripped into his like a kid on Christmas morning.

"Hmm," he said, looking at the leather-covered book he held in his hand. “A Bible?”

“It’s beautiful,” Olivia said sincerely, examining hers in turn. The bibles were bound in soft brown leather, with each of their names stamped on gold lettering on the front. The paper was thinner than rice paper, so thin the light shown through and highlighted the words on the page. The ink was gold as well, resulting in the open book shining under the fluorescent lights like treasure.

“It is,” Matt admitted reluctantly. “Just not sure what I’m going to do with it.”

Olivia chuckled. “Put it on your bookshelf, of course, with all the other books!”

“I suppose.” He sat his gift on the table, seeming disappointed.

Lt. Martin was grinning. “Okay, that might be St. Agnes’ idea of a reward, but I have something for you that you’ll appreciate just a little more,” he chuckled, pulling something else from his briefcase and handing them to both Detectives.

“Hey!” Matt said, delighted. “Now this is more like it!” Both he and Olivia were holding promotion orders raising them to the rank of Detective First Class, effective the first of February.

“I thought there was no funding for promotions right now,” Olivia said suspiciously, holding her document up to the light as Elaine laughed at her through the videochat.

“I pulled some strings,” Lt. Martin said imperiously, puffing out his chest, “but now you both owe me your first-born children.”

“Done!” said Matt instantly, drawing a laugh from everyone.

“In all seriousness,” the Lieutenant continued, “your work has not gone unnoticed. I know this case was a difficult case for everyone, for many reasons, but we all appreciate what you’ve done.”

“Hear hear!” Lt. Acevedo piped up, giving Elaine a hearty pat on the shoulder.

Olivia was touched. "Gosh, I wish we had brought Whitney with us," she mused, not really meaning to say it out loud.

The sudden silence was deafening. She looked up from her promotion order to see a strange, sad look on Lt. Martin's face.

"Uh…." Matt had the same look. "Olivia…."

"Dr. Johansson passed away," Lt. Martin said quietly. "She's been gone for a long time, Olivia. You know that."

Olivia's vision blurred for a moment as the world slipped, and when her eyes cleared the world had broken in half. She found herself divided, her mind's eye watching from the other side of the room as Lt. Martin and Matt gazed at her physical self, still sitting in the chair. Their faces were sympathetically, waiting to see how she would react.

"Of course I do," she saw her other self say, in a perfectly measured voice. "I meant, I wish she could have been here."

But I see her all the time, her divided self protested; but no one could hear and after a long moment the world slipped again and she was back in her chair. Her head was pounding and she took a long drink from her water-glass, the ice clicking painfully against her front teeth. She hoped no one noticed her hand shaking as she set the glass back down. It seemed too much effort at that moment to even try pondering over what was happening inside her mind, and so to break the tension, she took a deep breath and turned to the videochat with a smile plastered across her face.

"So, is there any news on Betty Huntsmen or Maggie Hofstedt?" she asked brightly.

Lt. Acevedo cleared her throat. "They are both in custody," she nodded. "We are still working with Lt. Vepp and the Minnesota D.A. on bringing Albert Thompson over here. Thank you for all the work you did on going through the security footage from the processing plant and the surrounding businesses. Our District Attorney has verified that the footage you found of the three of them, along with Albert Taylor, taking Anna Taylor into the back of the processing plant is sufficient to place everyone at the scene."

"Is anyone talking?" Matt asked curiously.

"Yeah, we've gotten quite a bit," Elaine confirmed. "Everyone is claiming it's an accident that she actually died, of course, but we've pinned down motive and means. They all blame Betty, say that she convinced them that Anna was drawing Seamus and Melissa into some kind of black-magic, Satanic ring, that the only way to save the two kids was to have Albert perform one of his 'rituals' on Anna."

"And what is Betty saying?" Olivia asked.

"Well, that's the funny part. Once we got past all the tears and drama, the first thing she did was lawyer up. Her lawyer is asking for full immunity in return for testifying against Albert Thompson, who Betty claims is the real cause of Anna's death." Elaine's eyes sparkled. "But so far it's looking like we don't need her testimony against him at all, and the DA is probably going to deny the request."

"Good!" Olivia said emphatically.

"Albert Thompson is definitely liable," Lt. Acevedo added, "and the footage confirms that he was the last to leave and so was probably the one who left that back door open, allowing Anna to freeze to death. However, the other two are most certainly accomplices. We found the drugs in Betty's belongings, along with this." She held up a black iPhone. "It's Melissa's missing phone."

"Did she take it?" Matt asked.

"She says no, that Melissa must have left it at her place by accident, but we ran the phone records and there were multiple outgoing calls made while it was known to be in Betty's possession," Elaine said.

"Last question," Olivia said, "at least from me. Why the hell did they carve up her face like that?"

Both Elaine and Lt. Acevedo shook their heads. "No one will claim that one. Our guess is that it was an attempt to keep her from being identified, as little sense as that makes."

"Okay, last question, for really-real," Olivia amended. "What about Kevin Murdoch?"

"Oh my gosh," Elaine said, shaking her head. "When you initially guessed some kind of love triangle, you weren't far off. Talk about screwed-up relationships. So, Kevin Murdoch – who *is* Maggie Hofstedt's kid, by the way, by her first husband - was dating Betty Huntsmen, but she really wanted Seamus, his cousin, who wanted nothing to do with *her.* Betty was convinced that Seamus was only throwing her off because he was in love with Anna, but Seamus and Anna were not in a relationship, at least of the sexual kind." She paused to take a breath. "It was Melissa who was in love with Anna, not Seamus. Betty convinced Kevin, her boyfriend, to help her get rid of Anna."

"So he's implicated?" Matt interrupted.

"He is the one who folded up poor frozen Anna and shoved her into the back of the Mini Cooper," Lt. Acevedo nodded. "Lord knows what he thought he was accomplishing by helping Betty with her sick plan, but he's not the brightest light bulb in the box and he sure has a thing for her."

"Meanwhile, Betty was doing her manipulating of everyone *else*," Elaine continued. "I kind of feel sorry for Maggie Hofstedt, who believed both her son and her nephew were falling prey to some kind of Satanic black widow."

“Yeah, well, she’s not the brightest light bulb in the box, either,” Olivia said uncharitably. “What about Seamus? Did Kevin kill his own cousin?”

Lt. Acevedo and Elaine exchanged uncomfortable looks. “Our gut feeling is that he did,” Lt. Acevedo answered. “But so far the evidence is thin.”

They all chatted on for awhile longer until their food arrived. Everyone waved goodbye and Lt. Martin closed down the videochat, putting away his tablet and giving the wifi device back to the very flirtatious waitress.

When Olivia got home that evening, she was ready to go straight to bed. Their lunch, much larger and heavier than her usual cold sandwich, had left her feeling uncomfortable and logy all afternoon. Her head still hurt from the strange discussion about Whitney, the memory of which had faded into a vague feeling of distress and emotional discomfort. She had barely been able to keep her eyes open on the short drive home. When her head finally hit the pillow, it was like being in the arms of a long-lost lover. She sighed luxuriously, nestling into the mattress with the warm radiator at her back, and closed her eyes exultantly.

“Finally,” she whispered to no one. “Sleeeeep.”

When her eyes opened again, seemingly only a moment later, to see Anna looking back at her from the bathroom mirror, Olivia felt punched in the gut.

“No,” she said sternly, staring back at the dead girl. “This case is *over*. I’m sorry you are dead, I really am, but there’s nothing I can do about it.”

Anna’s lips parted and a small beetle crawled out onto her chin. “It was never about my death,” she whispered.

“WHAT THEN?” Olivia shouted, nearly pulling her hair out in her angered frenzy. “*What the hell do you want from me?*”

She watched, bewildered, as in the space of a single breath Anna decomposed before her very eyes. Brilliant blue eyes turned white and then gray, clear pink skin turned mottled white, then gray, then green as moss began to cover her. Red hair filled with mud, earthworms wriggling between the curls and dropping on to her shoulders.

Dead-Anna leaned forward, reaching out to Olivia through the mirror. “He won’t let me go,” she gurgled, her dirt-covered brown fingers reaching for Olivia’s face. “*And he wants you too.*”

Olivia jumped back as fingertips grazed her cheeks. A voice she’d already heard too many times boomed in her head like a sledgehammer. Words that she couldn’t even understand resounded in her ears, threatening to split her head wide open.

“No,” she groaned, eyes pressed tightly shut, squeezing both hands against her temples. She felt a presence behind her, pressing against the whole of her body, as two hands slid up her back and rested on her shoulders.

She didn’t want to look, but she had to. She opened her eyes and the mirror before her showed the one that she knew to be Iblis. The very act of laying her eyes on its dark visage was painful, like having nails shoved under her eyelids. Darren was standing just to the side of the demon, laughing at her as she screamed in horror and agony. She took a step back, holding her hands out in flat rejection, and her scream was cut short by a startled gasp as cold gripped her with the fierceness of winter incarnate.

The mirror and the bathroom were gone. The world around her was gray and flat to the horizon. She stood knee-deep in ice cold mud that roiled with both life and death. She saw the corpses of fishes and small animals floating, their dead eyes staring lifelessly up at the black sky. Around them, tiny worms with teeth-lines mouths as big as the end of her pinky finger twisted and turned in the icy, watery mud as they fed on the bloated corpses. Rivers of decaying body juices and sticky black blood ran from the dead creatures as the worms chewed into their bloated flesh.

Olivia felt herself beginning to decay as Anna had, before her very eyes. She looked down at her naked body and watched as the skin sagged, then puffed out with the gasses created by decomposition. Her skin darkened and blackened with death, small insects and worms poking out here and there of holes made in her body by scavengers. Her long black hair began falling in tufts, gathering around her feet in small piles of death.

"No," she whispered, feeling herself begin to sink in to the despair, to let it carry her away on a tide of death and decay. It seemed so much easier than fighting; but as the world turned to black, she saw far in the distance a spark of something bright.

Fighting against the wave of cold sludge, beetles and worms forcing their way from every orifice in her body, dirt trickling from her ears and mouth and from between her legs, she gritted her rotting teeth and forced her puffy, death-bloated legs to move. They finally began to carry her forward towards the spark and as she got a little momentum, it became easier, like peddling a bicycle through wet sand.

After an eternity of slugging through an endless lake of death, the spark began to get a little closer. After another eternity, it got closer still.

Finally she got close enough to see that the spark was actually several colors, blending into one brightness as the object spun. It gave off sparks, each one flying off to shine briefly in the dark before fading into oblivion. As she slogged closer and closer, the center of the brightness became even more difficult to gaze at head-on, but with her head tilted to the side she could just make out the shape of the object. The core of it, she was surprised to see, was neither spherical nor symmetrical, but vaguely human-shaped.

Sometime during this surprising discovery, she realized the sludgy water around her legs had warmed to body-temperature. Her toes, nearly frozen, were painfully tingly as they began to defrost. She gritted her teeth in agony but kept moving forwards, spurred on by a desperate need to reach what was the only life-giving source in this whole dead world.

Finally she was so close that even seeing the object in her peripheral vision was too bright, and she was forced to squint and turn her head as if she was fighting against a head-wind. But the brightness was not painful; it was more from a lifetime spent protecting fragile eyesight during the blindingly bright, snowy winters of the Dakotas that she refused to stare at it straight-on.

At last, the water – now quite warm and so clear she could see her own purple feet – gave way to a soft sandy bank that made a foundation underneath the spinning object. As her feet touched the sand the object began to slow. Olivia came to a halt, watching in awe as the brightness dimmed to a manageable amount and the spinning object stilled, revealing itself to be a woman with her arms wrapped around her middle and her chin to her chest. Her skin was the color of the sweetest of light chocolates, lit from behind by the light of her own life-force. Her hair, a shiny black so dark and clean it was almost purple, fell to her waist. Her eyes were a warm cocoa brown, and they reflected the smile that shown from her face as she raised her head at Olivia's approach.

"Khéya," she said, and her voice was warm milk to Olivia's love-starved soul. "My sweetheart, my little *bloskúya*."

She used to call you her bloskúya*...her sweet potato,* John's voice rang in Olivia's ears. "M-mom?" she asked hesitantly, holding one dirt-covered hand up to shield her eyes.

"Yes," the woman said, holding her arms out. "It is me."

"Is this real?" Olivia asked, for what seemed like the hundredth time in the last two weeks. "Or is it just in my head?"

"Just because it's in your head, doesn't mean it isn't real," the woman admonished, still holding her arms open.

Olivia's heart plummeted. "I'm just dreaming," she said sadly. "You are a memory, or more likely, something my mind conjured after hearing about you."

The woman sighed and dropped her arms. "You've always been *čhaṇtéšil'ič'iya*," she said mournfully. "I suppose you have good reason to be."

"I don't even know what that means," Olivia said, growing distressed. Yet she did know; *making herself sad*. "How could I possibly know that word?"

"You know many things, things that you don't realize, or have tried to forget," her mother pointed out. "Things that hurt you. But it's time to remember, my dear."

"Are you saying that I…that I remember what happened to you?" Olivia asked hesitantly.

"Only you can answer that," her mother said, reaching out as if to wipe the tear from her daughter's cheek. "You must learn to forgive."

"Who? The person who killed you?" Olivia said angrily. Dirt and worms splashed into the warming water as she clenched her other fist in frustration.

"To forgive yourself, my dearest *bloskúya*," came the answer. Her mother's voice seemed to be fading, and Olivia found she was able to lower her hand. The brightness had dimmed considerably and the sand beneath her feet was turning dark. "To forgive yourself and those you care for. You must remember, and to remember, you must forgive."

"Remember *what?*" She asked, frustrated, but it was too late. The light faded away and she was left to stand in darkness, up to her knees in water that was cooling as fast as it had warmed. All around her she could suddenly hear little splashes and she realized the spinning had created an associated hum that was now gone, leaving a deathly silence broken only by the feeding of the sludge-worms.

Left to stand in darkness, she gradually became aware of a light behind her, back the way she had come. She turned around and began the long, long slog back. After a million heartbeats she began to see a square of light, and as she approached it coalesced into a room; her bathroom, in fact, when viewed from behind the mirror.

At long last she reached the mirror and without hesitation, as if knowing exactly how to deal with this oddest of situations, she wearily hefted herself onto the sill of the mirror and climbed through. She was extraordinarily tired, exhausted through to her bones; and somehow, even knowing all of this must surely be a dream did not make a difference. Her bathroom seemed the same as always, and her dirt and decay fell away as she set bare foot on the cold tiles.

She stepped into her living room, and she knew she was still in the dream because Whitney sat in the recliner, reading the latest copy of *Wicazō Ṡa Review*. Olivia couldn't imagine Whitney giving the faintest crap about a journal of Native American studies, despite being best friends with a maybe-Lakota *(no, wait, I'm Dakota, confirmed)* person.

Whether it was real or not, she was glad to see her friend. Olivia threw herself down on the mattress, heaving a sigh of relief as she hugged her pillow. She was once again clean, clothed in pajamas, as she had been when she laid down the first time.

"Thank goodness," she sighed. "Sleeeep." *How many times can I say that in one night?* She wondered drowsily.

"Now, hun," Whitney admonished, flipping a page. "You know you aren't done yet."

"Hmm?" Olivia's eyes were closed, already beginning to carry her away to a happy land of clouds and jumping sheep. "Whuzzat?"

Whitney sighed and turned, laying the journal down in her lap. "You haven't *remembered*," she said firmly. "I can't go until you remember."

"Huh?" Something about that jarred Olivia out of her descent into dreamland and she propped herself up on one elbow. "What'd you say?" Whitney just stared at her, obviously waiting for something.

"Oh, forget it," Olivia flopped back down. "I'm still dreaming and you're just in my head anyway."

"Just because something is in your head-"

"....doesn't mean it isn't real, I know, I know!" Olivia wrapped her pillow around her head in frustration. "Just let me sleep, for cryin' out loud."

In the next moment, Whitney went from sitting in Olivia's recliner to being in her face, her curly red hair tickling Olivia's mouth as she flinched back, startled.

"But *I* want to sleep too," Whitney said urgently, staring deep into her friend's eyes. "*I want to sleep too!*"

Olivia stared back, mesmerized, her reflection in Whitney's eyes seeming to encompass the whole of her vision. She was falling into that reflection, lost in the world she saw looking back at her, and as she fell she saw a world unfolding before her; a world she had once been in. These were her memories, she realized, being reflected back at her from the twin mirrors of Whitney's shining dead eyes.

Dead eyes....she saw before her a party scene, two women – one redhead, one black of hair – here in Olivia's apartment. It had looked much different then; the living room had been full of furniture – a sofa, pictures, other chairs. The mattress had been tucked away in the bedroom, like regular folk, with a frame and bottom mattress to boot. It was late afternoon, end of an early work day, and she and Whitney had come back to her place to wind down with a few drinks. A few drinks had, as usual, turned into many, and at some point Whitney had looked at her watch.

Holy crap! She had exclaimed. *How did it get so late? I gotta get the kiddos before daycare closes!* Her ss's were slurred and they had both stumbled to the door, laughing, and Olivia had waved goodbye as Whitney nearly fell down the stairs, trying to walk and get her car keys from her purse at the same time.

And then she was gone, and she had driven to pick up her children from daycare and on their way home she had fallen asleep, or zigged when she shoulda zagged, no one would ever know for sure, all anyone would know is that she had driven off the road and into a tree and died. They had *all* died, her best friend and her best friend's beautiful little boy and her adorable little girl, they were dead, and it was *her fault.* She had invited Whitney back for a drink because Olivia hated to drink alone, although she was doing plenty of that too in those days, and she knew Whitney could no more turn down a drink than she herself could and so they had drank together, in the middle of the afternoon on a weekday.

And they had died, and Whitney stared at her now accusingly, her dead eyes shining in grief and sadness. "I'm stuck here because you wouldn't let me go," her friend said. "I've been here all this time and I'm tired, Liv, I'm so tired, please let me sleep."

Oh....ohmygod. Her heart tried to stop in her chest and Olivia could barely get a breath in, the enormity of it all hitting her with the speed and ferocity of a runaway freight train. Memories came now, quicker and quicker; the phone call, arriving at the scene of the accident to realize it was Whitney's car, that the children were already dead. None of them wearing seatbelts or in child-seats; Whitney had gone through the windshield and was lying half-inside, half-outside the car, her bloody outstretched hand inches from the tree she'd hit as if trying to fend off the inevitable. The youngest child was found twenty feet away where she'd come to rest after being launched from the impacted car, her broken and bloody body looking like a red snow angel against the fresh white snow. The older child, the boy who had been the light of his father's life until the man was taken by cancer and their mother found solace in the bottle, he was still inside the car, miraculously, but clearly his luck not been strong enough to outwit the power of the air-bag that had snapped his fragile neck like a twig. The entire scene was like a cautionary tale for every safety commercial ever played; *don't put children in the front seat. Wear your seatbelt. Put your children in child or booster seats. Don't drink and drive. Watch your speeds in snowy or icy conditions. Don't drown your sorrows in the bottle.*

And then there had been the children's funerals while Whitney lingered in Intensive Care for weeks, Olivia by her side. The funerals had scant attendance because, who would come? Their whole family was now dead or dying and the rest of the world continued on despite witnessing the terrible tragedy. The trains kept running, the world kept turning, people had to work, who had time to mourn two little human beings whose lives were cut short, two little people who had not even had time to learn what it meant to be human before they were no more. *Whitney called them her little puppy dogs,* Olivia remembered in the midst of the sudden rush of memories. *It was a joke, she meant it lovingly, but it was almost true because they bounced around mindlessly like puppies, all snuggly love and unending energy.*

Then, finally, the third and last funeral. It had been that night the Department had gone out drinking, and Matt had kept her from leaving with those four men. He had been so careful, they had all been so careful around her, watching every word where Whitney was concerned.

I killed....I killed my best friend and her babies, I killed them, I killed them all. Tears rolled down her cheeks and she turned away from Whitney, leaning over the edge of the mattress just in time to vomit up everything in her stomach.

It was the smell that made her decide she wasn't dreaming. Whatever had happened earlier in the night, perhaps that had been a dream, or perhaps not; in any case, no dream could quite match the extreme sourness of fresh vomit, a smell so terrible it made one want to throw up all over again.

She could barely get the words, out, wiping strings of drool from her chin, but it had to be said. "I'm....I'm so sorry," she sobbed, wishing she could hug her friend and realizing now *(duh!)* why it was they hadn't actually touched in a year. "I'm so terribly sorry, Whit, if I could take it all back, if I could change anything...."

"Oh – oh honey!" the ghost that was Whitney seemed surprised. "Sweetie, I'm not here to make you feel responsible. I'm here *because* you feel responsible." She sighed, and it was all Olivia could do not to throw up again. "You didn't kill me or my children, sweet pea. *I* killed us." Whitney reached forward as if to stroke Olivia's tear-stained cheek, but her hand passed right through. It felt to Olivia as if a cold breeze had just whispered across her face. "You just have to let me go, honey, let all of us go. Let me move on, let *yourself* move on."

"But I – I..."

"No." Whitney's voice was firm, and was it Olivia's imagination that her friend was beginning to dissipate, her here-ness turning into an amorphous otherworldliness? "No," she said again, just as firmly. "I've been patient, and I've waited for you to do this on your own, but I can't wait any more. I miss my babies, I miss my husband, they are all waiting for me, I'm sure of it, and I need you to *let me go.*"

Olivia was out of protests, out of excuses, and out of reasons. All in a moment, she heaved a tremendous sigh and it was as if an enormous shawl of concrete fell from her shoulders, leaving only the weight of her own self behind. She felt lighter, more free, than she had in many a year.

"I love you," she said sadly, gazing up at a fast-fading Whitney. "I'm so sorry."

"I know, sweetie," the ghost of her best friend agreed with the last bit of voice she had remaining. "I love you too, Liv. I always will."

And then she was gone.

EPILOGUE
HEARTS IN WINTER

Isn't it crazy, child, how love sometimes leaves you
As dead as yesterday?
- *As Dead As Yesterday* (Black Label Society)

EPILOGUE

One Month Later

When life is hard, you have to change.
- *Change* (Bind Melon)

She went into the station early, hoping to avoid running into anyone in particular, but especially Matt. It was just her luck that he had picked that one day to actually come in early, and he cast a sad gaze upon her as she approached her desk with empty cardboard box in hand. She initially avoided his gaze, but couldn't avoid hearing the tremendous *poor-me* sigh he kept casting out over and over, the bait to her fish. Finally, she bit.

"Alright, what's up?" she asked abruptly, the box half-full.

"Weren't you even gonna say goodbye?" he asked mournfully.

"I'm not much on goodbyes," she said shortly.

"Well, that I already knew," he said, rising from his chair. "But I'm not let you going without a hug." He opened his long arms, and from her vantage point it was like the entrance to an animal trap, the kind that would cause a wild animal to chew off their own foot to escape.

After a long moment, during which she continued to ignore him, he finally dropped his arms awkwardly. "I can't believe you're walking out on a promotion," he said morosely. Subtext, which she heard clearly, was *I can't believe you're walking out on me.*

"I've made up my mind," she said firmly, filling the rest of the box quickly and slamming drawers shut. "I've got things to do, things to figure out, and I can't do that here."

"I don't understand why not," he said, and something in his voice made her turn and look him in the face; something she'd been avoiding of late.

"Look," she said softly, "this has nothing to do with you. I know that we've been through a lot together and I know…." She gulped, unwilling to say it out loud in case it wasn't true.

"Know that I want more," he finished for her, looking her straight in the eyes.

"Yes," she nodded. "And under different circumstances….I think that I would too. But being here, being with you, would require me being somebody that I'm just not able to be right now." Elaine's words from weeks before rang in her ears; *I finally realized that I'm not* supposed to be *anything….I'm just me.* The brand-new tattoo inked just above Olivia's left breast, nearest to her heart, throbbed in response to her momentary quickening blood flow. *Incipit vita nova*, it read; *Here begins the new life*. She had put it there as homage to both of the Annas and a visible reminder of her determination to make her life her own, no matter what might come.

She hefted the box and walked away, knowing if she looked back she would be tempted to walk into his arms, to let them close around her forever and invite all the heartache that would bring.

She met the L.T. for lunch that day, her last meal in Grand Forks. Her car was already packed with the few belongings she had left, and as she waited for him to arrive she kept looking at the clock on her phone impatiently. Her family was expecting her by late afternoon and she was eager to get on the road.

"Matt's pretty despondent," were the L.T.'s first words to her. She gritted her teeth and somewhere in the back of her mind made note of the fact that it was the only time he'd ever referred to Matthew by his first name.

“He’ll get over it,” she said firmly.

“So, your plans?” L.T. asked, moving on to the next topic as was his nature.

She nodded, grateful to put Matthew behind her in more ways than one. “A few days with family. Then I’m visiting with Elaine for a bit, and then I’m going down South Dakota way for a while.”

“Job or school?” he asked.

“Both,” she hedged, and was relieved when he let it drop. She had been offered a job teaching Criminology at Oglala Lakota College, but had asked for a semester to think about it while she worked on other things. Her mother’s murder was now a constant song in the back of her mind, and colored every decision she made. Whatever her mother, or Olivia’s dream of her mother, had said about forgiveness, didn’t mean that the murder didn’t need solving.

“We’ll miss you,” he said, and she surprised both of them when she responded, “I might be back. We’ll see what happens.”

That afternoon, as Grand Forks receded in her rear-view mirror, she pondered the strangeness of her life. Who was this person that nearly everyone else called Olivia, the person she was already starting to think of, in her own mind, as Khéya? She felt that she would never again look in a mirror without seeing a glimmer of Anna Taylor looking back at her; a girl so determined to do the right thing that she literally sacrificed her soul to save a friend. Whitney would always be there, too, as would Darren, for better or worse.

Her mother was there as well; and the little girl that was Khéya, a child still trying to remember who she was. All of them made up some part of the adult Olivia, the person she was now. The rest of it was up to her, and as the red road unwound underneath her wheels, she felt a sudden glimmer of excitement at the discoveries that were still yet to come; a life that was hers and hers alone, to make of as she desired.

END

Olympia, WA – Denver, CO

Oct 2011 – Oct 2015

The author looking out at the Flatirons in Colorado, February 2015.
Photo c. Shawn Swanson 2015

About the Author
Cara J. Swanson was born in Colorado somewhere around thirty-eight years ago, and immediately leapt to work on her first story. She has lived in numerous places throughout the United States, including five years in Grand Forks, North Dakota, and a total of nine years in western Washington State.

This is her fourth novel and her fifth book.

She can be found on LinkedIn and Facebook, at her homepage www.carajswanson.com, or contacted at raven@thewritingraven.com.

Made in the USA
Lexington, KY
22 February 2016